ONE SHILLING.

ARAB JACK.

THE ADVENTURES OF A LONDON BOY IN THE SOUDAN

LONDON: HOGARTH HOUSE, BOUVERIE STREET, FLEET STREET, E.C.

ARAB JACK;

OR, THE

ADVENTURES OF A LONDON BOY

IN

EGYPT AND THE SOUDAN.

——————

FULLY ILLUSTRATED.

——————

LONDON:

HOGARTH HOUSE, BOUVERIE STREET, FLEET STREET.

ARAB JACK:

OR, THE

ADVENTURES OF A LONDON BOY.

CHAPTER I.

A RUN FOR LIFE. — UNDER THE DARK ARCH BY THE RIVER.—A TERRIBLE RIDE ON THE UNDERGROUND.—A LIVING DEATH.

"HOORAY! Hooray!"

Such were the shouts of the wandering young Arabs who poured down Villiers-street from the Strand, their tatters flying like pennons in the wind, as they chased a poor miserable ragged object, on to the Thames Embankment.

"Hooray! Hooray!"

The shout sounded like a death-knell, as it rang out under the dark railway arch, and died away in echoes on the cold cheerless bosom of the broad murky river.

"Help, save me, spare me, don't kill me," were the next accents, uttered in feeble tones. "Oh God—I am fainting, I feel I am about to die."

The yelling crowd, however, showed no signs of mercy.

The stronger thrust aside the weak so as to get near the crying victim, and with such garbage as their hungry stomachs refused pelted the ragged mud-stained waif, who seemed as if each moment was about to be his last.

It was a motley throng that gathered around that poor sickly boy.

A score in number of London's wildest street Arabs, as scantily clothed as any wandering savage.

The scene lasted some time, when a new comer, clothed like the rest, clambered over the palings and dropped into their midst, which act showed he was quite a head taller than the rest.

"Hullo, my kiddies, vot's up now?" said he, "Vy Dick's on'y bin avay for a veek, an' 'ere you're all a goin' mad."

It was Dick of the Dials who thus spoke; he was king of the waifs and strays, a very monarch amongst the London Arabs.

At his voice they all drew back and disclosed a poor miserable object, with such clothes as remained to him in rags, and his face bedaubed with blood and mire, which gave him the appearance of a veritable tattooed Indian.

"Vot's he done, kiddies?" said Dick in an authoritative tone, "murder'd henny body or split on some ov our gang."

"Not he," answered one of the crowd. "He's a pigeon of light-fingered Luke's; he borrowed his old daddy's coat, and now he's afraid to go home."

"Oh, a lay kinchin is he," said Dick; "did he share out henny hof the swag?"

"Luke had it all, an' now he's left the kiddy to be bonnetted. I on'y wish I could git horf his shirt, they might chuck 'im in the river then for what I'd care."

Emboldened by his words the young ruffians again closed around their trembling victim, but by this time the spirit of a young lion was aroused.

The boy Arab was not what he seemed.

He was not a mean cringing cur to be trod and trampled on without making an effort to rise.

He sprang to his feet, and though hatless and coatless, prepared for a gallant defence.

"Cowards," he yelled, goaded by the pain he was suffering, "It was not the coat alone that I was tempted by flash Luke to steal—but the pocket-book, which contained notes and gold. He has ruined me. I dare not go home; and now you have robbed me and brought me to this. I care not if you kill me."

This speech called forth a loud derisive shout.

"Punch him, knob him, kick him," shouted several.

But as they prepared to bury him in a general rush, the young Arab rose from his knees to his feet, and doubling his fists dealt desperately about him.

In an instant two were floored, and a third half-blinded staggered back; but a fourth caught the young hero by the shirt, and endeavoured by all the means he knew to throw him.

But the struggle was fierce and brief.

The shirt, though of the finest texture and strong, gave way, the left arm of the Arab was bared, and from the shoulder to the elbow it presented an appearance of having been dipped in fresh blood!

This sight shocked even the most callous of the horde of waifs.

They drew back aghast and uttered a cry of terror.

By this means they made a lane of which the ill-used waif took immediate advantage, and with the swiftness of a hunted deer sped towards the railway station, through the doors of which he like lightning disappeared.

A burly porter prevented his pursuers from following him, and two policemen arriving at that moment quickly dispersed the rabble mob.

Jack Martin, such was the name of the young Arab who had sought sanctuary in the railway station, on entering it, glanced timidly around, and observing the staircase, bolted down it with all speed; thence along the platform he ran, jumped on to the line, and finding a hole beneath the platform crept in.

The hole was dark, dry, and evidently spacious, so that if it had not been for the sounds overhead warning him that he was being searched for and was likely to be discovered, he would fain have gone to sleep there.

Terror, however, lent him strength, his first act was to strip off his shirt, turn it inside out, and put it on again, by which means the sleeves became reversed, and thus hid the terrible disfigurement of his arm.

Although in darkness, Jack shuddered when he thought of that blood-red stain on his fair white skin, and in fancy he could see it through the impenetrable gloom.

Like the mark of Cain it haunted him, and for why ? there was a terrible mystery attached to it !

A tale that would cause one's blood to curdle, and turn one's brain at the recital !

What it was must for the present remain in darkness, we have enough terrors and perils before us now, and Jack Martin's boyish life is already become chequered. His position in that dark hole under the flooring was anything but enviable ; without money and having no ticket he was puzzled as to how he should get out of his captivity without being handed over to the police.

Whilst puzzling his brains he was startled by the sound of an approaching train, which ran into the station, puffing and snorting, and the brakes having screeched and groaned, the train stopped just a little way past the hole in which Arab Jack was concealed.

The train only stayed a few moments, but in that time a thousand thoughts flashed through our hero's heated brain.

" Fear, such as of death, I have none," he soliloquised ; " shame and dishonour is to me worse a thousand times. I have done wrong and I repent of it, but how can I hope to be forgiven ?"

During this time it seemed that a sudden impulse urged him to quit the hole, creep underneath the break van, and seize hold of one of the axletrees, upon which he leaned, drew himself up and fixed himself as if he were preparing for a long journey.

" Good heaven !" he gasped when the engine shrieked and the train prepared to move on. " Good heaven," then the brakes were released, the machinery clashed and groaned, and he gave himself up for dead.

How it was he escaped being killed seemed a miracle.

One portion of the cold iron passed close to his head, and produced an icy chill, while another portion of the brake caught his leg and held it, as if it were in a vice, between the brake and a portion of the woodwork.

Jack would have fainted off hand had not the pain kept him in a morbid state of consciousness, which served to fill him with dread of a most shocking and painful death.

The agony the poor boy endured, both bodily and mentally, was excruciating. No victim upon the inquisitorial rack could have endured more torture.

The vibration and jerking of the train seemed to dislocate every bone, whilst the close sulphurous air of the "Underground Railway," made his brain burn and swim to swell as if it were about to burst.

The stoppage of the train at the next station was still worse, for the putting on of the brakes and the sudden jerks seemed to turn his frail form inside out.

It was then that the overtaxed nature of the poor London waif gave way ; the dark cloud of oblivion blotted out the terrors of the scene, and Jack swooned as piercing cries rang out from those assembled on the platform.

CHAPTER II.

A RAILWAY MYSTERY.—SAVED BY THE WAIF. —AN ADVENTURE ON LONDON BRIDGE.— A STRANGE MEETING. — FRIENDS, YET DEADLY FOES.—SNATCHED FROM THE RIVER.

WHEN Jack returned to consciousness, he found himself lying on a locker with a bundle of oily waste under his head and a regiment of lanterns and lamps around him on every hand.

" Another railway mystery, Jem," he heard someone say. " It's a mercy he wasn't smashed or cut to pieces."

" Aye, that it warr, and I bet ye he'll think on't all his loife. It's a good job we found his ticket, and 'twas lucky that young chap left thay soot o' togs."

" Ah !" ejaculated the first porter, glancing in the direction of the waif, " He's coming too, now. We must obey orders and get him washed and out of this if he's able to travel."

" Well, youngster, how are you ?" said he, approaching Jack. " Does your head ache, and your heart throb as hard as it did when I picked you up off the line ?"

Jack stared at him in utter bewilderment for a moment, and then he bethought him of the terrible ride.

" Have I been talking a lot of nonsense !" he asked eagerly.

" You've been raving about a coat and pocketbook," said the man. " But it beats me how you got atwixt the metals. It's a mercy you warn't killed ; are you hurt much ?"

" I feel bruised all over," Jack replied, " but I don't think I've got any bones broken."

" That's all right, then. Here's water and soap, get a wash, and then toddle home as fast as yer legs 'ull let yer."

This was sound advice, but our young adventurer was too stiff and sore to jump about much. Having moistened his parched lips with a glass of water—which smelt strongly of ammonia and spirits—he had a refreshing sluice, combed his hair, and put on a waistcoat, jacket, and trousers, which had been left for his use by some kind passenger.

He then learned that a lady had taken an interest in his case by paying for the brandy and leaving the change of half-a-crown.

" And she left this 'ere card with her address, in case it might be useful to you," added the porter, placing the card in the inside watch pocket of the waistcoat. " There, now you looks quite smart ; why them clothes looks as if they'd been made to fit yer."

The porter grinned at the joke, for the jacket was as short in the arms as the trousers were in the legs.

" Beggars mustn't be choosers," said a third party who had been a quiet witness of the scene. " You've had a lucky escape, lad ; it's a wonder we haven't had to gather you up in fragments and put you in a basket."

Jack's heart was too full for him to give vent to his gratitude in words.

He was anxious to quit the scene, and longed once more to breathe the air of freedom. At the same time he was thankful that matters had turned out as favourably as they had.

Upon the line, close to where the boy was found between the metals, a ticket from Paddington to Moorgate-street was found, which ticket had evidently been dropped by some affrighted passenger during the affecting and terrible scene.

The officials, however, thought it belonged to Jack, and not wishing to get up an excitement for the papers they considered it wise to gloss over the affair as quietly and smoothly as possible.

From a number of bruised felt hats Jack selected one that fitted his curly head, and then looking like a homeward bound schoolboy growing out of his clothes, he evinced a desire to depart.

"Hi, hi," said the porter. "The next train to the City's about due, here's yer two bob, come along. I thought when I picked yer up, we should 'av had to a measured you for a corfin."

Our hero was profuse in his thanks and offered the porter a shilling, but the man for some reason refused it, and placed Jack in a second-class carriage.

As it whirled along the young waif thought of his providential escape, and compared his present position on the soft cushioned seat with that of his last dreadful ride.

He trembled fearfully as the train reached its destination. Carefully alighting he gave up his ticket, and rushed up the staircase into the cool open air.

Then he was at a standstill, but not caring whither he went, he bent his steps towards London-bridge, which bridge of all others many a poor friendless adventurer like himself had sought and gazed from the broad parapet on to the river.

It was a fine, bright afternoon, bustle and activity were on every side, if we except the recesses where a number of half-starved miserable looking wretches were crowded on the stone seats asleep.

"Thank God I have not come to that yet," muttered Jack with an inward shudder. "I must have courage and endeavour to get some honest work."

As he mused, a faint cry, a sort of agonised scream, caused him to start and turn, and then he beheld a female who in endeavouring to cross the road, had slipped in the confusion of the traffic, and fallen in front of a heavily laden waggon.

Jack's keen eye measured the danger of her position in a moment.

The front horse was nearly upon her, and if his hoofs should miss her as she lay on her face, in one second more the broad wheels must go over her outstretched neck and crush it.

All this, as we have said, the young Arab took in at a glance, and with one swift bound he seized the bridle of the horse, and turned it towards the centre of the road.

Then, momentarily, he stooped down, caught the young girl beneath the armpits, and drew her on to the path. A loud cheer from the onlookers greeted this act, and then a distracted voice sounded in young Jack's ear. It was that of a man, a young soldier in the uniform of the Grenadier Guards, who held a light cane in his trembling hand, and forced his way through the excited throng.

"Thanks, thanks," he gasped, "God in heaven, I thought she was killed. And if so, how could I have rejoined my regiment, knowing that through my inattention she had lost her young precious life."

The young Guardsman was exceedingly agitated, and big drops of sweat oozed from his manly brow, as he placed his strong arm round the young girl's slender waist, and relieved our hero of his precious burthen.

"Thank you, young stranger. I thank you from my heart, accept a soldier's gratitude," exclaimed the soldier, warmly grasping Jack's hand. "When next we meet Tom Atkins will not forget the hero that saved the life of his bonny lass."

He glanced around him in bewilderment, the crowd hemmed them in on all sides, and the girl, pallid as death, had fainted.

At that opportune moment, the man whose cab had caused the almost fatal accident by separating the soldier from his lady love, drew in to the kerb, and he offered to convey the young couple clear of the crowded bridge.

His offer was gladly accepted by the Guardsman, who rewarded our hero with another grateful glance as the vehicle drove away.

Arab Jack stood for a moment dazed, scarcely comprehending the act of gallantry he had performed, and in this state when the traffic resumed its course, he was unconsciously borne back to the City side of the bridge, again; a number of errand boys, with bags, baskets, and parcels followed him, and pointed him out to others as a boy hero, and recounted with much gusto the story of the soldier and his lass.

Wearied with their importunities Jack turned towards Monument-yard, and as he drew near the majestic pile raised in commemoration of the Great Fire of London, he beheld a dark, full-bearded sailor, with grog aboard steering a zig-zag course in the direction of the bridge.

Presently a fashionably-dressed lady, with a hat and feather which seemed to take the sailor "all aback," stepped before the jovial-looking tar, just as if it were by accident, and barred his way.

The tar of course made a thousand awkward apologies.

"Hang me for a lubber, I ought to be keel-hauled," he said. "Why Venus never had such a pair of lovely blue eyes as yours is."

This incident, trivial as it was, afforded a tall, thin, genteel youth a favourable opportunity of dipping his fingers into the sailor's jacket pocket and fishing out a purse.

Arab Jack recognised the dexterous youth in a moment.

It was flashily dressed light-fingered Luke.

Through his oily tongue and evil persuasions Jack had been led to forsake a good home, and was now an outcast of society, a friendless waif on the cold, cold world.

Jack no sooner saw him than a fiery impulse seized his seething brain. To bound forward, spring upon the thief, and clutch him by the throat, was but the work of a moment.

"Help, murder, help," gasped the astounded prig, gasping hard for breath.

The sailor hearing the cries of distress, turned round, as he naturally would, and thinking Jack was in the wrong he doubled his fist.

"Damme," he roared, "a pirate in our midst, stand aside, let me give him a red-hot shot."

"Yes, do, sir," implored the lady as she clung to the sailor's arm, "he'll kill the young man, I'm sure he will."

Such words, spiced with a few crocodile tears, decided the sailor that he was quite justified in dealing summarily with the waif, and so he gave Jack, a broadside from the shoulder.

Jack, who still held on to the throat of his enemy, rolled in the gutter just like a skittle-pin, Luke falling on top of him, when both engaged in a desperate struggle.

"I'll kill you, cuss you," hissed Luke, who found that the grasp of his assailant was relaxed; "you are the Demon of the Dark Arches."

This was uttered purposely to reach the ears of the boys gathered round, many of whom had heard of the Dark Arches of the Adelphi, and therefore concluded at once that Jack was one of the terrible gang that was reputed to haunt that resort of criminal London.

Consequently, Jack, who had a short time before been lauded as a hero from the skies, to be praised, was now regarded as a desperate Jack Sheppard sort of character, who would one day dance on nothing in the air.

It happened, too, that at that moment Luke in the desperate struggle let fall the purse, and the sailor catching sight of it, and recognising it, snapped it up with a double-shotted oath.

"Shiver my shoes if that arn't sharp work for a Chinee juggler," vociferated the tar. "Bust you, I'd like to boot your piratical figger 'ed off."

There was considerable commotion amongst the crowd, and—"Here comes the bobbies," was passed from mouth to mouth.

Flash Luke heard this with alarm, his portrait was quite familiar to many of the police. With a well-practised wriggle that would have done credit to an eel, he extricated himself from little Jack, and both of them rising together, ske-daddled like lightning out of sight.

Jack, as we know, had cogent reasons for shunning the company of the police, and he did not pause to look round, or even take extra breath until he traversed Thames-street, and stood on Tower Hill.

There he discovered a vendor of sherbet water of whom he purchased a drink, the man remarking that our hero looked hot, and declaring that if he was in the capital of the Shah he could not obtain a more cooling and refreshing draught.

"All right," said Jack, "let me have another, and then direct me to the docks where they load the big ships."

"There they is, right on afore yer sir; that's the Mint right over in yon corner, where they makes all the money, which I can tell you I'd like to get a pailful of. I wouldn't stick here then, benefittin' the public at a brown a time."

Jack laughed, the first time he had done so for a long time, then wiping his face with a grimy handkerchief which had been left in the jacket-pocket by its previous owner, went on his way rejoicing.

A smart walk soon brought him in sight of the tall masts and spars of the shipping towering above the grim walls of the docks, but the dock gates were closed, so that he had nothing to look at but the pictures of outgoing steam vessels posted about, and the dingy shops and public-house signs, all of which pertained to the nautical.

Jack, like many other boys, had often had an inclination for the sea, but now what he saw of it was anything but tempting to the west-end tastes to which he had been in a manner born.

A tempting cook shop whose window was full of cold joints and dishes of rolley-polley jam pudding attracted his attention, and having speculated in a huge portion of the latter, he pursued his way, little knowing and much less caring whither his steps were leading him.

The shades of evening, however, were begin-ning to close in, and he began to experience the awkwardness of being alone.

During the exciting scenes of the day he had had no opportunity of thinking of this, and he actually wished that some of the ragged fra-ternity would turn up to guide him to some place where he could "doss" for the night.

Hitherto he had not been called upon to pro-vide himself with a lodging,—the outcast waifs had always found him a hole where he could crawl in out of the rain. Now, as night ap-proached, the wind blew up chill from the river and angry clouds gathered in the sky.

He walked on a mile thinking of this, and also of how he was going to live when his funds were exhausted.

He had no one to talk to, no one to consult but his own inexperienced mind.

He saw plenty of miserable outcasts worse than himself, for he was tidily rigged, and his hunger was satisfied, but ——

He stumbled against a huge nail which diverted the channel of his thoughts, and put an idea in his head.

In their foraging raids the London Arabs often came across tins of preserved milk, which they opened with a nail similar to the one he had found.

This milk, spread upon dry toke (as bread was technically termed) was food and drink, very nourishing and pleasant to the taste.

Jack therefore speculated in a loaf, a small portion of cheese, and a tin of milk, all of which he tied in a handkerchief and slung in a loop on his arm.

Thus provisioned, he left the main track and darted down a narrow lane, in the hope of find-ing some place wherein to lay his head, but, alas! poor Jack was doomed to disappointment.

The lane was intersected with many smaller ones, all wretched in appearance, peopled with ragged dirty urchins, and guarded at the entrance with women, the very sight of whom made Jack shudder.

"Good Lord," gasped Jack, "this is worse even than the Dials, and Drury Lane is paradise compared with such ricketty slums."

After winding and turning, he at length hit upon some stairs leading down to the water, and he thought he would sit down there and rest, and watch the darkness fall upon the river. Suddenly he became aware that some parties in a boat were haggling about the fare that was to be charged for taking one of their number off to a big ship lying in midstream of the river.

"By George," Jack gasped. "That's the sailor that flash Luke robbed. I'm glad he hasn't seen me, for he believes I took his purse, and as he is as drunk as a fiddler he'd probably smash me."

Jack was about right.

If the sailor in his present state had seen him, he would have given him a red-hot shot, if he had not been tempted to pitch him neck and heels into the river.

"Now then, shove off," vociferated the sailor. "Hang the expense. I want to see my old top-mate aboard the 'Vulture,' afore I go down to Sheernest to join the guard ship."

The flood tide was running up swiftly, and as the man-o-war's-man stood up to push the boat from under the bows of a row of barges that were moored there, he by some means overbalanced, and overboard he went.

Young Jack uttered a cry of alarm, and heedless of all danger sprang across several boats, on to the barges, by which means he reached the one under the bows of which he had seen the sailor sink.

Well used to boating upon the upper reaches of the river, Jack knew that if the barge did not keep the body sucked under its flat bottom it must rise again astern, so he ran to that end of the barge and stood ready with the end of the vessel's sternfast.

Up came the sailor and down went the rope, just in bare time, and the drowning man clutched it.

"Good! bravo!" shouted the men in the boat when they saw Jack's action; "hold him up till we come, matey."

They had to pull right round outside the barges, and if it had not been for the hero's timely aid and presence of mind, the sailor would have been swept down under the next tier, and probably drowned.

As it was, he was hauled safely into the boat, and the watermen pulled off to the steamer.

A number of waterside loafers and river rats had assembled on the various craft, and Jack found to his dismay that he had incurred their displeasure.

"Cuss you for a meddlin' wampire," said one of the unshaven ill-looking scoundrels. "I've mor'n 'arf a mind to chuck you in, for being so handy aboard other people's wessels. It aint orfen we get a chance to drag for a dead body, and one as is likely to hold a few yaller flats in his locker."

Jack was dismayed.

The speaker had not only murder in his foul tongue but a devil in his looks, which so terrified the boy that he bolted off and put as many barges between himself and the loafer as he possibly could.

Then watching an opportunity he jumped down into the empty hold of one of the flat-bottomed craft, and endeavoured to hide.

"Ah," gasped Jack, "a door, by Jove that must lead to the cabin," and pushing it open he peered in and found that the dark chamber in the stern of the barge was unoccupied.

Jack very fortunately had begged a few lucifers at the chandler's shop, so he struck a light and then closed the door and bolted it on the inside.

He was now safe from interruption, for he had noticed that the hatch above was secured with a bar and padlocked.

Jack was too tired to eat,—he wanted sleep,—so stretching himself on a beam across the barge's stern, he placed his wallet under his head and thus pillowed was soon dead to the cares and troubles of the world, folded in the arms of Morpheus.

CHAPTER III.

ON BOARD THE "DROMEDARY."—THE PERILS OF A STOWAWAY.—FIRE! FIRE!—JACK IS ACCUSED OF A TERRIBLE CRIME.—A BULLY TAKEN DOWN A PEG.

"AHOY there! Yeo, ho! rouse out of this, shiver my shoe-strings, who'd a thought I'd dropped down the river with a ghost aboard?"

Little Jack was not only startled by the gruff voice, but the bear-like shake of a heavy hand, which made him for the moment imagine he was still pursuing his terrible journey on the iron road.

"Ahoy!" the voice again sounded, and this time Jack was seized roughly by the shoulder and jerked to his feet.

"Who are you? where am I?" were Jack's sleepy questions as he rubbed his eyes. "Where's my ticket,—you won't rob me and then lock me up?"

"I'll knock you down if you aint quick out o' this. I'll not wait for the water p'lice to charge yer. You're one of the river rats as nicks all our headfasts and fenders, I reckon; and if you're not smart a walking your chalks, I'll pitch you over into the river."

Jack began to thoroughly wake up at this.

He slung his bundle on his arm and climbed up from the hold, to discover to his astonishment that the barge was in a broad part of the river, and that a large vessel was alongside.

"Good man," said he to the lighterman who had followed him up, "you will put me safely on shore, sir, I beg of you."

"Can't you swim?"

"I can, sir, but not in a place like this—I, I——"

"That'll do, stow your gab," said the man, eyeing him up and down, "I can read you to a tin-tack, you've run away from home to go to sea, broke your parents' hearts, and done the same as a heap of others."

"There now, that 'ull do," he added, as Jack was about to speak. "Clear out o' this, I've got to take them cases up to the Wictoria Dock, so jump ashore or else I'll chuck you overboard."

He seized hold of Jack as if he were about to put his terrible threat into execution, but softening down, he said—

"Look here, now, I've got cubs of my own, and as I hope the Lord will give some one a heart to do them a good turn when they has to rough it, I'll do one for you."

"Thank you, sir," said Jack, whose mother had fully impressed upon him the value of civility.

"Well, then, that wessel alongside is bound foreign, so if you want to go to sea jump aboard on her, stow yourself down below as far as you can forard, and all as you'll get when they gets to sea and finds you out 'ull be a good tanning."

"Quite enough," thought Jack, "but it is Hobson's choice, so I'll accept it gracefully."

"Good day, sir," said he to the lighterman.

"Good bye, my lad, God bless you. I can see you're not what I took you to be; have you a copper about yer?"

"Yes," said Jack, producing a penny.

"There, now, that's a knife for you; it 'ull help you to carve a way in the world, and when you get down 'arted read the name on it, and think o' my 'couraging words, do ye see it—Will Wiggles? I've got a boy about your stamp knocking about in the world somewheres."

Jack exchanged his penny for the knife, and then shook hands with the rough but well-meaning lighterman, who began to cast off, and Jack clambered up through the port-hole into the big ship.

Jack Martin had had a good sleep and was much refreshed, but for all that he was not particularly happy.

At each step he was widening the distance between himself and his home, that home he might never see again, nor hear the sweet voice of his kind indulgent mother. But with the buoyancy of youth Jack's heart soon bounded again to the surface, his eager feet trod the firm 'tween decks of the magnificent steamship, at whose tapering masthead as he peeped up the hatchway, he could see the transport flag flying.

There was a deal of bustle on the upper deck, he could hear hurried feet moving about, the "click, click, click," of the pawls of a winch, and loud orders being given by the various officers.

It was his desire, however, to seek some place of concealment, and so after picking his way among bales, cases, and huge barrels, which were part of the cargo, he crawled in on top of some merchandise which appeared to be wedged and stowed for good, and made himself as comfortable as he could under the circumstances.

Whilst he lay thus snug, he learned that the ship was the " Dromedary," that she was now lying off the T. pier of Woolwich Arsenal, and that as soon as some soldiers and blue jackets were embarked she would be towed down the iver on her way to Egypt.

Jack's heart beat wildly when he heard this.

Egypt, the land of his dreams, the land of Wonders, from which the Needle on the Thames Embankment had been brought at so much expense and risk, that he had so often gazed upon in admiration and wonderment.

" Bang!"

A gun fired as a signal for starting. The drafts for the Mediterranean were evidently on board.

He could hear the cheering on shore and on the piers, on the steamers and boats alongside, and the returning volley from the throats of the men on board,—the Reds and the Blues,—who were going to fill up vacancies in the regiments and men-of-war, from which invalids and time expired men were to be sent home.

At sound of the loud huzzas the heart of the wandering waif swelled nigh unto bursting.

" Huzza, huzza," he shouted from his voluntary prison house, where he sat uncared for and alone.

At length the whistles of the tugs were heard, the vessel began to move and Jack knew he was on his way to distant climes, leaving those he might never see more without so much as a word of parting,—the fond farewell, and the sad good-bye.

Jack fairly cried,—he could not help it,—not from sorrow or grief at going away, but from that inexplicable and holy feeling which every one,—and more especially a true Britisher—experiences on first bidding adieu to his own dear native land.

But soon the cheery song of the chanti-man was heard, to which the sailors jovially chorussed

as they got the heavy anchors over the bows and secured them to the cat heads ready to drop into the river's bed when necessity needed.

Jack would fain have been on deck, his forced imprisonment was irksome; he listened to the ship's bell as it proclaimed each passing half-hour, until he could tell by the motion of the vessel that she was fairly out at sea.

Then he began to experience the inconveniences of those who journey on the ocean highway—the close hold, the odour of tar-barrels, cordage, and so forth; but he had the consolation that he was not likely to meet with the awful sufferings and death of some stowaways he had heard of, who had been literally roasted through creeping in too near the boilers.

Nevertheless, he was spared the horrors of sea-sickness, although for days he could not eat, but when his appetite returned he quickly demolished the whole of his tiny store.

Hunger then seized upon him, accelerated by a burning thirst; added to which, each night, (that is according to his reckoning, for he was in perpetual darkness) he was troubled with a mysterious sound just like the scratching of a number of rats.

In this dire strait he determined on crawling about and seeking for a means to reach the deck, for he concluded that all the rope's-ending he could get would be nothing in comparison with what he must eventually suffer.

On the day after making this resolve he was startled by the appearance of a streak of light, and while he lay on a bale of serge watching and wondering, a board was removed from the bulk-head which partitioned off the hold, and a man bearing a lantern passed through the aperture and made for one of the cases which were stowed near to the hole.

With a small crowbar the man opened the case and took therefrom several boxes of sardines, which he stowed away in the bosom of his shirt, when hearing a noise without he fixed the lantern and crept back through the hole, closing it after him.

Jack was then like a hungry wolf.

The sight of the sardine boxes set his stomach yearning.

Creeping to the case, which had not been properly secured, he helped himself to some of the contents, just as a heavy wave caused the vessel to give a lurch, which toppled the lantern over and sent it rolling.

Jack gave a startled cry, for the glass of the lantern was broken by the fall, and the burning wick coming in contact with some light fabric set it in a blaze.

Our young hero did all he knew to extinguish the fierce flame, but without water he was powerless.

The dry stuff seemed to court the hungry element, and there was every likelihood of the ship falling an easy prey.

With blistered hands and burning brow the brave boy did all that remained in his power, and that was to tear down the board from the bulkhead and shout for help.

But he might as well have called to the winds if it had not been for a fortunate circumstance.

The ship was in danger and all hands were on deck, so that his voice was not likely to be heard.

One of the men, however, came down below

to take off his boot, his foot having been severely crushed between a stanchion and a deck spar which had broken loose, and he thus fortunately heard the voice of the young stowaway.

"Shiver my jib!" exclaimed the injured seaman, forgetting the pain of his foot and glancing towards the passage that led to the bulkhead, "that's a human voice I'll swear, or Long Tom's not a seaman aboard this boat." He listened again.

"Fire! fire!! Help!" he heard shouted in feeble accents.

Then he saw a flare of the dread enemy, and clambering up the ladder again on deck he informed the second officer.

He quickly saw how matters stood and quietly gave the alarm, which resulted in the fire being extinguished and the stowaway being taken on to the quarter-deck.

The captain, though a brave and hardy seaman, and one who could command the calmness of a stoic in the wildest storm, lost his temper when he learned that the vessel had been set fire to by a young stowaway.

In spite of the danger of the ship, and the howling of the gale which had suddenly burst upon her, he gave vent to a big oath, and stamped his foot vehemently on the deck.

"Take him below," he thundered ominously. "Put him in irons. The young whelp shall bitterly rue the day he set foot on board the 'Dromedary.'"

The passengers in the saloon, who, could not sleep in their berths for the violent motion of the vessel, gazed on each other with pallid cheeks in silent awe.

Horror of the diabolical crime reigned in every heart, and not one there, in the feeling engendered for the moment, would have stretched a hand to save the waif in the event of the captain essaying to throw him overboard.

Eight bells, twelve o'clock at midnight, the hour when most folks on shore are peacefully slumbering or preparing to go to bed.

Then the gale was at its height.

The black, foam-crested waves rolled and rose like giant mountains in the Bay of Biscay.

No one on board the ocean steamer slept a wink that night.

Jack was placed in the spare sail-room, which was the temporary prison, and his legs confined in the bilboes—a long iron bar running fore and aft of the deck, to which the prisoner is shackled by the ankles and padlocked.

This was a cruel farce in the case of our young waif, for by slipping his shoes he could draw his feet through the shackles, a fact which Marcus Fortescue, one of the arrogant mids, was soon to learn to his discomfiture,

This cockey young sprig, like many others of his class, thought he could ride rough shod over the stowaway boy before one atom of guilt had been proved against him, or he even had had the opportunity to speak for himself. The venomous, ill-looking, and overbearing beast thought to play his pranks on our little hero.

"Little" we say. Jack was about the ordinary stamp of his age, a boy of fourteen, but the bully was two or three years older, a disparity which of course would make a deal of difference in their height and size.

The storm, towards daylight began to abate, a circumstance which, if it had not been for the cold cheerlessness of the morning, would have put the night-worn watch in good spirits. And in the meantime, Jack, who had free use of his hands, opened the tin of sardines he had secured and devoured the contents ravenously.

"By George," he muttered, "I feel as strong as a lion after that feed ; didn't the oil let them slip down, and ain't it greased the machinery of my stumjack."

"Hallo, who's that talking?" said a voice. "Well, I declare, if every dog don't bark and whine when he feels the chain."

Jack no sooner heard the voice and its unpleasant jarring tone, than he conceived at once that the words were intended as an insult towards him.

"What poodle is that snuffing about my summer-house?" said he.

This was quite enough to rile Marcus Fortescue.

"Where is the poodle?" said he, opening the door, which had been bolted on the outside.

"In your skeleton case," replied Jack with aggravating sang froid. "Turn up its pretty little ears and let me see whether they need to be cropped."

Marcus bit his lip, and tried vainly to hide a scowl.

"Turn up the little cur's nose and let me judge whether it needs pulling," sneered the bully, at the same time moving forward towards the imprisoned boy, and stooping down as if he was going to spit in his face.

Jack was seated on the floor with his back against the panelling, and his monkey, being up, he warned Marcus to keep a safe distance for fear he might be tempted to land him one on the eson.

Eson was a slang word Jack had contracted during his sojourn among the London Arabs, and Marcus Fortescue quite understood its significance if he did not its meaning.

"Bow, wow," he hissed, "you naughty little puppy ; " at the same time pretending to pull Jack's toe, just as a mischievous boy would make a feint to pull the tail of a snapping terrier.

Little Jack could stand no more. Slipping his ankles from the bilboes, he sprang to his feet and dealt the bully such a stinger on the nose that he not only yelled, called on his mother, the captain, and the cook, but actually bellowed like a disconsolate town bull.

It is only fair to say that Marcus was taken at a decidedly unfair advantage.

For instance, he was quite unaware that the prisoner could slip his irons, and he was totally unprepared for such a telling blow without the necessary preliminary of boxing.

Arab Jack was quite satisfied with giving him one blow. His big fat nose went "squash," and split like a ripe tomato, whilst the claret ran just as if a bottle of that liquid had suddenly come to grief.

"Bravo, younker, you deserve a putty medal," roared the boatswain, who was watching through the slide or peep-hole in the door, and was quite pleased with the chastisement of the arrogant and ignorant bully.

Not so the captain ; when it came to his ears he raved and stormed about the young castaway. "I'll have him keel hauled," he said to the mate. "D——n him, it was through him we had last night's gale."

"I don't see how that can be," replied the mate, who was quite a gentleman in speech and manners. "There were other vessels in the storm and they could not all have a stowaway on board."

"Probably not, nor a young incendiary. If the flames had reached the magazine we should have gone like a rocket into the air, and——and——"

"Midshipman Marcus would not have played his monkey tricks," interrupted the mate.

The captain scowled and turned away on his heel at once.

The bastard lord was his favourite, although he was as ignorant of seamanship as the pig on deck in the stye, and could no more take the sun's altitude or work a dead reckoning than could Jack; therefore he was a smart object to crow over the friendless waif. But the secret of the captain's favouritism was, that he got well paid to look after the illegitimate snob, and that there was a young lady—save the mark—also of doubtful origin, but with plenty of money, on whom the captain had cast his speculative eye in the case.

Little Jack was therefore looked upon as the very acme of all that was bad, in the eyes of the captain.

"Lash his fiendish limbs to the bar," said he to the second officer, who informed him that Jack had slipped his ankles from the bilboes. "I'll have this matter sifted in the course of the day, and then I'll give the carcase of the young reptile to the sharks."

———

CHAPTER IV.

ARAB JACK IS BROUGHT TO TRIAL.—THE SCARRED CHEEK AND THE MAIMED HAND.— AN AWKWARD SQUAD.—JACK CHIRRUPS UP ALOFT.—A FIRST DAY IN EGYPT.

CAPTAIN CORMORANT was one of those who if it suited him failed not to keep his word. During the forenoon watch, when the vessel was bowling along under sail and steam, he ordered the prisoner to be brought before him.

Jack was almost paralysed when a corporal and two soldiers with muskets loaded and bayonets fixed entered the sail-room, and informed him that he was to be tried, by what they termed a drum-head court-martial, for attempting to destroy the ship.

The corporal undid the lashings from Jack's feet, and the soldiers taking a position on either side of the terrified boy led him in military fashion to the state cabin.

There an imposing scene was prepared. A file of soldiers with bayonets fixed was ranged along one side, and a couple of blue-jackets with drawn cutlasses resting on their shoulders guarded the door.

The captain, surrounded by the officers, had already taken up his position at the further end, and having delivered an elaborate speech, in which the crimes of the prisoner were set forth, the enquiry commenced.

Jack, as we know, had very little to tell or confess.

He explained how he found himself alongside in the barge, his treatment by the lighterman, and his sufferings in the vessel's dark, stifling hold.

All this was listened to by the officers with an air of belief, but when he described how the man with the lantern had broken through the bulk-head and broached the cargo there was a murmur of disbelief.

The face of Captain Cormorant flushed with indignation.

"Such a story, such an abominable and bare-faced lie might do for the marines," he exclaimed glancing at the officers around him, "but as we have none of that gallant arm of the service on board—why ——".

"Halt, sir," interrupted Colonel Fitzalwyn; "give the prisoner a fair chance; if he saw this man, as he says, surely he can give us his description."

Encouraged by these words, Jack drew himself boldly erect.

"The man I saw," he said, "had a blue scar on his cheek like a cross, and only three fingers on his right hand."

This settled the matter.

There was a stoker on board answering that description, a man who had been injured in a boiler explosion.

He was on duty at that moment below; but the chief mate had him quickly called up, and little Jack, to the man's great astonishment and alarm, swore that he was the one he had seen enter surreptitiously into the hold.

This coupled with the fact that a lantern of the description Jack described was missing from the lamp-room, and also the second mate's evidence that a wire-guard, such as might have encircled the lantern, was found among the charred debris, fixed the guilt at once on the stoker.

He, therefore, was placed in irons in room of the boy, and Jack's crime was thus reduced to that of defrauding the company of the passage money, and the striking of a ship's officer.

Marcus, with the rest of the middies who were not on duty was present, and a gleam like that of an exultant savage shone in his green, tiger-like eyes.

Arab Jack at that moment caught a glimpse of his fiend-like features, and the brave boy hurled him back a defiant glance.

The cabin was then closed, and Jack, having been supplied with a drink of cold water and a hard biscuit, was sent up aloft to the crosstrees, there to atone for what the captain described as his dastardly attack on the middy.

Jack had never been aloft before in his life.

He had climbed many a tree and flag-staff on shore, but that was far different to climbing the rigging of the lofty masts of a steamship, which plunged into the heavy head-seas in a manner that made the position aloft unbearable to a landsman.

Jack, however, made the ascent.

His brave heart quailed not at the danger.

One slip—one false hold, and he would be precipitated into the boiling sea; yet he clung to the shrouds like grim death.

Up, up, he went; slow certainly, but surely, the eyes of those on deck following his every movement, until he reached the spot pointed out to him by the vindictive captain.

Once there it took him all his time to hold on.

The huge sails occasionally flapped, the ropes

creaked under their heavy strain, the mast rocked from side to side, causing a sensation in his stomach similar to that when a boy first goes up in a swing.

At times, when the bows of the vessel rose on a billow and then fell into the deep hollow of the sea, Jack's perch, to which he clung with the tenacity of a monkey, described a complete circle in the salt-laden air.

But our hero had no fear.

Though he felt the qualms of sea-sickness he did not show it.

He felt that the eyes of the sneaking middy were upon him, and that strengthened his nerve, so much so, that he munched away at the hard biscuit, and glanced about him at the numerous vessels which, like the "Dromedary," were plunging and rolling in the troubled ocean.

Jack was in hopes of getting a glimpse of the land, but he saw nothing but water on every side, from which, on the port bow, a misty vapour seemed to arise.

Presently a bright flash darted out of the mist, and the report of a gun in that direction made him start almost out of his skin.

"That's the 'Gib,'" said a gruff voice in his ear, and to his surprise he saw that he was not alone.

One of the seamen had been sent aloft to keep an extra look-out ahead, and he quickly pointed out to Jack's inexperienced eye the dim outlines of the stupendous rock of Gibraltar.

As the mist cleared Jack was enabled to see the flag-staff on the lofty peak, from which signals were made to the vessel he was on, and after speaking for some time, the "Dromedary's" flag was dipped, and her head was turned towards Malta.

Jack was so pleased with being aloft that he was quite sorry when he was called down.

As he was a stranger to all on board, and was looked upon as an interloper from the captain down to the cook, he felt anything but comfortable.

But a fresh misery awaited him upon deck.

As he dropped from the rigging he was confronted by one of the gruff man-o'-war's men, who nearly terrified him out of his life.

"Dash my sister Poll's cat's mangy tail, if you ain't the cockroach as pressganged my pus."

Our hero started, and had only time to duck and elude a broad-handed blow, which, as it missed him and struck the hand-bitts, assured him that his head must have been knocked off at once.

The tar rapped out an oath, for the blow stung his fingers, and he was about to resume the attack when Jack bolted away and dodged behind the mast.

"Hallo, avast there, matey!" cried the seaman who descended at that instant from aloft. "What's the younker been up to,—prigging some one's bacca?"

"A hanged site wuss, cuss him. He stole my pus as I was boarding a saucy fire-ship, alongshore there, up at the moniment."

"Stole it!" exclaimed the sailor, starting back. "Come now, let's hear what the younker has to say about it. Hi! Carey's Chicken, heave up here."

Arab Jack gave a flat denial to the accusation, and explained satisfactorily the mistake of the bluff honest sailor.

"Well, boy," said he, "as I've wronged you, I'll be your friend. I'll make a man of you while we're shipmates aboard this wessel."

Jack thanked him, although he was not in the slightest aware in what way he was going to make him a man. In the first place he gave him a good tuck-in of grub and a basin of hot soup, the first meal the London street waif had partaken of for many a long day.

That evening Jack was delighted with the yarns spun by the jolly tars, and next day, Tom Trysail, his newly-made friend, put him, as he termed it, through his facings.

"Here," said he, putting a mopstick into his hand, "this is supposed to be a musket. I'm going to learn ye rifle drill."

"Anything for a quiet life," Jack thought. "If it's no good to me, it can't do me any harm, so I'll do my best to learn."

He little imagined how useful the knowledge would be to him in after years.

He little thought that the tide of fortune was drifting him towards a scene of perils and adventures that would make his name famous in the annals of life.

So he progressed joyfully under the tuition of old Tom, and in time he could not only handle the rifle and bayonet with many of the soldiers, but also acquired a useful knowledge of the cutlass and boarding-pike exercise.

Jack's drill-mates were only two in number, a black pickaninny who waited on the cook and a curly-coated dog belonging to one of the passengers.

This awkward squad caused much amusement among the crew, especially the canine one, who, with a cocked hat and feather, stood on his hind legs and shouldered his little gun with as much sedateness as any Christian.

Mocho was the dog's name, and Jack and he were the best of friends, perhaps for the reason that they drilled together when Sambo was engaged in the caboose.

Marcus viewed this happy family with considerable distaste.

Discontented, malicious and envious in himself, he could not bear to see others happy.

One of his chief annoyances was the absence of a moustache, which his overhanging sallow lip gave no sign of bearing.

His fellow-mids, however, were blessed in that respect. They all had a little down, and one, Alf Athol, had quite a dark silken fringe, which was the admiration of all the young lady passengers.

Marcus, who was death on lady-killing, hated Athol, and in the endeavour to cut him out he bought heaps of bottles of the so-called hair producers; but none seemed to act with the required efficiency. Sambo, the black boy, acquainted Jack with this, and the pair had many a good laugh over the recital, which always ended in the desire of the negro to "Pay out the dam bad massa, who frowed knives and forks at him when he went into de cabin."

Tom Trysail chanced to overhear this, and as he was a sworn foe to what he termed lubberly, upstart, fresh-water sailors, he offered his aid and advice to upset the foppish middy.

"Try and get me one o' the bottles," said he to Sambo. "And by the mother of Neptune I'll make him have a lip on him as 'ull be worth looking at."

That night Sambo captured an empty bottle, and also narrowly escaped a broken head. As he was coming up the steerage ladder from below, a heavy block was dropped from the hatchway above and struck him on the shoulder.

Sambo just had time to catch a glimpse of a receding head, which from its outlines he felt certain belonged to Marcus, and making for the forecastle he acquainted Jack with the dastardly trick at once.

"Dere be a debil in dat fella," said the darky. "Him try to poison Mocho toder day; but Sambo watch 'im, an den 'praps he gib 'im little sumfing dat make 'im belly squeak."

Jack and Tom broke out into a hearty laugh.

The picaninny rolled his large black eyes and showed the whites of them in such a ludicrous manner, as he held both hands to his stomach, that they could not restrain their merriment.

Before the "Dromedary" reached Malta, Marcus Fortescue's cup of bitterness was full to overflowing. His lip was blistered and green, and a sickening pain seemed occasionally to gnaw his vitals.

The cantankerous spirit was not, however, crushed; but his power to do evil was so weakened, that it made him fret and fume like an angry porcupine.

No one pitied him except the captain, and his pity was more for himself than for his angelic charge.

At Malta the soldiers left the ship, and orders were given for the blue-jackets to proceed to Alexandria, which port, in due time, the "Dromedary" safely reached.

Tom and his shipmates were greatly excited when they saw the British and French fleets quietly anchored in the harbour, but evidently keeping an anxious and watchful eye upon the shore.

"There, Jack," said Tom, pointing to a couple of ironclads, "that's the 'Monarch,' there's the 'Sultan,' and yonder little gunboat's my old ship the saucy 'Condor.'"

According to Jack's idea the "Condor" was a mean-looking ship for such a stout-hearted seaman as Tom Trysail to be aboard of, and he said so, to the evident disgust of the hardy tar.

"Never mind, Jack," said he. "It's not allus the big ship that's the best, d'ye see. Why, that craft's more like a eel, and I guess it could give some o' they forts a dose o' pepper."

The "Dromedary" fired a gun and hoisted her colours as she steamed into the inner harbour, where, before she had time to drop anchor, she was surrounded by a crowd of boats.

Jack in the meantime took great interest in the place, the Pharo lighthouse, the numerous forts, and above all, the strangely mixed-up nationalities of the shipping.

"Jack," said Tom, in a regretful tone, "I shall now have to leave you; here comes the launch for me and my chums. Good-bye, and may God A'mighty bless yer."

With a sinking heart Jack then found himself on the deck alone; but he buoyed up his spirits with the hope that he might perhaps get on shore and obtain some sort of employment. From what he could see of the place, with its tall minarets, palaces, and nice whitewashed buildings in the distance, he concluded that it must be healthy and clean, and, moreover, abounding in wealth.

Tom had told him of places he had visited which abounded in gold, diamonds, rubies, and so forth, and where fruit was so plentiful that they could have loaded their ship with it, and yet not have diminished the store.

But of Egypt Tom spoke very little, so that Jack was astonished to see so many people of various colours.

As he stood thus gazing into the water, thinking of crocodiles and other hideous sea monsters, Sambo crept to his side.

"Oh, dear, massa Jack," said he, "captin speak berry ill ob yoo; say 'im send yoo to one Arab man's polis station, hab yoo beat, and put yoo in prison."

"Will he?" vociferated Jack, glancing at his sturdy arms, and looking down at his long straight limbs, which had so developed that it seemed as if his clothes were skin-fits. "Will he? I'll swim ashore first; I'm not afraid of the sharks."

"Plenty boats, Jack; but Arab big tief dey say. Oh lord! 'ere dey come. Good-bye, Jack, if Sambo see yoo no more."

A tear stood in the negro boy's eye as our hero wrung his hand, and then taking advantage of the confusion on board, and the clamouring of voices alongside, Jack crept down the side and concealed himself in one of the boats.

How he evaded detection and landed on the wharf would have puzzled him to tell.

Once safely on shore he took to his heels and fled from the water-side.

But his idea of the town was altered when he got into the narrow squalid streets, and he sighed as though his heart was about to break, when he heard nothing but a strange language from every one around.

CHAPTER V.

THE MAN OF MYSTERY.—JACK FINDS THERE IS CORN IN EGYPT.—THE THREE BEAUTIES OF THE SUMPTUOUS DIVAN. — A STARTLING PROPOSAL.—JACK SIGNS THE MYSTERIOUS SCROLL.

"WELL, God knows what will become of me," said Jack, as he drew near to the Greek quarter of the town; "every one I meet offers me an insult, and on all hands I am met with threatening frowns."

He muttered unconsciously aloud, and the next minute a hand was placed lightly on his shoulder.

He turned and confronted a pair of eyes that had haunted him everywhere he went—eyes that once seen could never be forgotten.

"Silence," whispered the strange man. "You are a Frank, an European, I would caution you not to utter your thoughts too loud. There is trouble brewing in Alexandria, so I bid you beware if you don't wish to be murdered."

"Thanks, I am English, and you speak my native tongue full well. Say, how am I to avoid this terrible injustice?"

"Allah be praised," said the strange man. "There is one God and one prophet."

He dropped his head so that his turban partly concealed his features, and folding his hands devoutly across his chest, gave our hero a nudge to do the same.

Jack inclined his head, and then saw by a

"MY TURN NOW, ONCE IT WAS THINE!"   *p.* 24

shadow on the ground that some one was approaching, so he remained dumb until the muffled figure passed them and entered a narrow passage.

"There, that's how you have to do in this country," said the stranger. "Mum's the word. You must have as many creeds as there are days in the year, for in these perilous times no one knows his friend."

"Who was that, then?" Jack asked. "I have seen some rum customers here. Some look like women in bedgowns with a sheet folded round their heads, whilst others are dressed in damask window curtains."

"Just so, every one to his creed and nationality. You see that group of women yonder, they are Turkish wives, that white cloth over their faces covering all but their eyes is the yacmash. Their loose silks don't look very fashionable to you, and the slip-shods they wear over their beautiful slippers, no doubt, give you the horrors to see them drag along. But tell me, what's your game in Alexandria?"

"Plunder," said Jack, with a grin. "I've run my ship, now I want employment."

"Just as I thought, hanged if it ain't. I saw you come up the wharf, and, thinks I, that's a runner disguised in some other kid's togs. If you'd gone down the Jew's quarter in that rig they'd have locked you up for a thieving young Arab."

"Very pleasant," said Jack, " and exceedingly complimentary. Were it not for the pleasure of conversing in my own language, I should quit your society for being too civil."

"Tut, tut," whispered the man of mystery, "don't be too hasty, my friend; we are talking loud here, and though the walls are high and thick, the roof is flat, and big ears may be up there listening."

Jack's spirit was roused, his eyes flashed, and he stood up looking the picture of health and vigour, the man could not help admiring him.

Our hero was puzzled to make out the strange being who took so much interest in his welfare. He kept rattling the coin in the capacious

2

pockets of his big baggy trousers, so seemed unlikely to have designs on Jack's evidently lowered exchequer.

The man was rather tastefully dressed. His baggy breeches were of blue cloth, his waistcoat was of green silk, heavily braided, over which he wore a kind of corsair jacket trimmed with red and gold, his feet were encased in patent leather boots reaching to his knees, and a turban of purest whiteness encircled his head. He had a long dark moustache, somewhat after the style of the Greeks, but of what nationality he was, Jack could not, of course, determine.

Jack's solitary store was a sixpence, and the formidable knife he bought of Will Wiggins.

This he determined to use upon any one who molested him, and possibly, if he had been by himself in those crowded streets, the opportunity would soon have occurred.

"Well," said Jack, when he had well eyed his friend up and down, "what do you think of doing? Can you direct me to any English place where I can board and lodge until I get some employment?"

"You shall share my own house," replied the man, extending his hand. "I like you, whatever your name may be, and I can probably inform you of something to your advantage; you seem plucky, and you would, possibly not object to a little travel and adventure."

Jack's eyes blazed again with that peculiar fiery ardour, as he replied, " just my mark, lead on, I will follow you."

He led Jack up many strange streets, showed him the Grand Square, or Place Mehemet Ali, pointed out the mansions of the different consuls and ambassadors, and described to him the difference between the Egyptian soldiers and the police.

At length they arrived at the stranger's house at Attareen, in the suburbs, a dingy looking building externally, with venetian blinds, but beautiful in the exterior.

They entered by means of a key, and having passed along a dimly lighted passage, they entered a room in which were several ladies, who, on seeing a stranger, made a movement towards a damask screen which concealed a door.

"Sit still, don't be alarmed," said Jack's guide, "I've brought a husband for one of you disconsolate maidens."

"For one!" exclaimed one of the ladies whose beauty astounded our hero, and whose dress reminded him of the princess in the "Arabian Nights."

"For one! who is that celestial that Allah has so vouchsafed to bless?"

"Well, he may marry you all in time my good sisters," said the man, jocosely. "But as he is an Englishman, and his Allah will only allow him one wife at a time, he cannot marry you all at once."

This speech elicited such peals of sweet silvery laughter, that Jack felt his heart fairly bound.

He quite forgot the bashfulness and shame he experienced when in his grimed shabby state he found himself in the soft lighted chamber, thickly carpeted, with the sumptuous divans or low cushioned couches that lined the richly draped walls.

Jack was not only enraptured with the lovely females, three in number—fair, dark, and olive complexioned, but he was delighted to have discovered people who spoke his own tongue.

"Oh Hassan," said the fair girl, throwing her arms about her brother's neck, "how cruel of you to introduce an angel into our sanctuary without giving us timely warning to prepare for his reception."

"There is time for you to do so, fair Lily, while we perform our ablutions," said Hassan. "Summon the dwarf and let him prepare all that is good for our English guest; we have broken bread and eaten salt on board his vessel, so he is quite entitled to our hospitality."

Jack was astounded to find so much social familiarity, in a country where he was taught all matters were carried on with such restraint.

It was plain to him that Hassan could not be a true follower of the Holy Prophet; perhaps he was a renegade, a Greek, but there, what mattered that to him?

Jack was quite refreshed when he had bathed and perfumed himself in one of the marble baths, and glad enough was he to find himself clothed once more in clean linen.

He was startled when he viewed himself in the massive mirror, for Hassan had ordered the slave to provide him with a regular Arab suit, and a turban that would have taken him all the days of his life to have folded into shape.

The repast was simply sumptuous; in a word, every delicacy of the season was provided, and Jack certainly imagined himself in heaven as he lounged on the cushioned divan, surrounded by the ladies sipping coffee and eating sweets.

"Now, ladies," Hassan said, "I leave him entirely in your care, look after him well, and don't let him want for music and amusement during my absence."

With that Hassan left them, and Arab Jack made himself at home by answering the curious questions of the ladies, who in return taught him their various names, and actually told him their respective ages.

Hassan returned some hours after, as the gong of the time-piece struck the hour of midnight, then the fair bevy retired, leaving Hassan and Jack to sip coffee, smoke their chibouks, and enjoy an uninterrupted chat.

If our hero was previously astounded by what he had heard and seen, he was more so now, for Hassan after a roundabout conversation, came to a point that startled Jack.

"Well," said Hassan, "I have unfolded to you Arabi's plot against the Khedive, and how he proposes throwing off the Turkish yoke; now I must ask if you will go with me to Osman Digna, in the Soudan?"

"Where's the Soudan?" said Jack, who felt rather jolly.

"Hundreds of miles from here, right away the other side of Egypt; you'll see some fine sights on the road, and I'll teach you the Arabic language."

"Good," said Jack, throwing himself back on the soft yielding cushion, and puffing at his chibouk with as much ease as if he were the Sultan. "What's the row out there?"

"No row at all; the row will be *here* very shortly, I expect. I have a little diplomacy to work, and if I could only get a private letter to the Mahdi, I could get as much gold as would purchase the Suez Canal."

"Good again," said Arab Jack, who had not

the remotest idea how much gold that would take although, from what he had heard, he knew that it must be an enormous quantity. "When do we start, do we travel by road or rail?"

Hassan nearly choked himself with laughter. "We shall have to travel by boat, on horses, camels, and any mode we can; across deserts as bare of water and vegetation as the palm of your hand, and ——."

"Is there any fighting? I can shoot and handle a scimitar," interrupted Jack, who considered the journey too tame.

"Of course, there will be plenty of that, there will be danger enough, but I know by your looks you are not frightened, so say you'll go, and just sign your name to this roll of parchment." Jack's eyes glistened.

The document was written in characters that were to him perfectly unintelligible.

There was a strip of green silk through a hole in the parchment, and the two ends were fastened together with a large red seal.

"Is it right?" queried Jack, as he took hold of the pen. "It looks like the scribbling on the stones I've seen in the British Museum."

"Very likely, but it's all right," said Hassan, and our hero thus assured, wrote in letters of red ink—"ARAB JACK."

CHAPTER VI.

JACK BECOMES A VERITABLE ARAB.—SHOW-ING THE LION'S TEETH. — SELA OF THE GOLDEN HAIR SERVES JACK A TRICK, AND PAYS THE PENALTY.—SECRET SERVICE, A VISIT TO ARABI PASHA. — THE MASSACRE IN ALEXANDRIA.—JACK'S PERIL AND GALLANT RESCUE OF A LOVELY ENGLISH GIRL.

ARAB JACK, after signing the mysterious document, remembered no more until he awoke the following morning and found himself, fully dressed, stretched on a soft downy ottoman.

The handsome chibouk, with its long cherry-wood stem and amber mouth-piece, was by his side just as he dropped it, and a cup of rich coffee, on which floated the cream, was within reach of his hand.

Jack was loth to fully open his eyes; to him it seemed that he had been blessed with a delicious dream, and he feared to dispel it.

Strains of sweet music, however, floated seductively on his ear, and as his eyelids became unsealed and he looked about him, he beheld the three graces of the preceding evening seated on a divan, opposite him, touching their lutes and smoking their cigarettes.

There was a time when such a sight would have shocked our hero, but in his visits to the Haymarket with flash Luke, when he first made his acquaintance, he had seen the so-called ladies smoking with as much gusto as their dupes the profligate swells.

All the young ladies were playing some dulcet instrument, but as soon as they discovered he was awake, Lily, the fair one with alabaster skin and hair of silvery whiteness, dropped her guitar and leaped into the centre of the divan.

Nina, the dark one with pale cheeks, black eyes, and jet crimped hair; and Sela, of the olive-tinted skin, and gold red locks hanging in a profusion of curls over her shoulders, remained seated

Had Jack been of the same temperament as Marcus Fortescue, he would have had a fine opportunity of airing his love sonnets, as it was our hero knew not how to reply to the flowing language of the fair Lily.

"Awake and kiss the morn, apple of mine eye, garden of my heart," said she, drawing nearer to the dumb-stricken boy. "Allah has sent me to conduct you to paradise, and prepare you for the seventh heaven."

"Hang it," exclaimed Jack, "I can't stand this any longer. I have not come here to make love; where's Hassan, has he started on his journey without me?"

"He'll be here soon," replied Lily, tantalizingly. "You seem dull, and yet my brother left you here to make us happy; come, join us in a dance, a can-can. If you look so glum and sorrowful you'll cause us all to cry."

"You may cry your eyes out," thought Jack, whose mind was troubled concerning the mystic document. What if he had signed his own death warrant? What if Hassan had led him into some fearful snare?

He wished to be quiet to collect his thoughts, but the girls would not let him; at a signal from Lily, her sisters also dropped their instruments, and joined her in the centre of the carpeted floor.

Then they took from their pockets their castanets, and danced to a Spanish air which gradually developed itself into one of those wild outbursts practised by the dancing dervishes.

Jack in his own mind wished the whole three of them were in Hades. The tobacco of the previous night had not done his head any good, as he was unaccustomed to smoking.

It was quite a relief to him when Hassan returned. He brought home news of the dark doings in the city. "My sisters," he said, "you will all have to keep within the house very close, the doors and windows must be securely barred. The Arabs have risen and are slaughtering all who have a white skin."

"Good gracious!" exclaimed fair Lily, gazing anxiously into the brother's sun-tanned features, this is bad news if you are going to leave us here alone."

"You will be as safe as in a castle," said Hassan. "Koro," alluding to the hunchback, "will do all your outing, and I shall have a strict watch kept upon the house of a night."

Thus assured, the young damsels became as playful as usual, and one of them, clapping her hands danced and whirled herself out of the room.

Presently Koro entered and approached our hero, and after saluting him with a profound salaam, informed him that water of the purest, from the grand canal, was waiting ready for him to lave his hands and face in.

Jack could not help smiling at the demure face made by the black, deformed, yet faithful attendant, and immediately he followed him to the bath, where a basin stood on a marble pedestal, containing, as it seemed, water that had just been drawn from a filter.

Jack rolled up his sleeves, taking care, however, not to expose his left arm above the elbow, and sluiced himself well, sponging his chest and rubbing the water well into the roots of his hair.

"Dere, now, dat do massa lubly lot good," said the hunchback, handing him a turkish towel, and then assisting him to dress.

"Ah, that's proper and cool," Jack said, as the dwarf handed him his turban. "I wonder what they'd think of me if they saw me in London?"

He looked in the mirror to adjust his turban, when he drew back in horror, perfectly shocked.

His face was like a disc of polished mahogany, and his hands were the same.

Jack, thinking that the hunchback had been playing him a trick, turned upon the dwarf to soundly abuse him, when he saw that individual almost white with terror.

"Hoo-hoo!" gasped the dwarf, in accents that clearly proclaimed his innocence. "Who do magic—turn massa's white skin in dat manner?"

"I should like to find out," said our hero, gazing abstractedly into the font, the water in which was now of a clouded amber colour.

The dwarf procured fresh water; but all the washing failed to remove the stain from his hands and face.

In this state he returned to the saloon, where Hassan was in conversation with Lily and Nina, who, on observing Jack, burst into loud peals of laughter.

"This is Sela's mischief," said Hassan. "She is always acting some sorcery; but it will do no harm—in fact, it will serve our purpose admirably. You are now Arab Jack without further paint or——"

Hassan's speech was shortened by a strange apparition which suddenly appeared in the doorway, pressing aside the folding arras.

It was Sela, with her bright golden hair thrown back, dressed in the discarded suit of our young adventurer.

Sela was about Jack's height, so that she looked even more ludicrous than he did in it, as, with her ringlets streaming behind her, she bounded into the room.

"Jack," said she, catching our hero by the hand, "now we are both boys I can kiss you, and I will too, in spite of your dirty face."

Jack was quite powerless to resist her. She placed one arm round his neck and gave him such a sound smack on his lips that it brought the hot blood to his cheek, and made the others roar more loudly with laughter.

"Now," exclaimed Hassan, looking full into the mischievous eyes of his sister, "I'll turn the laugh on you. As you have donned the raiment of our guest, he is entitled to claim the garments you have thrown off, which during our journey may be useful to us should he have to act the *role* of a Soudanese lady."

When the mirth had subsided the gong sounded for the midday meal, which being over, Jack and Hassan repaired to a small room in which there was a case of handsomely-bound books and rolled up maps, one of which Hassan opened, and, having laid it upon the table, pointed out to Jack the route he proposed taking.

"This," said he, pointing, "is where we now are. This is the true Nile; here is Cairo"—and so on to Khartoum. "But," he added, after enumerating several places, "the Mahdi may not be in any one of these fortified towns, and in that case we shall have to visit Berber, Sinkat, and even Suakim."

"What a long way!" said Jack, wishing in his own heart that he might be able to get a look at the Red Sea.

"The Mahdi," he said presently, "as you call him, must be rich if he owns all that region. I suppose he has plenty of soldiers. What do they fight with—guns and swords?"

"Anything they can get hold of—mostly spears; and they're devils to fight."

"Oh, then," said Jack, his fine eyes sparkling "I shall be able to use my knife if they come any nonsense. I know how to fence, you must know."

Jack in his excitement took out his knife, opened the long formidable blade, and showed Hassan how he could cut and slash on an emergency; and in his imaginary combat he became so demonstrative that Hassan was compelled to defend himself.

Drawing a short Damascus blade he always carried up his left sleeve in a sheath, he parried one or two dangerous thrusts, and then with a turn of the wrist he disarmed Jack, whose knife was wrenched from his hand with such force that it flew across the room and stuck in the panelling of the opposite wall.

"There," said Hassan, "you young Turk. With your mad blood, you ought to be a soldier; you could go in and win then."

"So I could; but I don't like being under restraint. I had a cousin in the Fighting 24th. He was killed at Rorke's Drift, when the men guarding the hospital were surprised."

"Oh," said Hassan, rolling up the map. "Well, if we have any fighting, I hope you won't get killed. You've damaged my fez, but no matter. I have to pay a visit to Arabi the Great, the General of the Egyptian army, and you may accompany me."

An hour later they stood at the palatial residence of the great man, and Hassan having delivered a folded missive to the officer of the guard stationed at the entrance, he and his companion were allowed to enter.

A grave grey-headed official led them through the vestibule into the reception-room, and after Hassan had informed Jack that, as civilians, they would have to tread the general's carpet with stockinged feet, they were in due course ushered into the august presence.

Jack was much struck with the oriental grandeur of the place, but on hearing Arabi pronounce his name, he quickly gave up staring about and gave him his attention.

"So you are the young gentleman, who signed this agreement," said the general, or pasha, as he was styled, in good English; "by it you engage to assist Hassan-el-Ahed to convey a private message to Mahomet Achmet, the Mahdi, and prophet of the true God, who is friendly with your people, and wishes they may do well."

Here the pasha made a devout sign, which his chief secretary and other subordinates faithfully copied, and after explaining how secrecy and expedition were imperative, concluded by naming the promised reward, about £5,000.

"To you Hassan-el-Ahed," he added, raising his eyebrows as a sign of exalted admiration, "all praise is due for the manner in which you have obeyed our imperial mandate," shifting his eyes towards Jack, without deigning to move his head. "Allah preserve you, Allah be your guide. Dervish Tewfik shall honour you both with verses of the Koran, which will guard you from all harm."

The pair, who had listened during the interview with bowed heads, now prepared to depart, and as they backed towards the door, the pasha utilised every moment by impressing upon Jack, the service he was about to render his country,— whose ships were now in Egyptian waters, to show respect for the Sultan and the Khedive, —whose military servant and councillor Arabi Pasha was.

Arab Jack, quite innocent of the meanness, treachery, and subtlety of the Orientals, was entirely ignorant of the lying propensities of Arabi.

He was not aware that the military general had come by stealth on the previous night from Cairo, to hold an audience with his equally evil councillors. Therefore, Jack thought he was doing a good thing, embarking on a holy mission, instead of on one of the most infidel and disastrous to the cause of Christians.

As they proceeded towards Hassan's house, crowds of unkempt Arabs came from the Moslem quarter, and formed into knots in the bye-streets, casting ugly glances at any who passed dressed anything at all respectable.

"Keep close, look out sharp," whispered Hassan, " these roughs, as you'd term them in your country, are not over honest and civil."

Further on they saw a Greek gentleman pushed and insulted by two ragged young Arabs who were leading donkeys.

Jack's monkey was up, and, without a word to Hassan, he ran forward and interfered.

On this two shirtless bare-legged men rushed out of a doorway, and reaching over the backs of the donkeys gave our hero a blow on the shoulder and one under the ear.

Jack was in attitude in a moment.

"Hallo! two to one ; this way you bully mongrels, I'll soon settle you."

So he did, and with one blow too. But that blow was laid just like a sledge hammer on the tallest bravo's huge nasal organ.

"Oh, Allah," exclaimed his companion, as the blood spurted on all sides, and spattered his grimy face. " Oh, Allah, that was surely a kick from a camel."

Hassan-el-Ahed was unable to stir for laughter.

" Damme, Jack," he vociferated, " I can't help using flowery lingo, you've smashed his conk, he won't be able to take snuff for a month."

The bravo himself was apparently quite satisfied.

He put both hands to the injured organ, just as if he was holding it on to his face, and with a grunt such as one might with difficulty squeeze from the snout of an over-fed pig, backed to the doorway and disappeared with the rapidity of a shot.

His mate had already taken to his heels, and then Jack took one of the ragged urchins by the greasy neck, with each hand, pressed the toe of his boot against their seatless trousers, and hoisted them along the street.

Passing along the Rue des Sours, they evaded another gang, most of whom were armed with narhouts, or stout staves with iron ferrules on them.

As Jack was about to make some remark, an upper window of a tall house opened, and a shower of these formidable clubs was poured out, but no person was seen, the thing was done so unexpectedly quick.

A number of Arabs seized upon these and then made for the centre of the town, striking many white men as they went, and killing one right straight off.

One terrible blow given by a stout naked arm, with one of the narhouts, had split the man's skull and let out his brains.

Hassan spoke to a police-guard about it, but he only shrugged his shoulders and made no reply, so the dead body was left there.

As Jack and Hassan stood at the corner of the rue or street, a carriage full of Mustafazin soldiers, dressed in blue uniform, passed, and looking up at the windows shouted out words of encouragement to those who looked out.

In the square, or Place Mehemet Ali, matters were still worse.

A line of carriages with notables in them was proceeding towards the Caracol Libau chief police office, whither Amar Pasha Lufti had summoned them. These carriages the rabble stopped, and dragging the Christians out into the road, beat them to death.

One carriage in particular they made a dastardly raid upon.

It was a splendid open vehicle with a pair of horses of Arabian blood, driven by an ancient coachman, who had all his work to keep them in hand.

These horses were seized, the carriage doors wrenched open, and the occupants, an English gentleman of high standing (some said it was the English ambassador), with his fair and lovely daughter, superbly dressed, were dragged out to be beaten with the clubs.

Jack, however, was in amongst the ruffians in a moment.

Giving one a scathing kick with his toe on the bare leg, Jack seized the cudgel from his hand and laid about him smartly.

" Bravo, give it them, Jack," yelled Hassan, and rushing to his assistance he played such havoc among the swarthy crew that they were compelled to retire.

But it was only for a moment ; the thirst for blood and plunder was too powerful to be resisted without a struggle, and that struggle—to the death as it seemed—commenced.

This resulted as it always must do when right and a good cause is in the balance. Broken heads and bleeding scalps were on all sides, and many useless appeals were offered up to Mahomet.

Hassan succeeded in rescuing the venerable gentleman, and Jack did the gallant to the young lady, both of whom would have been stripped and robbed, if not murdered, had it not been for their timely and plucky interference.

Our pair of worthies then turned the horses' heads, and guarded the carriage and its occupants back to the mansion from whence they had started, and then left them after a profusion of thanks, and an invitation to call at some other time and be rewarded.

Hassan then made for his own home, but he did not take the usual course, he saw that a crowd of the disappointed Arabs were following on their track, so he took a zigzag course to baffle them.

This served his purpose as he imagined, but to his surprise, on turning a corner by which means they would double back, they came upon a party of half drunken Mahouds, who at once fell upon them without mercy.

Jack drew his knife, and Hassan bared his sword, and then a fierce fight ensued, in which several of the Arab horde were severely wounded.

CHAPTER VII

JACK STARTS FOR CAIRO—A MYSTERY AND A BLACK BAG—IN THE EGYPTIAN GUARD-HOUSE—LOVE, JEALOUSY, AND MURDER—THE INJURED HUSBAND AND A FAITHLESS BRIDE.

THE rising of the Arabs caused quite a sensation in all circles. The Khedive, Tewfik Pasha, seemed to be losing all control, and strange stories were afloat concerning the intentions of the English and French fleets.

To Arab Jack, however, this was all as Dutch. One pasha, to his disinterested mind, was quite as good as another.

As to Hassan, he was eager to get away, for fear he might get into some scrape which might detain him, and cause him to lose the favour of Arabi, who seemed likely to be the overruling power.

"Well," said he to Jack, when they were safely home, "we have had a narrow escape of being murdered and robbed; you the more especially so, as the rascally bravos could converse in words you could not understand."

Jack laughed.

"They might have murdered me, but I had not much for them to rob; a knife and a holey sixpence is all the treasure I possess."

"But, small as it is, you wouldn't like to lose it, I suppose?"

"Certainly not. This knife, like Whittington's cat, may turn me up a fortune, and the sixpence will always keep me in mind of three great things."

"Allah be praised! what are they?"

"Firstly, its colour reminds me that I am a white man. Secondly, the word sixpence impresses me with the language and nationality of my birthplace; and, thirdly, the Queen's head reminds me that I am a loyal subject of my gracious sovereign, Victoria."

"Good!" said Hassan, who, by-the-bye, was not quite of the same opinion; for, by entering the secret service of Arabi Pasha, he, Arab Jack, was signing a political contract without the sanction of Her Majesty's consul or ambassador.

Our hero was not to blame for this, he was ignorant of such matters.

He longed to be on the move, and visions of the Nile, crocodiles, caravans and such like, haunted him.

He sighed for the desert, and was pleased when the bare-legged, shirtless Arabs packed their mules with the luggage which they were to convey to the railway station.

Hassan and Jack then took an affectionate leave of the tearful girls, and our hero experienced a pang as if he were actually taking leave of his own sisters and his home.

The railway station was thronged with passengers, most of them flying for safety to Cairo, as hundreds of the panic-stricken Christians had sought shelter on board the ships in the harbour and fairly crowded them.

And yet our hero failed to realise the seriousness of the panic, and actually hummed a tune.

" I'm off to Ki-ro, so early in the morning;
I've paid my railway fare, I hear the people say.
I'm on the track; I've left those lovely, weeping girls,
I'm going to the Soudan, and I'll whistle all the way."

This was Jack's refrain, purely of his own composition, which he kept humming, much to the annoyance of several Armenian merchants who were discussing events with bated breath.

It was a long stretch to Cairo—over a hundred miles—and it was not reached without many stoppages, and the serious danger of Jack being funked out with the Turks' chibouks.

Hassan spoke very little. He was full of thought, and appeared to be indifferent to all that was passing, instead of which he was drinking in every word, and even started when the names of the Mahdi or Arabi was mooted.

From this he gleaned that the majority was of opinion that Arabi was at the bottom of the disturbance, and that, although he was not seen in it, he was answerable for the massacre.

Jack having hummed till he was tired, amused himself with looking at the tall minarets and splendid dome of the mosque of Mehemet Ali and the fortifications of the citadel, until the station was reached, when he had enough to divert his thoughts with the shouts and bustle.

"Come," said Hassan, "our luggage will be forwarded," and turning into the nearest bagnio he ordered sherbet for our hero and coffee and brandy for himself, after which they proceeded towards the interior of the town.

"Where are we going now?" Jack asked, at length. "I am fairly dazed with the sight of so many asses, mules, and camels."

"Ah, you'll get used to that, lad. Stay here; this is a nice little out-of-the-way nook, and mind this bag till I return, which will not be long."

"But, should I get lost—miss you?"

"Oh, no fear of that. You stick here, and stick to this bag also, and don't let it go from your possession on any account."

Jack promised to do that; but he did not relish the idea of being left amid such motley throngs and such a Babel of languages. He felt a sort of mistrust, which amounted almost to a presentiment, that something ill was about to happen.

Why Hassan should leave him thus he never explained, and Jack had only time to catch sight of his fez above the heads of the crowd as it turned a corner far along the street, when one of the Armenian merchants who had ridden with him in the train tapped him on the shoulder.

"My bag!" said the Armenian, with fiery eyes, and tugging at his huge moustache. "My bag, you Arab dog, confound you!"

Jack was startled. He could see that the man alluded to the bag; but he was determined not to part with it.

A few more hot angry words and a crowd gathered round, when Jack was soon made to understand that the merchant accused him of theft—that a bag similar to the one he held was missing from the station, and that the merchant swore the bag was his.

Our hero was in a pretty predicament. He could tell by the shrugs, gestures, and angry vociferations that he was looked upon as an Arab cad, but he could not find words to explain his innocence.

The mob bawled and jeered and caused quite a riot, when suddenly a file of Egyptian soldiers on their way to mount guard at the gate came on the scene.

The officer of the guard was a French renegade—a man who in his own estimation knew a great deal.

Having explained his views on the subject, and expended a deal of high-handed talk, he decided that Jack and the bag should accompany him to the guard-house, where the matter could be very soon settled.

"Now," said he, when he had relieved the guard and disposed of his men, "this bag is locked. Which of you holds the key?"

The merchant, with a good deal of bustle, produced a huge bunch from which he selected a key of peculiar make, but it was too large and would not go near the lock, which caused the officer to look at our hero with a smile.

Jack was however fairly nonplussed.

He had no key, and therefore the officer decided that the bag belonged to neither of them, suggesting that the black bag might contain combustibles, dynamite, for what he knew, and might be actually on its way to the Suez Canal, to aid in its threatened destruction.

He smiled proudly to himself, and considered that he had hit upon a clever suggestion, and, striking the iron, as the saying is, while it was hot, he expressed his determination to detain the bag until something more definite was known about it.

Expostulation was vain, and so the claimants retired, glad enough to find themselves at liberty after hearing the officer's dangerous opinion.

To describe our hero's feelings at that moment would be impossible. Find his way back to the place where Hassan left him he could not, and as all the streets seemed to him alike, the upper floors of the houses in many cases overhanging the pavements, and as he knew not what street to ask for, his case seemed utterly hopeless.

He had money—a small bag of gold his friend had given him—but what was that when he had lost his benefactor and the opportunity of fulfilling that which his whole mind and soul was so fully bent upon.

As he wandered down one of the streets that appeared to be quite deserted, his brain all of a whirl, and his bosom full of reproaches, a startling scream aroused him from his reverie.

This was succeeded by a despairing cry, a shower of oaths, and then a man emerged from the door of one of the houses, and darted wildly down the street.

He was immediately followed by another man, splashed with gore, flourishing a broad-bladed yataghan, dripping with blood, who rushed after the first man with the speed and fury of a maniac.

Jack was horrified at the sight, but worse was to come.

At the door, which was raised a few steps from the ground, appeared a female, fair as a Circassian, her hair streaming down her back in wild dishevelment, and her raiment, once of the purest texture and dotted with pearls and gold, blotted with deep red stains.

A gash in her fair throat, from whence the ensanguined stream was flowing, showed that she had been subjected to some fiendish violence, and as she held her small white hands over the cruel wound to staunch the vital flow, she fixed her large blue eyes upon those of our hero in such a manner as to transfix him to the spot as if he were made of stone.

Meanwhile the men flew on, pursuer and pursued, when the former gaining upon the latter, who was already wounded, gave him a swift blow with the keen edge of the sword, which sent his head rolling on the uneven stones, whilst the headless trunk fell to the earth with a lead-like thud.

This fearful tragedy occupied but a few seconds in all, but in that space a score of men and boys had made their appearance, and murder was shouted in as many different voices.

Jack, appalled at the sight of the lovely female, fled the spot, rushing in his wild delirium in the direction of the men, when coming in contact with the slayer, the wronged husband of the frail but fair one, he in his blind fury slashed at our hero, and sent him reeling against a post, where he lay stunned and bleeding from a ghastly wound.

CHAPTER VIII.

JACK FALLS INTO THE SNARE OF A CRAFTY OLD SINNER.—THE DRUGGED ELIXIR.—FOLLOWED BY FOOTPADS.—JACK IS ROBBED AND GETS SOUNDLY CUDGELLED.—A MODEL LODGING.—IN THE HANDS OF THE YOUNG ARABS.—RESCUED BY AN OLD FRIEND.—THE RESULT OF A STARTLING ADVENTURE.

WHEN our hero returned to consciousness, he was lying on the floor of a dimly-lighted room, the walls of which were hung with dingy coloured drawings of anatomy.

This was the sanctum of Ben-Ali, a crafty old sinner who had been kicked out of the harem in which he was chief eunuch for some breach of the rules.

His crime was such that it should have been expiated by death, but in consideration of his age and some particular service he had rendered his master, a terrible torture was substituted, by which he was to be deprived of his eyes.

This sentence, however, was not strictly carried out; the torture left his black bloated face horribly scarred, but there remained a small gleam of sight.

He now practised as apothecary and leech to the poorer classes, who, being blessed with a scarcity of money and an overflow of brawls, gladly sought his aid.

It was to him that our hero was conveyed, under the supposition that, in addition to the wound on his head, he had received a terrible cut on the muscle of the left arm, and he was thus left to the tender mercies of the leech.

Ben-Ali had only one remedy for such wounds, a substance much resembling boiled pitch, which he plastered on thickly with a brush, and then covered with a cotton rag.

In this manner he anointed Jack's head, and then stripping off the sleeve of his jacket, and rolling up the sleeve of his shirt, he anointed the mark on his arm, and bound it round with part of an old greasy turban.

Then administering a draught, extracted from some miraculous herbs, he left his patient, for Nature to do the rest.

Jack no sooner awoke than he sat up, which caused the old man at once to pray:—

"Allah be praised! through his prophet Mahomet he worketh miracles."

"Hang it," said Jack, "what has Allah to do with this bump on my head?" then observing that his arm was bandaged, he felt and pinched it to ascertain if there was any wound.

It so happened that there was not, for the point of the yataghan only had caught the cloth and rent it, disclosing the terrible birth-mark which Jack took so much precaution to conceal.

Ben-Ali, owing to his defective eyesight, considered there was a desperate wound, and he told Jack so, and in Inglese, for the man of science had picked up a spattering of that language.

"Thank you," said Jack, glad enough at having found some one by whom he could make himself understood.

"What is your fee, old man?"

"Anyting, vot you pleese, me very much poor, me want but leetle."

"Then this will pay you," Jack said, taking the bag of gold from its concealment, and handing him one of the pieces.

"Yash, yash, vera much tank you, tank you. Allah is good, he vera much bless de cure."

Jack had no idea that the old leech having caught sight of the bag was anxious to feel it.

He had done one of the most unfortunate and incautious deeds he could have perpetrated.

Ben-Ali, when an opportunity occurred, was not only a leech by name but a leech by nature.

Our hero was about to bid him "good day" when the old man checked him.

"Yash, yash; you Inglese, so good; so very, very good. Stay, I will give you von elixir dat make you well directly."

Jack obeyed, never dreaming that the old devil was so iniquitous. He took the colourless draught which Ben-Ali desired him to drink while in a state of effervesence, and drank it off.

It was cool and seemed delightfully refreshing, and Jack walked out wondering whither he should next bend his steps.

Hitherto Jack had seen nothing of "El-Massel-el-Kaherah," or "The Victorious Metropolis," as old Cairo was orientally named.

He had wandered about a labyrinth of lanes, up and down, in and out, and in some places, owing to the narrowness and the overhang of the houses which nearly touched each other, as dim as torchlight even in day time.

But now he wended his way to the broad streets, where the tempting bazaars shone out gaily, and where wealth and oriental fashion reigned in all its glory.

Jack, however, soon grew weary of the gaudy sights and the picturesque company.

The busy Egyptian shops, the coloured walls, and the untiring guttural cry of the ubiquitous donkey drivers, made his head swim.

Turning into one of the less bustling streets, he engaged a tailor, who, seated cross-legged on a board in the open window of his shop, was engaged on a pair of celestial bags, to mend the rent in his sleeve.

Jack did this more with the view to get small change wherewith to purchase a melon than anything else, as he was seized with a sudden and parching thirst, the result of the drugged elixir which the avaricious old sinner, Ben-Ali, had recommended him.

There were plenty of melons about, so ripe, so tempting, that on a hot sultry evening the very sight of them made one's mouth water.

"Oh, melon pips! solace of the uneasy!" shouted one of the vendors, thrusting one of his finest into the very mouth of Jack, who bought the tempting fruit and devoured it eagerly.

But he had no sooner done so than he became drowsy, and being tired he sat down on a doorstep to sleep, which act was witnessed by two evil-visaged ruffians, with an exultant chuckle.

Like two shadows of evil these men had watched our hero from the house of the leech, stopping when he stopped, and regulating their pace by his.

As soon as he dropped and closed his eyes, they knew that the drug had worked, and creeping stealthily up to him they dragged him into a dark corner, and searched for the coveted bag.

Having discovered it, and secreted it in his own capacious rags, one ruffian wanted to take Jack's knife, but the other, more scrupulous, pointed with a significant nod to the name on the plate, as much as to say that it was dangerous, as it might supply evidence against them if any bother ensued.

Jack's sleep remained undisturbed until the bagnios and wine shops were about to close, when all respectable citizens retired to bed, or to their homes, if they had been on a visit or to witness some amusement.

Then it was that a youth about the size and clad similarly to our hero, reeled up the entry, and stumbled over Jack's prostrate form.

This unceremonious salute aroused Arab Jack, who rolled over and gave a loud snore, which startled the young wine bibber, who thought it must be some geni or devil, called on Allah to save him, and shambled off much soberer than when he came.

He had barely disappeared, when two other personages came upon the scene, one a middle-aged man, whose head and whiskers were turning to an iron grey, and his wife, whose face was covered with a blue cloth and who wore a loose dress down to her heels.

The old man carried a lantern, and grasped a stout stave, two great necessaries in Cairo after dark; and as soon as the old man thrust his lantern into the entry to ascertain whether it was all clear, its wretched light revealed the figure of young Jack.

"Allah! Allah!" gasped the aged man. "Allah! Allah!" and then turning to his wife, he said, "The curse of the wine-press is upon your son, now shall the bine of the vine sweeten his slumbers."

Thinking Jack was his son, who had returned home inebriated and fallen helpless in the entry, thus disgracing his father's house and his doorstep, the old man, whose arm was in no way feeble, commenced to belabour young Jack, calling him all the disgraceful and ill-conditioned young Arabs he could think of, whilst his staff rattled loudly against his bones.

Thus aroused Jack started to his feet, but could not stand.

"Moses, scissors," he yelled, "leave off, you old gudgeon, or I'll throttle you."

"Will you," gasped the old man, worn out with his exertions, mistaking Jack's words for some drunken threat unintelligibly uttered by his reprobate son. "Allah! my arm is weak."

It was joy to our hero when he found the old man's exertions began to flag, and his breath grow short and thick. With the effort of despair he rose to his knees, and on all fours, like a goat, butted the old gentleman in the waistcoat, thereby causing his rotund stomach to cave in just as though it had been an India-rubber ball.

"A-a-al-lah," grunted the old man. "Fat-Fat-Fat-i-ma, k-k kick him, my darling, I, I'm killed."

Fatima, however, was reluctant to kick, as she

supposed, her beloved son, so she pretended to faint, when thinking she was steadying herself against the wall, preparatory to giving him a warm 'un, Jack butted her in the legs and sent her on her beam-ends with a flop.

If the old gentleman was out of wind, his spouse was not ; she shrieked, yelled at the top of her voice, set all the mongrel dogs barking, aroused the sleepy watchmen, and awoke the very echoes.

Once clear of the entry Jack glanced up and down the street, from both ends of which he could see the lamps of the watchmen approaching, and hear the sound of their long staves as they beat them on the stones.

This was the general custom of those plucky guardians of the night. In that quarter murder and robbery was frequent, and as they were not paid so well as the soldiers, they cared not to be wounded or shot, so they made plenty of noise so as to warn the bravados to clear off.

Jack, had he remained, however, would have received a good cudgelling, being alone, and have been locked up in the caboose into the bargain, as it was he climbed over a low pair of gates and found himself in a donkey-yard.

For a wonder the animals were all still, possibly worn out with their labour of the previous day, and Jack, who had no time to investigate the cause, looked about and discovered what he considered a safe retreat.

It was a large iron tub or butt, which was swung in a wooden frame, on wheels, with shafts thereto in the fashion of a cart.

The butt was broad at the bottom, and gradually narrowed towards the top, putting Jack very much in mind of a conveyance he had seen used for hog swill, but as it was clean and sweet within, and Jack did not particularly care what was its use, he clambered up it, crept in, and settled his aching bones on the cold iron.

Being a sultry night, Jack rather liked it, and he listened in glee to the angry railings of the outraged Fatima, who called not only the watchmen, but her husband, all the horrible unchristian names she could think of.

In the midst of this Jack went off to sleep as soundly as a top, and he doubtless dreamed, and like little Benjamin down the pit, thought of his dear native home.

But from this sweet bliss he was hurriedly aroused by a sudden chill that seemed to freeze the very marrow in his aching bones, and to his horror, he found that his bed-room was converted into a receptacle for water.

Scrambling to his feet, he dashed the water from his eyes, and looking over the brim discovered a dozen swarthy Egyptians who were engaged in drawing water from the canal and filling the locomotive cistern, to which was attached a number of donkeys.

No sooner, however, did the water-drawers observe Jack, who looked like a half-drowned duck, than they dropped their bucket skins and set up a yell as if the very old Nick had suddenly made his appearance.

"Allah, Allah," they all yelled, and then leapt into the canal, leaving Jack in the hands of the Arab boy drivers.

These mischievous young imps were not so easily frightened ; one of their number remembered seeing Jack's features on the previous day, and having shouted lugubriously to his chums,

they with their long donkey whips began to beat our hero most unmercifully.

It was Jack's turn to yell in good earnest now, and he hopped about, as the long hard thongs twined round him, just as if he were a whip-top.

At this juncture a European gentleman on horseback appeared on the scene, and charging in amongst the ferocious young rascals forced them to desist from their cruel sport.

A twitch of his riding whip brought one of the dusky imps, bellowing for mercy, alongside his saddle, and then the rider, a person of quality demanded the cause of their brutality.

"He spoil our water," snivelled the Arab. "He no pay for waste of time, and rob us of pay for breakfast."

"Here," said the rider," throwing down a coin, and turning angrily away he motioned Jack to him.

"My lad," said he, "I am sorry to see you in this plight. I know by your voice you are a countryman of my own, which discovery I made when you so gallantly risked your life in saving mine, and that of my daughter, from the mutinous Arabs in the Square in Alexandria.

Jack bowed and acknowledged the recognition.

"Since then, sir," said he, "I have been cruelly beaten and robbed. If you could put me in the way of retrieving my lost fortunes you would confer on me a great and special favour."

"Bless you, my boy," said the gentleman, "I am wealthy, and my purse is entirely at your disposal, and as you seem above the common caste, although you choose to robe as an Arab, I will put you in the way of earning a sumptuous living."

"Indeed, sir, if you do, I shall be for ever grateful. I would rather eat the produce of my own toil, than live on the bread of dependence."

"So you shall ; get on that horse, behind my attendant you see there. I am about to visit a friend, who is in want of a courier and aide-de-camp."

Arab Jack was delighted ; wet as he was, he easily climbed on to the quarters of the Arabian barb, and the trio pushed their way through the jostling crowds.

At length they gained the open Boulevard, Mehemet Ali, and passing the splendid portal of the Sultan Hassan mosque, they at a brisk canter reached the mansion of Signor Varnoni.

Our hero, wet, dishevelled and mud-soiled, just as he was, was admitted to the house of the Italian signor, with no further introduction than the *open sesame* of the English gentleman, to the evident disgust and astonishment of the richly-dressed attendants.

Once in, however, he was ushered into a bathing chamber, the surroundings of which were chiefly of Alabaster, and from thence into a magnificent wardrobe, where, upon pegs surrounding the polished walls, hung costumes of every nation.

Jack looked at several, but though they were costly he spurned them all, and preferred to wear the dress of an Arab, as it was the most suited to his taste.

A stiff dish of maccaroni, washed down with coffee, and some pastry very much resembling English tarts, were next operated upon by our hungry Jack, after which he was summoned to the presence of the signor.

The wealthy Italian laughed when he saw Jack so modestly attired, for he could have had a black velvet suit with buttons of real gold, silk stockings, Spanish leather shoes, and a cap with a golden tassel, if he had liked.

Jack, nevertheless, took care that what he chose was good.

His scarf was sumptuous, his linen and turban of the purest whiteness, and the gold chain he put round his neck, and to which he fastened his knife, shone with sparkling brilliancy.

"My lord," said the Italian, addressing Jack's English friend, "This youth appears to me like that casket on yonder bureau, not of so much value from its outward appearance as from what it contains."

Lord Woodberrie nodded assent.

"You will find him, Signor Varnoni, just as I described him, full of British pluck, and honest, so far as I believe, both of action and speech."

"Then he shall not lack my patronage," said the signor. "What is your name, noble youth ?"

"Jack," was our hero's reply, colouring to the very roots of his hair.

"Jack, eh, that's sharp, and to the point. What else ?"

"Arab Jack."

The Italian raised his eyebrows in surprise. "Arab Jack ! well that will suit my purpose as well as any other. But tell me, have you ever been to Arabia or the Soudan ?"

"Never," said Jack, "but I'd like to, though."

The Italian seemed pleased with Jack's blunt and unwavering answers.

"Since you choose to be thought an Arab," he said, "let me advise you to use an Arab's precaution ; be not too communicative, listen with both eyes and ears, and, like the camel of the desert, always be grave and thoughtful."

"To-morrow," he added, turning to his lordship, "I shall start for Port Said, take passage by the Canal to Suez, from thence on to Jedda, and thence taking passage by the Red Sea, call at Suakim and Massowah."

"Then you will not go to Mocha," suggested his lordship.

"That will, presumably, be my destination, but I am not going to traffic for coffee when I can traffic for gold ; from Massowah I may cross the desert to Khartoum, as I have business at Omdurman, and I may visit the Mudir of Dongola."

The signor would have proceeded further with the disclosure of his intentions, had not Lord Wooberrie given him a warning glance, as much as to say, "We'll discuss further matters in private."

Jack was all of a glow with excitement. He drank in every word of the signor, for he had taken such a retentive view of the map Hassan had shown him, that he could picture the places he heard mentioned in his mind.

"Well," he muttered to himself as his presence was temporarily dismissed, "I wonder what ups and downs and perilous adventures are yet in store for Arab Jack ?"

Could he have foreseen events, it would have given him a startling surprise.

CHAPTER IX.

JACK CAUSES A SCENE WITH THE EGYPTIAN ARABS. — ASTONISHING A RUSSIAN.—HOW JACK OVERHEARS A SECRET AND IS MISTAKEN FOR A FAIR ONE'S LOVER.—IN THE DEATH CLUTCH.—JACK'S COURAGE IS PUT TO THE TEST IN A STRANGE MANNER.

"PORT SAID ! and so this is the Suez Canal, over which they make so much trouble," exclaimed our hero as he glanced significantly around. "Well, hang me,—hallo, what's up ?"

The noise and clatter of a tribe of young Arabs startled Jack, a tribe of incarnate demons, almost nude and covered with dust.

"Ha, they come this way," he added, thrusting his hands in his pockets, and assuming a listless attitude. "' Baksheesh ! Baksheesh !' the dusky demons have spotted me, and take me for an Arab swell, no doubt."

Jack had rightly guessed ; the grimy beggars, led by a tall thin lad, whose feet and hands were of giant proportions, "went for him," as the saying is, at a brisk pace, waving their sticks on which pieces of coloured rag were tied in imitation of pennons.

In an instant Jack was surrounded.

"Baksheesh ! Baksheesh !" again yelled the crowd. "Coppers, coppers, one piece," and they immediately began dancing around him.

"Aha ! now for some fun," laughed Jack. "A race, a race, look out," and having scraped together all the coppers he could find, he tossed them into the air in the direction of a pool of mud and water.

A yell of delight followed Jack's words and actions, and then like a flock of geese they darted towards the pool, using both arms and legs in their frantic endeavours to be first.

The tall lank youth led the way, his long broad feet assisting him rapidly over the ground, and, without hesitation or demur, he waded into the thick black mud, and stooping groped about with both feet and hands.

But alas for him ! although he won the race he had to pay dearly for his victory, for the pressing mob being brought to a sudden standstill on the bank of the pool closed up, and then, impeded by the force of the shock, they all went in pell-mell, and the lank youth was thrown completely over.

"Wah-ha-yah," yelled the discomfited one as the foul fluid poured into his ears, mouth and nostrils. "Yah-hoo, hold me up, or I shall be dead."

"Shout away," cried Jack, who was awfully full of mischief, "give him a good ducking and I'll find some more coppers."

His words were heard and would have been obeyed if the small fry could have kept their feet, as it was they could get no foothold on the slimy bottom, and they slipped and tumbled about as if they were in a glorious state of inebriation.

Arab Jack roared with laughter till he almost split his sides.

His eyes watered and his cheeks glowed, whilst his feet irresistibly went through the motions of a breakdown.

"Bravo, bravo," he shouted, when he could find breath to speak. "Soap him well ; what would I give now for a cellar flap !"

The soap Jack alluded to was the thick greasy

mud of the pool, which in handfuls they daubed on the unbleached linen of the lank one, whom in their endeavours to save they clutched hold of to save themselves.

"Ah, boo, dash it! why don't you fellows rout those devil-skins?" said Jack, turning to a party of native boatmen, who, busied in conversation about something that was going on at the sea gate of the canal, had not troubled as to the cause of the odour that began to assail their nasal organs.

"What's the row?" growled one.

"Well, we are all liable to an attack of cholera; look yonder, hang you. Is that the way you let the young urchins stir up a pestilential infection?"

"By the bones of Mahomet, no," replied the man, giving his shoulders a suggestive shrug. "I'll murder the whole lot, thank 'ee; here, mate, hand me your boat-hook."

Jack had slipped a piece of silver into the man's hand, and the effect of that talisman was magical.

Putting his hand to his mouth and having pointed to the grog store, he seized the boat-hook and beckoned his mates to follow him.

His movement towards the pool was the sign for a general stampede, and as he edged his way to windward of the awful stench, the writhing demons fought their way to the opposite edge of the pool, and emerged from the pestilential slush like so many rats taking leave of a tar barrel.

"Now I'm off," muttered Jack, who had wisely made up his mind to slope. "If I remain I may get more than that for which I've bargained. Hallo! my eye, what a dose of ships! ironclads, too! why there seems to be a naval representation of every country."

True enough; the bay outside the canal was dotted with men-of-war with their flags flying, and some that had not come to an anchor, still under steam.

One ship, flying the Russian eagle, was close up to the lock, her commander shouting and gesticulating most horribly against a Turkish gunboat having been allowed to pass through in presence of his own man-of-war.

A large crowd had collected to witness this altercation, among whom were several Egyptian merchants and a group of Frenchmen.

They were laughing boisterously at the antics of the exasperated Russian, who, wielding his speaking trumpet in the fashion of a sword, swore that he would swim on shore and murder the whole lot who dared to insult the dignity of the mighty Czar.

Jack, still ripe for fun and mischief, edged his way into the throng and found himself alongside a discomfited Muscovite, who pulled vigorously at his moustache and began to abuse the canal officials, whom he strongly denounced as French and English frogs and dogs.

"Yaw, got dam! the von bad Inglese," he vociferated, casting wolf's eyes at the English flag hoisted above the consul's house. "Him carrion, or me eat him vid a pinch of Russian salt."

"Would you?" thought Jack, his eyes flashing and his bosom swelling at the stinging insult. Then he added aloud, "What a vile smell—a stink; one would think the old Russian barge was loaded with putrid bear's grease."

The Russian turned round on Jack with a look of scorn which was fierce enough to be annihilating.

"Vot you speak for grease," he hissed huskily, "is ball and powder; my countree good, reech, and plenty fight."

"Oh!" said Jack, taking his dimensions with the same astuteness as if he were about to measure him for a coffin. "Oh, my angelic don, I suppose you are one of the mighty smashers."

"Me am von dat take no insult," replied the Russ. "I could, if me loik, eat you; you be not one mouf-ful for me, you Arab swine-hog."

Jack's British blood was raised to boiling heat. Like most impulsive and ambitious boys he longed to resent any insult offered by a foreigner to his country, even if the aggressor was double his size and likely to give him a good thrashing.

The Russian wore a green cloth coat reaching down to his heels, trimmed with fur, and girted in at the waist, half boots with fur also round the tops, and a sable skin cap shaped like a pail turned upside down.

Such a dress on an Egyptian summer's day was quite grotesque and conspicuous enough, without its owner doing more to attract attention.

The words he had uttered, however, as to the eating of Jack stuck in our hero's throat, and in a haughty tone he replied:

"Most noble smasher, I presume you would rather eat me dead than alive. Have you any objection to give me a specimen of the way in which you commence your terrible slaughter?"

The Russian was startled.

He was a head and shoulders taller than Jack and proportionately broad, therefore he looked disdainfully down upon him, just as a mastiff would at a Skye terrier.

Jack drew his well-built form proudly erect and glared full into the green wolfish orbs of the Russian, at the same time planting his foot upon his toes, throwing the whole force of his weight upon them.

"Yaw, hog," hissed the Russ, grinding his teeth like a grizzly bear. "Yaw——"

"Hog, swine, this in your teeth. Take that lot and count them."

The Muscovite staggered as though so many sledge hammers had been hurled at his frontispiece.

The crowd drew back. The indolent Turks and the sleepy Egyptians opened their languid eyes in wonder.

"Allah! Allah!" exclaimed the Turks, as they gazed on the crimsoned visage of the once blustering but now totally extinguished Russ, whilst the Egyptians muttered the names of their favourite saints.

All this took place so suddenly that no one had time for comment, our hero himself being in wonderment as to how it was done.

But he was determined not to give the Russian a moment's time; before he could rally Jack was at him again, and polished him off as easily as a London shoeblack would have polished a new boot.

The last blow Jack gave him sent him sprawling over a fruit-vendor's stall, where he struggled for a few seconds amid the dates and melons, and finally collapsed on a sherbet stand, terrifying the owner almost out of his wits and sending the stem of his long pipe half way down his throat.

Jack saw the damage, which created laughter, groans of anguish and horrible threats, but without waiting to estimate the cost, he, acting on the wisdom of the east, took his departure and was soon out of sight.

As he rambled along through a row of shops he suddenly bethought himself that he had a letter for an agent who lived somewhere thereabout, so, producing the document from one of the many receptacles in his Arab dress, he tried to make out the superscription.

"Ah! Signor Antonioni—that's the name, and here's the very house. Hi, ho, there! you parley Italiano?"

The individual addressed was standing at the door of Antonioni's house, smoking a cigarette and eyeing Jack curiously, but he made no reply.

"Well, old man, you seem all optics. Have you no tongue and ears? I want Signor Antonioni."

Jack shouted loud enough to be heard a mile off and then discovered that the man was both deaf and dumb, a circumstance of which he was made aware by a little Italian organ boy, who held out his hat for his reward all the time he was giving the information.

"Well, if there's no one to show me in I must needs be my own servant," said Jack, pressing past the mute, expecting to find the office door open; but it was closed and fastened, so that Jack went further into the passage and ascended a flight of stairs.

There he found a door partly open, and, peering in, he beheld a sight that set his young blood all of a glow.

In an elegantly-furnished room, with stained glass windows, and a luxuriously carpeted floor, sat two ladies on an ottoman conversing in such tones as could barely reach our hero's ear.

"Ah! Maria," with a sigh, "do you not think it a dangerous game to play to have two lovers, when your heart cannot be given to both, and above all things to allow an infidel to pay you his addresses."

"But he is not an infidel, although he is not of our church, and he is so handsome; his features are as perfect as those cut by our most famous sculptors, and his eyes, Isabel, are of that melting nature that I am sure you would love him."

"Then why does he not attire as a Christian. I dislike this bal masquery in every-day life, and if he were ever so handsome and he were here I would tell him so to his face."

"Then, Isabel, you and I differ; but I won't quarrel, for I can tell you that I want him all to myself, and since I have told you he is of English birth I——"

A creak of the door suddenly checked Maria's speech, and, turning her head, she beheld two such eyes as she had been describing, and a pair of bronzed cheeks such as in Egypt are considered by the fair sex the very pinnacle of beauty.

Without a word, and as if urged by some supernatural agency, the beautiful Italian girl rose to her feet, and with her dark eyes sparkling as brilliantly as the diamonds in her hair, and her voluptuous bust heaving as gently as the bosom of a summer sea, she flew to the door.

Then her round pink arms, which shone through their gauzy covering, trimmed with lace, were thrown round the neck of a turbanned head as two palpitating hearts were brought together in a fond embrace, and warm lips met in an ardent kiss.

Maria, thinking it was her lover she had thus embraced, was about to chide him for his coolness, when suddenly she discovered her mistake.

It was our hero, Jack, whose lips had been so fondly pressed to hers, and she, blushing with confusion, was about to chide him for the intrusion, when he raised his turban, and said :

"Lady, I feel unable to apologise in adequate terms for being the innocent cause of this—well—pleasantry, and I freely forgive you for having shocked my too—too sensitive feelings."

Jack assumed such an air of injured innocence that the lovely Italian girl knew not whether to smile or frown.

"Sir," said she, in silvery accents, "for what object have you intruded on our privacy, and for all I know acted the eaves-dropper? do you know ——"

"That you are one of the sweetest of creatures, and I am sorry I am not the favoured one permitted to dwell within the sunshine of those bright eyes for ever, and, for that matter, a day longer."

Our hero put on one of his most fascinating smiles, and looked what is termed impudent, and the lady rather appeared to like it.

The novelty of the situation quite emboldened Jack.

The sweetness of those cherry lips made him long for another kiss, and, without asking leave, he helped himself to one, very much to the envy of Isabel.

"Sacre," suddenly exclaimed an angry guttural voice. "Sacre, accursed devil worshipper, what are you doing here? Have you come to rob me of my treasure before my eyes? Hound, I will take your despicable life in her guilty presence."

Jack had not time to move or speak.

A strong wiry hand had grasped him from behind, by the muscles of his neck, and held him with a vice-like tenacity.

Then our hero saw a stiletto dazzle before his eyes, and in another instant the cold blade would pierce his heart.

Jack was no coward, as we know; to submit tamely to be murdered in cold blood was not his nature, but as he was so held what could he do?

The girls were both terrified, and uttered piercing screams.

"Lorenzo, Lorenzo," they cried in the terrible accents of despair, but the enraged lover seemed not to heed them, as with flashing eyes, which seemed to start like beads from his dark pale face, he brandished the keen-pointed weapon above his victim.

Jack at the moment, however, thought of his knife, he had no other weapon, and quick as thought he silently opened the blade and drew its edge across the fingers that held him.

"Ah, sacre, fiend, take that."

As the enraged Lorenzo withdrew his hand with pain, he made a fierce deadly thrust at our hero's heart, but Jack turning quickly evaded the blow, and springing at his adversary he cried :

"My turn now, once it was thine, now what mercy can I show you? Why should I not take the life of him, the hound, who would deprive me of mine?"

"Hold, thou shalt do no murder," commanded a deep bass voice; "this house is mine, who has dared to turn it into a shamble, a slaughter-house, where female delicacy is not even respected?"

The combatants with one accord drew back and

"THIS IS BETTER THAN GOING TO THE ZOO."   *p.* 30.

hid their sharp weapons behind them ; the stern rebuke of Antonioni cooled their fiery ardour in a moment.

A deep and painful silence ensued, which was broken by the voice of our hero :

"I am subdued by your venerable presence, signor," said he, "but I am not conquered ; this gentleman, if I may so style him, is the aggressor, I am the wronged."

"How so, explain ? "

The fine dark eyes of the Italian wandered from face to face, and then he listened until Jack had finished his recital.

"It is all a mistake ; thanks to the Virgin that it has not terminated fatally. This letter, Signor Arab Jack, explains all. My friend, Signor Vernoni, will be here later on, for the present you are my guest, and you will enjoy the evening in the company of Lorenzo, and my niece and daughter."

"Shake hands, then, and be friends," said our hero to the fiery Spaniard. "I feel that the life of Arab Jack will be sacrificed in some far better cause."

"Amen," said Lorenzo, and the pair, who so recently were ready to shed each other's blood, shook hands with a grip which promised they would be fast friends in the future,—but time reveals all.

CHAPTER X.

A BRACE OF VILLAINS.—JACK OVERHEARS A COWARDLY PLOT. — ARAB JACK WARNS THE CAPTAIN OF THE "ADAMANT."—THE TREACHEROUS PILOT.—PIRATES ON BOARD. —A COLD-BLOODED MURDER.—ALL IS LOST.

THE Mail Steamer, "Adamant," had scarcely started on her journey through the canal, when Jack made a discovery that the vessel was to be run aground, all hands murdered, and the cargo plundered by the wandering tribes who infested the banks.

Jack's suspicion was aroused by the movements of a couple of Greeks, who prowled about the decks, and seemed to him to be in every hole and corner of the ship.

3

"I'll have my eye on you, my jokers," said he, as from a dark corner in the steerage he watched their movements. "I never saw two such cut-throat looking rascals in all my life, and from what I have heard and read I'd bet my life that you are a brace of Ionian pirates."

As though in confirmation of his words, one of the two, who were both seated on the arm chest, took out the formidable knife he carried in a sheath stuck in his sash and ran his thumb along the edge.

"It's as sharp as ever," said he to his companion, "but it needs a little fresh work to keep the rust from eating in. It's done nothing since it severed the windpipe of that confounded Venetian woman who gave us so much trouble, and see how it stained the blade."

Jack shuddered as the ruffian held the blade in a streak of light that came down the hatchway.

"That's a blood stain," muttered he, "sure enough. How horrible it looks, and as black as ink, a fit memento of the dark deeds perpetrated by such villains."

Jack lay perfectly still, he could not move just then if he wanted to, but when the pair had talked over their plans and left, he crept from his concealment.

"Aha," he muttered, "so the pilot's in the swim; I'll on deck at once and acquaint the captain."

It so happened that the captain at that moment left the deck and Jack followed him into the saloon.

"I want a word with you, sir," Jack said, approaching him deferentially, "I have something of importance to communicate."

The captain looked at him amazed.

"Why, what's the meaning of this? you are entered on my books as an Arab, and yet you talk English as fluent as a native? What is it you have to say? Come, pay out the yarn quick, for I have no idle moments."

The captain laughed when Jack told him about the knife.

"Don't let such trifles trouble you," said he, "we have plenty of ugly customers travel this road; why, bless you, murders are as plentiful as rain drops among the Grecian Isles, and pirates are as thick as poppies in a corn field."

"Yes sir," said Jack, "but those men have a design against the ship, and those on board, I'm certain of it, I wish you would let me speak to Signor Varnoni."

"I can't, it's against the rules; the private saloon is closed to all but passholders. If you have nothing better to do, my lad, turn in and go to sleep."

"Not I," muttered Jack, "I mean to watch. I'm not going to have my throat cut in my sleep, I'll go on deck."

As he walked forward, his mind filled with visions of the terrible knife, an old salt tapped him on the shoulder.

"Hallo, my young Arab," said he, "What cheer, my hearty? Why you look down in the dumps—and ——"

"So would you," Jack replied, "if you knew what I do."

"Oh, my hearty, what's that, eh?"

Jack drew him aside and told him what he had heard and seen.

"Oh," exclaimed the old tar, "then the pilot's in it, my lad. They're a nice lot, there's few on 'em as hasn't been pirates in their day."

"I thought so."

"Aye, and that crafty shark as you gave a drubbing to, that Rooshun bear, is as bad as any on 'em and I'd bet my old baccy box he's one o' them Greeks as you speak on."

"What, in disguise? Well, now I come to think of it, one of them is awfully marked. I took them for old scars, but they may be fresh cuts painted over."

"That's it. You've guessed it. It's just the same as you having your face done over with that stuff, why, Lord love yer 'art, the games as is played on this canal's a caution."

"A caution to the Greeks, I suppose," said Jack, smiling.

"Jes' so, and they'll find it out too, no gammon if they plays their hanky pankys, or my name arn't Breakwater Ben."

Jack was cheered by the old sailor's words, "I'll go aft," said he, " and just hear what's going on ; you look up the handspikes, and keep them handy in case of alarm."

"Aye, aye," replied the old salt, and Jack walked on to the quarter deck.

The captain was there, talking to the pilot.

"It will be dark to-night, pilot," Jack heard the captain say, "and although I want to push on, I'm afraid I shall have to bring-to off Ismalia."

The pilot looked about as if judging the weather, but in reality to gain time for a reply.

"Ismalia," said he, at length. "That, sir, is an awkward spot; you see the freshwater canal joins us there and causes an awkward current. If I were you I'd push on to Lake Timsah, and then ——"

"Well, well, we shall see how the moon looks. I don't like riding between Lake Timsah and the Bitter Lake."

"Oh, it's safe enough," said the pilot, with an ill-concealed smile.

"Ah," thought Jack, "That's the place we're to be run aground, it will take us till ten o'clock at this speed to reach there."

He went below then to try if he could see any thing of the Greeks, and, listening at the door of their berth, he could hear them snoring as if they were fast asleep.

"That seems as if they were innocent enough," muttered Jack. "But they may be only getting a snooze preparatory to the job; I'll hear what Ben says, and then I'll get an hour's doss myself."

Jack turned in "all standing," as the sailors say, that is with his boots and clothes on, so as to be ready to jump up in an hour's time, but instead of that he snored double that time. He was worn out, in fact; he had been moving about a good deal, boy like, watching the sights, and studying the various languages.

In his troubled sleep Jack dreamed of his terrible ride on the train, and he was awoke by a tremendous shock, and a grinding sound just like that when the train was brought to a stand-still.

His blood froze, his brain whirled, and he rolled from his berth reeling like a drunken man.

"Oh, God—mother," he cried, "Oh that I had never sinned!"

"More you ain't! come on, Jack, the ship's ashore jes' as you prog-knob-stick-ated."

The sound of Ben's voice brought the dazed boy to his senses.

"Is she aground, Ben?" he gasped, grasping the old tar's arm.

" Aye, lad, and them Greeks as ye call them's gone on deck, I just caught sight o' that scar face ugly-looking coon, as acted the grizzly, and I'd lay a tot o' rum he ships false whiskers."

There was a commotion and shouting on deck that caused Jack and Ben to hurry up.

The captain was tearing his hair and rushing about, whilst the pilot in his hideous language, was cursing the rudder of the ship.

Some old Turks and Jews who had been gambling for heavy stakes, thinking that their last hour had come, began to pray with all their might.

One old sinner of an Israelite, in his alarm, actually swallowed some of his gold, so that he might take it with him to the promised land.

The " Adamant " was only going under easy steam at the time of the mishap, but the crafty pilot had set her on the shoal in such a way that she could not be got off.

When all efforts failed the captain ordered a kedge anchor out fore and aft, so that the vessel was moored head and stern.

The anchor watch was then set, the third officer and two seamen taking the first turn, whilst the scoundrel of a pilot stuck to the wheel, bewailing his fate as an injured man.

Arab Jack stood in the waist of the ship and watched this fellow's movements.

He saw him strike a fusee and wave it in the air as if expostulating with himself before he lit his cigar.

Ben crept to Jack's side at this moment. " Where are your Greeks now ?" he whispered, with an incredulous grin. " Do you think we've been mistaken ?"

" You'll see ; keep a good look-out on the shore. I could swear I saw a dark object in the water just a bit ago, and some black specks moving along the sand hills in the gloom."

" A crocodile may be, and the ghosts of some of Farer's old crows."

" All right," said Jack, " I'm not in a humour for larking," which speech made Ben a little huffed and he stole away.

Jack, however, kept his eye on the shore, and by that means failed to notice a muffled figure sneak forward on the opposite side of the deck.

He had almost fallen into a reverie, picturing fantastic shadows in the hazy mist, when he was startled by a dull thud and a stifled groan.

In a moment a horrible presentiment flashed across his mind.

" The fell work's commenced," he muttered as he crept forward towards the look-out man, and found him crouched down near the bows. " Is he asleep or ——"

Jack started, he had placed his hand on the sailor's breast, and found it sticky and wet.

" Blood," gasped Jack. " The pirate's weapon has pierced his heart. Where's Ben ?"

He glanced wildly around, and just caught a glimpse of a raised weapon, and a cloaked figure bending over a prostrate form.

" Curse you. fiend of darkness !" Jack cried, as he sprang forward and dashed aside the weapon, of the would-be double-dyed assassin.

One glance showed him that the intended victim was his friend, Ben, and so, seizing one of the handspikes the old seaman had placed ready to hand, he gave the ruffian a crushing blow that seemed to break in his skull.

The red-handed villain sank on the deck without a word or a groan, and then, by the light from the galaxy of stars, he recognised in the assassin the Russian and the Greek both in one.

" Ben, Ben," cried our hero, " Rouse up ! now the Philistines bear down. List, hearken, can you not hear a rippling on the still waters ?"

But Ben could not move, even to save his life ! he was drugged ! some one had given him some rum to cheer him during the night watch.

Jack rushed down into the forecastle to arouse the men, and on returning to the deck he found the hatch was closed, and the bar put over it.

He tried to force it, but it resisted his efforts, and he again endeavoured to rouse the men, who were exhausted with the previous day's toil.

" Great heaven !" he gasped, as he heard a footstep overhead, along the deck. " All is lost—lost—lost !"

CHAPTER XI.

AN INCARNATE FIEND. — HOW ARAB JACK ACTED WHEN STRONG MEN QUAILED.—A DEATH STRUGGLE WITH THE MURDEROUS GREEK. — BOARDED BY BEDOUINS. — JACK PREVENTS A TERRIBLE MASSACRE.

A STILLNESS, such as that of the chamber of death, reigned in the ship, when Greek number two, if we may so describe him, left his post near the cabin door and crept forward to see what had become of his confederate in guilt.

Like all those whose hearts engender evil he was superstitious, so that when he beheld the bloodstained, crushed and crouching form of his dead companion, his heart for a moment sickened, and he felt his own time was come.

But it was only for a moment that this qualm took possession of him, for soon a guttural sound escaped him, and an expression of glee burst from his unholy lips.

" Ha! ha ! the devil is not good to all, he deserts him, whilst I take his roubles and dollars."

With these fiendish words, he closed the hatch which our Jack had descended, and was actually kneeling upon it, listening with demoniacal delight, when the brave devoted boy was thumping away at it underneath.

" Ha-ha, me stifle dem," he exclaimed, whilst his callous ears gloated on the sound. " Fire, smoke. Aha ! den dey roast while I feast on de gold."

Jack heard these words, and his blood fairly boiled with rage.

" You demon !" he hissed, grinding his teeth in despair, when suddenly he remembered the cowl that gave air below.

It was a large one, yet not sufficient for a man to climb through ; but Jack having found it, by aid of the dim smoky oil lamp hung from a beam, by dint of sheer pluck, and the tenacity with which young blood clings to life, struggled upward until he clutched one of the stays.

" God help me !" was Jack's prayer, and, although it was a tight and terrible squeeze, he drew himself out clear and dropped gently on the deck.

Then he paused for breath and glanced cautiously around him.

Horror ! a dozen dark heads lined the rail of the bulwark opposite him.

It was fortunate it was not yet light, and

also that those to whom the heads belonged, doubtful about the signal dropped down on to their raft, were waiting its being repeated.

The pilot took no further part in the affair; he had "done his bit," as the saying is, and so, like a crafty dog as he was, he leaned over the wheel and pretended to be asleep.

Jack breathed more freely when he saw the black murderous heads depart, and creeping from his concealment he searched for old Ben.

"It's no use going aft to arouse that old fool of a captain," Jack thought. "I warned him once, and he mocked me, now he may look out for himself, and—ah——"

At that instant he caught sight of the old tar, just as he had left him, and horrible to relate the demon who had closed the hatch was leaning over him.

One hand was over Ben's heart, feeling whether it had any pulsation, whilst the other clutched a long dagger or creese, with which, if he lived, he would speedily let out the life-blood of the prostrate tar.

At that moment Ben opened his eyes in a half-dazed manner, and, although his limbs seemed dead and useless, he caught sight of the gleaming blade and tried to clutch it.

And that action nearly sealed his doom !

It betrayed he was living, and but for our hero, the weapon would quickly have done its work; already the bold tar felt the point of the cold steel pierce his flesh, and his blood curdled as he thought of his cruel doom, when Jack suddenly appeared, and witnessed, as he thought, the bloody deed.

To one of less mind and action the sight would have been paralysing, but to Arab Jack it gave renewed vigour.

Like a young lion he sprang at the burly Greek, and before the ruffian caught the light sound of his bounding footstep, he dealt him a blow between the eyes and sent him rolling over on his back.

Jack was upon him then in an instant, and being unable to use his knife, he caught him with both hands by the throat, and by sheer pressure caused him to turn black and green in the face. But the pirate (for now he had shone up in his true colours) was not one that was soon deprived of the vital spark.

He struggled desperately for life, and the pair rolled over and over, Jack still continuing his deadly grip, until the veins of the pirate's neck stood out like ridges of cord, and his eyes protruded wildly from their sockets.

Ben by this time was again on his feet, but he had not the chance of rendering Jack any assistance, for a dozen heads suddenly appeared again above the bulwarks, and as many dusky forms like shadows dropped upon the deck; no noise, not a sound did they give.

Their bare feet trod like velvet on the stout planks, whilst their tiger-like movements precluded all possibility of their being heard.

It was only a question of a few moments, and the black-skinned Bedouin Arabs would be masters of the vessel, and the crew and passengers be brutally massacred.

Jack's keen eye glanced for one instant from the hideous visage of the gurgling foe, to the dusky figures along the deck, who, armed with matchlocks and spears, were considering which end of the ship to begin at first.

The sight put fresh vigour in Jack's flagging arms.

With one mighty effort he squeezed the life out of his formidable foe, and secured his weapons,—the long dirk and a brace of Damascus pistols.

The latter were splendid weapons, handsomely mounted and carved, but Jack had no thought of this. They were loaded, that was all he cared to know, and as he caught sight of a herculean dusky demon, who was advancing spear in hand upon old Ben, he sent a ball crashing through the head of the treacherous foe.

All this was but the work of a few seconds, and the false pilot, who was ignorant of the death struggle going on forward, was wondering what had become of the Greeks, when the report of the pistol startled him.

That sound also startled all on board of the ship.

The sailors clamoured to get on deck, and used their efforts to burst open the hatch, whilst the captain and his officers seized their revolvers and rushed up from their berths.

Taken thus by surprise the dastardly horde, who anticipated an easy victory over sleeping men and innocently-dreaming women, found they had entered the lion's den, for the captain and mate apprised of the treachery by Jack's shouts, showed no mercy or quarter to the demons, but blazed away.

"Unfasten that hatchway," cried Jack to Ben, "then take this boarding knife and follow me."

"Ah," exclaimed Jack, a moment later. "A fresh supply, come on you myrmidons of darkness and test a British boy's powers and pluck."

Another gang was swarming up the bows and Jack was in among them in a twinkling.

It was not so dark now, the mist had cleared a little, so that Jack fired his second bullet with accurate aim, shooting one Bedouin right through the head, carrying away another's left jaw, and wounding one who was scrambling over the cat-head in the abdomen.

"Bravo, Jack, a good shot, that," roared old Ben, who, with a long iron bolt in one hand and the murderous knife in the other, rushed to the assistance of our daring boy-hero.

"Bang ! bang ! bang ! "

The matchlocks of the Arabs were at work, but the male portion of the passengers who had courage sufficient rushed upon deck with their weapons. Ladies screamed and called on the stewardess for aid, thus adding to the confusion, whilst the sharp crack of the revolvers and the agonised shrieks of those hit, added terribly to the midnight scene.

The crew and passengers including the women did not comprise more than forty in all, whilst fifty or more at the least of Bedouins got foothold on the deck.

They floated alongside on rough rafts hastily constructed, but capable of conveying on shore a vast quantity of loot, whilst a herd of camels on the bank were ready to transport it across the desert.

Arab Jack was unceasing in his prodigies of valour, and the manner in which he beat back the dusky crew as they clambered the side, with the butt of his empty pistol, encouraged the sailors to use their handspikes and other miscellaneous weapons with good effect against the long deadly spears.

Blood and brains were spattered about on all sides, and our hero had many narrow escapes from losing his life. He had a spear wound in his arm and leg, and an ugly graze on his cheek from the ball of a matchlock.

Old Ben had a spear wound in one cheek, which laid it open to the bone, and two sailors, f faint heart, were killed outright, whilst a oker who helped to support Jack's party was lled from the blow of an Arab's gun.

But the tide of battle was soon run, the Bedouins who had the chance of escape, seeing nothing before them but defeat, turned about and sprang over the bulwarks into the canal.

In one hour from the onset the clamour was toned down, and then the decks presented a ghastly appearance.

Dead, dying and wounded strewed the deck, whilst the blood pouring from the scuppers told how terrible had been the carnage.

Arab Jack was now considered a hero of some note, and well had he earned the appellation.

The captain called him aft when the conflict ceased, but Jack took no heed until he had given an old sheikh who was being poled ashore on a raft a parting shot.

"There now," shouted the indomitable boy. "Take that for a keepsake. Aha ! you are forced to accept the gift ; may you never sit down comfortably the remainder of your life."

The sailors gathered near the side all laughed heartily at this, for they considered it a capital joke,—but it was the reverse for the Bedouin sheikh.

As the bullet struck him in the rear, he leaped into the air several feet, performing a perfect somersault, before dropping like a baffled shark into the water.

When Jack appeared on the quarter deck, those assembled gave him a ringing cheer, and the captain, taking him by the hand, thanked him warmly for his services.

"I feel honoured by your compliments," answered Jack, taking the blood-stained turban from his head and making a graceful bow. "I have done no more than the youths of my country should do. I fought in a just cause, checked the cupidity of those fiery untamed savages, and punished the treachery of the Greeks."

A loud shout of approval greeted Jack's plain-worded speech.

"Three cheers for our boy deliverer, Arab Jack," shouted the captain.

"Hurrah ! hurrah ! hurrah !"

Three cheers then rent the still air and rolled over the dark waters of the canal, such cheers as had never before been heard in those dreary wastes.

The bold handsome boy remained uncovered during this ovation.

When it ceased, he again bowed his acknowledgment, and was about to resume his blood-smeared turban, when an Indian, magnificently attired, stepped forward.

Jack looked with veneration on the wrinkled face and long white beard and moustache, which contrasted strongly with the dark piercing eyes, filled with gratitude.

"An Indian noble," thought Jack, as the stranger drew near, leading by the hand a most beautiful female, clothed in a rich mantle down to her very feet.

Jack gazed upon her with speechless fascina-tion, whilst those gathered around stood rooted in silent wonderment.

"Who can she be ?" Jack muttered, as her clear blue eyes shot their rays into his, and the rich gems sparkled in her sunny and neatly-braided hair.

He was soon enlightened.

"You are surprised," said the Indian noble, as Jack gave an involuntary start. "This is my daughter, the child of my dear departed wife, who was of your own country, and whom I saved from the carnage in Lucknow."

Our hero bowed gracefully, and a murmur of astonishment burst from those assembled.

"For that deed, she became mine," continued the noble, a tear of remembrance starting from his eye. "And now, since you have been instru-mental in delivering me and my peerless daughter from, not only death, but a fate ten times more horrible, she is yours—as her mother was mine."

The aged sire, strong as he looked in physique, broke down under the terrible strain, as he pressed his daughter a step nearer our hero.

Jack, young as he was, was not invulnerable to the powers of beauty and love, but what was he to do with a wife ?

He knew that they married young in India's torrid clime, and the girl, whose beauty he felt sure could not be surpassed, was just budding into early womanhood. A nabob would have given half his wealth for her possession.

The lustful eyes of the Turks and Assyrians, wandered from the proud form of Jack to the girl's splendid figure,—the exquisite contour of which was discernible through the light texture of her loose-fitting robe,—with expressions of envy and disgust.

Our hero, however, viewed the lovely vision with naught but boyish ardour.

"Mine is a roving disposition," he said, in-clining his head courteously to the noble. "Your daughter, like myself, is but a child, and it would be madness to bind myself for life, and thus quench the adventurous spirit I have within me."

"But," he added, observing the old chief's pained look, and the pallor of disappointment that overspread the fair cheek of the girl. "I may love her as a sister ; and I now take the liberty of sealing that lasting friendship, which in this British boy's heart shall never cease."

Arab Jack, carried away by the impulse of the moment, stepped forward, placed his arm round the delicate form of the thrilling girl, and drawing her gently to him, until her heaving bosom pressed against his swelling breast, im-printed on her delicately-chiselled coral lips a kiss so pure, so fervent, that the lips of the sensual Turks fairly watered.

"Allah, Allah," exclaimed one old sinner, roll-ing his lustful orbs. "What would I not give to have her in my harem !"

Our hero heard the remark, and turning sharply on him, would have spurned him with his foot, when his impetuosity was restrained by a hand laid on his shoulder.

It was Signor Varnoni who thus interfered.

His dark cheek was flushed, and he spoke to our hero in trembling tones. "Senor Jack," said he, "we must at once quit this scene, the pasha's yacht comes this way, and will soon be alongside. In her we must depart."

"I am ready," said Jack, laughing at the

ludicrousness of the scene and the astonishment evinced in many of the faces around. " I have undergone my ' baptism of fire.' If I remain here I may be captured by love."

CHAPTER XII.

ON ARABI'S YACHT.—JACK MEETS WITH AN OLD FRIEND. — TAKING IT OUT OF AN EGYPTIAN.—ARAB JACK AND THE PASHA'S BEAUTIFUL NAUTCH GIRL.—AN ATTEMPT TO DESTROY THE CANAL.

JACK looked not unlike a pasha as he stood on the saloon deck of Arabi's splendid yacht. No boy was ever prouder than he was then ; his hands were ablaze with massive diamonds, and a heavy chain of exquisite Indian workmanship was round his neck.

" Ah," said he to himself, as he tapped the jewelled hilt of a costly yataghan that hung by his side, and glanced down at the emerald-handled dirk and the brace of silver-mounted pistols which were stuck in his gorgeous sash, " what would they say at home if they saw me now ? What would Flash Luke and Dick of the Dials say if they beheld such a turn-out as this ? No tinsel, all pure and worth enough money to buy up the Burlington Arcade."

Jack then relapsed into a dreamy state, thinking of the vociferous cheers that hailed his departure from the ship, the showers of presents that were heaped upon him by those on board, and the face of the Indian noble with his peerless daughter by his side, whose wistful orbs followed our hero until the daring boy was out of sight.

Jack was leaning on the rich carved work of one of the skylights which overlooked the grand saloon, and glancing carelessly down he beheld Arabi, whom he recognised at once, in deep converse with the signor.

" I wonder what they are talking about," thought Jack, who in spite of his rich attire and glorious surroundings, was still an English and inquisitive boy. " I'd give a crown down just to find out the gist of their little game."

But although he strained his ears he could catch nothing but a confused mumble.

Arabi was seated on a throne-like divan smoking a costly hookah, and the signor lounged on a cushioned couch puffing thin clouds from a Pequitta cigar.

A third party was also there, Mustapha Ali, one of Arabi's greatest generals, whose bushy brows and heavily-haired upper lip, from which the smoke of his hookah incessantly poured, showed that he neither lacked cruelty nor cunning.

" Confound it," said Jack, turning away in disgust, " those heavy hangings, though they look nice and must cost a good lot, are nuisances, they deaden the sound so that a slave might be flogged there without any one hearing his cries."

" Yah, um get flogged plenty sometimes," muttered a voice in Jack's ear, and on turning he beheld a barefooted fez-capped Egyptian boy, who was grinning from ear to ear.

" What a mouth for a tart," Jack exclaimed. " I wonder whether you could eat spotted duff."

" Me eat, yah, ah ! " grinned the lad, his eyes starting out of his head. " Dere, hark dat bell tinkle for you. Go quick, den you hab plenty nice t'ings."

Jack could not resist a laugh, although at the same time he eyed the poor boy in pity as he shambled away with a keen eager glance fore and aft to ascertain whether he was watched by any of the officers or crew.

Jack was then ushered below by a smartly-dressed Nubian, a slave evidently by his dejected appearance, into a room where a table was laid with every luxury.

" Do I partake alone," asked Jack, on seeing that plates and so forth were laid for only one.

" Yas, sur, you hab all dis," casting his eyes round the sumptuous room, " to yourself."

Forgetting that the slave was not an English waiter, Jack gave the fellow a fee, which delighted him very much, and caused him to bow and scrape until he was clear out of the door.

" Scissors," exclaimed Jack, when he foun himself alone. " My eye ! here's a treat Wouldn't this be a feed for a pack of hungr school-boys."

He took a survey of the various dishes, wonde ing which to begin at first.

" They all look nice, I'll taste of each," h muttered, and having discovered that all wer equally choice, he added, " I'll fill up with thes splendid cheese cakes, omelettes and jam."

" Yas, dem good. berry," exclaimed a voice i the very feeblest of tones, " cheese cake and jam awf'ly jolly."

" What ! " said Jack, glancing towards the door, " that voice sounds familiar ; come in."

The curtain was drawn aside, and then our hero beheld the woolly head and white gleaming teeth of little Sambo, the cuddy boy on board the " Dromedary."

" Hallo, what brings you here my young scarecrow ? " Jack exclaimed. " You've run away I suppose, and been sold in the market for a slave."

" No, me 'tolen, sar," whispered the negro boy. " When you run, captain beat me berry much, Middy Fortskew speak bad—say I know all 'bout it, and then pay bad man 'teal me."

" Good heavens," exclaimed Jack, indignantly, " who would imagine such rascality could be carried on under the British flag ! How do you feed here, plenty to eat, eh ? "

" Black bread, water, sometime onion, bit ob salt."

The little urchin cast such a devouring glance over the sumptuously laid table that Jack felt it a cruelty to starve him any longer.

" Here, fall to," said he in his John Blunt way. " Yaff all you can, you savvy."

" Me do," mumbled the darky, thrusting his grimy hands into one of the porcelain dishes and devouring its contents with the avidity of a wolf.

Jack was so delighted to watch him that he could eat no more himself, but any qualm that our hero might have felt that too much of the good things would be left and taken away, was dispelled by the appearance of young Zip.

Zip was the boy Jack spoke to on deck, a boy with a mouth that Jack compared to the opening in a sack.

" Come in," shouted our hero to him, and pushing the table towards one of the cushioned seats, he bade them both mount thereon and peg away.

Zip needed no second invitation, like Sambo his duties were in the culinary department, where they both had plenty of work scouring kettles and pans, but little to eat.

" This is better than going to the Zoo," exclaimed Jack, laughing right out, a laugh, however, that brought a third party to the sanctum.

This party was no other than Majoud Akan, the son of a dignitary connected with the Sublime Porte, a lieutenant on board the Pasha's yacht, and also a favourite of Arabi's.

When he peered in and saw the plebeian guests of our distinguished Arab, his dark blood mantled his cheek, and he uttered a very profane oath.

Jack affected to take no notice of this, and in his most cheery tone cried—

" Hallo, what another hungry swab ! Enter, thou famished one, partake of that which is left ; the more of us the merrier."

Majoud Akan was not accustomed to this kind of talk.

To be thus addressed by what he considered a dog of an Arab, quite upset his polished dignity.

" Dog of an infidel," he exclaimed. " Is it thus you insult the son of my illustrious father ?"

" Dog yourself," cried Jack, unmindful of where he was. " I'd insult you, and your father too, if he is as insolent as yourself."

" Would'st thou ?" was the disdainful response. " Dog, I spit on thee as I would on the beard of a Jew."

" Eh, is it so," cried Jack, his fine eyes flashing with choler, " you paltry son of a cobbler. Why with one of my meanest gems I could buy you up, from the tassel of your fez to the smallest button on your tinsel uniform."

Jack was putting it strong, but he did not care now, and turning to his affrighted guests he bade them go on munching without the slightest fear.

Majoud gave the young urchins a withering glance, and expected to see them fall down at his feet in abject fear.

He was disappointed in this, and so to enforce his authority he caught hold of Sambo by the ear, and drew his scimitar, with the threat—

" Confound thee, thou whelps of asses, I'll slit both of your assinine ears."

Jack shook with rage.

" Sambo's ears were of the mulish type, but Majoud's were more of the shape and size of mushrooms, so that Jack had no difficulty in reaching over the table and seizing one of them by the rim just as he would a willow pattern plate.

" Now," said he, " execute your threat, and I will transfer your apish lug to this dish and make you eat it for a pancake."

Majoud quailed for an instant under Jack's fierce frown, but he had power on his side. At one word he knew he would have plenty come to his assistance, and Jack would then have to sing small.

It so happened that at that moment Arabi ordered the band to strike up, to drown some dull foreboding that distressed his mind, and Jack taking advantage of this resolved upon humbling the Egyptian pagan.

" Now," said he, " we can talk without fear of being disturbed, will you fight, can you box, or are you any hand at fencing with that gewgaw of a weapon of yours ?"

Majoud, was not over surfeited with pluck, but, as we said before, he depended in the event of a tussle and his being worsted on calling for assistance.

" I can fence thee," he hissed savagely, at the same time releasing Sambo's ear. " Come on ! No Arab shall ever conquer this Egyptian."

" Good," cried Jack, with a smile. " I feel chock full of fight. Now, mind those wind-flappers you carry each side of your head."

" Curse thee," yelled the coxcomb, slashing at Jack while he pushed the table aside ; " the devil and thou shalt be partners before many minutes are over thine——"

He had no time to finish.

Arab Jack's bright blade flashed like lightning from its sheath, and, parrying the Egyptian's deadly blow, he smote him in the cheek with the flat of his jewel-hilted yataghan with such force that he fancied his ears were on fire and his head completely blown off.

The boys crouched in a corner, not knowing whether to cry or laugh, for Majoud's dusky cheek puffed up, and they saw the rattan in the perspective.

Jack gave his adversary time to get breath and feel the smart of the blow.

He hoped it would sting him to madness, as Jack wanted to test both his own arm and his steel.

He was gratified, too.

The Egyptian finding no blood had been drawn was emboldened, and, with a cry that was meant to be awe-inspiring, he flew upon our hero like an infuriated tiger, brandishing sword and dirk, thinking to dazzle Jack's eyes by the last-named weapon.

Bold Jack, however, was too wary for him.

He met the onslaught with a coolness that would have excited admiration.

Then, guarding the doubly-dealt blows with exquisite skill, he with the slightest ease imaginable sliced off the tip of Majoud's left ear.

The howl that he gave when he felt the smart and the hot blood trickling down his neck, was astounding.

He had received a mark of disgrace that would burden him through life and cause him to be scoffed at in society.

In his mind he regretted that he had ventured on the job, but now Jack gave him no chance of retreating.

" One dog's lug," Jack said. " Now, shall I put the other on a plate ?"

" Avaunt, thou fiend of darkness," was the retort, " I will crush thee like a worm in the earth."

Jack's reply was a taunting laugh.

He saw his way clear for doing just as he pleased with the Egyptian.

Giving his arm the twist which he had learnt from his friend Hassan, he wrenched the scimitar from Majoud's hand, and then sent his poignard flying in an opposite direction.

" Good ! that is well," exclaimed a female, at that moment.

Jack turned his head in astonishment, and to his increased surprise saw the figure of a lovely Arabian girl standing in the opening of a secret door.

It was one of the Nautch girls, or dancers, that Arabi carried on board his yacht to kill the *ennui* that at times oppressed him.

Believing Jack to be one of her own country as he spoke the tongue moderately well, she had looked on without fear, and watched with interest Jack's conflict with the Egyptian.

Our hero doffed his turban, and bowed to her as she made him a graceful salaam, and he took the trophy she offered him, the emblem of her country, a delicate white flower.

Jack looked the ideal of beauty as he stood there, with the wind of the desert (which blew aside the silken curtains of the window) fanning his cheek.

Whilst the Arabian girl stood talking to him in all the gracefulness of her native beauty, the report of a musket overhead startled them.

Sambo and Zip, vanished like two spectres, and sought the lowest part of the ship, whilst Jack, who was gently pressing the hand of the witching girl, imprinted a kiss on her soft, voluptuous lips, and hurried on deck.

"Well, Jack," said Varnoni, who had preceded him, "there seems to be trouble wherever we go. Here the rascals have been trying to blow down the banks of the canal."

"Ah, that accounts for the rifle shot," Jack exclaimed, as he saw on the distant sands the figure of a native, lying stiff and stark. "And, there, I can see a group of Bedouins on camels, and another party in the hollow of that ridge mounted on fleet Arabian steeds."

They were watching the pasha's yacht as she seemed to fly through the rippling water, and appeared to be waiting until she had passed.

Jack saw no more of Majoud during the trip.

He heard from the lovely Arabian girl that he had been seized with a pain in his bread-bag, and that cholera was likely to set in.

"Choler-a, rather," suggested Jack, indulging in a well-deserved laugh, "I dare say he will cut the sea if he recovers, and become a ear splitter, as clever as he who split the bank notes."

When Suez was reached Jack took an affectionate farewell of the dancer, and also allowed her, as a souvenir, a lock of his curly hair.

In return she gave him one of her own silken locks, and her photo, which had been done by an Englishman at Port Said.

Sambo and Zip almost cried when Jack stepped into the pasha's gig.

They thrust their heads out of a port-hole under which the boat lay, and shook hands with the noble-hearted boy, who gave them each a valuable coin to keep him in their remembrance.

Jack only had a short run at Suez, just to look at the ancient place, for as soon as the baggage was transferred to the P. & O. boat which was waiting, they steamed for Aden and the Red Sea.

Jack now found himself mixed up with a motley crew, Arabian sheikhs, caliphs of Bagdad, East Indian nabobs, and Turkish pilgrims bound to Jedda, on their way to Mecca.

The smells were just as varied as the people.

"They are enough to stifle one," said Jack. "One moment the garlic is so powerful as to almost skin one's nose, and the next the odour of frankincense and myrrh is enough to destroy one's senses." Worse had to follow however.

CHAPTER XIII.

AN ADVENTURE IN THE PALACE AT SUAKIM.
—THE ABDUCTION OF A NUBIAN BEAUTY.
—JACK PURSUES THE MYSTERIOUS FIGURE.
—FACE TO FACE WITH OSMAN DIGNA.—
ARAB JACK COMBATS WITH THE SOUDAN
STANDARD BEARER.

"WELL, signor," said Jack, one morning on returning from a stroll round the market place, "how long are we going to stay here in Suakim before we start for Massowah."

"I cannot at present say, it will all depend on events," replied Varnoni. "You can make yourself comfortable here, no doubt; you have money, and if you need more come to me. So far you have given me entire satisfaction in obeying my commands, and now I trust you will continue to do so."

"All right. Then I am not under any restraint? I am to live in the governor's house, and can go in and out as I like."

"That's just it, my lad. Make yourself happy and at home; the hot weather don't seem to hurt you and the mosquitoes don't trouble about your young blood."

"No," said Jack, laughing outright, "the dark rolling eyes of these lovely Soudanese girls trouble me most."

"Be careful," said the Italian, giving Jack one of his most meaning looks. "You bid fair to be a gay Lothario; mind it don't get you into another scrape."

"If it does I must scrape out of it," laughed Jack, "I feel I am only fit for love and war."

They stood in the garden of the governor's house while thus talking, and when they parted the signor repaired to the council chamber, whilst Jack sauntered across the court.

Stopping at a fountain, he viewed himself in the clear crystal flood, and appeared satisfied with the result, when suddenly the sounds of distress aroused him.

It was a female voice, and the heart-piercing shrieks cut him to the quick. But whence could they proceed? This puzzled him.

The windows were too high from the ground for him to look into any of the apartments, and most of them had the lattice-work closed.

He was driven to despair when the cry was repeated.

"Ah, that is the window," he cried, suddenly, having glanced wildly around. "But where is the door? Good God, it may be murder, and here I am fixed like a Johnny Gilpin."

To add to his anxiety he remembered that on the day of his arrival he had caught a glimpse of a round-cheeked, chubby-faced Nubian girl at that very window.

So beautiful was she, though black as the purest jet, that Jack had dreamed of her through the night, and now he could picture to himself her shiny, well-oiled skin, and the silver rings that pended from her ears and nose as she sang a song in one of those strains which delight the heart and charm the most callous ear.

It was a strange fancy of Jack's to take a liking to such a being, but he could not help it. "I feel like Don Quixote," he said, "bound to aid the weak and oppressed, but how am I to proceed in this case?"

A row of palm trees at that moment caught his attention, and quick as lightning he sprang towards them, and climbed one of the slender stems.

He could not ascend far, but just high enough by craning his neck to get a glance into the apartment, and then he saw a sight that made his young blood boil.

"Ah, 'tis the Nubian girl in the villain's grasp," he exclaimed, excitedly. "See, he stifles her cries; she will faint, she will fall victim to his horrible designs. She must yield to the dark-skinned, gloating fiend, if no one renders her assistance."

Jack's excitement was so intensified by the sight, that big beads of sweat poured from him, and his hands clutched at the tree just as if they were at the scoundrel's throat.

Suddenly he remembered there was a passage across the paved court, and dropping to the ground he eagerly sought it.

This led to a terrace in which there were numerous doors, all leading to apartments belonging to the palace, and selecting one which he supposed would lead him to the chamber of the distressed damsel, he mounted the stone stairs. Here he was at fault ; there were several doors, but which was the right one.

"This is ajar," he muttered, selecting one that was partly open, but the room was unoccupied, and various articles were strewn about in confusion.

"Curse it," he muttered, in despair. "I shall be too late. What a fool I was not to count the trees and the windows, which would have assisted me."

He sprang to the window and looked out, and then he saw where his fault lay.

He recognised the tree he had climbed by the drooping of its branches, and by these means he took the bearings of the window he wanted.

Quick as thought he turned and left the room to seek the other chamber, when lo, the sound of a sandalled foot caught his ear, and a muffled figure bearing some object under its cloak brushed past him and nearly threw him down.

Jack was so unprepared for this that he was some seconds recovering his equilibrium, thus giving the cloaked figure time to descend the stairs and get clear of the terrace before he could follow in pursuit.

"By Jove!" cried Arab Jack, "I'll not be thus shamefully beaten. The fellow, for I know it to be a man by his turban, is of herculean figure, but this boy shall try his strength against him, even though I should be beaten."

Jack loosened his yataghan in its sheath as he bounded down the stone stairs, thence he fled along the terrace, through the passage, across the court, and made his way out of the precincts of the palace.

As he left the gate the astonished sentry was too surprised to give him the challenge—he was gaping after a flying figure, who seemed to speed along like the wind.

"Ah ! there he goes," cried Jack, darting off in the same direction; "he makes for the city gate. I will after him ; I guess his object is to escape with his precious plunder across the plains."

Jack was not far out.

The city gate facing the hills was in that quarter, but had he known who he was following the knowledge might have deterred him.

Unmindful of this, however, the daring boy sped on, but owing to the narrow streets that at intervals intersected the way, he lost sight of the flying form on several occasions.

This caused him to lose ground, and a further delay occurred at the gate, where he was questioned by the Egyptian sentry, who allowed the fugitive to cross the open space without the walls and gain the mimosa bush.

Our hero here begun to lose trace of the pursued owing to the rocky nature of the ground, but soon he came upon a heavy imprint in the sand, which told of some one carrying a burden.

Following this up, and guided here and there by a trampled shrub, he came at length to an open grove where the sight he saw startled him.

A dozen or more splendidly-accoutred camels were tethered there, feeding on the foliage, and a party of well-armed natives were squatted around smoking.

A couple of low tents attracted our hero's attention mostly.

"It is there the ruffian is concealed," he muttered ; "if I have to fight a score to one I must put up with it."

So saying, he placed his yataghan between his teeth, and dropping on all fours crept noiselessly through the prickly scrub which encircled the clearing until he was right opposite the gayest-looking tent, the canvas of which was striped white and red.

Wriggling on his stomach, then, more like a Red Indian than a British boy, he gained the opening and peered in, when he saw a dark, heavily-bearded savage gloating over a prone, listless form which he at once recognised as the bright-eyed Nubian girl.

Jack's heart was in his mouth, as the saying is, but his proud spirit kept him up.

"Curse you," he hissed, "you are a devil in human form, you are——"

"Osman Digna."

The voice which finished Jack's speech sounded harshly in the brave boy's ear, and the cold steel that was placed against his throat, as a hard hand clasped him by the nape of the neck, made him shudder.

Startled and annoyed by this unwelcome intrusion the dark, black-bearded wretch raised his gloating eyes from his victim and fixed them upon Jack.

For a moment our hero was horrified. Never had he seen a face so satanical, except in a likeness, and that was in a sketch-book in the house of the signor. Jack needed no further confirmation that it was Osman Digna himself who glared at him with those black, stony eyes—Osman Digna, the mighty chief, the terror of women and even babes, the fierce and indomitable tyrant of the Soudan.

"Yes, it is he," Jack thought, as, held in that terrible position, he rested on his hands and knees. "Just heaven, how do you allow such monsters to pollute the air with their foul breath ? "

But our hero's meditations were cut short.

At a sign from the Soudan chief, he was jerked like a babe to his feet, and the savage who held him clutched at his jewelled yataghan.

"Not yet," thundered Jack, his eyes fairly sparkling with fire. "That trophy I won with my blood, and will defend it to the last inch of my life."

Osman Digna was startled.

Astonishment beamed in his hitherto expressionless face, as he gazed upon the handsome young Arab.

"Allah, preserve us," he muttered, "the boy speaks with the tongue of a warrior ; has the holy camel appeared, that we are blessed with this miracle ? "

At the mention of Allah, the fellow who held Jack released his grasp, and made a devout sign to the prophet, a movement of which Jack took instant advantage.

Shaking himself together, and throwing his

half dislocated shoulders into their place, he drew his yataghan from its sheath, and springing upon the fellow caught him by the burly throat.

"Now, demon of the lowest pit," Jack yelled, in frantic accents, "beg your craven life, or by the prophet's holy beard I'll strike off your accursed head."

The man was alarmed.

He was a true Arab and a devout follower of the prophet, and to be bearded by a mere puny boy, as Jack seemed beside his huge, massive frame, was unbearable.

But to die by the hand of one whose soul, though it might be as pure as that of the holy prophet, was not permitted to enter beyond the first gate of paradise, made him feel as if a nest of snakes were writhing about his vitals.

He stood paralysed with fear, until Osman Digna pronounced his name. "Abdul Ahad," cried the chief, "what is this qualm? Awake, strike to the heart of our foe. Is it thus I see my standard bearer tremble?"

The words were magical.

Abdul Ahad drew his crescent-shaped sword, and like a lion shook off the grasp of our hero.

Jack recoiled from the shock, but he gathered himself together again on the instant.

"Foot to foot, blade to blade," he yelled. "I defy you, come on. Let Osman Digna see that the boy whose chin is as bare as the scorching sands of the desert possesses the spirit of a man."

Osman Digna had no need to be told this twice, he could read it in our hero's face, and he would fain have stayed the conflict, which he felt sure must end in favour of his stalwart standard bearer. But curiosity impelled him to let things take their course.

"Go on," he said, "let your fight be to extermination. Begin."

Osman Digna's commanding voice was such that it had only to be heard to be obeyed.

Mechanically, it seemed, the combatants faced each other at the front of the chieftain's tent, and the struggle commenced.

It was no child's play that followed. The arm of Arab Jack was strong and supple, and his wrist was as flexible as steel.

How it was he kept off the fierce onslaught of the standard bearer, however, was a mystery.

Each blow from that terrible crescent-shaped sword was sufficient to cut a man in twain, and yet Jack warded it off, and gave Abdul some trouble to guard himself.

Aroused by the clash of steel and the fiery sparks that emanated from the contending blades, the Arabs, who had sat peacefully smoking, arose, and in a body rushed towards the tents, keeping, however, at a respectful distance.

These men were Osman Digna's own bodyguard, and were the very pick of the fighting men of the various tribes, so that they were good judges of warlike skill. Therefore, when they looked on and applauded Jack it might be taken that he was no dunce at the sword.

The chances, however, varied on both sides: at one time it seemed that Jack had the standard bearer fully in his power, and at another Jack was equally at his mercy.

At length, and even when the onlookers thought the brave boy must give in from sheer exhaustion, Abdul Ahad threw up his arms and feebly cried for quarter.

Jack was about to lower the point of his yata-

ghan to the ground, or, as it is termed, bring it to the rest, when the thought struck him that this might be construed into an act of tameness.

"I will at his throat, as I have sworn," he cried; "whatever his name, whatsoever his rank or station, he is conquered by Arab Jack."

As the standard bearer lay on his back, his arms outstretched and his weapon dropped from his pulseless hand, our hero placed one foot on his broad upturned chest, and stood over him with his yataghan raised, ready to sweep off his head.

Jack would have made a good actor on the theatrical stage.

He went through this performance with such an air of reality that Osman actually thought his flag bearer was about to lose his head.

"Hold!" he yelled; "by the beard of the prophet, I conjure you."

Jack's mind was actively at work all the while.

His life was in the balance, and the weight was against him for many reasons.

He had drawn swords with one who from what he had heard was high in office, and beaten him, which gave good excuse for Osman Digna to take his life; then, again, he had been sued to for quarter, and if he granted it would not Abdul Ahad be indebted to him henceforth.

"These are both cogent points," Jack muttered, when with rapid thought he considered it over. "I must be brave and demand my terms." Without moving an inch and without blinking an eye, and still holding his gleaming yataghan in that death-dealing attitude, he cried:

"Osman Digna, chief of the Soudan, leader of many tribes, by the beard of Mahomet, whose bones we both worship, I demand of you my rights."

The great chief started.

He was literally astounded at the boy's audacity.

"What rights are they?" he demanded, his brows contracting ominously over his cold, stony eyes.

"Those of conquest. If I spare this caitiff's life, mine must be spared also."

Osman Digna bit his lips.

The boy by his presence of mind had baffled him for the moment, so that Osman had to call forth all his powers of perfidy and tact.

Turning his gaze upon his followers, who were grouped around with their spear staffs planted in the sand, he with a gesture ordered them to seize the daring boy.

But Jack instinctively read the meaning of that look. Stringing his sinews for the blow, he pointed to the wretch beneath his feet, and shouted in a tone of thunder:

"Halt for your lives; stand back all of you; let not one of you move forward one step, or the breath of this carrion shall cease."

It was a terrible moment that.

A moment not only of suspense, but portentous and direful to all.

One of the warlike party, the robber sheikh Taher, bolder than the rest, essayed to move.

But Jack seemed to possess a dozen pairs of eyes, and as his sword, like that of Nemesis, prepared to descend, Taher stood rooted like the rest.

The group, now statuesque, was worthy the artist's brush or the chisel of a sculptor.

Such an impressive scene had never before

been witnessed in the Soudan !—one single arm, and that a boy's, keeping those desperate, savage sheikhs at bay !

CHAPTER XIV.

ABDUL AHAD PREDICTS THE RISING OF THE SOUDANESE. — THE VISION OF THE HOLY CAMEL. — OSMAN DIGNA AND HIS FOLLOWERS START FOR HASHEEN.—A SCENE IN THE PALACE OF THE MUDIR OF SUAKIM.

HOW long Arab Jack would have held that mystic sway is questionable, had not an unforeseen circumstance happened at that critical juncture.

Abdul Ahad began to show signs of returning life, and in wild and terrible accents commenced to rave and tear his beard.

One of the party, a dervish or holy man, held up his hand and enjoined them all to silence, whilst Abdul yelled : " Oh, Osman Digna, son of the faithful, thy meteor is on the wane. The star and the crescent are in the ascendant, the Soudan is lost, because Mahomet has withdrawn his light from it, and for why ? Ye have neglected his word, the infidel is not yet stricken with the sword."

A dead silence reigned.

Not a word broke the stillness, not so much as a breath of wind stirred the leaves of the stunted palms, whilst the group stood wrapped in awe and wonderment.

This was a revelation, and all longed yet dreaded to hear it.

Arab Jack was as eager and curious as the rest. To him it seemed that the standard bearer was inspired as the wise men of old.

Jack eased the pressure of his foot, which was still planted on the broad, heaving chest of his foeman, and allowed him more freely to breathe and proceed with the prophetic incantation :

" O Arabi ! Arabi ! the land of blessedness is forsaken—Christian dogs laugh thee to scorn—the root of thy glory is withered. Soon the sun of the Mahdi shall shine."

Abdul Ahad ceased, but only for a moment. The beaded sweat poured from his brow like peas, and his features worked strongly, as though they were convulsed with pain.

Arab Jack gazed on him in silent pity. His magnanimous heart would not permit him to gloat over the miseries of a fallen foe.

That pity, however, nearly cost him his life.

Suddenly Abdul Ahad began to writhe as if wrestling with some powerful demon, and before our hero was aware of his recovery, the standard bearer sprang to his feet with the strength of an ox, and hurling our hero some yards away, he began to rave :

" O ye Arabs, tribes of the Soudan, arise, arise, the light of Ismail burns dim, sharpen your spears, strike for the Mahdi—the white camel of Mahomet comes to bear you to paradise."

He paused for a moment, and stood gazing wildly into the thick bush between him and the palms, and then shouting :

" It comes, the white camel of Mahomet ; I shall die, I shall die, and on this the fatal spot." He fell down, then, thoroughly exhausted, and presenting the appearance of one dead, a circumstance that warned Osman Digna that he must push on to Hasheen.

Let us now see what was passing in Suakim.

The mudir, or governor of that place, on learning that the Nubian girl, his niece, was missing from the palace, and that all search for her had been vain, sent for the commandant of the garrison and chief of the city watch to appear before him.

The inquiry was held in full divan, or in other words before a full bench, on which sat all the high dignitaries of the place to make a strict investigation of the mysterious affair.

The first witness called was the *femme de chambre*, a lady of colour and obesity, who superintended the terrace chambers in that part of the palace from which the girl disappeared.

She declared that " about dat hour when all good Mussulmans go to the mosque and pray, and all holy 'gipshuns go to dare shrine to worship, den me see sperrit, geni, come take somefink away, den Olibyah faint."

This evidence was tested but not shaken, and the soldier on guard at the palace gate at the time was also sworn and cautioned.

" Your highness," said he, trembling in his soleless shoes, " as I stood at the gate, seeing that no one should enter and disturb your highness's devotion, an apparition looking like a wild horse walking on its hind legs, erect, passed me, and when I looked at it, it flew away."

" Allah preserve us," exclaimed one of the grave old Turks in the divan, taking his chibouk from his mouth. " Art thou sure it was not the holy camel ?"

" It was like a horse," said the Egyptian, trembling, and looking awfully pale, " and it stuck out each side as if it had wings."

This sworn evidence caused much comment, but no one cared to dispute it, and the slaves who stood ready with their courbashes seemed annoyed that they were not called upon to use them on the witness.

The sentry on guard at the principal city gate, the only one open at that time, came next.

He was a big, bushy-whiskered fellow, who could scarcely see out of his eyes for hair, and he declared by all the saints of the calendar, that he saw no one leave the city except an old grey-headed Arab whose face was sheltered by his robe, and who carried a bag of old clothes.

These witnesses stood aside when Signor Varnoni, entering the justice chamber in haste, informed the mudir of Suakim and the lawgivers seated on the divan that his courier, Arab Jack, was missing also.

The mudir looked grave.

" Have you searched for him ?" he asked. " Are you sure he is not within the city walls ?"

" I have searched everywhere, and even sent the crier round, and I have also visited the harbour, thinking he might be there."

" That's strange."

" And awkward, as you know, for I have my papers, and must leave at once for Massowah."

" Yes," answered the mudir, drily, " It is very awkward ; in my opinion this is an elopement, or, worse, an abduction ; and signor, I furthermore suspect that your Jack is the prime mover in it."

Signor Varnoni began to expostulate, but the mudir, as the saying is, shut him up.

" I have only seen your secretary once," said he, " and then I declare to you that I thought he had got them all on. Why, bless me, I declare he was dressed equal to an Indian nabob."

The signor was proud of Jack, therefore he was pleased to hear him thus spoken of, but he could not bring himself to believe after the admonition he had given him in the morning that Jack had run away with the Nubian girl.

He endeavoured to explain, but the mudir's mind was fixed, for, said he :

"I did the same thing myself when I was young, and I believe that, if any one around me were put to the test and tempted of the spirit as I was, they would do the same."

Some of the wizen-faced Greeks essayed a laugh, the Turks grinned demurely from behind their chibouks, and the sallow-faced Egyptians, fancying themselves in Pharaoh's house, winked at each other as much as to say :

"Not for Joseph."

The mudir, a jolly old cock, smiled benignantly from beneath his bright red fez with its long silken tassel, at the idea of his having raised a joke, and there is no doubt he would have stood wine all round on the strength of it.

But the presence of the Mahommedans restrained him, they being forbidden by the Koran to drink wine, and so, as a set-off, he bade the slaves strip and courbash each other.

This they did with as good a grace as they could command, and they howled in concert to the stripes, whilst tears, unmingled with joy, rolled down their elongated cheeks.

CHAPTER XV.

ARAB JACK'S FIRST RIDE ON A DROMEDARY, AND HOW HE LIKED IT. — WHAT HE THOUGHT OF HASHEEN, AND HIS FIRST STEPS TOWARDS BEING A DERVISH.—JACK HAS AN EXTRAORDINARY VISION, AND THE GOVERNOR LOSES AN EYE.

"BLOW you ! stash it ! what are you up to ?" exclaimed Arab Jack on arriving at Hasheen, when he was aroused from a sort of lethargy by a sudden jerk.

"Yah ! yah ! all right, lilly warrior, you fight massa sheikh."

Jack opened his eyes in mingled astonishment and alarm.

His hands and feet were bound, and he was hanging head downwards across the saddle of a dromedary that was kneeling.

This accounted for the jerk, but "how did I come in this position ?" he mused.

"Come, be quick," he halloaed to the dusky driver, who was undoing a tortuous thong, "or I'll fight you. Who put me here ? Am I in the hands of the pirates of the plains ?"

"Yaas, yaas, you fight well ; Massa Abdul 'trong, him trow you, and if you turban not be good, you have calabash smashed to dead certainty."

"Thank you," sneered Jack. "Now play sharp with that confounded thong, the blood's all flying to my head, and I'll go mad and kill you if you don't."

The black fellah was so agitated that he could not undo the rope, but by Jack's desire he loosened his hands, and then Jack took out his knife and cut it.

"There, that's better," said Jack, dropping on his feet. "I'm awfully stiff ; undo my legs, and give me some water."

The fellah laughed.

"No much water here, Hasheen wells no berry good ; look, two tousand men, camels, horses—all big lot."

Jack looked through the opening pointed to in the prickly bush, and beheld a sight that almost took away his breath.

In a plain beyond, and stretching right away up a road between two hills, was a whole army of camels, horses and men, most of the latter being mounted and armed with matchlocks and long broad-bladed spears, on which floated pennons of various hues.

Some of the camels were loaded, and were forming in caravan order for a journey ; others were being watered, and those of the men who were not employed in the task were smoking, complacently looking on.

"My eye," said Jack, "what a host ; where have they all come from, and where are they bound ?"

"Some, not loaded, go Sinkat, some Tamai, some Berber, some go all ways ; I live Berber."

"You do ! is that far ?"

"Yaas, long way. Me born Kassala. Sheikh take me away."

"What sheikh ?" asked Jack, growing inquisitive.

"Sheikh Taher ; him big chief, much people, rob caravans, buy slaves, fight plenty, starve poor fellah, and make him work like nigger."

Jack burst out laughing.

"Well, what are you but a nigger ?" he said.

"Me fellah, no nigger, me poor Kassala man, born free, have to work in fields when Nile go down, but sometimes go long journey caravan—Khartoum, El Obeid and Mettameh."

"I should like to go to those places," said Jack, incautiously.

"You would ? Were you born any of dem, den ? you Arab boy ?"

"Yes," Jack answered, with his usual ready wit, "I come Mocha. Savoury that."

"Yaas, plenty coffee ; me like dat—taste him once ; make fellah feel like in paradise."

The fellah rubbed the front of the dusty cloth that was wound round his loins, the only covering he had, and went through the motions of an extravagant schoolboy who had just indulged at some famous tuck shop.

This little incident set Jack thinking of home, and he longed just then for the chance of gingerpop and a cranberry such as had often made his belly ache, for his stomach very much represented the empty waterskins he saw lying around.

He was about to put other questions to the fellah, when a voice sounded in his ear and he beheld the dervish.

"Come on, my son, I have been looking for you. I want you to repeat to me a few verses of the Koran. I have taken a fancy to you, and I mean to make you a little dervish."

"The devil you do," thought Jack.

He was about to make some dissenting remark, when he bethought himself that it would be wise to dissemble, so he followed his guide.

Jack was disgusted with what he saw of the town ; its beauty consisted, as he described it, of a few miserable huts, looking like square blocks of mud, with flat roofs and a few holes to let light and air in.

Earthen pots, gourds and water jars stood about the hutch-like doors ; women and girls making mat bags for dates and other market produce filled the narrow lanes, working amid

A DARK, SINISTER VISAGE PEERED IN.   *p.* 46.

the cries and laughter of the naked piccaninnies, who rolled and gambolled in the muddy pools just as if they were offsprings of the lordly crocodile.

"My eye," said Jack, as they reached an open space, and came upon one of the primitive granaries ; "there's corn in Egypt, pasha dervish."

"Allah be praised ! He is bountiful !" returned the holy man. "But that corn is not yet in Egypt," he added, with a sinister smile.

Although Jack was much amused with all he saw, he was glad when they got to the centre of the town, where they came upon a house of less mean pretensions.

It was shaped like the rest, but there was a paving of coloured tiles before the door, and a flag with a black border was hoisted on the housetop.

Armed men with gay turbans and particoloured suits lounged about the door, and a party of grim-visaged, warrior-looking Arabs came out as Jack followed the dervish in.

One glance around showed Jack that he was in the presence of the governor of Hasheen.

At one end of the large apartment a sumptuous carpet was spread, and on it were seated Osman Digna and pasha Taher, between whom, on a hassock sort of dais, squatted Mahbu Teb, richly dressed, all of them smoking the glorious hookah or Eastern pipe of peace.

Jack took off his turban and salaamed, as the dervish, taking him by the hand, led him forward.

"In the name of Allah and his glorious prophet," said he, "I ask of you this boy. Allah sent him, and I am commanded of the prophet to receive him."

Osman Digna looked as sage as a barn-door owl, and waited for the governor to speak, but, as he did not, he said :

"We have seen his powers, and he fights like a true believer ; but why should I relinquish my claim on his head?"

"Because it is so written in the Koran. Hark you and he shall repeat a verse."

Jack was taken aback by this.

4

"Here's a mess ; how shall I get out of it?" he thought.

"Allah is listening—go on ; the ear of his prophet is now open," continued the dervish.

"I wish I could fire a pea into it," thought Jack ; "but here goes—I'll say something."

Fortunately for our hero he had profited by the importunities of a missionary on the voyage from Suez, that person having pointed out to Jack several verses in the Arabic Bible which tallied very much with our own.

"O, ye followers who are faithful, feed my flock ; give unto them who are athirst, water ; and raiment to those who are unclothed."

Jack delivered this with much gusto and to the great delight of all, who remembering they had not eaten for some hours decided upon doing so at once.

Arab Jack laughed in his sleeve.

"My first sermon," he muttered, "has made me a second Spurgeon. If they ask me for another I'll give them an extra touch on the raw."

Jack then sat down, or rather squatted on his hams, to a vegetable dinner, the first actual vegetable feed he had ever partaken of.

It consisted of lentils, Indian corn, a species of haricot beans, and garlic, all mixed up, stewed in salad oil.

This was considered a grand dish, especially as the dervish partook of it, but Jack did not relish it much.

It almost choked him to get it down, for the smell of the garlic kept bringing it up again.

"Hang the vegetarians," he growled, "I'd rather have the flesh pots of Egypt. I feel as if I could eat a stuffed camel ; this stuff's neither good for the teeth nor the appetite. I'll have an olive when I can reach one, they look nice and green, and makes a fellow think of a feed of greengages."

"I shall want you to repeat another verse of the Koran," said the dervish, presently ; in fact just as Jack captured a nice preserved olive and thrust it into his mouth.

Jack, however, found he had captured a Tartar instead of a greengage, for at the first bite his stomach turned, and up it came with a gush.

"Whoa, Emma," were the first words in Jack's mind, but he was unable to say, "whoa" to anything. It was "woe" to him, and the three who sat opposite him and received the full shower in their horror-distorted faces, sang out in chorus, "woe to you."

What the dervish thought he never expressed, and whether any of the sparks from Jack's miniature mortar assailed his olfactory organ was never known. Certain it was that something seriously disturbed his equanimity, and set him violently sneezing.

"Tish-ew ! Tash-ew ! Tash-ee !" he commenced, until big drops of agony rolled from his sanctified orbs into the dish, when suddenly changing his note, he with tightly-closed eyes and convulsive jaw, gurgled out, "Ha, ha-sh, hash-cew."

This over, they all glanced at each other in askance, wondering whether to be angry or not, when Jack with that presence of mind which never deserted him even in the midst of his direst danger, exclaimed, "Allah be praised, the prayer of thy servant hath been answered."

"W-w-what !" gasped Osman Digna.

"I was conversing with the prophet," said our precocious young hero.

"Ah, blessed be his beard," exclaimed the dervish, suddenly recovering. "What did he say to thee? I knew by thy manner that thou wert blest with a vision. Thine eyes told me when I first beheld thee that thou were gifted with second sight, what did'st thou ask him ?"

"Now for a lie," muttered Jack, as, looking straight at the trio opposite him, he drew his eyes into what is commonly known as a squint. "A big 'un it must be, a whopper as would choke a camel."

"I asked," said he, folding his hands, sanctimoniously, "how it was that Arabi's star was on the wane," and he answered, "because he had forsaken his people, partaken of the flesh pots of Egypt, fattened on the words that were forbidden by the Koran—and ——"

"Allah, Allah, forgive thy erring servant."

"And," continued Jack, "he, as a punishment, will fume and pine seven moons, until he becomes as Pharaoh's lean kine, when if he alter not he will wither."

"Allah, be merciful," gasped the dervish, "was that all ? Try, my son, try and remember."

"I am," thought Jack, " I'm putting the heavy on my brain pan. Here goes, it's sink or swim with poor Phil Garlick."

"He said, bless his name, that the flag of Moslem would arise and bud and flourish green and fruitful as the olive tree, and that those upon whom the spirit fell were his chosen ministers, whose duty it was to prune and trim the branches."

"Oh, Allah, Allah," cried the dervish, as big round tears gushed from his eyes, "this is the water wherewith that tree shall be nurtured, Osman Digna, Mahbu Teb, and Sheikh Taher, thou art pruners chosen of the prophet, now am I confirmed that Mahomet Achmet is the true mahdi of God."

Our hero had heard of the mahdi, but he was totally ignorant of the flame he was fanning in the Soudan.

His untruthful invention was the outcome of pure innocence, and it in all probability saved his life, for the olive with the force of a bombshell struck the governor of Hasheen full in the left eye."

"But what of this ?" he asked of the dervish, removing his left hand, which covered the damaged optic, and pointing to it with the spear he had hastily snatched up to hurl at Jack.

"Am I to go to paradise to dwell and revel among the houris in this maimed condition, without an eye ?"

"Allah be praised, no," answered the artful dervish. "In place of that sinful eye which hath hitherto gazed upon worldly lusts, thou shalt have two, so that thou shalt see more of the lovely houris than thy neighbours."

Mahbu Teb clasped his hands, and rolling his remaining cod-fishing orb up to the roof, as if he could see through it to the promised haven, uttered a prayer of thankfulness, and repeated sixteen verses of the Koran right off.

Arab Jack pinched himself and screwed himself into all manner of forms to keep him from laughing.

"The old fool," he muttered, "I'd like to knock his other eye out, and ram a hot baked tater in the hole."

CHAPTER XVI.

ARAB JACK AND THE DERVISH EXCHANGE SECRETS.—OSMAN DIGNA'S THREAT.—A RIDE IN CHAINS.—JACK COMBATS THE ROBBER SHEIKH, AND SAVES THE GOLD AND THE CARAVAN.—AFTER THE BATTLE.

"WELL," thought Jack, as he lay on a mat in a corner of one of the mud houses to snatch an hour's sleep, "I wonder what will be my next adventure. I've had some narrow squeaks, gained and lost many friends, and here I am, thousands of miles from home."

"Home !" he sighed. "Shall I ever see it again ? Each day I widen the distance, like a broken reed cast into the brook, borne into the river, and drifted down to sea."

"Now," he added, "what sort of company have I fallen across?—pirates, robbers, fanatics, for all I know. I can say of Osman Digna that he is a ruthless abductor and a thief, if he is not a right down cut-throat."

Jack rolled over on the mat as he recounted his wrongs, and if it had been light enough to have seen them, his eyes were staring and bloodshot.

"They have got my yataghan," he exclaimed, half aloud, "and they would have stolen my chain and other valuables if I had not left them in Suakim. I wonder what Signor Varnoni will think of my protracted absence."

"And the girl, too, what of her ?" he mused on. "Has Osman taken her to grace his harem or to sell her for a slave ? But, there, I must look to myself. I am alone amongst these wild and lawless fiends. I must escape ; I will. I cannot be many miles from the Red Sea coast."

"You'd neber find your way back, sar," said a voice in the darkness that startled Jack.

Our hero rose to his knees.

"Who are you, eavesdropper ?" he exclaimed. "Let me feel you—let me twine these fingers like serpents round your villainous throat."

"Sachem no villain—you lie," was the answer.

"Then what are you ?"

"Dervish-boy, fakir—goodee as you."

"Good God, another dupe !" gasped Jack ; "another victim in that viper's toils. Just Heaven, as thou abhorrest the wicked, why don't thy thunderbolts crush them, or the dark, burning sands scorch them up ?"

The boy who accosted our hero heard every word he said, and he shrank in terror from the corner whence Jack's voice proceeded.

Jack, worn out though he was, could not sleep now that he knew some one else shared his prison with him.

"What would I not give for a light !" he muttered ; "one match—one flamer, of which I sold so many in London streets."

Scarcely was the thought born when a light streamed into the gloomy cell, and by its rays our hero beheld the tall draped form of the dervish.

"Do you sleep ?" queried a voice, as the figure moved into the dungeon—for to Jack it was little better, the air being thick, close, and stifling, whilst the musty odour made him sick. "Do you sleep ?" whispered the dervish again.

"Why ?" Jack asked, rather suddenly, seeing the question was addressed to him.

"Because I have words of import for thee. You are young, proud, and ambitious. How would you like to go to Arabi and tell him your vision ?"

"How would that serve the pride and ambition of a youth ?" asked Jack.

"It would make you rich."

"Worldly, or how ?"

"It would win you gold, favour, power, and, above all, freedom, such as I possess."

"I would rather go to Khartoum," said Jack, thoughtfully. "I have seen Arabi Pasha."

The dervish started.

"Seen him ! What, you—where ? "

"In Alexandria."

"Allah ! thou sayest not so. Thou art an Arab, and I have learned that you come from Mocha."

"Even so ; but for all that I have seen Arabi ; and, as you are so hard of belief, know that I steamed with him in his yacht on the Suez Canal not six weeks since."

The dervish rolled his eyes and seemed fit to drop.

"What miracle is this ?" he gasped ; and raising the skirt of his garment, he took from beneath it a flask.

Putting it to his lips he drank deeply, and observing that Jack's lips were feverish and parched, he handed him the flask also.

The boy clutched it with avidity, and, thinking it contained water, drank freely, gulping it down until his craving was satisfied.

To his joy there was wine mingled in it, and when he took the flask from his lips he felt its invigorating effects course through his hitherto placid veins.

This wine-drinking by the dervish was a secret worth knowing to Jack.

The dervish, then, did not believe in the precepts laid down in the Koran any more than he did himself.

"Where shall I find Arabi ?" he said, now once more himself. "I am not afraid to travel. I would do anything, risk anything, rather than remain a prisoner pent up in this horrid place."

"Zagazig," whispered the dervish, placing his fingers on his lips. "I have a brother there, a fakir, who will receive you well and direct you how to proceed when you show him my seal."

Jack passed into the further corner to ascertain whether his fellow-occupant of the cell was listening.

He was only a boy of tender years, dressed in the long, coarse, gown-like habiliments of a dervish, and he was fast asleep.

"When shall I start ?" said Jack, speaking with less restraint, and in a tone which testified his eagerness.

"Not yet, not from this place. You may be followed. The Egyptian soldiers may venture here from Suakim to look after the Nubian girl whose abduction caused you to be here. And now our forces are weakened by the departure of Abdul Ahad with the main cavalcade to visit Sinkat, Kassala, and the small villages around, our object might be frustrated."

"Why has Abdul, my inveterate foe, gone to those places ? "

"Because they have not sent in the tithes. If they refuse to part now, either in money or kind, he has a force sufficient to compel them. To-morrow we start for Tamai, and, once there, I will unfold to you my plan of the secret expedition."

He then left, and next morning Arab Jack was aroused from his slumber by the beating of tom-toms, the clashing of cymbals, and a confusion of noises such as might have been heard in Babel.

"This way, sar," said a voice. "Come on you. Where de piccaninny dervish? Me look after him—see Christian no steal him away and kill him. Fakir-boy soon be killed if 'Gypshun man get hold of him."

"Good gracious !" thought Jack, "what a land of superstition !—what a nest of demons for a fellow to fall into ! They are taught to believe the Christians are devils. How fortunate for me that they have not by any means discovered my white skin ! If they do, God knows what horrible torture I shall be subjected to."

Jack's flesh fairly crawled as the thought struck him, and a sensation of scalding-hot water went down his back.

"I have heard of a Christian martyr being flayed alive," he added, "and I dare say they would not scruple in thus serving me."

Jack was just in that humour in which a boy who has been baulked in his object is likely to conjure up all sorts of horrible things—a state of mind in which they sometimes suffer more agony than they would if they were actually subjected to the dreaded and terrible ordeal.

"Ah, this is better," he exclaimed, as he stepped into the open and took in a gulp of fresh air. "I wonder what kind of breakfast I shall get."

It was better than he expected—parched corn and dhoura beat into pulp ; and instead of thick, muddy water, as he anticipated, he by the influence of the dervish was indulged with a cup of good, strong coffee.

"Ah, there, now I'm a man," he said. But he reckoned without his host ; for a couple of fierce-looking Soudanese laid hold of him, and carrying him to one of the dromedaries, hoisted him up into a sort of pannier and tied him there with ropes.

He then found that the little dervish-boy was similarly fixed in a pannier on the other side, and then both were attached together by means of a long light chain fastened to a wrist of each.

"Hang it ! this is worse than being a galley-slave," cried the indignant boy ; "they have the use of their limbs. I would like to have my sword and just five minutes with that Osman Digna ; he should either kill me or I would him."

"Massa no speak so loud," grunted a voice in his ear. It was the fellah, and his warning came not one moment too soon.

Osman Digna himself, clad in the gay panoply of war, approached our hero.

"So my orders offend you," said the chief, with dangerous calmness. "If you object to ride, I will have a rope adjusted to your neck and fasten it to my own saddle-bow. We shall travel at good speed over the loose sand, so that it will afford you splendid exercise."

"I acknowledge your favour ; I did not think you capable of so much generosity," Jack replied. "One day, however, I hope to be able to pay you back in your own coin."

"I trust so," was Osman's reply. "Since you are gifted with second-sight, you can do me special services."

He rode to the front then, and gave orders for the formation of the cavalcade, which, amid the yells of the drivers, the groans of the camels, the neighing of steeds, and the jingling of brass rowels and steel scabbards, moved slowly over the stony road through the prickly-pear bushes and mimosa.

Although Jack listened patiently to the words of Osman Digna, his heart throbbed with the convulsive heavings of a volcano.

"To be made prisoner and bound in chains like a felon," he hissed, "is more than British blood can bear. Something will happen, and when it does it will be something big."

"What you do, den ? " queried the little dervish-boy, who could hear perfectly well what he said, the chain by which they were attached conducting the sound and acting as a telephone.

"Be a fakir, of course," answered Jack, evasively. "I suppose you can work miracles—read the stars ? "

"Yaas, leetle," answered the boy. "Me go school of Faki, very learned man ; village Hoghali, close Khartoum."

"Oh," said Jack, gradually becoming enlightened ; "then you know plenty of verses of the Koran. Let me hear you repeat some of them."

Once started, the little fakir went on at a terrible rate. Jack listened intently.

"All right," said he to himself ; "I shall have no hard task to compete with him. Like the street spouters, he has one set code—promises of reaching the realms of the blest or descending to the regions of the damned."

This amused our hero for some time—until, in fact, the uneasy gait of the animal on which they rode, owing to the deep shifting sand, made Jack's bones ache and his hips and shoulders sore.

The whole retinue was shrouded in a cloud of dust or particles of sand so minute that it tickled Jack's nose, and made his throat feel as if he had been swallowing powdered glass.

"How about the water, Mahoud ? " he yelled to the driver, who sat on the dromedary's neck.

"Aha ! me got none. Have to wait till we get to Tamai wells. Yah, ha ! what dat ? "

The report of matchlocks and a shower of bullets announced that they were attacked by a band of robbers.

Several of the animals around Jack were hit, and the one to which he was so cruelly lashed fell with a groan.

"It's all up with me," thought Jack, who had previously witnessed the dying throes of one of the huge beasts, and now expected the wounded animal to roll over and crush him. "I'm a gone coon. Mahoud, come here, you beggar, and set me adrift," he shouted.

He might as well have called upon Mahomet as Mahoud. The driver was all of a tremble for his own safety, and seemed very much inclined to crawl into the animal's mouth out of the way of the shots, which still hurtled around them.

Then the clash of contending swords sounded, and Jack, who was looking around for some deliverer, beheld through the filmy mist the stalwart forms of Osman Digna and the robber chief, Sheikh Taher, engaged in mortal combat.

The truth then at once flashed to Jack's mind instinctively.

The animal to which he was still helplessly made fast carried the treasure-chest—a huge portmanteau-shaped affair made of stout rhinoceros hide.

For the possession of this the treacherous Sheik Taher had had a party lying in ambush, which accounted for the strong guard of Arab horsemen who had ridden on either side of our hero since they started.

Jack groaned with anguish, and the perspiration poured from him in streams. The dromedary, now still in death, pierced with a dozen balls, was not lying upon him very heavily; but one of the hard corners of the treasure-chest was pressing into his shoulder, causing him excruciating torture.

Some of Osman Digna's warriors were now dismounted, and on foot strove desperately to keep the robber horde at bay, whilst Jack's terror was increased by the prospect of having his brains dashed out by the hoofs of the restive horses.

The torture of suspense was so great that Jack even longed for something to put an end to his existence, when suddenly the band of the saddle-girth to which the pannier was attached gave way.

"Thank God!" was his mental prayer when he found the thongs that bound his hands had also become loosed, and, having gained his feet, he at once released the groaning dervish-boy from his critical position.

The yells and shrieks on all sides were now terrific.

The robber horde, bent on plunder and thirsting for the gold, fought more like fiends than human beings, whilst the voice of Osman Digna called loudly on his warriors to defend the treasure.

Arab Jack, once free, paused but an instant to consider with which side he should take part.

His blood boiled with indignation at the outrage Osman had practised upon him; but considering within himself that he would receive no more honourable treatment at the hands of the robber sheikh, he decided upon doing his utmost to protect the gold.

At his feet lay an Arab weltering in his gore, and from his hand he wrenched the matchlock he had newly-fired; but Jack could not find that he had any ammunition.

By this time a dozen or more robbers had broke the phalanx of Osman's men, and were forcing a lane towards the coveted treasure, when Jack, clubbing the matchlock, leapt on to the dromedary's hump, and with one foot planted on the gold-chest prepared to defend it with his life.

"Whizz! bang! crash!"

The weapon wielded in Arab Jack's sinewy hand had already begun to do terrible work.

Three dusky bandits bit the dust—one with his face entirely smashed, another with his jaw broken, and a third with the crown of his head fairly crushed in.

Jack got a mouthful of blood and a spattering of brains over this; but it only seemed to incite him to fresh exertions, and down went a fourth before the robber could get his huge sword anywhere within reach of the maddened boy.

How Jack performed these prodigies without receiving a scratch was a wonder to himself.

The surging throng at times seemed to press right in upon him, and whistling balls appeared to mock him with their sharp "ping" as they flew about his head.

Jack, however, was delirious with excitement.

He laughed hysterically in the very face of the grinning foe as they leapt with their sword-spears towards him, and he silenced them by the dull crashing thud that laid them low at his feet.

"Ha! ha!—die!" at length yelled a fearful voice that seemed to emanate from some fiend who had just escaped from the bottomless pit. "Die, demon—this to your very heart."

Jack had barely time to ward off the fierce thrust that was aimed at his chest—a thrust which if it had taken effect would have settled his account in this world.

But Jack's prowess and good luck stood him again in need, and the mighty Sheikh Taher fell bleeding and stunned under the brave boy's unerring blow.

This valorous act put an end to the bloody contest.

"Whose hand did that?" cried Osman, forcing a path to where the robber sheikh lay in his gore.

"Mine—Arab Jack's!" cried our hero, lowering his blood-stained weapon with all the pride of a victorious gladiator.

Osman Digna gazed at him with mingled awe and admiration—for he presented a ghastly spectacle just then.

Blood, brains, and pieces of flesh (still quivering, as it seemed) adorned him from head to feet, whilst his face, with the blood and dust, appeared as if covered with an ensanguined mask.

"Well done!" cried Osman Digna, seizing our hero's reeking hand. "This is our dervish that is to be. Let his name be reverenced at the tomb of our sacred Sheikh Hoghali."

The fall of the robber sheikh filled his followers with the utmost alarm. Had they been victorious, their reward would have been great; but their defeat was likely to be attended with the most serious consequences.

Those who could at the first outcry took alarm and fled to the shelter of the distant fortresses, whilst those who were hemmed in were made prisoners of war.

A look of withering scorn or of sullen moroseness settled upon the dusky visages of those whose weapons were taken from them by force, and many would have preferred death to the lingering tortures that they knew awaited them at the hands of the implacable Osman Digna.

CHAPTER XVII.

OSMAN DIGNA ASTONISHES THE ARTFUL GOVERNOR OF TAMAI. — CROSSING THE DESERT.—THE MIRAGE—A GLORIOUS REPAST.—ARAB JACK IS MADE UP FOR A YOUNG MAHDI.—THE SOUDAN DURBAR.

THE village of Tamai was thrown into the utmost alarm when the Soudanese chief arrived there with his broken caravan.

The governor quite forgot his gravity, and used expressions that were strictly forbidden by the Koran as Osman in the most imperative tone informed him that extra tithes would be levied from the neighbouring towns and villages to recoup the loss occasioned by the raid of the notorious robber.

"Most excellent chief," began the governor,

whom Osman knew of old to be a most practised pleader of poverty, "our crops are so bad—and——"

"That will do," said Osman, checking him. "A caravan passed here on the way to Suakim only yesterday, and poor as you were you traded for ivory and gold dust. See here," he added, turning over a bale of hemp, and another of camel's hair, "these fine tusks were never grown in Tamai, nor covered for any honest purpose."

The governor's venerable beard went a shade paler when Osman disclosed the concealed treasure, and Jack, who with the dervish had been admitted to the audience, began to wonder whether Osman or Sheikh Taher most deserved the title of bandit.

Jack was astounded when the chief with audacity continued:

"This youth, this boy, as I may term him, has rendered us both a service, and you especially; the gold dust is his by law; through his prowess the robber has been captured red-handed."

"What is that to me?" exclaimed the astounded governor.

"Everything," replied Osman in his calm but dangerous way. "If he deceived me with his protestations of friendship, how much easier might he have deceived you, and sacked the village."

Jack was pleased when the palaver was over, and something in the shape of substantial food was served, after which, he was still more delighted by Osman Digna returning to him his jewelled yataghan.

Arab Jack entertained not the slightest idea that the gold dust would ever be his. He saw it and the ivory packed on one of the best camels, and a double guard placed over it for its protection, but that was all.

Our hero was allowed to be one of the guard also, and he was permitted to ride a splendid cream-white Arab charger, which was richly caparisoned, and gave his boyish heart exceeding delight.

A forced march brought them to Handoub, where a message from the Mahdi awaited Osman Digna.

It was a supreme notification that a holy durbar would be held, on the open plain within easy distance of three of the principal cities, and that all true followers of Islam were to attend it, or be subject to eternal torments hereafter.

The Imam of Handoub was a devout follower of the prophet, he sent princely offerings to the Mahdi, and ground his people to the lowest to secure the happiness of eternal life.

He had a carpet that came from Mecca, which was supposed to be woven on the same loom as the holy carpet of Mahomet, and repeated the name of Allah every hour each day from early dawn to the setting of the sun.

When he was acquainted with the sacred firman, he was, of course, all on thorns to start on the journey, but the crafty Osman persuaded him to delay until his own "ships of the desert" were fairly under weigh.

Arab Jack was mounted on his cream-coloured steed as before, but in what direction they proceeded he was totally unaware, save for the position of the rising sun.

Far and wide on all sides stretched the hot glaring desert, and here for the first time Arab Jack beheld that wonderful atmospheric phenomenon, the mirage.

They had advanced far into the desert waste, where water was a thing unknown and vegetation was entirely out of the question, and yet to unaccustomed eyes it seemed that the vast waste was broken up into innumerable creeks, and rivers abounded, and vast lakes rippled by refreshing breezes, were not far distant.

"Are we going towards the Red Sea again?" Jack asked of the dervish, who rode by his side on a sturdy camel, "or is that winding stream the Nile?"

"Neither," replied the dervish, scarcely restraining a laugh. "We are going towards the Nile above the cataracts, but that reflection in the sky is caused by water hundreds and hundreds of miles away."

"By jingo," exclaimed Jack, "I thought it was near at hand, and that there would be a chance of having a bath. But, there, I suppose there are crocodiles and other sublime quadrupeds in that water out yonder."

The dervish was too intent on his prayers to answer Jack's further questions.

"Allah Akbar, God is great," he kept repeating in a low-toned voice, keeping time to the camel's jingling bells or the occasional clank of a sabre.

Otherwise it was a silent march, and awfully tedious to our hero, who, to keep himself awake, at length struck up the popular air of the "Rat-catcher's Daughter."

Osman Digna and the Dervish were astounded. To them it sounded like some new Moslem song of praise, so that Osman desired the tomtoms, the clarions, and the cymbals to keep time to it.

Jack roared himself hoarse, but he cared not, for he found that his ranting procured him an extra allowance of water, and whiled the time until they reached a spot where a clump of emerald verdure broke the monotony of the sandy plain.

This oasis, or green clump, was sighted by the headmost camels long before the eyes of their riders recognised it, and although they had journeyed so many miles, they quickened their pace on perceiving it, without regard to the extra jolting of those who were mounted on their lofty humps.

At this spot the party dismounted, and having tied one of the legs of each camel to prevent its straying, a few tents were pitched, and some lit their pipes or partook of the mid-day meal.

Arab Jack took out his handful of dried dates and washed them down with a gourd of muddy water with exceeding gusto.

"O Lord," said he, "this is a treat after toke and fried fish. Wouldn't the cockney yobs relish this in preference to a bag of London mysteries."

"Allah Akbar," exclaimed the dervish, thinking that our hero was offering up a prayer, "Allah Akbar," and he touched the dervish boy with his foot to make him repeat the thanksgiving.

The meal was soon over; in fact it was hurried by the sudden appearance in their rear of a moving column of dust, which wound its serpentine course across the plain.

"Allah, tis the Imam of Handoub," cried Osman. "Fagish," turning to his leading chief,

・arise, take your caravan to the fastness of Upper Kordofan."

Arab Jack heard this order given, and he at once saw through the craft of Osman Digna.

"I tumble to it, just like a bird," said he; "the gold that was to be the reward of my prowess is going to swell this Osman's horde, and the Mudir will get only the tithes that have been wrung from the poor and needy."

The cavalcade was soon divided, and then taking separate courses as from the point of a letter V, they widened their distance rapidly.

Jack was tired before they camped for the night, and had never ridden on horseback so far before, much less on a fiery, champing steed who was all the time eager for a spin.

He dropped down on a knoll under some palm trees and went to sleep, not noticing the ripe fruit until a fresh breeze in the morning caused one to drop on his nose.

Then he awoke with a start, and looking up, cried out in the most comical manner that can be conceived.

"Hallo, little Dotty, where are we, dossing under the trees of the Thames Embankment?"

The dervish boy to whom this was addressed, imagining that he was meant by little Dotty, began to laugh, and beckoned with his finger to another fruit, as if he was inviting it to fall, when Jack caught him behind with his Spanish leathered toe, and sent him rolling down a sandy slope.

"Come here, you nigger," cried Jack, quite forgetting his own tawny hue; " how far do you think we are from the Mahdi's encampment, just now?"

"Dere, ober dere, where you see dat lot tents," replied the boy, affectionately rubbing his behind.

Jack looked—but all he saw was apparently a deep hollow, the slope of which was to all appearance dotted with varied coloured stones.

"Where's the tents, the people?" queried he.

"Dere—heaps," exclaimed the excited boy. "Tousands, tousands;" and being unable to enumerate further by speech, he did so by closing his hands, until he described about six hundred thousand.

"Those are all tents, then, I suppose," said our hero to himself. " I shall be glad when I see this Mahdi. From what I have heard he must be an extraordinary man."

Jack had his wish; but, first of all, he was put through his facings by the dervish.

"Arab Jack," said he, you are not such a coffee-roaster as you seem. You are up to snuff, I know, and you were not such a molly as to be born in Mocha."

Jack felt as if his breath was suddenly taken away.

What ever could the dervish mean; he had never heard him speak in that ribald manner before.

"Who dares say I was not born in Mocha," said he; "and who will find cheek enough to aver I have not rode on a moke in Mocha?"

"Good," whispered the dervish, tapping him in the stomach, and giving him the wink, " That turban assures me that you are a true born Arab, and your polished cheeks are just of the hue of a nicely-roasted coffee-bean."

"Allah !" exclaimed Jack, thrusting his hands into the depths of his vast pockets and stamping his tiny foot, "the fellow is mad, surely.

Come, I say, dervish, what is your little game; what's your blooming kokum?"

"Do Arab boy want to make money?"

"I would like to have some hooftish," Jack replied. "How can I get it, dervish? Why blow me if you don't look as jolly as old Friar Tuck to-day."

Whether the dervish knew anything of Friar Tuck Jack did not deign to ask.

"Come, I know you have some secret to divulge," he said, "so out with it."

"Well, how would you like to be a young Mahdi, ride on a sacred camel, and hail from Mecca instead of Mocha?"

"Just my hammer," replied Jack, who was wondering all the while whether the dervish understood his horrible lingo; "chuck out yer mouldy highdears—two up for a brown."

The dervish led him away to a dark-coloured tent, sheltered in a deep sandy dell, and unpacking a huge leather trunk, he began robing our hero in prime style.

A gorgeous turban of varied hues, and a snow-white suit composed his under attire, which set off at great disadvantage his travel soiled boots.

Jack buckled on his yataghan, which was an article inseparable now, and turning to the dervish, with a laugh, said :

"Now for the Nubian touch; I'll just show you how to put on a Soudanese polish."

Taking a small earthen vessel, he mixed a paste composed of palm oil and lamp black, the latter taken from the sacred lamp which burned in the tent.

"There, now," said Jack, quite forgetting the character he assumed, "that polish would be worth a diamond to a London shoe-black boy. He'd fancy he was in Nixey's land, I'm sure."

The dervish tried hard to maintain his gravity, but was forced to turn his head to give vent to a quiet laugh, which caused Jack to fancy the holy follower was not altogether what he seemed.

"Come, finish your toilet, Jack," said the dervish as soon as he could frame his lips to speak, and then having encased him in a purple robe heavily bound with Damascene lace, he finished him off with a brilliant waist scarf of green and gold.

The Soudan durbar was one not to be equalled in magnitude and splendour by anything of the kind that had ever been seen.

Mahomet Achmet, in a curtained howdah inlaid with precious stones and literally ablaze with gold, rode on an enormous elephant, whose trappings might have vied with the regal splendour of any of the former Egyptian kings.

The noble creature was cream-coloured, with a dark patch on its trunk, signifying the one black spot of iniquity which the Mahdi's forces were massed together to blot out.

On his right sat Mahoud-el-Khin, his governor deputy; and on his left Dervish Pasha, a chief of the dervishes, on camelopards, who bore the reputation of having visited Mahomet's tomb.

Ten thousand dervishes of various orders and degrees filled up the background, from the high dignitaries clothed in purple and fine linen, whose costly-sandalled feet were prepared to walk in the realms of bliss, to the half-nude fanatics whose feet were bare, and whose vestments consisted of a loin cloth and a cloak of camels' hair.

In the foreground extending for miles were the mudirs, imams, and sheikhs of the numerous tribes, with their followers as numerous as the sand on the seashore.

A little to the left, and dividing the dervishes on that side from the vast multitude, was a tent or lofty pavilion, surmounted by the green flag of Islam, whose heavy silken folds floated out lazily at times, disclosing the following inscription in gold :—

"ALI, ALLAH, MAHOMET."

"There is one God, and Mahomet is his Prophet."

"And the MAHDI is the Saviour of his people."

CHAPTER XVIII.

THE MAHDI IN STATE AMONG HIS PEOPLE.—ARAB JACK AND THE LIGHT OF SYRIA.—JEALOUSY AROUSED.—THE MAHDI VISITS JACK IN MUFTI.—A WOULD-BE ASSASSIN.—HOW JACK PUMMELLED HIS FRIEND IN MISTAKE.

WHEN the Mahdi drew aside the curtains of the howdah, the cry of welcome that arose was truly deafening.

"Allah be praised!" the dervishes shouted in a breath, and the whole concourse turned and bowed reverently towards the east.

Then the Mahdi unrolled a parchment scroll and read a proclamation, signed by Arabi Pasha, in which the true believers were exhorted to rise as one man and smite with the holy sword of the prophet, both the Frank and the Jew, and drive the Christian dogs into the sea, which went on :—

"We have already begun, and gained a victory, the Narbout has done its work. The blood of the believer mingles with the dust, arise, advance ! Victory is sure and the golden gates of paradise are open."

Then the cymbals clashed, the tomtoms sounded, the clarions burst forth, and the dancing and howling dervishes commenced their diversions.

In the midst of this the opening of the pavilion was rolled back, and with a guard of pennoned spearmen the sacred camel, spotless as the driven snow, was led forth.

Mounted thereon was a handsome youth, bearing in his hand a banneret on which was embossed a verse of the Koran and a motto signifying that the bearer was straight from the holy shrine, and bore testimony of the good will and belief of the inhabitants of Mecca.

"The Mahdi, is the true prophet," it added, "and the bearer is a disciple under him."

The young Mahdi was no other than Arab Jack.

"Well, blow me, this is a novel position to be in," he soliloquised. "What a mighty host ! I declare it eclipses that of Pharaoh when he pursued the Israelites across the Red Sea."

It was indeed a sight to make the young boy thoughtful. To think, imagine, that he, the poor street waif, should have drifted so far from his home to become a sojourner in the desert, a stranger in a strange land.

In spite of the ebullition of joy that set his heart bounding with ambitious hopes, Jack could not help heaving a sigh.

He thought of his mother just then.

"What would she think of her boy if she saw him now," he muttered.

With silken cords the grey-bearded attendants led the sacred camel into the open, and at a sign from the Mahdi every head in that vast assemblage was bared, and those who were near bowed until their beards swept the dust and their faces touched the sand.

"Ali, Allah, Mahomet," again burst from the lips of the dervishes, after which the Mudir's deputy governor desired those who were prepared with offerings for the poor to draw near with them, and receive in return that solace which the weary so need on this earth.

A large carpet was spread, and the head dervishes having formed in a square around it, then commenced taking the offerings, which in bags, bales and jars poured rapidly in on all sides, the dervishes taking note of each donor, the value of the donation, and rewarding each with a certificate of indulgence according to merit.

The dervishes in the background then made way that those who were served could take their departure, and a cordon of dervishes having surrounded our hero, presents of gold and precious stones were received by him to take with him on his return to Mecca.

Jack, then, having handed his banneret to his flag bearer, distributed with his own hand tokens and favours which were supposed to have been brought from the holy shrine, and the prayers of the most grateful Irish mendicant ever heard would have paled beside those of the grateful Arabs.

For hours this continued without intermission.

The sun was sinking low, when a falling off of the donors gave signs that the golden harvest was nearly reaped.

Jack was growing tired, too, of stooping and doling out favours which in his own mind he, of course, knew were swindles.

"Jerusalem," he muttered. "This would suit General Booth. Wouldn't he weep and pray if he commanded the Salvation Army of the Soudan ? wouldn't pious Captain Mary Walker trot around here and gather up the pieces ?"

Our hero was actually grinning to himself, when suddenly he looked up, and discovered a lovely pair of eyes gazing softly upon him.

They were those of a lady, evidently of extreme beauty, although her face, all but the upper part, was hidden by the yacmash.

Jack, guided by instinct, was about to raise his turban and salute her with European courtesy, when suddenly remembering himself he resumed his gravity.

The lady was seated in a sedan borne by a splendid gray palfrey, which was led on either side by attendants of some dignity, one of whom from the likeness he bore to the Soudan chief, Jack concluded was the son of Osman Digna.

"Lady," said Jack, with a most extravagant Oriental salaam, "although I am a stranger in the Soudan, yet can I see by your exquisite form and loveliness that you are a princess ; eyes more lovely and divine I have never beheld, even among the pilgrims who visit the holy shrine in Mecca."

The lady smiled, and as the rays of her dark, piercing orbs shot into his, she replied :—

"I am Nur-el Sham (Light of Syria), only sister of Mahomet Achmet, the true Mahdi of

God, and I give thee welcome to our yellow sands."

Arab Jack bowed, and in accordance with the native custom remained silent. They, however, exchanged loving glances once more, and the palfrey was led away.

"Allah's curse upon you," muttered Digna the younger, in whose heart the fierce passion of jealousy was at once awakened. "Curse you, you Meccan dog; I thirst for your heart's blood, and I will drink it!"

Jack caught his dark, lurid eye, but he had no idea he had given offence. To him even the Light of Syria was not half so lovely as the Nubian beauty he had followed from Suakim.

The durbar was over at length.

Our hero caught sight of the vast concourse melting away without regret, for the glare of the rich panoply, gilded by the setting sun, dazed his senses and bewildered his youthful brain.

"Well Jack," said the dervish when they were once more alone in the pavilion, "how fares it with thee now, lad; are you prepared for a journey northward, or do you prefer visiting Khartoum?"

"I care not, I have no particular choice," answered the boy, stretching himself on the sumptuous divan and giving a deep yawn.

"I thought we were supposed to be bound for Mecca."

"We! You mean to stick to me then, and not bolt and leave me."

"I never desert a friend," said Jack, eying him rather askance. "How about the gold? Is that going into the Mahdi's coffers the same as the gold dust went into Osman's?"

"I should say not: that is the very thing I want to talk to you about. I want to get to Cairo, and thence on to Alexandria. I begin to feel anxious about my sisters."

"Oh," said Jack, more amazed than ever, "have you sisters, then?"

"Of course I have; you ought to remember that. Have you forgotten the bright-eyed Sela, who exchanged garments with you?"

Jack gave a start and sprang to his feet.

"What! are you Hassan-el-Ahed, then?"

"I am," whispered the dervish, hoarsely; "but breathe not the name again. The lives of us both depend upon secrecy. You have served my purpose, and I have done you a good turn."

Our hero could scarcely believe his senses.

"Hassan-el-Ahed," he muttered, "whom I lost in Cairo, and find here in the Soudan."

"Eh," replied the dervish, who just caught the purport of his thoughts, "I am he whom you left in Cairo, and got into trouble through that precious black bag."

"You wrong me, Hassan," cried Jack, forgetting the dervish's caution not to call him Hassan, "I did not leave you. I am perfectly innocent of that."

Jack then explained what did happen, and narrated the whole of his adventures until he reached Suakim, and the deadly combat waged between him and Osman's flag-bearer outside the walls of the town.

"I know of that," said the dervish, "and also that you are a fiery termagant. But, mark you, I did not recognise you for a long time as the young swashbuckler who nearly settled me in my own house until one day I saw you using that formidable knife."

"Good! Shake hands friend," returned Jack. "But how came you here, and by what means were you made a dervish?"

"My own wit," said Hassan, proudly; "and by that wit, you see, I have also gained you the proud title of the Young Mahdi. You have acted your part well, and in one hour from this you shall be thanked in person by the true Mahdi."

"Shall I?" said Jack, rubbing his hands excitedly. "Shall I?"

"You shall; but craft, cunning, deceit, and circumspection are the rule here. The Mahdi really believes you to be a native of Mecca."

"Then I won't undeceive him," said Jack "My future movements shall be ruled by you. What do you propose?"

"That you be anxious to start on your return journey, and I will volunteer to accompany you part of the way. 'Twas I who brought that proclamation from Arabi, and of course he will expect me to carry an answer to it in return."

"Bravo, that's good iron. Hassan, may your inventive genius never rust."

"Hist! hark! Have I not forbidden you to address me by that name. I am a plain dervish, a follower of the learned and influential Fakir of Dongola, Mahomet Saleh."

"Is that a name for the devil?," said our hero placing his finger beside his nose, "or——"

A rustling of the tent curtains brought Jack's speech to an abrupt termination, and a tall, slim figure closely muffled entered the sacred pavilion.

It was the Mahdi in mufti, or more commonly speaking, incog.

He glanced hurriedly round to ascertain that no fourth party was there.

"Allah blesses the faithful," he said, which was the preconcerted signal between him and the dervish. "Are we alone?"

"We are, your holiness," replied the dervish. "Have you prepared the holy firman."

"I have! it is here; it must be delivered to Arabi, and then——"

He paused, looked round, and listened mistrustfully, as if a sound had disturbed him.

"Dervish," he whispered, producing from beneath the folds of his robe a dagger with a formidable serpentine blade like that of a Malayan creese, and pointing his fore finger towards a portion of the arras, "doth the asp of the Egyptians lurk there?"

Hassan moved with noiseless tread towards the spot indicated, and drawing his long thin dirk thrust it about the spot, but not a sound emanated from it.

The Mahdi seemed satisfied then, and turning to Arab Jack he explained, "This edict is for the true believers of Mecca. With it you must return to your people; and guard it, mind you, as you would your mother's life."

Arab Jack winced at this.

Recovering himself quickly, however, he replied:

"My mother's life is not in my keeping. When this you confide to my care," pointing to a small scroll the Mahdi held in his hand, "my life-blood shall not be to me more precious."

As he spoke he had good opportunity of regarding the Mahdi's appearance.

He had strangely basilisk-like orbs, the iris of which seemed, chameleon-like, to change in colour as the various emotions or passions worked in him.

"There's a strange fascination in the man," Jack thought, "that I rather like. I don't wonder he holds such power over a mass of ignorant people. I believe if I looked at him long he'd mesmerise me."

He had to avert his gaze from him more than once during the interview, which lasted some time longer, and then the Mahdi left as mysteriously as he had come.

"Well, dervish," said Jack, "when do we start on this twofold mission? I long for something more exciting. It's evident this Mahdi means to stir up war, and we shall just be out of it."

"Shall we, though. I fancy there will be plenty of it about; but we've got the gold, you know, Jack, and that's all I care for at present."

"Are you sure it's safe."

"As the bank; if you look out you will see we are surrounded with a strong guard, and none but a pagan would venture to put a hand on our sacred casket. To-morrow soon after sunset we shall be sailing away across the desert."

"Then I'm on for a snooze," said Jack, giving another yawn. "So here goes."

Arab Jack took off his turban, and throwing himself down on the soft divan, was soon asleep.

Not so the dervish.

He from a secret corner produced a gourd of wine, and pouring out a good cupful drank it off.

"There," said he, "such liquour is too good for the faithful," and thus soliloquising he replaced the gourd, and was soon asleep as soundly as if he had been one of the pyramids.

They were now both snoring against each other at a tremendous rate, which might have caused an impression that they were exerting themselves for a wager.

Suddenly a portion of the tent on one side was raised gently, and a dark, sinister visage peered in.

"Asleep, eh, and as fast as a tent peg," muttered the intruder; then creeping cautiously inside, he rose to his knees.

Whoever this was his purpose was plainly evident. Glancing towards the curtains which concealed the treasure he gave a self-satisfied grin.

"It is safe," he hissed. "Now for the other treasure which haunts my burning brain. Allah! To think that a dog of a stranger should dare to gaze amorously on her I so madly love."

It was Digna, the son of Osman, who thus stood gazing on his prey like a desert wolf.

He took a poniard from his girdle, and approached the sleeping boy, and waited until he turned so that he might bury it in his heart.

"One, two, three," he counted, and then raised his arm to give the fatal blow.

Then, like a flash of light, the blade descended, and Jack might have been no more, only that the blade of the weapon shivered in a dozen pieces close to the hilt.

Our hero was awakened, and sprang to his feet in a moment.

"Fiend," he hissed, and recognising his foe, he caught him by the throat and struggled with him for the mastery.

But Digna was strong. His powerfully-knit frame was like that of a lion.

"Boy," he muttered, savagely, between his grinding teeth, "your life I must have; I have sworn by the prophet to slay you."

Arab Jack, however, was not quite so easy a victim.

Planting his feet like those of a wrestler on the rich carpet, he shifted his hands to his assailant's shoulder and hip, and threw him clean over his head.

With some such a floorer would have given our hero the victory; but the young sheikh, accustomed to the wild sports of the plains, sprang to his feet like the Nubian lion, and flew again at the boy.

"Whoa, Emma," shouted Jack in his excitement; "take that for your trouble, and that."

Jack's clenched fist checked the sheikh's wild career, and two sharp blows followed well up sent him staggering.

The would-be assassin was not prepared for this.

Such a mode of warfare was to him new and astounding.

He looked more like a demon as his two teeth followed each other down his throat, and the blood gushed from his nose and face in a purple stream.

Jack, however, gave him not the slightest chance to recover from his astonishment.

He was at him again in an' instant, and pounded him in sledge-hammer style about the ribs.

Digna cursed himself inwardly for not having another weapon, and fearing that the dervish might be awakened, he glanced about him for a means of retreat.

There was none so handy as the way by which he had entered, for the opening was closed effectually by means of stout silken cords tied across.

To attempt to crawl back under the canvas would be useless, as Jack would be upon him in an instant; but an idea suddenly struck him, and he acted upon it at once.

Seizing Jack's turban he hurled it up at the lamp and the place was immediately in total darkness.

Before lying down Jack had unbuckled his yataghan and laid it aside, but he still had his knife, which, until then, he had scorned to use against an unarmed foe, considering it unmanly and un-English.

Now he considered anything was fair. He would have used a pistol or a matchlock, but he had neither, nor could he see in which direction to aim.

Nevertheless, he groped about in the hope of falling in with his enemy, and after various exasperating mistakes, he came upon a recumbent body.

"Oh, I have you," he gasped, thinking it was the body of the sheikh crouched down, and without more ado he grappled the supposed villain by the nape of the neck and belaboured him most unmercifully.

"Hold, curse you. Help — murder! Jack, Jack."

Our hero recognised the voice in a moment. It was that of Hassan-el-Ahed, against whose ribs Jack's knuckles were rattling just like dice.

Arab Jack's anger left him in a moment.

"What, dervish," he said, "have you been lying here sleeping like a dead man whilst I have been almost murdered?"

"By the beard of the prophet, I dozed soundly. But who has attempted to murder you—whose dastardly hand was so nearly steeped in the blood of assassination?"

"Sheikh Digna, the eldest son of the villainous Osman, who robbed me of my gold and abducted that beautiful Nubian girl from Suakim."

"Then it is time we took a hurried departure; depend upon it he and his thievish assistants have a design upon our treasure. Behold you, the firmament is already tinged with the morning light."

He pulled a cord connected with an opening in the roof, and by the faint gleam that entered the pavilion they could see that Sheikh Digna had escaped.

Jack then explained how he had been awakened by the dastard's blow; the shivering and splintering of the well-tempered blade to the very hilt; the death grip and the struggle, and how he had pummelled the cowardly cur with that bulldog tenacity which was within him.

Hassan listened to his recital with glowing admiration, and rising suddenly from his seat he grasped his hand.

"Jack, my lad," said he, "I forgive you the rib-tickling you presented so gratuitously to me, my dear boy; I fancy you must have had the nightmare, or have been dreaming."

"See here, then," replied Jack, taking the lucky sixpence from a pocket in his breast; "look at that dent, and then step inside here and see if there is not another one similar to it in this left rib."

"Good God!" cried Hassan, turning awfully pale, "you have certainly had a narrow escape, and—ah! here are the very splinters of the blade. What have you done to incur the anger of the Soudanese?"

"Nothing more than you know of, I assure you; but if you, as you inferred, believe that our treasure-chest is their aim, why it is fortunate you were not first attacked instead of me."

"Quite true; but it is not so much for my own sake I care; my three sisters, I have to remember, are dependent upon me. I have a horrible story to relate, too—one connected with my parents, which to you I will some day narrate and make your very blood, as mine does sometimes, crawl through your veins like threads of ice."

Arab Jack shuddered.

A raw, chill air mostly heralded the Soudan dawn, and those who were exposed to the intense heat of the day felt it terribly then.

Hassan remarked Jack's cold shudder.

"Now, look here, Jack," said he, "all good things were sent on earth for man's enjoyment; what do you say to a toothful of wine?"

"Allah forgive me," exclaimed our hero, brightening up suddenly. "Let it be an elephant's tooth, an' it please ye, and do not let its smallness frighten me out of me wits."

They were both awfully jolly now.

The wine was excellent, rich and ruby, just the sort that the followers of Mahomet were forbidden to indulge in.

"It makes me dance like a true dervish," said Jack, mischievously, "and I'll just tip you that nautical hymn, ' Come fill the flowing bowl."

He had indulged in such a deep potation that he now roared at the top of his voice in such a way that Hassan became actually alarmed.

"Here, stop that; we shall both lose our heads if we are reported to the Mahdi, you young wine-swiller. If you go on in this way you will not reach, much less enter, the gates of the seventh heaven."

CHAPTER XIX.

DEAD, YET ALIVE.—THE STORM IN THE DESERT.—FIGHT BETWEEN THE ICHNEUMON AND THE SERPENT.

RAMADAN, the great fast or Lent of the Mahometans, was nigh when Arab Jack, Dervish Hassan, and the little dervish boy started for Mecca and Cairo with firmans from the Mahdi and the treasure.

They had a splendid retinue of well-armed Arabs, divine sheikhs and hoary-headed jellubs (slave dealers) whose souls were unpurified.

Most of these were pilgrims bound to the shrine at Mecca, and paid heavily for the privilege of being allowed to journey thither in company of the sacred camel.

Having struck the desert path, they journeyed for days without anything of interest occurring.

A few roving Arabs had at times turned up, but to Jack's disappointment there was no fight in them, owing probably to the pilgrim caravan being too strong for them.

These desert prowlers were mostly seen about the wells, their idea being to attack the caravans whilst the camels and horses were being watered and the waterskins filled for the next stage of the journey.

They were making one of these long stretches, with barely a cupful of water each to carry them the next twenty miles, when Jack, wearied with the anxiety of the guides and the groans of the almost exhausted animals, whistled a favourite popular air to drive away, as he said, the " blue devils."

Ali Lobah, a desperate outlaw, a big, burly Berbereen, with big, bushy, curly black hair, and a pleasant round face that could laugh, and murder while it smiled, was the chief guide.

"Allah curse you! May the devil and his donkeys run away with thee," he spluttered fiercely, as he rode to the side of Arab Jack. "All wells become dry because you make that noise like the simoon."

"I can't help it," replied Jack; "it's as hot now as any baker's oven. I feel like an animated biscuit; I am so dry and crisp that I almost wish somebody would take a fancy to me and eat me."

"Allah forfend! The Jew dogs might eat thee for roasted pork, and die," said the insolent robber. "My camel has had no water for five days, and now, see, the hot wind comes to scorch up the desert."

"Well, I won't blow any more," said Jack, "if my savoury breath is likely to do us harm. Your camel is not so precious as this sacred camel of the Mahdi. Go ahead, Ali Lobah; let us push on towards the holy city of Mecca."

"What's that confab all about," asked Hassan as he urged his camel forward to the side of our hero. "I don't like the looks of that rascal; I would not have had him if he had not been recommended by the Mahdi, who, by-the-bye, might have engaged him to suit his own purpose."

"Just my idea," returned Jack, "I'm certain our treasure chest is torturing Ali Lobah's vitals. What if the Mahdi made arrangements with him to rob us of it and return it to him again, for which he would get a good share."

"I hardly think that, Jack, for this reason : if the Berbereen is an outlaw under the protection of the Mahdi, and he is engaged to do the trick for us, I don't think he would have proceeded thus far without making a successful effort. No, no, Jack, the Mahdi in such a case might have done the trick himself, filled the chest up with stones and old iron, and just put a few shiners on the top."

"Very well, Hassan, we won't be careless in our watch. I shall look out for squalls. Hallo! what do you call that?"

The atmosphere, which before had been oppressively close, now became stifling and unbearable alike to man and beast, the throat became parched and shrivelled up, whilst a hot wind swept across the sands so seething that it seemed to sear the very skin.

No one could speak, no one could move—the cavalcade came to a dead halt : every one stood statuesque, as if they had been stricken by a hot furnace blast, or had been breathed upon by the lips of some volcanic crater.

What rendered it more appalling was that each one though rigid in limb, locked in jaw, and with eyes open, staring, fixed, and wide, held the power of thought untrammelled, thus condemning each object to a living death.

Arab Jack offered up a mental prayer for their deliverance, and, lo! it was answered at the very moment when the Moslems considered they were irrevocably lost, as they were unable to cry aloud to Allah.

Suddenly the sky became darkened, and masses of lead-coloured cloud rose up from behind the hills afar off, which gradually kindled into a dull, lurid glare, painful to the eye.

The flashes of lightning darted vividly from the overtaxed sky, loud peals of thunder shook the earth and made the very sands to tremble. The very atmosphere was charged with dust resembling a thick mist, which was pierced with big drops of rain that seemed to fall like balls of molten lead and were drunk up eagerly by the scorching sands.

What a relief!

Suddenly the big balls, as if seized with capillary attraction, joined hands and became one vast descending sheet! and the stricken caravan, aroused from their deathlike torpor, sought shelter from the deluge.

Never till then had Arab Jack experienced any of the real terrors of the great desert ; never before had he been in such a storm without the least sign of habitation or shelter. It seemed now that, instead of in the form of drouth, death would overtake them by water, for its descent was of such force that it seemed to beat them into the very earth, whilst the sand around them rebounded and covered them as it were with a shroud.

Arab Jack, novice as he was in such matters, was the first to make an effort towards deliverance.

He goaded the sacred camel into action, and like a spectre of the storm he rode about amongst the drivers, and with yells and blows made them form the camels into a sort of lager.

By bringing their heads together and exposing their flanks to the storm-tossed sand, he thus got the quadrupeds formed into a breakwater, so to speak, thus preventing their throats being choked and their eyes being cut out by the sharp, glass like pieces of flint that were worked up from the under surface.

"Now, dervish," said Jack, endeavouring to appear lively, "vot do you tink o' dat?"

"As before, as you were," replied Hassan, dolefully. "I've got the mullygrubs and the toothache."

"Oh, why don't you twist up a rope-yarn of sand and let me assist you to lug it out?"

"You can't, Jack, I've got a mouthful of it."

"What do you mean, blow you, a mouthful of tooth?"

"No, pain, Jack. I feel as if my mouth was choke full of pain and all my teeth were stuck into it."

"That's bad. Are they moist? Do they water much?"

"Oh, yes, awfully so—that is they water for a puff of the weed, which would make them much better, you know."

"There's no chance of getting a light now, so I'll summon a dozen water drawers to draw off the aqua, then I'll hitch on a camel to your refractory toosey pegs."

This so tickled Hassan that he laughed right boisterously, thus driving away the pain and causing the miserable pilgrims to look up in astonishment and alarm.

At first they imagined that a herd of wild beasts had been driven from their fastnesses by the fury of the storm, and were now come to be revenged upon the poor wretched travellers.

"Allah! Allah! protect us in the wilderness," they all echoed in one breath ; but when they looked up and beheld the risible features of Hassan they all hung their heads with shame.

By this time, fortunately, the storm had spent its fury, and as the sky cleared and the sun shone forth in its oriental splendour, Jack espied a green spot which seemed to grow up out of the earth like magic in the distance.

The sight was hailed not only by the men with joy, but by the quadrupeds, who as soon as the leader sniffed the air, snorted and started off in that direction just as if they were entered for a Soudan Derby.

Jack's camel was not only the emblem of sanctity but patience ; it allowed the unsanctified to tear and squabble whilst it leisurely strode to a spot where it nibbled the choice food without trouble or unseemly interruption.

The whole party was pleased to dismount, they were drenched to the very skin, and those unaccustomed to long rides felt as if the jolting had shifted the latitude of their internals.

"Now let us feed," said Jack, "for I fancy we have had the patience and endurance of our four-footed friends here. Can't we procure some dried sticks and indulge in a drop of warm Mocha?"

"Ah, yaas, me do dat," cried Daireh, the cook. "Mans feel awful chill after 'bath."

"Mans," exclaimed Jack, jocosely tapping the little dervish on the head, "what about boys, eh? Do they think we've a hide like a camel?"

"Like de drum-derry," chimed in Daireh "Dem want plenty tom-tom to keep their hides warm."

"That's shut me up," said Jack walking away. "I'll just take a squint at yon hollow."

So he did, and the sight he saw repaid him. Deep down between the two sloping hills there was a patch of refreshing vegetation, with one or two clumps of young palms, and hollows such as are termed surface pools filled with water.

"But what is that moving among the cactuses?

JACK COCKED THE LOCK OF HIS LONG GUN.   *p.* 51.

What is it causes the tall wiry grass to wave in the absence of the slightest breath of wind?"

Thus mused Jack as he took up a position to watch, and presently he saw an enormous serpent uncoil itself from the lower part of the stem of a cactus.

"My eye!" cried Jack, "I wish I'd brought my gun or pistol. What eyes! what a sting! and what a tremendous length!"

It was uncoiling itself sharp, and appeared in a state of agitation, the cause of which was soon shown by the appearance of an Egyptian ichneumon.

"By Jove!" our hero exclaimed, "I have seen one of them before; it was in the Zoo, but I have not had an opportunity of seeing these two deadly animals at close quarters as yet."

"Ah, dat mongoose," cried a voice at Arab Jack's elbow. "Him eat rats, bats, snakes, and ebery oder ting."

"Hallo, Daireh," said Jack, turning, "are you there?"

"Yaas, me look for dry camels' dung, make fire. Yah, yah, look dere, look dere."

Jack was looking, and with all his eyes, as the saying is.

The huge serpent, being confronted by its tiny enemy, endeavoured to charm it, and drew up its elastic bands ready for the fatal spring.

If things had gone properly with the serpent, the ichneumon would just have prepared his palate for a good meal; as it was, the little ichneumon beat his venomous foe, and Jack, boy-like, clapped his hands in honour of the victor.

"Bang!"

Jack spun round with rage. Daireh, dying for a shot at something, had pulled out his pistol, and sent a bullet through the conqueror's head.

"You idiot," Jack cried out, "to take the life of such a useful creature. At one time it was worshipped by the Egpytians, and then if you had wantonly destroyed one your life would have paid for your indiscretion."

"Yaas, me know dat; but mongoose good feed if you like."

5

"I don't," cried Jack, "I have not yet taken it into my dietary to eat cats, and I won't."

The coffee made by Daireh, however, set them all in good humour again, and greatly refreshed, the caravan party started again on their adventurous journey.

The arid sands, cooled for the moment by the rain shower, which on the sandy waste was no more than a drop of fresh water added to the sea, quickly heated again, and Hassan soon after showed signs of ophthalmia.

This was first made known by the following incident.

The cavalcade having wound their way round the foot of an extraordinarily high mountain, espied a small caravan of twenty camels and as many men coming in a direction in which both parties must at a given hour meet each other at the point of two irregular angles.

Hassan although this was pointed out to him could not discern it.

"I can see nothing," said he, "but the ocean and a few small ships."

"Then your eyesight is at sea," returned Jack, "and I am as pleased as a piper to hear of it."

"For why?"

"Because you will not be able to look after the treasure, and I shall have the whole of that horrible duty devolve upon me."

"What then?"

"I may have the trouble, and be put to the extra expense of hiring a cab and taking it to my lodgings at St. James's."

"St. Giles's," said Hassan, with a laugh, and his eyes watered so with the exuberance of his mirth that when he closed his optics he could see double.

"Can you see my cab?" said Jack.

"Yes, and the number of it, too ; it's a black one, and seems bound to the catacombs to deposit an Egyptian mummy."

"All right! sold again," laughed Jack. "But what's that thing reared up on yonder caravan—is it a cage?"

"Of course it is. A fellow with any sort of eyesight could see that, and there's a lion in it, too, I should say."

Arab Jack gave a quiet smirk.

"Can you make out its colour?"

"Red, I believe."

"Good, your eyesight, dervish sheikh, is improved a deal. That's a fresh lion on the way to replace the old one at Brentford. Just notice the curl of its tail."

Hassan-el-Ahed indulged in another good laugh, to the no small disgust of the sanctified pilgrims, who had prayed incessantly since the ceasing of the storm.

But how much more would they have prayed had they known how the dervish adulterated his water with wine !

Or had they been told that the principals conducting the sacred caravan were Christian dogs, and that the sacred camel itself was ridden by one of them !

But if ignorance engenders bliss, why should we seek to be wise !

CHAPTER XX.

THE GUIDE OF THE CARAVAN—A LION IN THE DESERT — HOW ARAB JACK FOUGHT WITH THE BRISTLY - MANED MONSTER AND DEFEATED IT.

AT the point expected the two caravans met, and at just sufficient distance apart to allow them to pass each other, when, lo and behold ! the lion, who had been nibbling at the stout wooden bars of his cage, suddenly broke out.

There was a diversion then.

Groans, yells and prayers ascended to Allah in the most confused order.

Ali Lobah, seeing that the noble animal made straight for him and his valuable beast, raised his matchlock, took aim and fired, but the charge, which had got damped during the deluge, was no use, and the dry powder only flashed in the pan.

The outlawed sheikh was no coward. He had fought against terrible odds in the battles between the rebels and the Egyptian regulars. He was the most daring crocodile slayer of any who practised upon the Nile, and he cared not for the wild elephant, the rhinoceros, or the hippopotamus of the far south. But this lion had something in its wild and ferocious appearance that made the bold outlaw quail.

Its mane was bristled and stood up like an enormous fan, and its long tufted tail lashed its sides with a thud which echoed far and near like the sharp peals of muffled thunder.

Then followed a most deafening roar.

The very earth shook under the bounds of its strong limbs and velvet-carpeted feet.

Ali's fate seemed now as certain as the setting of the noonday sun, for the fierce beast was upon him before he could draw the useless charge, much less re-load his long-barrelled gun.

Arab Jack saw his danger with a quick and calculating eye.

"My God ! he is slain," he cried in mental agony. "My gun, dervish boy ; hand me immediately my pistols."

But the affrighted boy could not undo the valise.

He clung like a dying negro to the fore-part of the camel saddle, with his eyes starting almost out of his head.

The confusion that reigned now was not only general but painful in the extreme.

Some cried, others laughed hysterically, whilst a few stood petrified and speechless with fear.

Hassan was nearly driven mad, for his division of the camels had taken fright and were on the point of making a stampede.

Bravest of all, however, was our hero, Arab Jack.

Though but a boy, his soul, fired by the exigency of the moment, made him more than a man.

Already Ali Lobah was in the power of the enraged beast, who had him down and was endeavouring to tear away his arm, which Ali, by the lesson of past experience, had enfolded in a blanket of camels' hair.

Through this tough swathing the huge jaws of the noble animal were unable to force their way, nor could the baffled beast disengage them from the textile fabric.

Meanwhile Ali endeavoured with his other

hand to clutch his dagger-knife, but the weight of the huge beast pressing on his chest almost squeezed the life out of him, and kept his arm at work endeavouring to ward off the pressure.

These were terrible moments for all.

The keeper of the escaped animal raved and danced like one suddenly seized with madness.

It was his fault that the beast had gnawed through the stout wooden bars of the cage, for he had neglected to use the long iron rod with which he was to probe him when engaged in such work of mischief.

Now he saw two chances of losing the animal altogether.

It would either be frightened away into the wilds, or be slain, and the body claimed as compensation for the damage it was yet likely to do.

The caravan to which the lion belonged, or, rather, of which it was part freight, mostly consisted of merchants who thought more of their own lives and property than they did of those of others, and so they pushed on, leaving the holy caravan to bear the battle and the brunt.

Our hero, Jack, however, was soon at the post of danger, and with his yataghan bared dazed the sight of the lion by flashing the bright blade before its glistening eyes.

This was to attract the lion's attention from the victim who was most unquestionably in its power.

The ruse was effective.

The lion looked up, and as Jack fixed its eye he endeavoured to thrust the weapon's point forward into the animal's throat.

This was not a success.

The trusty weapon would have done its work true enough had it not been for a tuft of tough hair which resisted the blade, turned the weapon aside, and by the impetus thus given brought Jack and the lion face to face.

Those belonging to the sacred cavalcade saw at once the deadly peril of the daring boy. With a cry which startled even the huge beast, they rent the air, and invoked the aid of Allah, his prophet, and the Mahdi to aid the daring boy.

Hassan's life, also, was in imminent peril now.

One of the fleetest footed camels had taken to flight, and the halter having in some way got entangled around Hassan's arm, he was dragged across the plain at an almost incredible speed.

Many of the guards had heard of but never seen such a monster before, and believing that it was some divine manifestation boding evil to the caravan of the sacred camel, they not only stood aloof, but incessantly implored Allah to forgive them their past misdeeds and to save them.

The little dervish boy was the only one that actually rendered any assistance to Jack.

Recovering from his fright he got the matchlock and the pistol, and bore them to Arab Jack, who being told they were loaded, seized one of the weapons to put a ball through the head of the lion.

But here again the will of Providence interposed.

The dervish boy, though he saw the weapons were loaded and primed, handed the pistol to our hero at half-cock, so that it only was of use when clubbed, and Jack manfully battered the beast's head with the butt end of the weapon.

Enraged at this, the fierce monster with but a slight movement of the body shook Jack off, and growling at the entanglement which now

held prisoner his teeth and paws, he got himself into such difficulties as enabled the outlaw sheikh to free himself from his dangerous position.

By this time Jack had thrust both his pistols in his sash, and had also cocked the lock of his long gun, the barrel of which was soon adjusted to his sight, and the bullet sped on its course.

A tumultuous cry then arose, "He's hit, he's hit!"

So he was, and staggered back as the blood gushed forth from the hole in his neck; but the king of the forest was not yet subdued; there was still a chance of resenting his untimely death.

Jack, emboldened by the success of his shot, and believing the animal to be weakened beyond further mischief, closed with it at once, and the struggle for victory that ensued made it doubtful which would gain the mastery.

Arab Jack from some particular cause scorned to use his pistols.

He clutched his knife, the weapon he had received from Will Wiggles, the lighterman of the Thames, and with it he endeavoured to give the wounded brute its quietus.

But Jack had reckoned without his host. The lion, though bleeding as if an artery had been severed, still wanted some killing, and seemed as if its rage was centered on Jack's snowy turban.

It may seem absurd, but it is, nevertheless, true, its teeth and claws seemed to vie with each other in endeavouring to get a grip on the idol of Jack's pride, and it required all his tact to prevent the fierce lion accomplishing its purpose.

But this terrible work could not last for ever.

Ali Lobah knew this, and as his gun was now reloaded, he at once set about rescuing the brave boy who had put himself in his place.

"Bang! bang!"

Two shots, fired almost simultaneously from the same double-barrelled gun, struck the enraged brute just above the eyes, and with a roar that caused everything living within hearing of it to tremble, the noble animal rolled over and breathed its last.

Arab Jack was now the object of a grand ovation.

No warrior fresh from the battle field could have received more plaudits and honours.

A large sum of gold was collected in a bag and given to him, and prayers of thankfulness met him on every side, much to the chagrin of the outlaw sheikh, who eyed the bag of gold with looks of unmistakable greed.

Hassan-el-Ahed was amongst those who lauded our youthful hero. By some miracle he could not himself explain, he brought the runaway camel to a full stop, and led it back in safety to the caravan, which when the lion was dead was soon put again in order and made ready to proceed.

The poor unfortunate keeper wept like a child, and fell on Jack's neck, overwhelmed with gratitude, when our hero informed him that he would not claim the skin of the animal as a trophy; and so leaving him there with his people, some of whom had returned when they heard of the lion's death, the sacred cavalcade again proceeded.

One danger was at an end; but another more terrible was in store for them.

CHAPTER XXI.

THE VALLEY OF THE SHADOW OF DEATH.—
ARAB JACK VISITS THE BEDOUIN ENCAMP-
MENT.—THE LEECH THROWS OFF HIS DIS-
GUISE.—THE RED SHEIKH, OR THE TERROR
OF THE PLAINS.—THE CARAVAN ATTACKED.
—DESPERATE ENCOUNTER FOR THE POSSES-
SION OF THE SACRED CAMEL.

AFTER the stirring events recorded in our last chapter, several days passed without anything extraordinary occurring.

One of the pilgrims certainly died of fright, or rather of delirium, caused by the terrific encounter with the lion.

It was a case hopeless from the very first, as a medicine sheikh, or leech, who travelled with them, described it. "For," said he, to Arab Jack, "you see that fever had set in, and in this latitude fever has every chance, or as you'd put it, has no chance at all."

"How is that, sheikh?"

"Simply because we are now in the region of the valley of the shadow of death, and the further we enter it the more the heat will increase, and those who cannot stand it, fall there, and are left by the wayside for vultures and hyenas to banquet upon."

"That's cheerful," remarked Jack, with a shrug.

"It is awful, and a terrible warning to those who have not embraced the true faith. Allah be praised that I was very early brought to believe in the doctrines of the true prophet."

"Amen," said Jack. "Are we obliged to go through this valley, then?"

"Yes, my son. I have travelled this path many times, and no other track have I known. One might call this Golgotha, for verily it is a place of bones and skulls."

This valley of death was a gorge hemmed in by steep mountains on both hands, and so narrow in parts that camels could not proceed two abreast.

"In places," continued the leech, "it is difficult to proceed at all owing to the loose stones that roll down from the mountains, and falling upon those that line the sides bound into the path."

In passing through this gorge Arab Jack felt anything but easy.

"This, dervish," said he to Hassan, "is just the sort of place one would expect to fall in with a nest of robbers lying in ambush."

"Yes, Jack; but don't fill us with more horrors than are necessary. Look at the bones; aren't they bleached? And those skulls, they look every one as if they were staring at us with their sightless orbs."

"Hang it all, it's you who work up the shudders," said Jack. "In my map which I am making of the route, I shall call this the Upas Valley of the Soudan. What a place it would be, though, for an ambuscade!"

"Yes, it would be proper—I mean for those who lay in wait. What a deathly smell! I don't believe a breath of pure air ever blows through it even in winter."

And so the dreary miles were traversed, taking them the whole day, and glad enough they were when they emerged into the open.

As the night was moonlight they travelled on till a late hour, in order to place as much distance as possible between them and the deadly valley.

After they had pitched their tents and tied the camels' legs, they discovered they were in the vicinity of a large Bedouin encampment.

"A nice lot of neighbours," said Jack; "but, there, I suppose they are not more dishonest than their traducers. I often wonder whether the two thieves who were crucified were Arabs."

"Not unlikely," said Hassan, giving Jack one of his sly, meaning looks. "I happen to have an Arab friend: one of these days I'll ask him."

Next morning Jack took a stroll to the Bedouin camp to see what it looked like, and very much surprised was he to find it literally alive with children, goats, sheep, mules, horses and camels, and numerous cocks and hens, the former of which kept the morning alive with their music

The Bedouin sheikh, who was seated in his low hut, crossed legged on a splendid carpet, received Jack civilly, but a sort of mistrust seemed to lurk around his restless eyes.

"Good morning, you are welcome," said he in the Arabic with which Jack was the most acquainted. "This is my wife, and he pointed to a fancifully-dressed little lady who was covered with gold, brass and beads lying in one corner of the tent with a carpet and camel's hair rug between her and the ground.

Arab Jack made a grand salaam to the little lady, repeated a verse of the Koran, chatted about the Mahdi, and eventually bargained for a dozen pairs of fowls.

The Bedouin was delighted to hear about the Mahdi, and especially from one who had seen him, shaken hands with him, and broken bread and partaken of salt—a great honour and a token of sincere friendship, by the way — with his devout excellency.

Our hero spun him a yarn quite as feasible as that told by the sailor who declared he had helped to fish up with the ship's anchor one of Pharaoh's golden chariot-wheels from out of the Red Sea.

When Jack took out of his bag and gave him a small piece of gold, the eyes of the sheikh grew as large round as tea-saucers, and no doubt, as Jack thought, he would have liked to have helped himself out of it.

A present to the little lady secured Jack further friendship, and he was actually presented with bread and salt, which he partook of with the illustrious lord and master of the desert mansion.

Jack's return with the fowls was hailed with shouts of delight.

Daireh was directed to prepare them at once, and as many as could breakfasted off of them, Jack himself and the little dervish boy just managing to get hold of a wing and leg between them.

During the night Ali Lobah was missing from his post, and no one knew whither he had gone.

Arab Jack regarded this at the very least as suspicious.

"Hassan," said he, "I consider it our duty to call a council of the whole party. I have a presentiment that we shall be waylaid and robbed."

"Sit down, then, fakir mahdi, and indite a firman. We may as well hold a durbar at once; and as for your presentiment that we shall be waylaid, I have a presentiment that I shan't be waylaid, nor robbed, either."

"We shall see."

"Of course we shall, unless we have bad eyes.

But, there ; perhaps you sent the hard-up outlaw to the rank to order your cab, and if so depend upon it I shall be able to scent you both out."

Jack was vexed ; he bit his lip and smiled bitterly.

"This is no time for jesting, Hassan. I am surprised that a man of your abilities talks with such levity at a time so critical and important."

"Aye, that is your view of the situation. Mine is that you are the only critical personage present, and the only one who introduces any importunity."

Arab Jack gazed into his eyes, and he soon saw what was the matter with his old friend Hassan-el-Ahed.

The dervish was elevated beyond the altitude of common sense, his eyes were red with wine, or, if it is necessary to speak plainer, he was drunk.

Our hero saw this, to his evident dismay.

If the pilgrims, holy as they were, and sanctified as they pretended to be, only found out by his drinking wine that Hassan was a false dervish, deluding them, and actually making a mockery of their souls, they would set upon him, torture him, and submit him to some horrible death, for which they would be applauded, instead of condemned, by every Mahometan in every country, without the least regard to shade or colour.

But what could he do ?

Hassan held his secret. He knew his skin was white, that he was a Frank (European), whose blood the Mahdi, with the salt of his fanatical creed, had set the Mahometans thirsting and hankering after.

What excuse could he make for the absence of the outlaw guide, who knew every inch of the road they were pursuing ? And how could he hire another and go on without giving some explanation to the Soudanese pilgrims ?

Our hero was in a tight fix.

He was in a false position, and a critical one. For what mercy could he or ought he to expect at the hands of the faithful if they discovered the deceit he was practising ?

Even the Mahdi, himself would proclaim him to strengthen his own cause, and make no scruple of ordering him to be flayed alive, as he had already done several others who stood in his way, and those not only Englishmen and white men, but men, and even boys, of his own township and his own dark blood.

Jack now looked seriously back to the one dark spot in his life.

He thought of the true proverb he had often written in his copy-book at school—"Honesty is the best policy."

"So it is," exclaimed Jack, as he started up, his brain on fire, his very soul melting under the anguish of the thought. "Honesty in speech, honesty in action, honesty and uprightness, in fact, in all the dealings I may have with my fellow-man."

Jack's soliloquy was now at an end. He had moralised so far that he had actually cornered himself.

There lay Hassan suffering from the fumes of the wine, and yet he had not the courage to deal honestly with his fellow-man by going forth and proclaiming the truth to the passengers of the caravan.

The medicine man before mentioned was not blind to the fact, however.

He secretly indulged in the same evil course, only he took pick-ups and other stimulants to counteract the effect.

Peering into the tent, where Jack was sitting in a state of bewilderment, he said :—

"Allah be praised ! His blessing aboundeth for ever ! What ails the young mahdi sheikh ?"

"I am not very bright. I am afraid our dervish is labouring under a fever caught during our journey through the valley of death."

"Allah, forbid ! May I just touch his pulse ?"

"Fifty pulses, if you like, learned father," replied Jack, vexed with himself at being compelled to tell so deliberate a lie.

The learned leech was, however, a man who knew how to dissemble.

"Allah be merciful, he is very bad. But thanks to the prophet, every hair of whose beard is wisdom, I have learned when the salt shalt lose its savour wherewith it shall be salted."

"I wish you would make haste about it, then," said Jack, "for I believe that the salt, the savour, and all the blessed lot of us will be gone when that outlaw guide of ours returns."

"Oh ! "

"Yes ; I believe he's gone to look after his fellows, and then he'll return with a host, and set upon and rob us."

"Allah forefend ! And in the presence of the sacred camel, too."

"Aye, in the presence of the devil for that matter," exclaimed Jack, bluntly, in his true English style, incautiously throwing off the Oriental suavity he had hitherto assumed. "He may even be negotiating with those Bedouins yonder, amongst whom I counted over a hundred fighting men, and what would we be to them ?"

"Allah, Allah—Allah is good," exclaimed the leech, sanctimoniously lifting his eyes and raising his hands towards the heavens.

"So is Ali Lobah, friend leech. But if you can do anything by cupping, bleeding or any other process known to yourself for our good dervish I shall be thankful."

The learned man placed his finger on his lip and glided away. But scarcely had he reached the entrance of the tent than a discordant yell was heard, and the sleeping members of the cavalcade were aroused by those who kept watch and guard.

To Jack's discerning mind the truth flashed in a moment.

"The Philistines are upon us," he cried ; "I knew they would be ; and now farewell to all our worldly treasure."

As he flew to the opening of the tent the crafty leech turned towards him and implored of him by all the saints he could name in the calendar to be calm.

"Allah will deliver us," he said. "Why should His followers dim the sheen of their swords when His word is so omnipotent ?"

Jack, however, saw through the fellow's oily craft.

"Stand aside," he hissed, "or by the God I worship I will cut you down." And drawing his yataghan from its sheath just like a flash of light he prepared to put his threat into execution.

The medicine man laughed.

"Puny boy," he said, scornfully. "I could have killed you many times ere this if I thought fit : poisoned you if I so chose. But I have watched you, and admired your plucky spirit ? Were the rest like you, even my arm and my followers would have no chance against such."

As he spoke he threw off the dervish-like robe that encased his hitherto bowed and patriarchal form, and stood before Jack as he really was—THE RED SHEIKH, THE TERROR OF THE NUBIAN DESERT AND THE SOUDAN.

Arab Jack drew back in wonderment and awe.

He had heard of this terrible scourge, but he never thought that he ever would see him, and now, when he beheld the tall, well-knit form, the broad shoulders as powerful as those of an ox, and the blood-red dress, in the sash of which a whole arsenal of weapons seemed located, he felt his brain fairly whirl.

"Boy," again spoke the bandit, "I could annihilate you at a blow, but I would consider it a sin to crush such a proud and implacable spirit in the bud. Here's my fist. I give you the offer, if you so choose, of joining my bold band at once."

Jack was astounded, yet he thought of the peril of his friend Hassan, and the caravan.

The latter was a mine of treasure in itself, whilst most of the pilgrims were of such note that they could be held for heavy ransoms.

But the Red Sheikh needed no telling of this. He knew all. It was his business, the hobby of his life, to satisfy which he roamed the desert like a hungry wolf, or as the bloodthirsty pirate ploughs the sea.

"Well, what do you say, boy?" he asked, as Jack paused to see how he could push by his burly frame, which completely filled the opening. "Do you consent, or am I to serve you as the Romans served the bold Caractacus, load you with chains?"

"That I leave to the decision of fate," Arab Jack haughtily replied. "I am free born, I am not a slave of the soil, I own no master, nor will I submit to any dictator."

The rover of the plains drew back in astonishment. It was his turn to be filled with wonderment now.

To see the young cub, as he termed him, with his puny yataghan, standing before him, pigmy-like, but valorous and defiant, just as the young David stood before the Goliath of old, and just as confident of success in a personal encounter with a giant as he was.

"Great Allah ! " gasped the red bandit sheikh, "is this really one of thy chosen—the coming Mahdi of thine own selection in the embryo ?"

Jack stood with his proud lip pursed, his Apollo-like form drawn up erect, his shoulders thrown back, and his feet planted just as if he was prepared to be modelled for a statue of Achilles.

In his right hand he grasped his yataghan, his left hand having sought the butt of one of the exquisitely-mounted pistols stuck in his sash.

The Red Sheikh was a perfect Hercules in form now that he was seen to full advantage, and there was that in his look and manner which showed that he was not to be trifled or played with.

"Arab Jack," said he in a sharp, short tone, "I have had my doubts as to whether you were an Arab or not. I have more than once taken you for a Christian, a Copt, a descendant of the ancient inhabitants of Egypt."

"Why so ?" demanded our hero, still maintaining his firm demeanour.

"Because I have noticed in some things a difference in your worship to that of the true-born Moslems of Arabia."

"Perhaps so ; and perhaps you would notice much more if you were granted the privilege to do so."

"Confound it, that's cheek," muttered the bandit. "So then," he cried aloud, "I am really to put you in chains."

This interview only lasted a few moments, but in that space the cries and the shouts had increased.

The guards, having stood to their posts until defeat and death seemed certain, had rushed in, and having no proper leader, so to speak, every one indiscriminately fought for himself.

Arab Jack, hearing a cry which sounded as if the possession of the sacred camel was being disputed for by the combatants, made a desperate rush for the opening of the tent, and forcing himself against the robber sheikh caused him to roll with the motion of a big war-ship when suddenly struck by a squall.

This act most likely would have cost Jack his life, or in any case it might have ended seriously for him had he not been as fleet of foot as a deer.

The Red Sheikh uttered a fierce oath, and made a flat-bladed blow at him as he steadied his towering form by the yielding canvas of the tent.

Arab Jack was in the midst of the fight in a moment.

"Hurrah ! Shout, you beggars," he yelled to the armed driver and others who formed the escort of the sacred caravan ; "down with the unbelieving dogs who dare lay hands on and outrage our sacred camel."

This speech, short and inspiriting as it was, had the desired effect.

The guards gathered around the sacred animal, which seemed to cry as if it knew it was being laid hold of by polluted hands, and with sword and matchlock they did much execution among the robber band.

Many of the pilgrims, aged though they were, fought also in favour of the dedicated beast, which for all they knew had often borne the holy carpet from the tomb in Mecca to the ancient city of Cairo, where once a year it is cleansed from all impurity and scented with frankincense and myrrh, and other costly perfumes.

To say that the desert band was not awed, and might not have been easily put to flight at first if the sacred caravanists had been well led at the onset would be false ; but when Jack arrived amongst them the Arabs had lost much of their superstitious fear, which wore off at every shot or clash of blade to blade.

The Red Sheik, leaving his men to complete their work, himself set about looking after the golden treasure, which day after day he had watched as it was borne along on its own particular baggage camel.

What became of it when they encamped by day or were compelled to halt by night he never knew, nor could he ever find out ; for on no account during the long journey were any of the caravanists allowed to enter the sacred tent.

That very morning when he peered into the tent disguised as a leech he was seeking about for it; but had it not been for Hassan's indisposition and Jack's dread of losing him by the way, the bandit sheikh would not have been permitted to enter the holy precinct except by force.

The Red Sheikh had all his work cut out for him even now, and so, leaving him in the tent there with his drawn scimitar, which he used as a sort of divining rod, we will watch the battle, which was now beginning to rage with Oriental fierceness.

Among the pilgrims were sheiks of tribes who were leaders of men, and therefore when all came to all and they saw that the wealth which was to be made the purchase of their souls and the instrument by which they were to procure a safe passport to the Mahometan realms of bliss, they threw off all fear of and banished all thoughts of mercy for their assailants.

To Arab Jack they clung like fanatics, obeyed the mandates uttered by his voice, and made the thieving Arabs yell with pain and grind their teeth with rage at being met by so fierce and deadly an opposition.

CHAPTER XXII.

ARAB JACK PROVES HIMSELF A WARRIOR.—THE GIRAFFE-SHEIKH CROSSES SWORDS WITH OUR HERO.—THE CAPTURE OF THE CARAVAN.—A STARTLING DISCOVERY.—THE CHARMED BULLET.—A SAND CLOUD MOVES OVER THE PLAIN.

HAD the Bedouin Arabs made their murderous attack before it was light, the peaceful caravan might have fallen a rich and easy prize, and every member of it have been slain or taken prisoner without the satisfaction of having dealt a desperate blow.

The arrangements for the surprise had been well planned, and if they had been as admirably carried out it must have proved an undoubted success.

Ali Lobah, the outlaw guide, as soon as his services were accepted by the Mahdi, sent a swift horseman by stealth to apprise his lieutenant of the route he should take and the probable strength of the pilgrim party.

"Collect our bands," was the stern command, "and on the seventh day of the moon lie in wait behind the ridges about one mile southward of the entrance to the Valley of the Shadow of Death."

Aben, Ali Lobah's brother-in-law, obeyed at once, but neither Aben nor Lobah had made allowance for the storm, which, by-the-bye, was rather unseasonable, and rendered travelling so dangerous in a defile they had to pass through that Aben deemed it prudent to seek a more open and circuitous route.

By this divergence they encountered a strong party of Egyptian horsemen, who after a short encounter routed them and drove them back, sending them flying in all directions over the plain.

Thus it was that the sacred caravan was allowed to pass through the valley unmolested. At the same time, Lobah, who was boiling over with disappointment and rage, left the encampment as soon as it was formed and went towards the mountains in search of aid.

During the long, tedious journey every movement of his had been watched with jealous eye by the disguised Red Sheikh, whose "get up"

was so faultless that even Lobah, to whom, of course, he was well known, failed to unmask it.

But now that Ali Lobah had brought his hired host, which now surrounded the caravan like a living wall, the Red Sheikh fearlessly threw off his disguise, for the Arab robbers were no other than a party who acknowledged his sway.

But our hero paused not to question them as to their leader, or even ask from whence they came.

They were there, and independently of their warlike array, their actions showed that their intention was to conquer or die in the attempt.

The jellubs, as the slave dealers were named, who had undertaken the journey to Mahomet's shrine as a set-off against the unholy traffic by which they amassed considerable wealth, more than once showed an inclination to fly rather than fight, so that Jack, hotly as he was opposed by the Arab horde, actually spat at them in token of his abhorrence of their cowardice.

But Jack had more important work in hand just then.

"It is fortunate," he thought, "that I ordered the drivers to hobble the camels when they lay down, or now there would be such a stampede amongst them as would make one imagine Satan and his host were let loose, and my efforts, puny as they are, would be totally crippled."

Had matters been less serious one might have laughed at our hero's idea of describing his efforts as puny.

Half-kneeling, half-standing in the hollow formed by the double humps of one of the recumbent baggage camels, he was cutting, thrusting and parrying with all his might.

His pistols, being muzzle loaders, when once discharged were too much trouble to reload; in fact, such an act would have cost him his life.

So with his yataghan in his right hand, and his cross-handled dagger-like knife in his left, he gashed and hewed at the merciless fiends, who fell upon him with hideous yells, and tried to beat him down, until the sand beneath the groaning camel, and even the very air, seemed to reek with blood.

"Red, red, everything is red," hissed Arab Jack. "My hands are sticky with the congealed gore, and I feel that my eyes are growing blood-shot."

And such really was the case.

The brave boy's hands were actually glued to the haft of his knife and the jewelled hilt of his splendid yataghan.

The one big diamond which formed the boss of the hilt of the latter, alone shone brilliantly in the rays of the morning sun, and as it reflected the dazzling beams it served to fire the avarice of the desert-robbers almost to frenzy.

It was as much for the possession of this, and perhaps more, that they struggled so savagely and determinedly.

Jack was almost mad.

To him, as he described it, every thing was red. One red glare seemed to surround him, and in that the dark image of his foes seemed to rise, sway about as they elbowed their way to the front, and then stand out in bold relief against the ruddy background.

"Slash—crash—whizz!"

Then as the flesh was cleaved, the bone cleft or splintered as the sharp, heavy, broad-backed yataghan descended with a force that was irresistible, and the blood flew in all directions, it seemed to the excited boy as if a shower of crimson snow was falling around him.

Already a pile of the turbaned slain or badly wounded lay beneath the breastwork, so to speak, formed by the huge side of the camel, and yet Jack unflaggingly pursued his deadly work, at times standing erect, and at others sunk down on one knee, according to the exigencies of the moment. He actually shouted for his assailants to come on, and they, led by the warlike spirit in which they were born, answered his invitation by appearing before him in person.

Those who know anything of the Bedouins, or children of the desert, as their name signifies, can easily understand the motive that prompted this, and also the reason why they did not take the brave lad at a disadvantage by firing at him.

The Bedouin Arabs are a race who glory in their feats of arms.

Like the ancient Britons, they are brought up to physical exercises, and trained to war from their cradle, so that they can fence, shoot, and manœuvre as well, if not better on horseback than they can on foot. Therefore they glory in deeds of daring, feats of strength, assaults of arms, and the like.

At the same time they are instilled while at their mothers' breasts with a hatred for every being outside the pale of their own caste, and a love of plunder.

And, if we had time to moralise, how could they exist without?

They roamed from plain to plain, pitching their tents sometimes in the mountain, sometimes in the valley, or far away from any other habitation on the dark, waterless and scorching desert.

It was this love of chivalry and sense of honour, which in a Bedouin Arab is innate, that saved our hero from being riddled by a hundred bullets.

The elders of that lawless tribe, even in the hour of conflict, with the fierce passions of war raging in their breasts, could not but pause and gaze in admiration on the Boy Mahdi, from whose lips they verily believed the words could at any moment drop which would consign them to eternal perdition.

But they had passed the Rubicon now. They had struck the blow, and retrogression would be worse than pushing forward.

"Boys," said the elders, gazing with protruding eyes at their young men, "see yonder. The holy Arab boy is valorous and full of courage. Cut him down, spear him, but use not a bullet against his breast; cut him down we all say, and charge you to do so quickly, or at a breath he may consign our spirits one and all to the lowest hell."

The young men thus stirred needed no further incentive. Thus it was that Jack was so hardly pressed, with scimitar and spear, until, as we before said, the very ground bore the appearance of the shambles.

Leaving Arab Jack thus, with his sword crimsoned to the hilt, and his clothes bespattered as though he had slaughtered a herd of swine, we will glance around at the other parts of the encampment.

It was oval in form, and occupied an immense space of ground, for in addition to the two hundred pilgrims, there were nearly as many slaves, attendants upon them, besides the drivers and guards, picked men of the Wahabee and Kababish tribes.

The camels, horses, and Nubian mules were all of the finest breed, having been selected by the governor-general of the Mahdi, and with the sacred camel, which was almost above price, the animals would have been a ransom for a Soudanese prince.

On one side of the camp huge boulders eighteen feet high and twenty feet apart assisted in its formation, and the camels with the less costly baggage formed the outer wall or edge.

Inside this were the horses and mules, then the tents, and enclosed within all there were the costly treasures, the produce of the wilds, consisting mostly of ivory, agate, jasper, and porphyry, with costly incense, such as the Greek and Romish priests purchase with avidity to use upon their altars.

To protect such treasures as these from the pirates of the desert, the slaves and drivers, instigated by the promises of freedom and large rewards, fought as only those who have life and liberty at stake know how to.

Armed with all sorts of weapons, even to scythes and sickles, with which they cut provender for the horses and cattle, they made a good stand against the murderous onslaught of the Arabs, until they were at length compelled to yield.

This was the signal for a glorious shout, "Allah is good!" "Allah is great!" and then they poured into the opening with an overwhelming rush, which was torture to the daring boy.

Turning from his assailants for a moment, he looked to those behind him, and shouted to them to re-form; but he might as well have shouted to the wind.

"Stand fast!" he yelled. "Allah is with us. Allah Akbar, God is great."

But his own battle-cry nearly proved to him his own death-knell, for on turning to the front again he found himself face to face with a tall, wiry sheikh, who not only stood considerably over six feet, but had arms whose length was greatly in excess of his stature.

"Good heaven," gasped our hero, as he mechanically guarded the down cuts directed at his head, "good heaven, give me power to hew down this man-giraffe before I am slain."

Jack's comparison was not out of place. The tall, thin, wiry Arab sheikh certainly looked like one of those graceful quadrupeds as he stood before our hero, and with his long, sinewy arms and broad-bladed scimitar, which looked like the decapitating sword of a Siamese executioner, he seemed to be the avenger of the blood of the young men Jack had slain.

"Curse you!" shouted the grey-bearded, cadaverous-looking man. "Allah has sent you as a plague to strike our first-born, our young warriors, and shed desolation over the hearts of our maidens, who mourn their loss."

"'Tis a lie, father!" Jack shouted. "It is they who are the locusts of the plain; and as for you, you treacherous old fiend, I will hew you down, aged as you are, as if you were but a worthless sapling."

Jack's passion was so great that he could scarcely frame his words, and, more, he hardly understood their purport when he uttered them.

The old sheikh, however, being fresh to the fray, weighed every letter of Jack's speech, and he fairly foamed with rage.

"The curse of Allah rest on you, false Mahdi," he hissed. "Who taught you to call the date palm a sapling, when it hath counted the overflowing of the Nile three score and ten times?"

"Well, it was a bit of cheek," thought Jack; "but then I am not going to retract. Three score and ten! Why, hang me, the thieving old sinner ought to have been choked long before this time."

The old sinner, however, required more choking than our hero could give him. He wielded his deadly weapon, heavy though it was, as if it had been a toy, and once nearly wrenched the knife from Jack's hand, firm as was his grip.

It took all Jack's time to watch his peculiarly-coloured eyes, and his elongated and wrinkled visage, in which, despite his cuteness, Jack could read his every move and thought.

At length our hero remembered having seen that visage before.

"Yes," he cried, half aloud, " it is the same, that of the old sheikh I beheld in the tent this morning. Allah preserve me, it is the infidel dog with whom I ate salt and broke bread in the presence of his lady."

Low spoken as were his words, and in spite of the clash of steel, the quick ears of the old man caught every sound, and he glared on our hero from under his pent brows as if he would eat him.

"Devil from the pit!" he screeched, "fakir from the land of Hades, I defy you! You visited me this morning to work upon me your devilish arts; but Ab-Akan is no geni's toy, so I will slay thee, and the soul of thy slayer shall dwell in the land of the pomegranate, the melon, and the palm, where fountains of sweet water play freely, and the honey of the wild bee is in plenty."

The aged sheikh was certainly blest with good respiratory organs, and as he kept up his tirade Jack could not help comparing his lungs to two pads of leather, for he never paused to renew his breath, but slashed and cut away until the edges of his and Jack's swords were notched and toothed like two saws.

At this juncture another diversion was raised. A shower of leaden balls began whistling about our hero's head.

"Confound it!" cried he. "I must get rid of this ugly customer for good, and at once," and he made such a lunge at him that it seemed as if his sword pierced his sinewy throat.

It was a miss, however. By a dexterous movement the sheikh escaped, but as he did so one of the bullets fired from the direction of the plain struck the edge of Jack's sword, and it was split fair in twain, one half striking the neck of the sheikh and burying itself in it in such a way as to sever the spinal column.

The old Arab chief threw up his arms, and uttering a wild, despairing cry, fell back on the ensanguined heap, where, with several of his sons, as Jack afterwards learned, he bit the dust, and lay stiff and stark in the arms of the grim monster, Death.

"I pity him," said Jack; "he deserved a better death. But now I must look to myself. Ah, I see the varmint who is playing popgun at me."

Arab Jack, serious as was the situation, took things all in good part.

The fellow whose bullet had struck Jack's sword and thus strangely rid him of a foe, was mounted on horseback, and was evidently manœuvring on the plain.

As Jack's glance sought him he was practising what the Bedouins call the retreat. That is, he was lying flat along the horse, his head sheltered and resting beside its neck, and holding a pistol in his left hand, which he fired behind him as his horse sped straight away across the plain.

That he was a good shot Jack very soon found out. His bullet, well aimed as it most certainly was, would have struck Jack in the eye had it not been for his clever instinct.

Drawing quickly back as he calculated the speed and distance, he, with the flat of his sword, struck the bullet aside with as much *sang-froid* as a school boy would play at rounders or feeder.

"Well, done! No athlete in the Roman arena could have excelled that, and no magician that ever appeared before his excellency the Sultan could have charmed a bullet aside in that manner."

Jack turned, startled by the voice.

In the rear of him stood the mystic chief, the Red Sheikh of the Desert.

Our hero blushed to the very roots of his hair with unaffected pride, and as another bullet passed close to his cheek he hissed :—

"Mystic being! Whoever thou art, or whatever is your mission, I defy you, as I have done before. See yonder"—pointing with his sword —" is my treacherous guide. If you mean me well why have you not endeavoured to silence his accursed weapon, which, as you see, has no power to inflict injury on one who is made invulnerable by my immaculate master the Mahdi?"

The Red Sheikh shrugged his enormous shoulders and placed both hands on his hips. "Boy," said he, "I place no reliance in priests or princes, so that thy words have upon me no effect. I believe I am as much the true Mahdi as Mahomet Achmet, and the name of Allah the true God is as often in my mouth as it is in his."

"Art thou a blasphemer, then?" asked Jack, eyeing him fearlessly.

"Nay, Allah knows I am not. I pray to him to throw such caravans as this in my path, and I then implore his aid in procuring me the victory."

"It is sacrilege," said Jack, "plundering a holy caravan, and it is murder to kill those who are on their pilgrimage."

"Bah! I have heard enough of such foolish talk, enough of such senseless arguments. As I have said, I believe in the true God, and follow in the footsteps of his holy prophet."

"Then I am done with you," Jack replied, "and I despise your carnal boasting. Did you not tell me that you knew with what to salt the earth if it lost its savour?"

"Yea, and that do I. Gold, my son, gold. That treacherous Ali Lobah dare not come near thee now he has recognised me; and should he dispute my power by which I have transferred the plunder of this caravan from his hand to mine, I would slay him or take him back in chains to Berber, from whence he escaped when being tried for complicity in some awful crime, and was outlawed."

"Have you a right, then, to slay him?" queried Jack.

"Decidedly. Every man's hand is raised against him. But few of those who possess the will to strike have the power. They fear him because he is mighty; but I can tell you that I, the Red Sheikh, the terror of the arid plains, am more feared, and, above all, more obeyed."

Jack scarcely knew how to reply.

He would have asked about Hassan, but somehow, although he kept up his proud spirit, he felt a strange sensation of awe creep over him when he gazed at the robber chief.

The caravan and all its belongings was now in the hands of the Arabs, who having overpowered or slain all who offered them opposition, were now plundering the tents.

Jack's heart beat wildly as he gazed on the scene around him.

Heaps of slain and wounded lay in all directions, and a strong guard was placed over the prisoners, who were marched out into the open, where they came bound with their own sashes, camel ropes and chains.

Whilst Jack took in this scene with a sickening and saddened heart, the pirate chief uttered a cry that startled him.

"There, my young inflexible," said he. "Look! Yonder is one of my mounted bands, my desert rangers, my rovers of the plains. Now bethink you what chance you would stand in putting your hand against mine."

Arab Jack cast his glance in the direction indicated by the sheikh, and then beheld a single horseman bearing a blood-red flag on his lance scouring towards them across the plain. Behind him came a dark moving cloud, which seemed to follow him like a wall. Jack soon made this wall out to be an enormous cloud of dust.

As it drew near he could dimly discern just within the sand-cloud a number of horsemen, twelve abreast, with their pennoned lances, following at full speed the single rider.

CHAPTER XXIII.

HASSEN-EL-AHED AND THE BLUE RIBBON.—
BROUGHT AGAIN TO LIFE.—THE RED SHEIKH
AND THE SACRED TREASURE.—ALI LOBAH,
THE TREACHEROUS GUIDE, IN CHAINS.—
BOUND TO THE DROMEDARY.—A DEATH
RIDE ACROSS THE DESERT PLAINS.

"THEY will be here shortly," said the Red Sheikh, alluding to the approaching horsemen. "Such steeds as they have come of no common stock. They are all females, and I fear not to back them and their pedigree against any others of the plains for any stake—even to that of my own right hand."

"That's a heavy wager," said Jack, eyeing him closely.

"It is; and as my right hand is more precious to me than the right hand of the Sultan is to him, you may judge that I make no idle boast."

"How is that?" asked Jack.

"Because it is with this right hand I control my desert subjects and maintain my power as king. But, there, if you accompany me to the pavilion, I will talk a few matters over with you there. Come on."

Our hero paused.

It galled him to be invited to his own tent.

The Red Sheikh, noticing his hesitation, gave a light cough, and like magic a dozen desperate-looking ruffians, with red fez caps, on which were emblazoned, in burnished silver, the skull and crossbones, appeared from various places and surrounded Jack.

This quiet but unmistakable hint was, our hero considered, sufficient.

"Lead on," said he, at the same time looking first about him, and then at the chief, as much as to ask if there was any luggage for the cross-boned ruffians to carry.

Not one muscle of the Red Sheikh's visage moved. It seemed to be carved out of stone.

Arrived in the tent, the sheikh requested Jack to be seated.

"Now, boy," said the sheikh, "as I have no time to waste, let us to business at once. Your friend, lieutenant, or whatever you term him, is as sound as a rock. In him we see the folly of wine-bibbing. Can we wonder at its being forbidden in the verses of the Koran?"

Jack was too disgusted to reply.

Not only disgusted at Hassan so far forgetting and lowering himself, but at the manner in which the chief spoke.

By this very manner he had no hesitation in pronouncing the sheikh not only a traitor, but a crafty, designing wretch; for he little doubted that the supposed leech had wound himself round Hassan during the journey, and given him the wine, which must have been drugged.

And now Hassan was bound hand and foot; and in very mockery of the prostrate man a blue scarf was tied about his neck.

"You see," said the robber sheikh, pointing to him "he has adopted the Blue Ribbon. Now I will give him an antidote to bring him to, so that he may give us some of his experiences!"

Jack felt very much inclined to hurl something at the sheikh's head, his words stung him so to the quick; but prudence warned him to refrain.

The robber chief then took from the folds of his turban a small stoppered bottle, and opening it allowed a quantity of smoke-like vapour to exude from it, after which he placed it beneath the nostrils of the snoring man, and afterwards to his lips.

Whatever the phial contained, it was so strong that Hassan returned to consciousness with a scream of agony and a start. Then his eyes opened, and he glared about him with the wildness of a madman.

"So I am here. Yes. Ah—this is the tent; but—but——"

He paused suddenly as his eyes rested on the red dress of the giant robber, and a cry of mingled horror and execration escaped him.

"Ah, the Red Sheikh; the terror of the Lybian desert; the despoiler of a thousand caravans; the — the — the — fellow-plunderer and confederate of Zobehr Pasha, than whom no greater rascal, I can vouch, ever existed."

The robber sheikh listened patiently to this effusion.

With bowed head and arms folded across his massive chest, he surveyed Hassan, who made desperate efforts to free himself, whilst the sweat oozed so plenteously from him that one would have thought he was lying on the heated plate of a furnace.

Jack's monkey began to rise again when he saw his friend Hassan struggling like a lion in the toils.

Turning to the Red Sheikh, he defiantly said :—

" Sheikh, what is the meaning of this outrage? Are you not satisfied with plundering us, but must also add this glaring insult to our injury?"

" Aha ! " laughed the robber. " You have seen nothing of my prowess as yet. I have not ordered your shoes to be taken off and the bastinado applied. I have not had you hung head downwards and flogged upon your bare back while your body dangled in the air."

" Hold ; that is enough," cried Jack.

" And," continued the sheikh, tauntingly, " I have not had you chained to a post and flayed alive inch by inch."

" Nor would you ever do so," exclaimed Jack, now strung to the utmost tension. " You have seen something of me ; but you have not seen all of the young mahdi."

" Quite true. But if through your insolence I am compelled to place you in chains, you will rue it. As to your drunken companion, I think he is cared for well. He can do no harm to himself or others while he is so tenderly nursed."

Arab Jack would have replied with a stinging retort, but the breath was nearly knocked out of him by feeling himself suddenly seized from behind and held in a strong, vice-like grip.

Two burly Arabs, at a signal from their chief, had slipped through the arras at the entrance of the tent and clutched him in such a manner by the shoulders and wrists that our hero was as powerless as an infant.

The Red Sheikh then walked to the other end of the pavilion, and drawing aside his blood-red flag, which was hung to the canvas wall, disclosed the treasure-chest, which he drew into the centre of the tent.

" Herein," said he, " is the treasure intended for the high priests and dervishes. It is mine now ; but as I mean to deal fairly with you, I will give you each a portion, and a couple of horses, so that you can go on your way in peace, and we shall cry quits until we meet again."

It took the sheikh, with his sinewy hands, but a few moments to open the precious casket, and whilst his eyes glowed with eagerness to catch sight of the bags of gold dust which he expected to find there, he raised the lid.

He gave a start, and turned almost pale when he gazed into the silent depths, for placed on the top were a few light bags, and the bottom was filled up with heavy stones.

This sight produced quite a shock to his system, and made him grind his teeth.

" Ha ! " he hissed, " either you or the Madhi have been here first. See, the gold is gone, and naught but stones and sand fill the place of that and the jewels."

Jack was astounded, but he hid his feelings under a quiet laugh ; whilst Hassan, who had thrown off his refractory behaviour and quieted down, gave a perceptible chuckle.

The Red Sheikh was terribly enraged.

He clenched his hands and invoked the curse of heaven upon the Madhi and his fellow-impostors.

" This is some juggling trick," he thundered, stamping his broad camel-like feet on the carpeted floor. " By heaven !——"

" Curse on," interrupted Hassan. " The prayers of the ungodly are registered in Islam. This jugglery, as you term it, is only the justice God's prophet, Mahomet, has meted out to you."

But the desert robber was not so easily pacified.

His business needed payment, and that payment was plunder, but now he was sold.

" Away with your cant," he yelled, " and your dervish mummeries. Did I not when on the plains of Kordofan, at the grand durbar called by Mahomet Achmet, see this treasure trunk lined with the most precious stuff, whose price would have paid the ransom of an Eastern prince, and is it not now transformed to a worthless bauble, than which the meanest package of baggage in the train is more precious ?"

" It appears so," said Jack (who was himself no less astounded at the transformation), as the sheikh threw down the two small bags that chinked, and emptied the stones upon the carpet.

" But," he added, " the transformation, as you term it, must have taken place here. And if I judge rightly, whilst the treacherous attack on our peaceful caravan was being made."

" Liar, infidel," roared the sheikh. " Had Ali Lobah, the accursed outlaw and treacherous guide, had his own way I must have confessed that it might be so, but he has been from here ever since the ships of the desert cast anchor on the sands, and returned again only in time for me to make him prisoner."

" Is he your captive," gasped Jack. " 'Twas a ball from his matchlock killed the hospitable sheikh."

The Red Bandit smiled archly and bit his lip.

" Hospitable " he hissed. " Yes, his hospitality was to take your gold, cut your throat, and then steal the very horse from under you."

Before Jack could utter another word, Ali Lobah was led into the pavilion. His clothes were blood-stained, an ugly gash nearly blinded his left eye, and heavy irons were upon his ankles and wrists.

The irons on his wrists were connected (by a chain rove through a ring) with a broad iron belt which was riveted round his waist.

The irons on his ankles were connected with the ring attached to his waist, and so constructed that on his attempting to escape, or even run, he could be thrown on his face without a moment's warning.

The outlaw scowled horribly when he met the accusing glance of our gallant hero. He seemed as if he would have given the world if he only possessed the power of sinking into the sand or rendering himself invisible.

As yet he had not seen Hassan, the dervish of the caravan. Coming in out of the glaring light, he did not observe him in the shadow lying on an ottoman.

" Well," said he, glaring fiercely at the robber chief, " now I am here what do you demand?"

" That you will give me the true history of this charmed treasure."

" What know I of it, a poor captive, a condemned sinner, against whom the very stars of fortune have set their faces, and against whom Mahomet has closed his ears and eyes ?"

" Would that he had closed thine eyes against this sacred casket, " thundered the Red Sheikh. " Had I more substantial proof that you are the plunderer I would have my executioners hack thee piecemeal. Eh, thou mayest frown. These stones are from the mountains of Ta-el-Raber, at the foot of which we camped on our second day out, and there the change was evidently effected."

"If so I know naught of it," exclaimed the outlaw, savagely. "Either you have been duped or I have been made the scapegoat of the foulest villainy."

The robber sheikh laughed.

Foam stood on his lips, and his eyes fairly blazed with fury.

"Again I say one of us must lie, and if I could discover the culprit Allah's own power would not screen him from the torture."

"Take him away," he added, motioning to the guard, some half dozen Tartar-looking rascals armed to the very teeth. "Take him away."

"Whither to?" queried the captain of the guard, bringing his sword to the salute, and bowing deferentially.

"Let him be tied to the fleetest dromedary ; set its head across the desert to the west, so that the outlaw may have a ride for life."

Ali Lobah ground his teeth with rage.

Such a ride across the desert was worse than ten thousand deaths.

He saw before him all the horrors attendant upon such a journey, and his stout frame shuddered.

"Sheikh," said he, "I am too proud to crave for mercy, or even to ask one favour at your hands. In store for me I already behold the scorching sun searing my very brain, the tightened thongs cutting into my swollen flesh, the pain intensified by every jolt and step of the beast bearing me onward like the wind— and——"

"Say on. Your speech falls upon ears that are as stone. Speak out and let these know the delightful paradisical dreams of a death-ride over the desert."

"I have already spoken," replied Ali Lobah. "I need not add that thirst, hunger, and the fangs of the maddened wolves will be my lot, but I wish you to remember how you terminated your journey after such a terrible ride, to which you were doomed by the Mudir of Dongola."

The Red Sheikh started.

"Allah," he gasped, "what has put such a fiendish thought into your brain, such words into your mouth?"

"Your loving mandate," hissed the outlaw, sarcastically. "Do you remember the branded felon, all in rags, who cut your bonds and liberated you from the maddened brute who would have crushed you in its dying throes?"

"Hold—cease," gasped the frenzied sheikh.

"Do you remember who shared with you his gourd of water, and how you gulped it down your parched throat, muddy though it was, and blessed him as your saviour and benefactor?"

"I do, and the very thought sears my brain like red-hot irons. But what has this to do with thee? Away with him, bind him to the dromedary and let him go free."

Ali Lobah, upon whose broad black brow the sweat of agony stood out like shining beads, gave a groan, and attempted to struggle with his captors.

But his efforts were futile if not feeble, for by a sharp jerk of the chain his arms were almost dislocated at the shoulders, and he was dragged away.

"One rival the less," gasped the robber. "Would

that all my enemies were as completely in my power !"

The Red Sheikh then motioned two of his servants to replace the stones in the leathern case ; then he ordered Hassan's release, and the front of the pavilion was drawn wide open by means of silken cords.

In that brief interval Ali Lobah, the treacherous guide, was strongly bound to the back of one of the fleetest and freshest dromedaries.

He was placed on its back with his upturned face exposed to the withering rays of the burning sun, and his naked limbs smeared with honey, as an invitation for the wild bees to settle thereon, and firmly lashed down to the sides of the maddened beast.

One cup of brackish water was then poured on the culprit's parched lips, and then the snorting beast, goaded by a dozen pointed spears, bounded with lightning fleetness over the barren plain.

Jack and Hassan gazed upon the terrible sight with fevered brows and firmly-compressed lips, gazed until the huge beast, leaving a cloud of dust behind, grew less and less, until it was but a speck, and then distance rendered it imperceptible.

"Now," queried the merciless chief, "what think you of that ? Remember that he who sent one could, if he so willed it, send a hundred on the same journey over the barren, pathless track."

"I see nothing miraculous in so cold-blooded a feat," Jack replied ; "should you serve us so it would only betray the demon that like a serpent lies coiled round your callous heart."

The sheikh was silent.

He evidently expected some such answer, and so would not trust himself to reply.

But that silence was but as the calm that precedes the storm, and Jack saw it in his looks ; but the brave boy's mind was not intuitive enough to foresee the troubles and horrors that were yet in store for him.

CHAPTER XXIV.

THE NIGHT MARCH OVER THE SILENT DESERT. —IN THE FASTNESS OF THE RED SHEIKH. —HOW JACK DECEIVED THE ARAB SOLDIERS. —IN THE JUDGMENT HALL OF THE ROBBER'S FORTRESS.—JACK WITNESSES THE HORRIBLE TORTURES INFLICTED ON THE UNFORTUNATE CAPTIVES.

IT was a beautiful starlight night. The full moon rode majestically in all her splendour in the clear blue sky as the cavalcade, which reached fully half-a-mile, wended its silent way along the trackless, sandy path.

Arab Jack, though somewhat cast down, endeavoured to amuse himself with the sublimity of the scene.

It was almost as light as day, and the varied hues cast by the knolls of sand and undulations which stretched away on either side as far as the eye could reach filled the mind of our youthful hero with a myriad of contending thoughts.

Strange sounds mocked the stillness of that calm, clear night—the almost noiseless tread of the elastic hoof of the camel, or the unshod hoof of the graceful Arabian steeds and mules, broke gently on the ear, with weird effect.

IT WAS A TERRIBLE RIDE. *p. 72.*

This was occasionally varied by the tinkle of a distant bell, the harsh clash of a sabre scabbard, or the still harsher voice of one of the Arab guards, whose quick eyes instantly detected the least irregularity in the line of march, and as speedily corrected it.

Jack, owing to the indulgence of the terrible chief, who secretly doated on the brave and daring boy, rode on the sacred camel, seated on a luxurious downy cushion, which yielded to every motion of the stately, graceful animal.

But Jack was in chains, and that galled his proud and haughty spirit keenly.

Unlike Hassan, who rode on a piebald dromedary, he was not so easily moulded to the will of fate.

He envied the dervish the pleasure he seemed to extract from the long-stemmed pipe, with the stolid and complacent demeanour of an emir seated on his divan.

Jack's long train of thought was suddenly broken by the Red Sheikh's voice as he rode noiselessly to his side.

"Boy," said the sheikh, "we are now travelling towards my citadel, where splendour reigns, next to myself, and happiness such as you have not witnessed for many a day abounds."

"What of that?" queried the haughty boy. "What pleasure can that impart to me when like a caged eagle I am chafing here in chains?"

A pained look crossed the features of the stalwart chief.

"I have a tiger here to tame," he muttered, "a tiger to whom I see no way of approach either by indulgence or the sword."

"Then why have these chains?" he said to our hero. "Were they not of thine own choosing? Have I not offered thee liberty and ——?"

"At what price?" thundered Jack.

"On easy terms," answered the pirate, coyly. "I have offered you a captaincy in my army, and slaves, male and female, shall wait on thee. Thou shalt have wives the most lovely and concubines the most charming if you will but take the oath and join my standard."

"And sell my soul to eternal torments," cried

Jack, frowning darkly. "What motive have you—for certainly you must possess something of that kind—in offering me all these ? "

"Simply a fancy. A strange infatuation draws me to thee, a fascination which I can no more resist than the peaceful llama can resist the charm of the deadly cobra."

"But you can repel."

"Aye, I can repel it, as you say, but I would not. To do that I would have to lower my princely dignity and crush you as I would an offending worm."

The Red Sheikh spoke with such fierceness and firmness that Jack, if their meeting had taken place in London streets, would have shivered and shook like an aspen.

As it was, a kind of devilry seemed to possess him, and caused him to delight in toying with the terrible chief.

That the chief could have crushed him, as he described it, like a worm, he never for one moment doubted.

That he could halt the caravan there and then and have him stripped and flayed alive there was no disputing.

But Jack, having discovered that he possessed that mystic charm which held the proud, puissant chief in thraldom, resolved to strengthen it by maintaining that obduracy which he knew so well how to assume.

Hassan, who rode at a respectful distance, and yet within earshot, was both astounded and alarmed. He expected no less than to see the sheikh raise his powerful arm and fell Jack, crushed and bleeding, to the earth.

Even as a man, and knowing the Red Sheikh of the desert as he did, evidence of which we have seen by the excited speech made by Hassan in the tent when he awoke from his drugged sleep, he would not have dared to utter such words.

Had the hands of the dervish been free, and his sash bristling with pistols and dirks, he might have opened his mind freely to the puissant robber, but then even it would have been at the risk of his life.

At a word from the Red Sheikh, a hundred scimitars would fly from their sheaths and hew him to pieces, or as many bullets would riddle his body as if they had been fired at a target.

And yet Jack evinced not the slightest fear.

He complacently asked the sheikh for a drink of goat's milk, adding :

"My lips are parched with replying to your unholy temptings, and my companion in durance vile must be as scorched as the sands beneath us through listening to your hellish offering."

The eyes of the Red Sheikh fairly flashed with indignant fire as the words fell upon his astounded ears.

A strong feeling of resentment rose within him, and he experienced an almost unconquerable desire to fell the audacious boy from his lofty perch.

But he was held by a sort of superstitious fear, which resulted only in his eyeing the boy mahdi with ineffable scorn and riding away.

The fierce Arab guard then re-formed in their previous close order until a couple of slaves appeared, each one carrying a couple of chased silver-mounted drinking-horns.

"Yah, sar," said one, holding the vessels above his head as he trotted alongside to keep up with the long, measured strides of the sacred animal. "Here's wine and milk, which you please. Yah, yah, sar, it am berry good."

Jack was really parched ; but for all that he made his selection very cautiously.

He smelt of both, returned the wine, and drank the milk with evident relish.

Hassan, however, was not so particular.

He partook of both, and drained the horn goblets to the dregs.

The consequence of this was soon apparent.

Both wine and milk were drugged, so that both recipients at once turned drowsy, and fell forward upon their saddles in a state of utter helplessness.

When morning dawned they were both as fast in the arms of Somnus as if they had had no sleep for a month, Hassan quite edifying the mules, who cocked their long ears and verily believed that a sojourner from Jerusalem of a similar class was regaling them with a specimen of his somnolent music.

The cavalcade was now heading towards a long range of cloud-crowned hills, whose summits, like pinnacles, seemed to pierce the very skies, and here and there the ground before it appeared rocky and broken.

This added to the rocking motion of the stalwart quadrupeds ; but Jack and Hassan slept on undisturbed, and, in fact, never woke until the caravan halted at night amongst those very hills.

The change of air aroused the sleepers simultaneously.

A brisk, bracing breeze swept down one of the gorges, rustling the broad palmated leaves of the date tree and the tamarind, which grew there in refreshing beauty amid the coffee plant, the gum acacia, the grape-vine, the light mimosa, the giant cactus, the prickly pear bushes, and the green patches of maize or Indian corn.

"Truly, I am in paradise," muttered Jack, as he opened his eyes in wonderment and alarm. "Why—why—where are those camels going to with all that baggage ? They seem to be swallowed up in the very heart of the mountain."

Jack could not make it out to see them led up to what appeared the solid face of the rock and then suddenly disappear, without so much as an "open, sesame " or a "good-bye."

But he had a hundred things around him more marvellous still.

The place was a fastness formed by Nature in the centre of lofty mountains which towered away in the distance, and had been evidently improved upon by the hand of man.

On one hand was a mosque, with its marble dome and whitewashed minaret.

On another, the turreted roof of a splendid palace, surrounded by a garden enclosed in its high red-and-white brick wall, and a fortress built of massive unhewn stones.

In one valley, on a ridge at the foot of which ran a foaming torrent which descended from the mountains, there were a number of neatly-built Arab mud huts, with children playing about the doors, and women engaged in various house-work or shaping arrows.

But what startled our hero most was the living freight of the caravan, who were drawn up in lines on a flat, rocky space in front of the fortress, over which floated the terrible banner of the Red Sheikh.

The banner was of blood-red silk, with a broad inner border of silver, in the centre of which, worked in silver cord, was the dreaded emblem of the robber sheikh—a skull and cross-bones.

Jack looked from it to Hassan, and from Hassan to the brown-turbaned slaves who tended their animals, and he was about to make some remark, when suddenly a flourish of trumpets awoke the echoes of the rocks and set every heart thumping at the vastness of the sound.

" Here he comes," cried Hassan, spontaneously. " Look out for squalls, Jack. I guess we are in for it now for the manner in which you cheeked his excellency."

" I don't care," replied Jack ; " I shall cheek him again. It may be all very well for him to play his tricks on slaves, but I can't see how he can stand to treating free-born personages worse than serfs."

" Don't you ? Then ask him. Here he comes, and I daresay he'll fall on his knees and beg your pardon."

" He'll have to before we shall be friends," echoed Jack. " But here he comes, as you say, and the coward's actually put on his armour."

So he had.

The Red Sheikh was now wearing a cuirass of chain mail, which shone like burnished silver, below which the skirts of his kaftan or Arabic dress looked peculiarly strange, being blood-red, like the silken banner, and heavily hung with silver braid.

His head dress, a sort of turban, was also immensely rich. A hundred precious stones of various hues adorned it, and a costly feather sticking straight up in front was held in position by an immense star formed of diamonds, and set in a brooch of solid gold.

He was surrounded by his head councillors, all superbly dressed, and everyone armed, and preceded by the band, which made every rock vibrate with the clash of its cymbals, the beat of the tambourines and drums, and the brazen music of its sound-lunged trumpeters.

Without deigning to look at Jack, the sheikh passed on from his palace into the castle, the gates of which were thrown open by the costly-apparelled guards, who when the retinue passed in again, closed the gates and issued some order to the captain of the watch tower, whose loopholes commanded the gates and the open space in front.

The captain of the guard-house, thus adjured, walked at the head of his twenty men straight up to Jack and Hassan, whom he ordered to dismount, and having looped up their chains, desired them to follow him.

He led them then into the tower, showed them a large vaulted room, which was evidently hewn in the solid rock, and pointing to a large stone bath, through which there was a constant flow of water, desired them to perform their ablutions.

Arab Jack, as may be naturally assumed, took every precaution on such occasions to conceal the white portion of his flesh.

He now gave the soldier strict injunctions to close the curtains, and rewarded him with a verse of the Koran, written on a leaf of the paper tree, which the Arab accepted with much glee,

and as a natural consequence showed it with awe and rapture to his fellows.

This had the same effect upon the ignorant Arabs as General Booth bestowing his especial benediction on one of his flock would have upon the rest of his hoodwinked followers.

The keeper of the bath was blessed beyond all mortal conception, for the boy mahdi and his dervish had smiled upon him, and he had actually been able to place his hand upon the hoof and gaze into the eyes of the sacred camel.

It was well, therefore, that Jack was thoughtful enough to guard the colour of his skin, for the menials who held office in the Red Sheikh's castle were as inquisitive as those who hold similar situations of trust in other castles.

In fact, they had peepholes in the arras, and they waged a quiet war with each other to get a glimpse of the inspired pair, the imprint of whose feet, like those of Paul and Peter, they expected to see left in the stone of the flooring.

It was well, too, that Jack and Hassan let not one word drop that was likely to betray their secret.

When they had done, and perfumed according to the custom of the castle, Hassan struck the gong, and a bevy of attendants rushed in, each one eager to conduct them to the large hall where the robber chief, surrounded by his retinue in their rich warlike panoply, sat in state to give judgment upon offenders and reward those who had done him signal service.

The Arab ushers threw off their sandals at the door of the judgment hall, a signal to the slaves working the punkahs, or large fans, to pull the silken cords by which the arras was raised to admit the hallowed guests.

Following the chief's eye, they ushered Jack and Hassan to one of the richly-covered divans, upon which Arab Jack and his friend soon mounted by the damask-carpeted steps, and seated themselves cross-legged, as demure and as comfortable as any brace of tailors.

The Red Sheikh was the only one covered, head or feet, before Jack and Hassan entered, and they would have been looked upon to do the same, only that their saintly calling excused them from this ; and after a deal of salaaming and other jimcrack formulæ, such as we see in our own courts of law, the business commenced in earnest.

The brazen band, seated in a raised balcony, ceased their noisy labours when the great gong announced that the culprits were to be led in, and silence reigned from the tesselated floor to the gilded roof as the surviving pilgrims of the sacred caravan were placed in order, according to rank and age, before the stern law-giver of the plains.

A dozen or so wise men with rosaries or strings of beads round their necks, squatted near the chief, by means of which beads they calculated the age, the probable wealth, the enormity of the crime committed by the accused, and the ransom that should be set upon each head.

All this was entered by the recorder or chief scribe, who squatted on a slightly-raised hassock, in his huge book, which rested on his knees, and when all was settled to the sheikh's satisfaction and the utter discomfiture of the pilgrims, especially the slave-dealers, they were led away to their cells or dungeons, as it might be, formed in the cavities of the rocks.

In this manner all were tried, and a set sum placed upon every head, the consequence of which was that the camel-drivers and slaves, who possessed nothing, were confiscated body and soul, and entered in the book for the slave market.

Some of these, however, had black marks against them.

They were accused of telling lies, refusing to deliver up the small store of valuables they had concealed about them, and furthermore with offering a stubborn resistance to the Arab robbers when they made their first attack.

For these and other crimes, therefore, they were to receive corporal punishment, and when the time came a large red curtain travelling on a brass bar with rings was drawn aside, and the culprits were handed over to the executioners.

Our hero now for the first time beheld the manner in which the bastinado was administered, and the sight he saw was one never to be erased from his memory.

A dozen or more burly blacks, naked as they were born save for the yard of brown calico twisted around their loins, with hair cut short, clean shaved, and their skin greased, so that the culprit might have no chance of grappling with them, stood ready to carry out the sentence which the chief scribe read out aloud from his book.

Not only the dropping of a pin could have been heard, but the fall of the ostrich feather on the bare stones was audible in the death-like stillness that reigned when the voice of the chief scribe ceased.

This was the signal for the executioners to commence.

With ready hands they seized upon as many of the culprits as they could, stripped them, and with knives notched for the purpose, hacked off the moustache, beard, and hair of those who wore it long enough for them to take hold of.

This torture, let alone the disgrace caused by such a disfigurement, was enough to wring tears from the eyes of the victims, who clenched their teeth and bit their lips to restrain the cry of agony that was by these means endeavoured to be extorted from them.

Then, naked as they were, they were thrown down on their faces, their necks enclosed and fastened in clamps of wood, their ankles secured the same, and a weight placed in the hollow of their backs, so as to curve their bellies down to the cold floor and bring their feet into such a position in the stocks as to incline the soles a little upwards.

Then an executioner taking his place on either side, one with his long supple rattan grasped in his right hand, and the other with it in his left, commenced the long, powerful, swinging strokes which soon produced on the tender soles hard weals and lumps, the pain of which drove the victim to a state bordering upon madness.

As four victims were thus operated upon at a time, it thus left four of the ebony monsters to look after the culprits' hands and prevent them using violence upon themselves by choking their windpipe and such like during the frenzy produced by the excruciating torture.

To have heard a cannon go off, much less a feather drop, would have been impossible amid the yells and screechings which were extorted by every blow, and as the eight blows were given almost in the space of a second, the five minutes that the punishment lasted rendered the place a perfect pandemonium.

Jack's heart sickened at the sounds and the disgusting sight ; but he bore up under the severe trial remarkably well, and strung his nerves to witness the punishment of the next batch without showing any outward appearance of being unstrung or moved to compassion.

CHAPTER XXV.

FURTHER TORTURES INFLICTED BY THE ROBBER SHEIKH.—ARAB JACK IS BROUGHT BEFORE THE SEAT OF JUDGMENT.—THE THREAT.—A NARROW ESCAPE.

ARAB JACK had such a specimen of the bastinadoing that his own feet began to tingle uncomfortably before it had ceased.

How the poor writhing wretches put on their sandals or crawled away he never knew, for when all had received their complement the curtain was again drawn, and a different class of offenders were put forward to receive chastisement.

Many of these were the jellubs (slave dealers), whose crime was concealment of worldly treasures, such as diamonds and so forth, which they had concealed in their neatly-braided hair or sewn in their garments.

For such a crime the punishment code of the mighty sheikh was terribly severe.

"The prophet's blessing" it was named, and was supposed to represent his coffin suspended in mid-air, as it is declared to be in the tomb in Mecca.

The very simplicity of this mode of castigation, coupled with its high-sounding name, made Jack shudder.

The chief executioner, whose head, wrists, and ankles were adorned with broad white bands to give effect to the solemnity of the scene, stood under the centre of the dome-shaped roof, and stretching his hands upwards as if in the act of prayer, he gave three low claps, in answer to which a fine thread-like cord descended slowly from the roof.

Whilst this mockery was going on, the executioners were preparing the victims by stripping them to the waist, and as only one could be performed upon at a time, owing to there being but one rope, the others were allowed the privilege of standing by and looking on.

Our hero, although he fain would have been away, was at the same time anxious to learn what this holy punishment could be.

He was soon enlightened.

Mahoud Akan was the first name called out, and as he toed the spot where the name of Allah was inlaid in the floor, one of the naked blacks crept behind him, laid a back, as a school-boy would describe it, and another of the executioners catching him by the feet threw him backwards over the stooping body of the black, thus making him a sort of see-saw.

Whilst in this position, which nearly took all the wind out of the wretch's body, the chief executioner, who held the looped end of the rope, formed it into a hitch, and having passed it over both feet of the culprit and drawn it tightly round his ankles, clapped his hands.

At this signal, with magical precision, the rope tightened from above, the culprit was drawn feet upwards, his head going with a sweep within an inch of the stone floor, and then he was raised in mid air about three feet clear of the ground.

There were no bonds to restrain his liberty, only the one hitch which held his feet together in the fine cord of Italian silk which suspended his quivering form in mid air.

The shriek that burst from the agonised wretch was enough to pierce the most callous heart, even though it might be of adamant or stone, and the violence of his agony-wrought throes made every muscle and sinew perceptible as it stood out in bas relief upon the surface of the swarthy flesh.

But this was nothing compared with what was to come.

As the shriek of agony died away, the inverted form became still as death, the blood having probably flown to the brain and thus produced insensibility, which the executioner soon counteracted by placing some strong aroma to the victim's nostrils, which restored him again to misery and to life.

"One !"

What a dull sickening thud !

What a horrid brain-seething yell !

It was the first blow from the basheeback, which the giant-like executioner held in both hands, and the ensanguined mark across the small of the culprit's back bore token of its being well applied.

The basheeback was a most formidable instrument of torture. It was about six feet long, with a broad thin blade of about half its length, and with a springy handle, made stout and firm so as to be easily grasped, with which the executioner could lay on from the weight of a heavy sledge hammer to the lightest touch of the downiest feather.

In the hands of a cruel monster, therefore, such an instrument was an abomination to the earth, although the Red Sheikh and his myrmidous regarded it as a delightful toy.

"Two !"

Again the well-oiled, heavy, supple blade fell upon the writhing flesh, and the victim swung to and fro like the bodies hung in gibbets on the heath when rocked to and fro with the pendulous motion imparted to them by the cold night wind.

"Good God," muttered Jack, as he ground his teeth to keep himself from crying right out, "Good God, is such torture considered more merciful than death !"

"Three !"

This time Jack heard the cry, and he nearly fainted.

The agonised wretch swung to and fro, and writhed with all the contortions of an eel when wriggling in agony on a hook.

If Jack could have had his will he would have put a stop to the hideous work at once.

He felt half inclined to spring up and face the cruel monster who by nods and inclinations of his jewelled turbaned head signalled the executioner when to strike.

Jack's idea when the last blow, number four, was struck was that the culprit's back was broken, but when he was lowered down no apparent notice was taken of this by the torture fiends.

Swooning, but with every nerve convulsed, the miserable wretch, more dead than alive, was thrown across the broad shoulders of one of the incarnate fiends, and like Ananias of old, who was struck dead for withholding part of the purchase money and telling a wilful lie, he was carried out.

Jack was so horrified and dazed that he scarcely knew how the others got on until he heard it announced that all were punished.

"Thank heaven," he fervently muttered. "Oh God, how can such wretches live and breathe the breath of life !"

Our hero, nevertheless, was pleased when he found that the hideous ceremony was ended, but he was very much surprised when the armed attendants of the so-called hall of justice approached him and bade him step on to the floor.

And he was still more astonished when, with brain reeling and his eyes filmed with the sights he had beheld, he was led into the dock which the former prisoners had occupied.

"Now, boy," said the chief, addressing him in the politest terms acknowledged in the flowery language of the Arabians, "you have seen what you have seen, heard what you have heard, and if you collect your thoughts you will probably be able to answer whether you have committed any of the crimes and transgressions that have been brought against the culprits whose light punishment you have witnessed."

Jack felt very much inclined to scratch his head.

"Light punishment !" he mentally soliloquised. "If that is light punishment for crimes only one-tenth part of those I have committed, I must sing small, for I don't believe that I could pass through such terrible ordeals without being fairly cracked up, or at the very least most seriously broken down."

The robber chief, with that keen perception which is only to be gained by hard-bought experience, read his thoughts in a moment.

"To a susceptive mind like yours," he said, "there is no greater punishment than leaving you to your own conscience. Guilty or not guilty, I discharge you with a caution and a promise that if you are brought before me at any future date the past and the present will be weighed in the scale with you and assist in turning the balance against your would-be innocence."

Jack stood abashed.

He could make no answer, neither could he frame his lips to speak.

He bowed submissively to the chief and those who sat in judgment upon him when the robber sheikh exclaimed :—

"Prisoner, stand down."

Jack was totally astounded to hear such words uttered in the mountain fastness of the great desert.

He could scarcely believe his ears.

"I must be asleep and dreaming," he muttered, "or am I reading some famed story of the 'Arabian Nights?'"

He took the opportunity of pinching himself to ascertain whether he was asleep, in a trance, or whether the circumstance was actually real.

The Red Sheikh suddenly evinced symptoms of alarm.

"He is working some miracle," he thought, as he eyed the daring boy, and remembered the wonders he had achieved. And as he looked he fancied he could see the strength of a Hercules in his bright curly hair.

The more he looked the more he imagined that the gallant youth grew up before him into a colossal statue.

Then he pictured to himself in his magnifying eye Jack, as a modern Samson, carrying away the massive gates of his castle and dislodging the columns that supported the cumbrous stone-work that formed the entrance.

Without a thought of what he was actually doing, he gave the signal for the court to close, and made a sign to the astonished servitors, who were still gathered around the astonished boy.

Without a word the men obeyed the silent mandate, and raising Jack on their shoulders bore him into the cool night air, where he instantly recovered. And our hero, Arab Jack, was once more himself again.

CHAPTER XXVI.

JACK AND HASSAN IN THE BANQUETING HALL OF THE PALACE — A STRANGE ADVENTURE — JACK LEARNS THE SECRET OF THE BEAUTIFUL SLAVE GIRL—PLANS OF ESCAPE—THE SERPENT CREEPING IN THE CORRIDOR.

HOW changed the scene. In the banqueting hall of the robber's palace all was joy, and happiness reigned supreme.

There was no festive board; but Jack and Hassan were privileged with small inlaid tables, which were spread with white cloths, and tended by slave girls of the rarest beauty.

Jack was quite charmed, and being blest with a good appetite, he did justice to all the good things, of which there was no scarcity, and even indulged in a portion of camel's hump, which was served up in real Oriental fashion.

There was wine in plenty, too, for those who chose to drink it, and, sad to say, those who refused it were few indeed, whether they were believers or unbelievers.

As to the sheikh, although he invoked the aid and blessing of Allah before partaking of each course, and made free with the prophet's beard every oath he took, he poured the wine down his thirsty throat with the ease and avidity with which a thirsty camel takes in its stock of water.

Our hero, when the eyes of the sheikh's retainers were not upon him, ventured an unholy draught, and he found it cheered his heart and made him both musical and merry. This delighted the pirate sheikh. He actually called upon Jack for a song, and he would have given them the "Battle and the Breeze," or something in that style, had not Hassan given him a dig with his elbow, which caused him to have a stitch in his side.

The sheikh, however, was not to be daunted. When the dishes were cleared away, and the dessert and hot coffee brought in, he ordered the band, which had been playing a soft lullaby sort of a tune all the while, to desist.

"Most noble guests," then said he, "if you do not object I will summon my dancing houris, who will sing and play to you until your very souls shall feel as if they are beating against the door of the highest heaven."

"Amen! Allah be praised!" burst from the lips of all, and the more especially from a small party of merchants, whom Jack instantly recognised as passengers by the holy caravan.

"Hang you," thought Jack. "Why you old sinners, you pretended to be the most devout of all, and now you are going in for the carnal as heavily as the greatest infidel."

But Jack with all his cuteness, was not in the secret.

These very merchants had under the cloak of religion undertaken the journey; but in reality they cared no more for the prophet's shrine than Jack did.

They took very little with them, and hoped to pick up a cheap lot of something that would sell well in the Soudan; and now having lost the little they possessed, they were hostages for themselves for a large ransom, the papers and signatures for obtaining which they had drawn up, signed, and given to the brigand sheikh.

Having lost in that way, they, therefore, were determined to get all the fun and pleasure they could for their money, and loudly they seconded the Red Chief's proposition.

Two slaves then entered with armfuls of pipes, and others brought hookahs, which they carried on silver salvers and placed by the side of the chief.

Two men then brought in the tobacco in a large porcelain vessel with handles at each side, and the beautiful slave girls who tended the feast commenced filling the bowls, and having lighted them from little oil lamps, handed them to the various guests.

Jack was almost afraid of the tobacco; but the winning voice of the lovely girl who tended him, and her coaxing way, soon made him decide to try a chibouk.

The wine was now working its effect on my young hero.

He laid back and stretched out his legs, putting his feet one over the other in the most easy and un-Mussulman-like manner, when the slave girl called him to order.

"Massa Arab, no do that," she said, in her sweet child-like voice. "It looks berry bad. See dere, squat like dat."

Jack could not help bursting out into laughter.

The anxious girl, fearing he might be noticed and probably snubbed for his breach of Oriental etiquette, put her plump arms around him, raised him up, and set him in the proper position.

Jack in all his travels never had had such attention paid to him before by the gentler sex.

When he felt those soft, yielding arms round his waist and her soft, glowing cheek touched his he was enraptured.

"By golly, Zela," said he, "if ever I have money enough to buy you I will make you my wife, and——"

"Shut me up in de harem same as sheikh does his wives. No, no; Zela rader be de slave or de concubine. Zela like plenty fun—plenty freedom."

Jack, elevated though he was, was astounded. The idea of a slave calling herself free was to him very much like a joke.

"Come here, then," said he. "Sit down here and tell me a fairy story. I shan't care much about the singing and dancing if I have some one pleasant to talk to."

The dancing girls were now on the carpet, and very handsome they looked as they played their tambourines and moved gracefully around in time to the gentle cadence of the lute or the sharp click click of the castanet.

"The Red Sheikh might well describe them as houris," thought Jack. "What busts, such slender waists ; what graceful limbs and delicately-turned ankles !"

The slave girl watched him with her soft, gazelle-like eyes.

"You like dem," she said. "Now tell me which one you love best ? "

Jack was puffing away at his long chibouk with all his might and watching the lovely dancers through the gauzy smoke.

"Love !" replied Jack, turning to Zela with one of his handsome smiles. "Well, if I loved one I should love the lot ; but priceless though they must be, I would not give the whole bunch for one such as you."

The eyes of the slave girl glistened, and she threw her arms around our hero's neck.

"Dere, den," said she, giving him a soft, rapturous kiss, as he took the pipe from his mouth for fear the large amber mouthpiece should choke him. "Dere now, Zela love you all she can."

"That's queer," thought Jack. "All she can, eh ? Perhaps there is another lover in the road. I'll just try her, for, by Jove, I was never so much enraptured with a girl in all my life, and if we were together long I fancy I should have to court her."

"How is it you can't love me altogether, Zela ? " said he. "If you were to love me so, you see, it would make us both happy, as we are both prisoners, and can't get away."

"Hush !" whispered the girl in terror, her soft bust throbbing against Jack's shoulder. "Speak low ; I want to tell you something if you listen."

"Yes, yes ; go on," whispered Jack, who was growing quite feverish with excitement.

"Hark ! You are captive ; want to get away ; Is dat so ? "

"Just it ; if I could do so without losing my head."

"Well, I hab lovers—two. One no good. One very good, brave, fight plenty, love much ; but he away ; prisoner, Cairo."

"Oh ! I am growing interested."

"Yas. His name Ababa ; and if he no come back Zela die."

"Of course. But that is not all, is it ? "

"No ; dere is one more, Ambri. Bad man, plenty house, money, very rich, plenty wives. He want buy me for his harem."

"Oh !" said Jack, opening his eyes. "Now I see."

"Yas. He want buy me. I no want. Sheikh take money ; say I go to-morrow."

"Against your wish, eh ? "

"Yas. Him no ask me no more. Him come, like all bad man, at night. Me wish me a man, den me cut him troat."

Jack gave an inward wince, and drew suddenly back.

"It's not very pleasant to have such a lady near one's throat," he thought ; "but I fancy I can see my way clear to turn this to my advantage."

He then placed his arm around her, drew her to him, and allowed her to toy with his silken hair. At the same time they were holding a conversation that was dear to both of them.

No notice was taken of this, for courting was the order of the hour, each guest sharing his seat with one or two dark beauties, and the sheikh having quite a bevy around him.

In the meantime the music still played, the dancing still went on, and songs of exquisite sweetness mingled in.

This, of course, deadened the sound, and prevented one amorous couple from hearing the conversation of another, which suited Jack admirably.

"Now," said he, when he found they were all in full swing, "what you want me to do is this —cut Ambri's head off when he comes."

"No, no ; then we all be killed. Me want you to be Zela—savey. He take you away in the dark. Den you be free, and he leave Zela here with her sisters."

"Ah ! You mean you would rather wait here with the other slave girls until Ababa comes ? "

"I do. Can we not manage ? Me find you clothes—ebery ting."

"I'll have a try at it," said Jack ; "if I don't hang me. Give me another kiss on the strengt of it, and teach me how to fondle, my rapturou lover."

That night the robbers' revelry was not only kept in the palace, but outside in the tents, in the huts, and in the lieutenant's quarters at the castle, a strong guard, however, being kept in all the ravines that led to the secret entrance to the stronghold.

Arab Jack, when all the revellers were drunk or sound asleep, found no difficulty in creeping from the banqueting-hall of the sheikh's palace.

Guided by the dark - skinned beauty, he traversed many of the gloomy corridors and secret passages, and actually paid a visit to the large, sumptuously-fitted chamber where the girls lived and slept.

It was an immense vault, draped with costly hangings, lighted on the top by skylights of coloured glass, heavily barred, and secured against ingress or egress.

Round the sides were numerous cells or rooms in which several slept together, and heavy crimson curtains covered the entrances thereto.

Zela led him into one of these, and showed him several ladies' suits, one of which fitted him exceedingly well, and having instructed him in the mysteries of the toilet, she showed him the place from which the slave girls who were sold or exchanged were supposed to be stolen.

"Stolen," said Jack, "eh ! Then they don't sell you as they do the slaves in the bazaars ? "

"Not openly ; the sheikh dare not. He stole me from my home when I was a child, and therefore, he has no claim properly upon me."

"Has he no papers, then ? " queried Jack.

"Yas ; him hab papers. Make dem. Ambri take dem when he pay. Him also hab pass to stronghold, and come here while I wait catch water, and lift me on horse, ride away."

"Good !" emphasised Jack. "He shall have something for his money. Now, another kiss, Zela, my darling. Lord bless you ! I do believe that I am just about beginning to like you."

Zela was good for a thousand kisses, especially when it purchased her freedom from one whom she thoroughly detested ; but just as she glued her soft lips to those of the noble boy, she gave an involuntary start.

Glancing over Jack's shoulder, she espied a dark figure gliding stealthily as a cat towards them.

Slipping her left arm, which was round Jack's neck, down to his waist, she, with a strength Jack never thought her capable of, wrenched him backwards, round, and pushing him violently into a dark closet, silently closed the door upon him.

Then she drew a small dagger from amidst the folds of her robe, and flattening herself against the wall, stole sideways towards the creeping figure.

As she approached it she suddenly made a spring, and grasping the sneaking cur by the throat, held the dagger over his left breast in line with his heart.

"A-A-Al-l-lah !"

The word was gurgled out in a manner which showed that the sneaking wretch was either choking or was half-dead with fear.

"Who are you ?" hissed Zela, pouring her hot breath into his ear.

"A-A-Al-lah !" gasped the wretch again. "Mahoud."

"Dat me know to be false," whispered the brave girl still more fiercely.

And without another word she pressed the point of her dagger through his scanty garment until it pierced his skin.

The affrighted Arab could have yelled out for very terror, but he was afraid to, for he had overstepped his bounds in his attempt to make some wonderful discovery, and thus rendered himself liable to chastisement.

The sneaking wretch, nevertheless, was quite right in his surmise in the first instance, for he fancied he saw a male figure, which he actually did, owing to the reflection cast by a coloured oil lamp.

But when he found that soft, plump, but sinewy hand clasp his throat, and hold him as tightly as if the fingers were a bow-string, he began to fancy he must have made a mistake, for the voice, he knew, was a female's.

A good shake, and a thousand interjected apologies, and he was gone, very much to the relief of our hero Jack.

"Allah be praised !" said he. "I thought I should be stifled in that hole. What place is it, for goodness sake ? "

"Dat prison for bad gal slaves," replied Zela, smiling. "Not berry nice ; smell much nasty."

"I should think so," said Jack. "Whew ! the odour of dead cats and pickled scorpions seems to have settled in my throat. Here, Zela, we did not finish that kiss."

"Dere ! Gib you anoder bimeby. Bad Arab with gun watch us."

"Hokey !" whispered Jack. "I must creep back again to the hall, then. It won't do to spoil our little game. I'm determined to change my sex this blessed night."

Daylight was breaking then, and as Jack, led by the girl, made his way back to the dissipated company, he fancied he saw a grey-clad figure following stealthily in their wake.

CHAPTER XXVII.

THE SLAVE GIRL'S STORY.—HOW THE CRAFTY MULEY ABON GOT CAUGHT IN HIS OWN TRAP. —THE GRAVE GUESTS OF THE RED SHEIKH GET A STARTLER.

OUR hero on returning to the banquetting-hall saw such a scene as made him long for freedom more than ever.

Upon the divans the half-drunken and drowsy guests lounged in all manner of postures, whilst the slave girls in attendance upon them fanned their heated brows.

"Allah be praised !" muttered Jack, sanctimoniously ; "the fumes of the forbidden wine hath raised them all to ethereal blissfulness, and our absence hath not been perceived."

"Zela," he whispered to the slave girl, "what has become of our lordly sheikh ? He is not on the daïs where we left him seated, and those two heavenly beauties who fanned him so gracefully are now folded in each other's arms asleep."

The slave girl was about to reply, when a slight movement of the arras that concealed one of the secret entrances arrested her attention.

"Look !" she whispered, giving Jack a meaning wink ; and the artful pair dropped down and pretended to be fast asleep.

Jack's head was in the shade, and his half-closed eye was as active as that of a lynx as he watched the rustling of the agitated damask, from the folds of which a black, close-shaven head soon appeared.

"Humph," thought our hero ; "that nut looks as if it were carved out of a solid block of ebony. I'd like to crack it. And what eyes ! One would think they belonged to a ferret."

Then a figure draped in a long sable vestment reaching down to his knees, and girded at the waist with a cord similar to that of a monk, glided in and crept towards the divan on which Jack was, and which during his absence had been moved a little from the cushioned wall.

Jack had not noticed this change.

He was not aware that the thing was movable, and as the cushions had been rearranged he had no suspicion that the divan had been tampered with.

But soon he became cognisant of the black's artful strategy.

Stooping down, the wretch raised the heavily-fringed crimson valance, and dropping on his knees, insinuated his fat, flabby form between the furniture and the wall with an ease that perfectly astonished Jack, and assured him that the intruder was no novice in such work, and laid himself down beneath the cushion that concealed the opening between the furniture and the wall.

"All right," cogitated Jack. "You are there, old fellow, and as I am certain you are after no good, I'll make you wish yourself out of this before many minutes are over your ugly head."

He could tell exactly where the fellow was ensconced by the subtle motion with which he wriggled into his place, and so, giving a long, drowsy yawn, Jack shifted himself right on top of the fellow's head.

"Allah, it is awfully warm," muttered our hero, as if talking to himself in his sleep. "I feel almost choked, I do."

Then he touched Zela's shoulder with his toe, and they both gave a satisfied grin.

"Him one bad eunuch," said the girl, as she crept up to our hero's side and whispered in his ear. "Him blackmail me ebery time we meet in dark."

"In what way?" whispered Jack, his bright eyes flashing indignantly.

"Him kiss me, and him great flabby lips I hate. He no dare look at beauties in sheikh's harem, but me him say he doat on, and he squeeze, kiss and slobber me all over."

"Right," said Jack. "I'll slobber him, the blubber-faced old villain. Come, hitch up higher, and just recline your delicate figure on his blooming windbag."

Zela was not very well versed in Jack's schoolboy vernacular, but she comprehended what he meant, and so imitating a yawn similar to that of Jack's, she settled her plump little figure on the most obese portion of the wheezing eunuch's anatomy.

Our hero and the delighted slave girl had quite a pantomime to themselves after that.

They could hear the crafty wretch puffing and blowing like a stranded porpoise, and every now and then struggling to get breath.

"Go it, old un," muttered Jack, just loud enough for his companion to hear ; and when the eunuch made the least effort to free himself he put on an extra pound, and nudged Zela to do the same.

In this manner they enjoyed themselves until the eunuch had sworn and spluttered himself almost out of breath, by which time the mellowed light streaming in through the ground glass windows overhead made the coloured lamps grow dim.

It was now ten o'clock by the massive timepiece which stood on a raised daïs at the eastern end of the hall, the face of which had till now been screened with a delicate curtain of green and gold.

Suddenly a loud boom, produced by the deep-toned gong which hung in the minaret of the mosque, awoke the sleepers, warning them to perform their ablutions and get ready for midday prayer.

This reminded our hero that it was Friday, the Mussulman sabbath, on which day all Mussulmans, especially those of note, go to the mosque to pray, and afterwards visit their harems.

The chafing eunuch, too, had extra duty to perform in the harem also.

He therefore coughed, sneezed, swore, and prayed to himself by turns, for he was afraid to move lest he should disturb our hero.

As the boom of the gong ceased its vibrations the slave girls took up their fans and repaired to their own apartments, and Zela having snatched another sly kiss and whispered in Jack's ear, followed suit.

Jack then with the mischievousness of a monkey settled himself down as heavy as he could, and motioned Hassan, who was aroused by the gong, to join him.

This he did, and Jack having told to him the fun, they both bumped on the eunuch with all their might, which conduct almost flattened the guilty wretch, and elicited from him a groan not unlike the roar of a goaded bull.

Such conduct was more than the eunuch had bargained for, and was decidedly more than he could bear, so that he made desperate efforts to get free, and his tormentors allowed him to struggle into the centre of the floor.

The solemn-visaged guests, whose eyes were barely open, gazed on the strange apparition in astonishment and alarm, and many of them evinced signs of displeasure on finding a eunuch, whom they knew by his close shaven head, disgracing them by his presence.

The cringing wretch was certainly anything but a handsome ornament to grace any society.

His eyes were bloodshot, and nearly starting out of his head, while his bald pate and ebony features fairly reeked with perspiration.

The look he gave our hero was angelic in the extreme.

Revenge and murder were written at once in that very glance.

As he shuffled away with his bare slipperless feet, he muttered threats of deadly vengeance, and later on dogged the footsteps of Jack and Hassan as they walked in the palace grounds.

The fresh air of the delightful garden, with its cool fountains, gravelled walks, and groves of cinnamon trees rendered it a paradise compared to the smoky hall.

Having sought the cool shade of a cluster of olives, Jack recounted to his friend all that passed between him and the slave girl Zela and asked him what he thought of the projected escape?

CHAPTER XXVIII.

A SNAKE IN THE FOLIAGE.—JACK CIRCUMVENTS THE TRICKY EUNUCH AND SELLS HIM A PUP FOR HIS PAINS.—OUR HERO CHANGES HIS SEX AND VISITS THE BLACK GIRLS' HAREM.

THE dervish listened gravely to Jack's recital, and then muttered a fervent thanksgiving.

"My boy," said he, "you have been within an ace of losing your young life—you have been on the very threshold of his lordship's harem, to violate the sancity of which is instant death, and the more so if he were to discover that you are a Christian."

"I can't help that, Hassan. The longer I remain here the more danger I incur. I want freedom, and I mean to have it at any risk."

"Do so, then. But I warn you that your life is in jeopardy at every step, and let me warn you that if your plot fails you will be put to a most agonising death."

"I don't care ; I shall chance it," emphasised Jack. "One may as well die a good death as a half-and-halfer."

The rustling of a leaf startled Hassan.

He glanced hurriedly round, but he could see no one, and then he led Jack hurriedly away.

It was well he did so, for the crafty eunuch, Muley Abon, concealed by a cluster of flowering shrubs, was creeping snakelike towards them, and his big ears were open and ready to drink in every sound.

He hissed like a serpent, and ground his yellow fangs as he watched Jack and Hassan ascend the marble steps leading to the entrance of the palace, and muttered a curse when the sheikh, clad in his vestments of crimson and gold, met them in the grand hall and saluted them.

The Red Sheikh was in wondrous good humour.

He had been enabled that day to make a costly offering to his patron saint, for which the priest, an arch-dervish, as we might call him, gave him an extra blessing and a promise of further success in his daring exploits in the future.

Jack took immediate advantage of the sheikh's hilarity.

"My lord," said he, bowing gracefully, "you seem as happy as those lovely plumaged birds, whilst I am pining like an eagle in captivity."

"How so?" asked the chief.

"Because I have not the license to roam about this vast territory at will, and also because you have dishonoured me by depriving me of my sword."

"Allah! if that is all that ails thee, I will make thee whole at once. Follow me; I will return to you your weapon, and allow you to range my fortalice on your parole of honour."

"Allah bless you," answered Jack, bowing until his head nearly reached his knees, and laughing within himself enough to split. "Then your servant will be happy and his heart once more merrily sing."

"That gladdens my heart," said the sheikh, who secretly hoped Jack would relent and become one of his chosen followers. "You shall accompany me to-day and witness a review of my desert troops."

"Thank you," replied Jack, "I accept your offer with glee."

Having sumptuously supped, the grand party, well mounted, rode to the distant valley far up in the mountains where the review was to be held, and the sight Jack beheld accorded well with his proud, martial spirit.

The display both of horse and foot was simply grand, for the robber sheikh spared no expense in mounting and arming his men.

The Red Sheikh watched the brave boy's sparkling and dilated orbs as they followed the manœuvres of the Arab horsemen, who on their powerful steeds performed such feats of arms as perfectly astounded him.

"Now," said the sheikh, "can I not induce you to swear allegiance to my noble standard, the blood red field and the bleached cross bones?"

"I will think it over," said Jack, evasively. "The sight is marvellous—so grand, it dazes me. In fact, I feel so indisposed that I still have to crave the indulgence of a few hours' repose on return to the palace."

"With all my heart," replied the sheikh, little dreaming of the artful dodge that was working in young Jack's brain.

Arrived in the courtyard Jack threw himself out of the saddle, and sinking into the arms of his Arab attendant desired him to lead him to his chamber.

This he did, and also summoned a leech, who at our hero's desire mixed him a strong sleeping potion and left him.

"Good," said Jack. "Fortune favours me thus far. Now for Zela, the disguise, and so forth."

As he cogitated thus, a faint shadow flitted along the opposite wall, and on turning his head a little aside he just caught sight of a dark figure gliding behind the curtains of one of the windows.

"The eunuch, by Jove!" muttered Jack between his clenched teeth. "I am right glad I caught sight of the skulking hound."

Throwing aside the quilted down covering the leech had placed over him to induce perspiration, Jack sprang to the floor, and without uttering a word strode over the yielding carpet and clutched the curtain with both hands, taking hold of the eunuch as well in its folds.

The discomfited wretch no sooner found himself thus trapped than he struggled desperately to be free, but Jack held him as if in a vice as he hissed ironically in his ear:

"Now, my black bauble, you have chosen your own setting; you have got into the finest straight waistcoat you could have done."

So saying, Jack held the eunuch's arms close down to his side, and with a sudden jerk, having caused the curtain to fall, he tripped the astounded black and rolled him over and over until the curtain presented the form of a ball.

"Well done, Jack," gasped our hero, drawing a deep breath. "Now, I must get the rascal on to the couch, give him the draught, and let him——Oh, not this time, my joker. You are not going to get away."

The eunuch by some means managed to get his head free, and was about to raise an alarm, when Jack dexterously seized the drugged potion, and nipping the eunuch's flat nose between his finger and thumb compelled him to swallow every drop of the noxious dose.

"There now, if that don't settle your hash before midnight I'm no true Mussulman," Jack said, as he deliberately seized the cords of the curtain and gagged and bound the terrified eunuch in such a way that he could do nothing but roll his large eyes.

Jack had all a job to raise him on to the couch; but he did it, however, and covered the patient up so carefully that any one might have imagined that Jack was a nurse.

"There, my dear, you've had one draught; and, by Allah, you shall not get another. A slight touch of cramp in the arms won't hurt you, though. And a rumble in your stumjack will do you good.

"There, there," added Jack, tucking the quilt tightly around the mummy-like form. "You can sleep for a thousand years now and no one will come and disturb you."

"Wa-hu-wah," was all the enraged eunuch could articulate, and Jack, with a light laugh, and mimicking a kiss, left him to vent his spleen at leisure.

"I must be cautious," Jack muttered, as he entered the marble corridor and descended the massive stairs. "I'm glad I fixed that sneaking rascal. I wonder where Zela is to be found?"

As if in reply to his thoughts, a secret panel at the foot of the stairs opened, and the slave girl's smiling face appeared.

She evinced no surprise at seeing our hero; but stretching forth her heavily-ringed hand drew Jack into the opening, when the panel again closed, and the pair were in darkness.

Jack, as may be supposed, felt rather strange in his novel situation. But his heart yearned for liberty, and he cared not what risk he ran or what sacrifice he made to attain it.

He felt awkward, nevertheless, when his companion informed him that he must change his raiment for female attire; for to talk about it and to practise it are two widely different things.

As it was dark, however, he speedily banished all reserve, and having changed his own clothes for those Zela brought with her, he secured his knife and yataghan, and donned the splendid head-dress which she gave him.

Zela then led him along several dark passages and down a staircase, when opening another door by touching a spring, they found themselves once again in the light.

"Dat good get up. You make splendid gal," said the delighted maiden. "Now put dis to fill out," she added, snatching Jack's turban from his hand and thursting it into the loose folds of the breast of his corset.

"I reckon I'm all a swell," said Jack, eyeing his richly-brocaded dress, and his trousers tied round the ankles, his pink silk stockings, and his sandal-shoes. "Now then, what's next? Remember the time is fleeting, Zela."

"Me know dat ; me anxious as you," replied the girl, who now that the time was drawing nigh was all of a tremble. "You must go into bedour where Zela's sisters sleep and wait until you are sent to catch the water."

"I'll do all that," said Jack, giving her a farewell kiss. And then pressing one of the golden petals of a beautifully-flowered column, as Zela directed him, a portion of it slid open and disclosed a spiral staircase that led into the chamber of the dark-skinned Hebes.

To say that Jack was awfully confused was a mild way of describing his feelings. His face flushed, and a strange sensation crept over him when he found himself in the presence of a dozen or so of the sisterhood.

Believing him to be Zela, owing to the head-dress he wore, and still further deceived by the mellowed light, several of them threw their soft arms around him, fell on his neck, and began to weep.

"This is warm," thought Jack. "How the dickens I am to go through this ordeal is a puzzler. I shall be glad when the old hag comes, for I can't stand these melting moments much longer."

In the midst of this scene, the old hag alluded to put her head through the curtained door, and showing her two yellow fangs that hung over her lower lip to their greatest advantage, called harshly on the name of Zela.

CHAPTER XXIX.

ARAB JACK GIVES THE OLD HAG A PILL.—
JACK'S VIGIL AT THE DRIPPING WELL.—
THE ABDUCTION OF OUR HERO AND THE
DISCOMFITURE OF THE VILLAINOUS MOOR.—
A WILD RIDE.—IN THE CAMP OF THE
EGYPTIANS.

ARAB JACK, with an outburst of well-feigned grief, tore himself away from the weeping beauties, who too well knew the meaning of the alabaster pitcher and the visit to the dripping well.

They had lost many of their sisterhood before, girls around whose memories their loving hearts were still entwined; and as Zela was their favourite, the heart and soul of their very existence, it is no wonder they so much regretted her going.

Jack was so well versed in the part he had to play that there was not one hitch until the old hag, with her well-practised suavity, handed him the pitcher, and bent forward to give him a kiss.

This was more than Jack under any circumstances could possibly stand.

Up rose his fist, and smash it went into her eye, making the stars to scintillate in showers and her head kiss the wall.

Two minutes later Jack was at the fountain, over which an inscription in Arabic informed him that the water, which dripped about a cupful in a couple of hours, was the tears of the prophet Mahomet, under whose influence all the sins and cares of the world would vanish as the darkness disappears before the rising of the sun.

"Good," said Jack, as the twilight closed in with Oriental suddenness, and left the alcove clothed in the sable vestment of night. "How awfully still it is. Why my heart beats faster than this steady drip, drip, which is enough to drive a fellow out of his mind."

Jack's ear was strained to the utmost tension. He was actually comparing the number of his own heart's pulsations to the Tantalus-like dripping of the font, when a soft step behind him caused him to turn, and he was about to utter a cry of surprise.

But before he could do so, the silk folds of a vestment were thrown over his head, strong arms were clasped about his waist, and he was raised from off his feet and borne swiftly away.

Then a sickening sensation crept over him, his limbs were suddenly robbed of their strength, his senses gradually left him, and he was at the mercy of Ambri, the ruthless abductor.

When our hero awoke to consciousness, he knew by the motion that he was on a jaded steed, which was making its way laboriously over a stony plain.

The covering was partly removed from his brow, upon which the cool air played. Strong arms held him, a hot breath scorched his cheek, and lips that even in his state of semi-consciousness appeared loathsome, pressed his own.

It took some seconds for Jack to fully comprehend the novelty of the situation in which he was really placed.

When he did, however, he quickly formed his plan of action.

Just as Ambri, the amorous Moor, saluted him again with his lips, and pressed to his own guilty breast the swelling bust, as he supposed, of the beauteous Zela, Jack threw up his arms and clasped him vice-like around the neck.

Then, before the astonished libertine could recover from his surprise, Jack bent himself forward, and exerting his whole strength reached the ground with his feet, and with a touch of the rein brought the horse to a standstill.

Jack had still one arm round the neck of the foaming Ambri, and with this he held him, as it were, half unhorsed, while he struck him in the mouth with such force as laid open his upper lip and caused him to swallow several teeth.

But the Moor was a stout built, powerful fellow, and nearly double the size of our boy Jack, which our hero had good opportunity of observing.

Therefore Jack had to use his wits, wrench himself from the wretch's grasp and draw his yataghan from its concealment to defend himself with.

Half blinded with rage, and smarting with pain, the Moor struggled desperately to free himself and regain a firm seat in the saddle, but Jack cut the girth and over he went, saddle and all, on the rough stony ground.

Jack's life was in deadly peril then.

"Curse you," hissed the Moor, as he sprang instantly to his feet. "I have been sold, and bought a Tartar. Take that! Thus I end the life I purchased with my gold."

Our hero sprang aside, for in the blindness of his passion Ambri would have cut him down, although it was evident he was not yet aware of the full extent to which he had been deceived.

He certainly discovered that the features before him were not those of the girl who held his heart captive, but never for one moment suspected that he had been lavishing his endearments on one of his own sex.

He was soon to be enlightened, however. Jack as he sprang aside and allowed the Moor to be carried forward by the impetus of the blow saw that the rowel of his spur was entangled with one of the stirrups, and the check thus given to him caused him to stumble.

"Waugh."

Scarcely was the word uttered when Jack was upon the Moor's back, and bringing him down on his knees struck him with the diamond hilt of his yataghan such a blow as stretched him bleeding and half-stunned upon the rugged ground.

"Now," said Jack, kneeling beside the prostrate form, "I must borrow your pistols, take care of what cash you have about you, and look after your horse."

Ambri could only groan, for the massive diamond had indented his skull, and blood was beginning to flow.

"Good day," added Jack, when he had secured the ruffian's long silken purse. "May Allah preserve you and teach you to be grateful to Arab Jack for thus graciously sparing your life."

Weak and in agony as he was, the Moor opened his eyes in astonishment, and endeavoured to get a view of his youthful conqueror, but Jack, anxious to lose no time, bowed gracefully to him and leaped on the back of the steed.

Jack's next thought was in what direction to bend his course; but in this matter he was not allowed so much as even a voice.

The beautiful grey mare scarcely felt him touch its back, when it gave a whinnying neigh, a tremendous snort.

And then with the hot breath streaming from its blood-red nostrils, its gracefully arched neck curved, and lashing its flanks with its long silken tail, it bounded away in the direction of the distant hills.

Jack had only time to fix himself firmly on its back and dig his heels into its quivering sides when it was off, fleet as the wind, whirling the sand up with its feet and driving it as it were before it.

The heart of our hero leaped with boyish excitement at every bound as the spirited Arabian steed cleared every obstacle in its path.

Onward, still onward, over the desert, with Jack clinging for dear life to both bridle and mane, whilst the perspiration poured from him and the showers of sand thus thrown up and whirling around him filled his throat. ears and eyes.

Jack had no power to speak.

He could hardly get breath, for if he opened his mouth it was only to take in a gulp of hot burning sand, so fine and yet so penetrating that it seemed to even enter the very pores of his skin.

It was a terrible ride!

Hour after hour it continued, and though every hair of the quivering creature was bathed in sweat, and its nostrils poured forth steam and its lips emitted flecks of blood-tinted foam, yet it gave no signs of relaxing the terrible pace.

Jack, nevertheless, began to feel that it was getting too much for his youthful frame.

The blood flew to his head, his lips, throat and eyes were dry and parched, his muscles were growing stiff, and the atmosphere was such as made him feel that he was in a fiery furnace.

"I can stand this no longer," he murmured, as he gave an involuntary gasp, and thought his last moment was come. "Good heaven! save my life. I die—die—I am dead."

As he in imagination uttered the last word, the foam-flecked steed was brought to a sudden halt, the form of Jack was saved from falling by the timely intervention of a stalwart pair of arms,—he was hugged more tenderly than before, and a hundred rapturous kisses imprinted on his parched and bloodless lips.

On this memorable occasion Jack was, however, spared his senses.

That is, he was conscious of being borne some distance into a tent, placed on a camel skin mat and having his head propped up with a roll of something soft for a pillow. Then water was poured between his lips, and there was a murmuring of confused voices all around, when opening his stiffened eyes he discovered to his surprise that he was in the encampment of a party of Egyptian soldiery.

Jack had only supposition to work upon, and from that he inferred that the tall Egyptian in the uniform of an officer in a favourite regiment of Arabi Pasha's, who was bending over him, and tendering the water to him, was the one who had wasted so many kisses over him in mistake.

"Well, my little Nubian queen," said the officer, chucking our hero familiarly under the chin, "what old parchment-visaged Arab sheikh have you taken in and bolted with his steed, eh?"

"None," said Jack, rising on his elbow. "That mare is mine, I won it in fair fight. But I see you belong to the Egyptian army."

The Egyptian laughed, as did also his companions.

"A nice little houri for our harem you'd make," said he, "if Arabi would only allow his brave troops to have one."

"I would make a better heirloom," said Jack, sarcastically. "Do you call yourselves brave soldiers, and deserving of the smiles of the fair, when you take a full blown double-moustached young Arab lad such as I am for a Nubian damsel?"

The Egyptian officers stared; and when Jack pointed out the very slightly perceptible fringe of down on his upper lip, they raised a laugh against the colonel, who pulled at his own long twisted moustache as if it had been a bell rope.

One officer just for a joke took up his field glasses and examined Jack's features, just as if he were in action taking a view of the surrounding country.

Jack's face was of the pure Nubian tint, for Zela had anointed it with the sponge with which the dark damsels obliterated any light-tinted spots they might have about their arms and neck, and upon this dark shiny surface the tiny hairs showed up, just like stubble in the harvest time, against a dark ground.

This, of course, raised another laugh, although it did not account for our boy hero's feminine

"ASSASSIN ! I ARREST YOU IN THE NAME OF THE KHEDIVE." *p.* 79.

disguise, which was well set off on his tall, graceful figure with the swelling bust which the amorous colonel had so gently squeezed against his own stalwart breast.

Jack joined in the mirth ; but suddenly recollecting that he had a mission to perform which necessitated his maintaining a manly bearing, he put on a serious look, and said :—

"Allah preserve us. Are the Egyptians and Copts, who boast so much of their ancient temples, more ignorant than the white-faced infidels who come from their homes across the sea to eat us ?"

"Ah," said the colonel, "where did you hear of this ?"

"It is well about, my people are not ignorant. I have a message from our mudirs, emirs and sheikhs for Arabi Pasha."

"Good ! We are on on way to Zagazig, from thence to Tel-el-Kebir. You shall march with us, and on our arrival, mounted on your proud Arabian, we will announce you as the Egyptian Joan of Arc."

This was followed by boisterous peals of laughter, which burst from all the officers now assembled in the colonel's tent.

Arab Jack took out his turban and placed it on his head, an act which brought down a shower of chaff on the brave colonel, for the voluptuous feminine bust which he had pressed so tenderly to his manly heart suddenly collapsed.

Good humour, however, prevailed, cigars and cigarettes were handed about *ad lib.*, and the wine flowed more plentifully than water.

CHAPTER XXX.

THE ADVENTURES OF OUR HERO IN ZAGAZIG. —OFF TO TEL-EL-KEBIR.—IN ARABI PASHA'S TENT.—THE FAKIR PERFORMS A MIRACLE WITH THE SERPENT, AND PREDICTS THE DEFEAT OF THE ENGLISH.

"ZAGAZIG ! Thank God ! We have zaga-zigged about enough to get here. My knees ache like the very deuce, and I am as stiff as a shot rammer all over."

7

"What, with only a three days' march?" replied the soldier addressed. "There is no stint of that in Arabi's army; but of pay, grub, and thanks we have very little."

"But you have the glory," suggested Jack; "and look at the beneficial changes of air. Now what a relief this is, with its flowery plantations of cotton, the mimosa, the canals, and the bright green dhoura fields, after the broad sandy desert."

The Egyptian ground his teeth, and eyed our hero as if he would pierce him through.

"All this beauty," said he, "may be changed in a few hours if the accursed Ingleese with their white faces should get here. Look at Alexandria, how they burnt every place, and pillaged the palaces and the bazaars."

"You don't believe that," said Jack, warmly.

"I do. They blamed our own people for it, but it was a lie."

Our hero was about to retort.

Like a true British boy, on hearing his own country thus calumniously assailed, he felt inclined to throw off his disguise and declare himself.

Fortunately at that moment an orderly rode into the field where they were halted, and galloping up to Jack, informed him that the colonel awaited his presence in the town.

"Lead on," said Jack, turning the head of his prancing steed in the direction of the tall minarets and the white and yellow washed walls of the houses in the distance.

As they entered the main road, which had hitherto been hidden by a row of date palms, Jack was surprised to see its warlike aspect.

Trains of baggage camels heavily laden, and parties of armed Arabs dressed in various costumes, were pouring into the town, and droves of unladen mules were jadedly leaving it.

War seemed the only object upon which every one's thoughts were centered. The fields and the husbandry implements were deserted, and women with children gazed in trembling fear from the doors of the mud huts.

On entering the town the main street presented one unintelligible jumble. Arabs, Turks, Greeks, and a varied mixture of Orientals lounged wonderingly about or jostled each other as they scrambled out of the way of the lumbering camels.

Many of the shops and hotels were closed, and the fronts boarded with stout planks, or guarded by their proprietors, beneath whose long loose vests revolvers lay concealed.

"Here we are, sir," said the orderly, seizing Jack's horse by the bridle rein, "Jump down and make your way up there," he added, pointing to an upper window.

Jack was so stiff and cramped, that he waddled just like a goose into the hotel, and elbowing through the crowd and up the stairs, found the colonel seated in a room surrounded by several of his staff.

Spread on the table before him were papers, telegrams, and such like, which he having signed handed to one of his staff, who placed them in a valise, and then the colonel turned to our hero.

"You have a dispatch for the pasha," said he; "let me have it. I will forward it by my special aide to the capital. We then push on to Tel-el-Kebir."

"I would rather deliver it personally," replied Arab Jack. "I shall go to Cairo and place safely in Arabi's hands."

The colonel frowned.

"You will do no such thing," he said, sternly. "I have no orders to search you and take the missive from you, but I shall certainly order you under arrest if you attempt any nonsense."

"Then I have fallen into a hornets' nest, and am likely to fare worse than if I'd met with a horde of robbers."

"You will not be robbed, I have given you that assurance. You will be treated as a friend so long as you act friendly, and be trusted as one who bears a friendly message from the Soudan chiefs."

Jack was silent. Acting on the maxim that discretion is the better part of valour, he retired towards the door and watched with eager eyes the hungry group who requisitioned the trays of food as they were brought up by the attendants.

Following suit he quickly captured a thick lamb chop, peas, potatoes, and a foaming jug of beer, which he devoured with great gusto, declaring it to be a feast fit to set before a king.

He had hardly finished, when the captain of the troop warned him that the assembly had sounded, and very soon they were on their way through the town, had passed the railway station, and once more gained the open country.

Twenty-five miles of silent travelling brought them to the lines of Tel-el-Kebir, where Jack was introduced to the commandant, who received him in his spacious and magnificently-furnished tent, and subjected him to a severe interrogation, during which his turban was taken from him and every fold of it searched. In it the dispatch for Arabi Pasha was found, and the zealous commandant was just wavering as to whether he should break the seal, when Arabi himself was announced, accompanied by his brilliant retinue.

Observing the seal of the Mahdi on the package, his brow lowered and a terrible frown settled upon his features.

"Before God and the prophet," said he, concentrating his withering glance on the abashed commandant, "if you had broken that sacred seal I would have sent you to Cairo in chains, and imprisoned you in the fortress of the citadel."

"Welcome, brave youth," he added, extending his jewelled hand to our hero, and giving him a grip that made the water start from his eyes. "Be seated. Thus do I receive the servant of the true God, who bears good tidings from the Mahdi, who is the emir of the dervish of the Allah of my forefathers."

He handed Jack to one of the thickly-piled carpets, and then seating himself cross-legged on a cushioned daïs, he reverentially broke the holy seal.

Jack could not help laughing to himself as he watched the pasha's hypocritical saintly visage, as he perused the cabalistic characters of the mystic missive, the purport of which he kept to himself.

Three times he perused it, accompanying his reading with devout signs, which were faithfully copied by the fawning satellites, who stood bareheaded on his right hand and on his left.

"Allah Akbar," he at length cried out, "Allah is good, Allah is great, the arms of our army shall be victorious."

As the words left his lips, the folds of the entrance slowly opened, and like a vision the

Fakir of Tantah, one of the most fanatical cities of the delta, stood in the tent.

The sight of this holy man filled the whole assembly with awe, and the zodiacal signs on his tall sugar-loaf-shaped hat, and his long flowing robe, wrought so powerfully upon them, that they prostrated themselves before him, and bowed their faces to the earth.

"What a devilish old rascal," muttered Jack, as he bowed his head and covered his face with his hands. "I'll not fall down and worship any man if I know it. Why, I declare he is going to make believe he can perform the miracles of Moses."

Arab Jack was practising the school-boy trick of peeping through his fingers.

To his horror he beheld the head of a huge serpent protrude from the broad sleeve of the sage, and its motions were plainly apparent beneath the coarse grey serge, as it coil after coil unfolded itself from around his body.

Jack could not help shuddering as he watched its glittering eyes, its open mouth, and quivering sting, and its long black neck, which gradually stretched forth until its green scaly body reached the carpeted floor.

Then followed a scene which changed Jack's trembling fear into one of mirth.

"Hiss, his-s, hi-ss !"

At the strange unearthly sound every prostrate head was raised, and the worshippers sprang to their feet with a yell of terrified rage.

But the sage made a sign with his hand intimating that there was no need for any alarm, and taking the reptile, which was fully ten feet long, by the tail, caused it to coil itself about his body and around his neck, into which it seemed to dart its poisonous fork-like fangs

The cry of intense horror that this elicited from the spectators, who like their chief gazed at the hideous thing with wide staring eyes and open mouths, brought a host to the tent, thinking that something dreadful had happened to their favourite pasha.

And this startling cry, as the fakir desired it, was echoed along the lines, reaching to the outer forts and trenches, until it aroused the sleepy gunners stationed in the batteries and forts.

During this confusion and alarm, the fakir waved his hands, a loud detonating report ensued, then a vapourous cloud enveloped the form of the holy man, which cloud on clearing away disclosed standing upon his shoulder a long-legged bird with a body about the size of a pullet.

The feathers of the bird were of snowy whiteness, with a pale pink tint here and there, by which our hero had no difficulty in recognising the sacred ibis.

This bird at one time was worshipped with deep veneration by the Egyptians, who at its death actually embalmed it and placed it in their sarcophagi with their hallowed dead.

The sight, then, of this worshipped object claimed the respect of all, inasmuch as it fixed its orbs on the fascinating optics of the serpent, and so transfixed it that before it could use its sting the bird struck it in the forepart of the head with its long sharp beak so forcibly that its head dropped listlessly on its breast.

Then its green scaly folds relaxed, and with a thud it fell lifeless at the foot of the venerable priest.

This scene wrought a startling effect on the audience, who called upon the name of the Deity, and then listened breathlessly to the explanation of this wonderful symbol.

"My sons," said the aged seer, "by this sign shalt thou know that thine enemy shall be crushed, the infidel who hath brought his ships and war engines against thee shall be slaughtered or driven into the sea. Yea, even as surely as their General Wolseley and their Admiral Seymour are now languishing in the water dungeons beneath the fortress of Cairo."

Every head was then again bowed, and the sacred ibis disappeared.

After which the fakir uttered a benediction in a low, impassioned tone, and left the tent as mysteriously as he entered it.

After a well-measured pause the crafty Arabi then addressed his followers :—

"Children of the Nile, you have heard the words of the fakir, and witnessed his holy works. Let your voices ring forth aloud. Should the Frankish dogs venture to attack us let your swords strike home, your loud-mouthed cannons proclaim their doom, so that Egypt may be freed from the yoke of the infidel, whose blood thus spilled shall purchase for you the firman which shall open to you the gates of paradise."

Arab Jack listened to this fanatical speech of the rebel chieftain in ill-concealed disgust.

He knew by the excitement it created that every word would be echoed from mouth to mouth, and that it would lose nothing by the long distance it must travel, as it would be added to by those whose interest it was to din it into the ears of the Egyptian and Arab troops.

But what could the gallant boy do? "I cannot escape from this," he reasoned, "and if I could how should I reach the English lines to warn them? I know not in which direction they lay, nor upon which point of these impregnable fortifications they will commence to bombard, even if they, as Arabi anticipates, make the fatal advance."

Jack at that time had no idea of the sights he was shortly to witness, the terrible carnage, the fearful slaughter, and the hand-to-hand conflict in which he himself would have a share.

CHAPTER XXXI.

ARAB JACK IS PLACED IN THE EGYPTIAN BATTERIES.—HOW TO SPIKE A GUN.—JACK CLOSES THE JAWS OF A BRAGGING RUSSIAN. —NIGHT IN THE REBEL LINES.—THE ATTACK ON TEL-EL-KEBIR.

"SO I am in for it nicely, now," said Jack, as he stood behind the earthworks of Tel-el-Kebir, watching the setting of the golden sun. "To what cruel fate am I devoted? I am here a prisoner, and compelled to fight, in the event of such taking place, not only against my countrymen, but my queen."

Jack felt in his breast for his lucky sixpence, which was suspended by a silken cord about his neck.

It was there, and the very feel of it cheered his spirits, for it had once saved his life, and it might do again.

He had been placed by Arabi's order at the front, and in one of the posts most exposed to danger, if the English were bold and headstrong enough (as the Egyptians termed it) to attack.

"I can't see why he should wish for my death," thought Jack, as he reasoned the matter over in his mind. "I saw the postcript, signed by Osman Digna, which recommended me for the front in the event of war, saying that I would fight the very devil and stick to him to the death with my trusty yataghan if put to the test."

Poor boy, he little dreamed that it was Osman Digna who compassed his death, out of revenge for the disgraceful defeat of his eldest son.

Osman never intended his reaching Mecca with the caravan.

As a fact he was in league with the outlaw Ali Lobah, and it was owing to his influence that the treacherous rascal got appointed to the post of guide.

Osman Digna, however, had not the slightest doubt that our hero would reach Arabi Pasha, and deliver the secret and important message to him.

He had seen enough of the young mahdi's daring spirit, to assure him that he would not relinquish his trust without a deadly and desperate struggle.

But he had not the slightest inkling that the Red Sheikh, in the crafty disguise of a leech, had attended the Soudan durbar, and actually joined the caravan, with the presumed intention of leaving his burden of sins at the holy shrine of Mahomet, or he would have predicted the fate of the caravan, which had not the slightest chance after it once aroused the avarice of the desert robber.

"But, there, such is life," soliloquised Jack, replacing his lucky sixpence. "Up and down, in and out, and I must follow its rugged course without repining." ·

"Yet for all that," he mused, as he gazed over the smooth sandy plain, backed by the purple-tinted hills in the distance, "one must have their thoughts. Here I am a wanderer, a waif, wafted far from my home, and to-morrow, September the thirteenth, is the anniversary of my birth."

Jack gazed along the ramparts down into the trenches, at the lines of strong and seemingly impregnable earthworks behind him, and the multitude of white-pointed tents, with their gay flags, flaunting in the background, and wondered what the morrow might bring forth.

It was quite a sight from where he stood to watch the multitude of turbaned and fez-capped heads, some motionless, others moving restlessly about, and to listen to the suppressed murmurings borne to him on the soft evening breeze.

What were they talking about?

Of what were they thinking as with dark piercing orbs they gazed anxiously over the parapets and eagerly swept the broad plain?

"Kassassin," said one of the Arab soldiers posted near to Jack, "lies in that direction," pointing across the plain, which on the right was edged with the embankment of the Sweet Water Canal. "Methought I saw a horseman yonder just now."

"Most likely," said Jack. "If any Ingleese are there they are bound to be out shooting; this is the very month in which they commence their sport."

"Allah, dey no sport much if dey play here," interposed a black-moustached Arab, smacking his hand on the breech of the gun. "Me load quick, fire so ; smash him all to leetle pieces."

"Yes, you'd make him wink like," replied Jack, laughing, "make him Zigazag, eh, Kus-his-sins, and so forth !"

The swarthy artilleryman grinned and showed his ivory immensely.

"Me fight ships big ; shoot ebery one out of de water. You no fight Alexandria, eh ? "

"No, I was donkey driving then," said Jack. "Are you one of the brave warriors that spiked his gun ? "

"Ah, yes," exclaimed the Arab, gleefully performing the feat in miniature. "This what I do it with. Cussed Frank no fire him off 'gain den."

Jack carefully noted where he put the spike, and then there was a general straightening up as one of the captains came along.

He hummed a tune, and seemed perfectly satisfied with himself, as with his sword dangling at his heels he peered into every nook and corner to see whether each soldier was on the *qui vive*.

Soon after darkness closed in—darkness so intense that to our hero it was really painful.

"Hang the pasha ; whatever did he put me here for ? If they come I'll not fight against my own country—that be blowed first. But how am I going on if they run against this wall in the dark ? "

Presently Jack saw a glimmer, a small light in one of the pits, and its momentary flash shone on the features of a man lying down lighting his cigarette.

"Dash it ! I know that face," muttered Jack. "Where have I seen it before ? "

A moment later the individual, shading the ruddy glow, came and stood by the side of the puzzled boy.

"Ah, smoking better than fight," said he, tapping Jack familiarly on the shoulder. "Dey British no face cannon, eh ?—vot say you ? "

"They'd be fools if they did."

"Yash, dat so I say. Big fools fight in dark ; British no big fools, I tink."

"What's he aiming at ? " thought our hero. "He don't talk like an Arab, he seems like a foreigner. Hang it ! if I don't think this is the Russ I gave the licking to."

At that instant an extra pull at the cigarette caused it to glow and reveal to Jack a broad white scar across the fellow's nose, which Jack recognised as if by instinct.

"So you really think ill of the British ? " said Jack, imitating him. "Arn't they a set of ugly Black Sea robbers ? "

"Yash. Me see dem fight Sevastopol. Bad every way : me shoot all down like wild fowl. Yah ! dey no like good man shoot at dem."

"No fools either," replied Jack. "You good shot I s'pose ? "

"Oh vary ; if British come here now I knock all down. Yah ! Vot's dat ? "

Jack in the darkness had snatched the cigarette from his mouth and placed the lighted end next to his nose, which, like the cigarette, being of extraordinary size, made a blister on its tip as big as a greengage.

"What's the matter, are you hit ? " Jack said, restraining a laugh. "Why don't you shoot, you half-bred pomatum pot ? If the British do come I believe you'll melt and run like a hogshead of Rooshun tallow."

"No, no, me no run—me Russ. Me like big fight ; but me no like burning like Moscow."

"Take that, then," muttered Jack, giving him

a dig under the ear which sent him headlong into the pit he had just vacated.

There he lay like a mouse, doubled up in a corner, unheeded by the drowsy riflemen, who cared not so long as he fell clear of them.

That night seemed awfully long to our youthful hero.

As hour after hour dragged slowly by he felt sleepy; and as he knew not at what hour he was supposed to be relieved his position was anything but pleasant, and bred discontent.

" I never did care for a soldier's life," he muttered ; " I hate this hanging about, doing nothing, only watching this big gun. But I would not care so much if I was with my own countrymen or riding about with those horsemen."

Jack could hear the Egyptian cavalry, as they scoured along the face of the lines, and to these he alluded.

But his grumbling was soon brought to a close.

A loud rushing noise and the order to fix bayonets, shouted in his own mother tongue, startled Jack and awoke the whole army into life.

Drums beat, bugles sounded, a Babel of voices shouted their orders all at once, whilst oaths and prayers mingled hoarsely with the din.

" To arms ! to arms ! " yelled the Egyptian officers. " Prime, point, fire ! " roared the Arabian gunners.

" Aim true, fire low," was thundered by those in the advanced trenches and rifle pits.

But the rush, effected at the proper moment, was too determined for Arabi's troops to resist.

The British, like one solid body, closed and pressed towards the works as firm as a rock.

The thunder of cannon, the bursting of shells, and the roll of the rifle volleys, mingled with the sharp whirr and hiss of the rockets, was tremendous.

Along the three lines of Arabi's boasted Plevna vivid sheets of flame canopied by dense clouds of smoke flashed here and there and lit up the grandeur of the scene.

The fight was commenced in earnest, and the groans, cries and yells of the combatants were terrific.

Arab Jack was completely startled.

A bullet from the very first volley of the British struck his turban, and in such a manner did it envelop itself into the folds thereof that the impetus caused the dazed boy to spin round and round like a teetotum.

Bang ! bang ! bang !

Three of the guns in Jack's battery were fired off, as it seemed to him, at once ; but the fourth, which Jack had taken the liberty to spike during the darkness, was useless, and so was the gunner, for Jack had given him a blow with the rammer and stunned him while he was asleep.

Crack, crack ! Cra-cra-cra-crack !

Platoon firing was going on on Jack's right, and as he staggered against the wall, a loud British cheer arose, and a hundred feet seemed to spring over the parapet or through a breach, Jack could not tell which, at once and carry all before them.

Jack had no other weapon than his sword, his trusty yataghan that had served him so often in such need.

With that he had to defend himself as best he could, and turn and fly, at times cutting down the Arabs who stood in his way, as they were now his foes.

Jack, however, would have been annihilated at once if it had not been for his wonderful tact and courage.

He shouted in English to those who were pressing upon him, and some by this means were induced to turn aside their bayonets.

But how it actually occurred that he was not trampled under foot, pierced through and through, or dropped by one or more of the myriads of shots was to himself a mystery.

All he knew was that he cut and slashed at every fez and turban that came within his reach.

His Arab frock, once white, was now like a butcher's smock. and he could scarce see out of his eyes for blood and gunpowder.

This was awful.

Ten hundred times worse than the fight in which Jack fought so well when Osman Digna's caravan was attacked by the robber Sheikh Taher.

It was actual warfare ; not a review, but the battle of Tel-el-Kebir.

CHAPTER XXXII.

IN THE EGYPTIAN TRENCHES.—JACK SUCCOURS THE LITTLE DRUMMER BOY. — HOW THE LITTLE BUGLER WAS AVENGED.—TOM TRYSAIL TO THE FORE AGAIN.—FATE OF THE GREEK GIRL ON THE SCENE OF BATTLE.—JACK ACCUSED OF ASSASSINATION.

THROUGH all these perils, although Jack went at times awfully giddy, and his heart felt ready to sink at the horrible sights that surrounded him, yet he never fainted, his good right arm never lacked its strength, nor did he feel the least wearied.

" Bravo ! Hurrah ! Old England for ever ! Hurrah ! "

This was all he kept shouting until his voice was nought but a squeak, and the thunder-like cheers of the British troops seemed to answer him.

Jack had no more idea of what regiment it was carried the escarpment near to where he was stationed than if he had never been there.

He had heard drums, fifes, bugles, and bagpipes all mingled in the confusion, amid the booming of the loud-mouthed cannon and the sharp crack, crack of the breechloader, heard the clash of steel as sword and bayonet met, and that was all he knew, yet around him stretched and falling he saw men of various nationalities.

Some were already dead, others wounded, and many were dying, and yelling in a delirium caused by the pain which drove them mad.

What a sight for a poor and now friendless boy to witness !

When another rush of soldiers had passed, just like the stampede of a herd of goaded buffaloes, Jack on glancing around descried a little drummer boy about his own age, who was still beating the " charge," but with an expression of concentrated agony on his otherwise handsome features.

Our hero made out the cause of his distress in a moment.

An Egyptian foot soldier, a very Hercules in stature, had fallen dead by the side of the boy, and in his descent caught his leg, which, doubling under the soldier sideways, brought the drummer boy down on one knee.

Then upon the Egyptian a tall Highlander had fallen also, with the sword still in his grasp with which he had slain the Egyptian just as his own breast received a mortal wound.

Arab Jack without a pause flew to the aid of the little drummer boy, who, mistaking him by his dress for an enemy, warned him to keep back.

"If you murder me," hissed the drummer boy, "I will still beat the tattoo, even when my fingers are stiff in death."

"I won't kill you," cried Jack, excitedly. "I will only rid you of your ghastly burden. I am an English boy like yourself."

Jack placed his yataghan, reeking as it was, between his teeth, and then released the brave little drummer by drawing the stark forms from off his stiffened limb.

"Is the bone broken, chummy," queried our hero, almost breathless with anxiety and fear.

"Nae, nae ; thanks, thanks," cried the boy, who was scarlet in the face. "Thou art a good laddie, I ken, after all."

"Not so good as they make them," said Jack, with a cheery smile. "Why what's up, are you going to turn chicken-hearted ?"

Jack saw the colour forsake the brave boy's face and his lips turn ashy pale.

"Water, water," he gasped. "I am fainting ; be quick, laddie. I got Tom Atkins to carry my water-bottle."

"Tom Atkins," said Jack, awfully flurried. "Is he here ? Well, I'm blowed."

But there was no time for thinking just then.

One glance showed him the water canteen of the prostrate Highlander, and seizing it he placed it to the drummer boy's bloodless lips.

"Drink, drink," exclaimed Jack, seeing him go paler still, and his eyelids beginning to close. "Bear up, sonny, bear up. I can't beat your drum for you, for I don't know how to."

The water, warm though it was, was refreshing, and brought the brave little fellow to, and in spite of the pain of his leg he sat down on the bodies of the dead, from whose weight he had been so recently extricated, and tattooed away as before.

The British forces were now making short work of the inner line, and Jack being of no further service to the drummer left him.

Stepping aside from the wounded, and leaping over the dead Jack soon caught up with one of the brigades of infantry, mixed with whom were several marines and blue-jackets, who were too hotly engaged to notice the young Arab in their rear.

The Egyptians were completely mastered now.

The British had the victory entirely in their own hands, and Arabi's troops who had not already fled in dismay were fighting with a stubborn yet hopeless desperation, sustained only by an inveterate hatred of the Franks.

Jack uttered a startled cry and muttered a vengeful threat as, after creeping through a gap made in one of the stone walls, he saw a youthful bugler fall by the treacherous blade of one of the stricken Arabs.

Exasperated at the sight, our hero sprang forward and with a blow struck off the cowardly hand, and then with a skill that surprised himself he sliced off the dastard's head.

Seeing the ambulance corps approaching he left the poor boy then, and the whirl of his own brain warned him that he was becoming the victim of exhaustion.

Water, the muddy stuff that had been served out to him by the Egyptian commissariat, was gone long since, but espying a flask which had fallen from the hand of an officer in Egyptian uniform whose features Jack declared to himself were those of a Frenchman, he seized it.

The top being unscrewed, he placed its neck to his parched lips ; but soon he dropped it with a burning sensation in his throat and a feeling as if he would be choked.

Its contents were brandy.

Fortunately, therefore, as he had only swallowed a small quantity it did him good, and when he had ceased coughing and his eyes no longer watered he felt ready to go through all the excitement over again.

"Hurrah ! hurrah !" he shouted, frantically, as a fresh cheer raised by the British soldiery announced that some new deed had been achieved, and then he careered on again until a swift blow from a hard, horny fist sent him spinning to the earth.

"Hang you," roared a voice, "you Harry-by-tated-petticoat-looking swab. I've a hundred minds this minnit to unship your ugly figgur 'ed."

Jack was astounded.

He could neither speak, move, nor open his eyes for some seconds.

"What have I done ?" he at length asked, never calculating the strangeness of the question on such a scene of the dying and the dead.

"Done, you Jim Crow - looking halligater ! done, you Mother Carey's chicken ! why you've sailed full steam acrost my poor wounded topmate there, and I've a mind to send you to Old Davey with a hole in your tarnal shot locker."

Jack ventured to look up, when he recognised the powder-grimed features in a moment.

Then summoning his sea lingo to his aid he spoke :

"Hold water, Tom," said he, "brail up your trysail, old tar."

The hairy-faced sailor, who seemed to be all eyebrows, moustache, and whiskers, started just as if a bullet had struck him between the shoulders.

"Who's this, blarm me ? Why what Harry-Bean swab is it knows Tom Trysail ?"

"Jack, the London Arab," replied the boy.

"What the stowaway as was aboard the 'Drum-head-hairy ?'" drawled the tar.

"That's him," replied Jack, picking himself up and rubbing one hand affectionately on his head and the other on his bruised knees. "Leastways," he added, "this is me—I'm Arab Jack, who saved your life off Wapping Old Stairs."

"I dessay you did if you can't tell a whoppin' good lie," said the tar. "Come, spin out a clearer yarn nor that—now shell out."

"Well, I once cut your head a'most off with a single stick, when you were teaching me the cutlass, and——"

"There, that 'll do, lad—I knows all now."

"And I've had many reasons to thank you for what I learned," added our hero, as the honest seaman grasped his hand and a tear moistened his eye.

"God bless you, Jack ! I'm sorry I hit you ; but, there, you've no right to wear that piratical rig. Who painted your bows, matey, and made you look like the doll as hangs over the cabin of the tagarine stores."

"I've been chawin' pigtail and drinking black

coffee, Tom ; but we mustn't stay here, or we shall get into a bother."

"That's sartin ; but my topmate's winged here, and I ain't going to leave him, so good-bye for the present. We shall meet again somewhere, you young dog, and if there's a grog shop anywheres handy you shall splice a brace wi' me as long as a foretop bowlin'."

And thus they parted, Jack making for Arabi's tents, which were deserted by their occupants of the previous evening, only pausing on his way to give some poor wounded fellow a drink of water or shift a shattered limb into a more easy position.

As our hero proceeded he became more and more accustomed to the ghastly scenes.

The filmed and staring eyeballs, the stiffened limbs, the vengeful expressions of hate on the upturned faces, and the clenched teeth, which gave such painful evidence of a violent death.

Jack therefore took more notice of the postures and forms of those he passed, and just as he reached the thickest of the dust, turmoil and smoke, he was seized with an involuntary shiver, and his yataghan fell from his hand.

Lying upon the breast of an officer, evidently a Greek, was a lovely girl, dressed as a common Egyptian soldier, with a sabre wound in her neck and her breast exposed.

"God ! can it be true ?" gasped Jack. "Has this beautiful creature lost her life in venturing on the battle-field seeking for her lover ?"

The sight almost drove him silly.

He had to bend over the dead girl, his cheek almost coming in contact with her now cold bosom, which she had bared in her efforts to get breath, in order to regain his sword, and a fearful chill as of death crept through his marrow and veins.

Recovering his yataghan, however, he was about to flee in horror from the spot, when a hand seized him by the shoulder and a voice hissed savagely in his ear :

"Assassin, I arrest you now in the name of the Khedive. You murdered that poor Greek girl, and like the Arab demon that you are you shall receive condign punishment."

Jack was astounded.

He was too horrified to speak.

The soldier snatched from him his yataghan, and holding it menacingly over his head led him towards the Egyptian tents.

CHAPTER XXXIII.

OUR HERO IS BROUGHT BEFORE SIR GARNET.—
FOR LIFE OR DEATH.—SENT TO CAIRO.—THE
JOURNEY TO THE CITADEL.—JACK DISCOVERS
A FRIEND. — THE FORTRESS. — JACK A PRI-
SONER IN THE LOWER DUNGEONS.

THE war, or more correctly, the battle of Tel-el-Kebir, was at end, so to speak, when Jack and his accuser entered Arabi's largest tent.

Sir Garnet Wolseley and staff had taken temporary possession of it, not only for the novelty of the act, but to get temporary protection from the humming mosquitoes, which were growing lively in the rising sun, and to issue further orders and dispatches.

Arabi's army was by this time completely routed and the victorious cavalry in hot pursuit of them in the direction of Zagazig.

The magnificent camp residence was divided into several compartments, in the outer one of which, with its front thrown completely open, awaited a number of soldiers under arms guarding the prisoners who were to be specially dealt with for extraordinary crimes on the scene of battle.

One or two were accused of cutting the throats of the wounded and robbing them, which crime to Jack's horror was charged to him.

"Sergeant Atkins," said the general when the time came, "is this young Arab accused of murdering and robbing his own people ? "

"No, general, but he was found bending over the body of a Grecian girl who must have entered the lines in disguise, and having discovered her dead lover, a rebel officer, was weeping over him, when the prisoner stabbed her in the neck."

"Oh," emphasised the general. "To what motive do you attribute so atrocious an act ? "

"Robbery, I believe, general."

"And the weapon ?"

"This toy—this yataghan."

"Not much of a toy ; it seems well lacquered with gore. Have you any proofs, or anything further to add ? "

"No, general."

"Did you witness the act ? "

"I did not," replied the sergeant, quickly. "I will not tell a falsehood, Sir Garnet, if I can help it. I never saw the Arab till a few minutes since, when he was given into my charge."

"Then who witnessed the deed ?" demanded the general, tartly, "Come, speak up, or some one shall suffer smartly for this."

At that instant another officer stepped forward.

"My name is Blinks, Corporal Blinks, your honour. I am in the light infantry, and this," pointing to a private, "is my prisoner."

The general raised his eyebrows, and turned to the staff-officers about him.

"Listen to this," he said. "Now, what have you to say, Corporal Blinks ?"

"That my prisoner, Luke Flashley, private in my own company, plundered the lady the Arab is charged with murdering."

"Indeed. Then let me hear what your prisoner has to say about it."

He did so, and Jack at once recognised in his features those of Flash Luke the London prig.

His explanation, however, rendered matters more unintelligible than ever.

He said that the girl on discovering her lover uttered a cry, which first attracted his notice.

Then having kissed the lips of the corpse, in an agony of despair, she threw open her bosom and drew a poignard, which she prepared to plunge in her breast.

"Proceed," said the general, when he paused.

"This horrified me. So to prevent the act I rushed forward, and she stabbed herself in the throat."

"Go on," exclaimed the general, growing deeply interested.

"I caught her hand just as the deed was done, and pulled the weapon out of the wound just as I was arrested, that's all, your honour."

"Then it appears to be a tragedy of errors," said the general. "This case must be tried by court-martial. Send both these prisoners under strong escort to Cairo."

"And what of my sword ?" said Arab Jack, speaking in broken English.

"Well, if you are innocent of the crime you ought not to be deprived of your harmless toy, and as there is a doubt about it, I give you the benefit."

"Thank you," said Jack, and he was about to remark further, when a sallow-faced Egyptian slunk up to the general and whispered.

Sir Garnet gave a start.

"What," he muttered, "one of Arabi's spies? he takes and carries between Arabi in Cairo and the Mahdi and Osman Digna in the Soudan? Well, he is a sparkling satellite, and attends on three of the brightest planets, undiscovered by Herschel."

The sallow-faced villain whispered again, and our hero catching sight of his eyes, recognised him as one of Arabi's chosen staff.

"No doubt," thought Jack, "he's the treacherous rascal who persuaded Arabi to place me on the advanced line, so that I might be wiped off at the commencement of the action."

"Take your prisoner away, Sergeant Atkins," said the general, sternly. "Let him retain his sword until he is confined in one of the strongest dungeons of the fortress of Cairo."

Arab Jack quitted the general's presence in the same state of mind that a London Arab leaves the dock when brought up for the first time before the beak for hawking matches without a license.

His brain swam, his eyes were swollen, and a big lump rose in his throat, almost choking him.

Just reason had he then to think of his home, and to regret the hour in which he became acquainted with Flash Luke, whose presence haunted him even now under the glaring sun of Lower Egypt.

Jack, however, although his heart was sad, was not absolutely cast down.

When he was asked on which he preferred to ride, a camel or a mule, he answered the sergeant with anything but meekness.

"Give me a horse," said he, "if you can't afford a train, or let me do the grand like Tommy Atkins, by riding free gratis in a cab."

The guardsman adjusted his helmet, and looking down at his dilapidated uniform evinced a deal of uneasiness.

"Look here, Mr. Arab," said he, "I want none of your check. If my name happens to be Tom Atkins, and I wear this abominable rig, I've a better one at home, a scarlet one, too, as bright as that old Turk's fez, and ——"

"Who said you hadn't? I said I would like to have a cab if you can't afford the railway business."

The railway station was in too much disorder to receive prisoners there.

At Zagazig it was no better.

General Drury-Lowe had already started from Tel-el-Kebir for Cairo, to invest that citadel, and by the time Jack arrived there the fortress alluded to by Sir Garnet would be in the possession of the British, and supply a prison for our young hero.

"This is cheerful," muttered Jack, as he listened to the various accounts, surmises, grumblings, and prayers of thankfulness which were uttered loudly by the crafty Zagazigians. "It's sixty-two miles from Tel-el-Kebir to Cairo, and I don't want to march all that way on foot, just for the sake of going to prison."

"No," said the sergeant, who overheard him.

"There's fifteen of us to go; but where to get fifteen mounts I don't know."

"There! Look yonder!" cried Jack, pointing down into a hollow; "there are horses, mules, and donkeys without number."

"Left wheel, forward, march!" cried the sergeant, and on reaching the hollow three men were left to look after the prisoners while the rest caught the animals.

The force numbered, besides the prisoners, one sergeant, one corporal, and twelve men, for use of which they captured six horses, the rest having to ride mules.

It was all a bit of fun, and Jack, although he was manacled and had to have his horse led, was as jolly as a grig to see the antics of the guardsmen.

Some of them had never been on top of a four-legged 'un before, as they expressed it, and therefore those whose lot it was to ride the mules had a slippery time of it, as they were off and on just as often as it pleased the obstinacy of the mules to send them.

There was no lack of traffic on the road—Arab donkey-drivers and water carriers—besides the military and camp followers.

Jack's horse was led for some miles, as a make-show, by a horse fastened to it on each side by the bridle, and then as Jack could ride as well handcuffed as not, he was allowed to do so.

Sergeant Atkins rode up to his side then. "Look here," said he, "I've been wondering what you were alluding to about the cab."

"Then you've a bad recollection of old friends and peculiar circumstances, or you're not the Tommy Atkins of the Guards whom I saw on London Bridge playing Villikins with his beautiful, bright-eyed Dinah."

"Dinah, be devilled to you; what do you mean? You must know something, or you could not chaff me like this. What were you doing there?"

"Well, I saved the young lady from being run over, that's all. You didn't seem to regret it much at the time; but perhaps if you ain't married, and have left her a little image of you in your place, you know, why you may wish she had been. That is my fakement."

"You are a confounded queer chap. My lass, God bless her, was saved by a brave-hearted boy from being crushed to death; but you cannot surely be he? Why, splinter my musket, you are a head and shoulders taller, and——"

"You are not Tommy Atkins; that'll do. He was a fine, noble-hearted fellow; he did not wait to describe my general appearance; he said as much that he'd never forget his benefactor, and that if it ever laid in his power to do him a favour he would."

"And so he would, too—he's no liar. But as to a rebel Arab acting with such presumption, why, a West Indee nigger might do the same!"

"Nigger or no nigger," said Jack, "I can show as white a skin as you. But I've got my accuser to contradict as yet, and if the Khedive is at liberty, and I can only reach his ear, I can tell him something that will win his favour, and I shall get him to punish the lying scoundrel for perjury."

"You're right in that. I have but done my duty. If you are the boy to whom I am so deeply indebted, I wish you well, and every success. At the same time, I will do all I can for you consistent with the honour of my country."

" Thanks, that will do. We shall see what sort of a crib I'm going to, and then a word from you to my gaoler might make things sit more easily."

" The roadway at this point became more thronged, and so the conversation ceased.

Cairo, on their arrival, was open ; but events had transpired so suddenly, and followed so quickly upon each other, that the people, especially the shopkeepers, were almost afraid to open.

For weeks every one respectable who had anything to lose had been shut up, expecting that Tel-el-Kebir would hold out, stand a long siege, and eventually the British, from want of water, would be compelled to retire.

In fact, Arabi made a boast to that effect, and his emissaries plundered and requisitioned the town, threatening those with death who demurred, and summarily punishing those who were too poor to dub up.

The fortress in which Jack was to spend his retirement was that close to the gate where he got into trouble with the black flag.

The entrance, like those of most Eastern fortalices, was very small, so that the old guardsman had to duck his head, unless he submitted to the indignity of doffing his helmet ; but once inside, matters were reversed.

Having traversed several long narrow passages dark as Hades, and as dust-grimed as if they were perpetually used for shaking mats in, they entered a spacious vaulted chamber, through which they reached a magnificent marble hall.

There a great deal of formula was gone through, by which the governor of the citadel transferred the prisoner from his special care to that of the warders of the dungeons, of which there was one for every day of the year, and three special ones for offenders during the fast of the Ramadan.

Sir Garnet, not having mentioned any particular dungeon, there was a difficulty, of course, to know which to choose ; but as he said a lower dungeon, it must be one of those which at seasons receive the drippings from the canal.

Jack listened to this with anything but pleasure, and when the janitor began to extol the beauties of El Kalah, as the fortress was named, he grew weary of the recital.

" Show me to my apartment," he said, brusquely, to the warder. " I have not come here to be tortured and played with like a wild beast."

" Allah forbid," exclaimed the janitor, making a devout sign, and motioning the sergeant to follow, he took his huge bunch of keys and a light and they commenced a journey through a labyrinth of passages, down stairs narrow, winding, and steep, guarded by doors which by the state of the locks and hinges seemed to have not been opened for years.

" Jerusalem ! It smells nice," muttered Jack, " and the walls look moist and slimy. Why, these are as bad as the water dungeons in the Tower of London. When shall we ever reach my abode ? "

Jack found all out in time.

As they descended farther water stood on the stairs and in the passages, and just as they were all about to complain the janitor suddenly led them upwards.

" There," said he, " now you have seen what I could have done for you if I liked ; but a true follower of the prophet is not so cruel as the Frankish general. Step in."

It was a huge key that opened the ponderous lock of that massive door, and the room they entered was equally large in its proportions.

" This is the private cell," said the gaoler, " that was once used for state purposes by the powerful Mamelukes, and when you lie here, as I doubt not by your bearing you are someone of superior quality, you will at least have the pleasure of knowing that no dishonour or degradation has been practised on your birth."

Jack bowed.

" No one will disturb me here, I suppose, but the rats. No ghosts, I hope, wander of a night in those delightful corridors and courts you have just brought us through."

" None, my good lord," said the janitor, grimly. " No footfall will you hear here but your own and mine. Nothing will disturb you."

" How about his bedding ? " said the sergeant, looking around the gloomy walls.

" There is a plank bed hewn from one of the plane trees of Solomon, a seat sawn from one of the cedars of Lebanon, and this table is a portion of the platform by which the animals entered the ark."

" Then my happiness must be almost complete," exclaimed Jack. " But first assure me on one point. Are there any bugs or other blessings of the ark hanging about my bed furniture ? "

" None, I assure you. I spent my only piastre last evening in procuring the antidote, for a vision I had a few nights since warned me that we should have visitors of note to the citadel."

So saying he repaired to a niche in the wall and took from it a massive silver lamp, which was suspended by a chain from the ceiling, which he lighted, and giving his own lamp to the soldiers who accompanied them, desired them to step outside.

" Now," said he to the sergeant, " let us understand each other. You are friendly towards my charge, and from your words I presume you do not wish me to be too harsh with him. Is that so ? "

" Such are my private orders, which I would not issue before my men. Use him well, or I, Tom Atkins, of the Guards, whose battalion is now stationed in one of these towers, will not forget you."

This was more a threat than a promise, but the sergeant having slipped an English half-crown in the fellow's hand he was very satisfied, and would certainly have backed his way out along the dark passages and up the narrow, winding stairs if he had been so desired.

Jack was then left alone in the solitary dungeon. The huge key grated in the lock, and all was as silent and as cheerless as the grave !

CHAPTER XXXIV.

OUR HERO PERFORMS A MIRACLE AND PRODUCES A RUBY.—JACK CIRCUMVENTS THE CUPIDITY OF THE GAOLER.—A GLORIOUS FEED.—TOM ATKINS PAYS A VISIT TO THE DUNGEON.—A MYSTERIOUS INTERRUPTION.

THE first few days passed by our hero in the dungeon of El Kalah were to him as painful as being entombed alive.

" Am I going to be kept in here for life, or will they bring me to trial ? " said he to the janitor one morning, as he brought him his coarse fare. "This black bread, onions without salt, and water which looks like muddy gruel, is not the sort of fare for a son of Mecca."

The gaoler bowed, but made no reply.

Sergeant Atkins had given him a hint that Jack was something superior to what he seemed, and the gaoler at once flew to the conclusion that he might be a distant relation of the prophet.

By this time Jack understood the character of the Orientals. He knew they were a lying, treacherous, and thieving lot, and that he, to keep time with them, must act the same.

"Friend," said Jack, on seeing that the gaoler had some henna flowers in the bosom of his dress, "I pray you give those to me. Allah will reward you and make us both rich."

"They are yours," replied the janitor, opening his eyes a deal wider. "Henna is the fragrance of the fifth paradise—henna, the sweet-smelling, with which the daughters of the river dye the nails and palms of their hands and the soles of their feet."

"In my hands they are precious in another way," said Jack, taking the flowers and smelling them. "They are delightful; but to me they are but as the head of Pharaoh's toad."

"Ah!" exclaimed the janitor, his black beady eyes glistening. "Have you the charm for finding the emerald?"

"I can produce a precious stone from this bunch of henna. Come near me, if you are not afraid, and bear witness."

Arab Jack then went through a lot of formula, such as blowing open the petals of the flowers, breathing on them, and putting them in his breast, from whence, after he had fumbled them about and muttered a prayer, he took out the bunch and desired the gaoler to open it.

At first the man felt afraid, but gathering courage, and urged by a feeling of avarice, he took the flowers in his trembling hand and parted them, whereupon, to his amazement, a ruby fell on the stone floor at his feet.

"Allah, Allah!" exclaimed the man, making a devout sign. "Is it real or——"

He raised it from the floor and would have placed it in his mouth, when Jack stopped him.

"No, no," said he, pretending to be all of a tremble. "You might swallow it, and then it would kill you! Now what do you think it is worth?"

"Allah alone knows, I am too poor to guess; but I will take it to the bazaar if you want it changed."

"I want its value," replied Jack, glancing searchingly into the fellow's eyes; "but I cannot produce one like it every day, so I should like to know to whom I dare entrust it."

"By the beard of the prophet, every hair, by-the-bye, of which was anointed with the essence distilled from the henna, I swear there is none more honest and trustworthy than your worthy friend here."

"Friend!" emphasised Jack. "Hitherto I have only known you as such by name. If I venture to entrust this mission to you, I hope you will prove yourself my friend by your every action. Take it and do your very best."

The gaoler took the precious stone and left.

"Adieu! Farewell to my ruby," thought Jack. "I've conjured for something. I lay he won't come back."

So confident was he that the gaoler, by the chuckle he gave as he closed the huge door and turned the key, meant deceiving him, that Jack walked up and down groaning to himself until he was fairly tired, and then he took his yataghan from under his bed and counted the gems in its hilt.

"It's still worth a lump," he muttered to himself. "It was as well I let this sanguinary crust remain upon it. Aha! If Tom Atkins or the gaoler had caught sight of the diamonds they would have deprived me of my toy, as they have the cheek to call it."

Jack went so far as to hug the precious weapon, and kissed the place from whence he had produced the ruby, and he had just tenderly placed it away when he was disturbed by the key grating in the lock.

"Allah be praised! Safe, once more safe," exclaimed the gaoler, entering and throwing himself on the prisoner's bed. "I have been robbed and nearly murdered."

Jack was silent; those awful words seemed to deprive him of breath.

"Who robbed you? Who attempted your life?" he demanded, after a painful pause.

"Aaron, the Levite Jew," was the reply. "When I told him that the gem had once graced the turban of our holy prophet he swore it was a lie, and declared by sundry marks upon it that it was stolen from his house."

"What, did he detain it then, old man?" exclaimed our hero.

"He vowed he would. He spat upon me, and actually tried to terrify me out of it with his dirk."

"Oh, he only tried to, eh?" said Jack, calmly. "Well, where is it now?"

"He has it."

"Liar! Did he take it from you without payment?"

"Allah be praised, he did not," replied the gaoler, awed by Jack's determined appearance. "But I got not the whole of its value—two thousand piastres were all he would pay."

"Two thousand! It is worth double. Where are they?"

"Here. But you do not expect the whole of them, do you?"

"Of course not," replied our hero, who was delighted to find he had bargained so well; "give me one thousand five hundred, and keep the other fourth for your trouble."

The janitor sprang to his feet.

He was overcome with joy at the liberality of his captive.

"Here," said he "is the sum," producing notes and gold for the whole amount.

"Thank Allah I am safe, for if the Levite had stabbed me in his rage, what would have become of my wives and children?"

"It would have been a bad job, very, in more ways than one, for that gem is a talisman, and if he had injured you the judgment would have fallen upon him tenfold, whilst I might have been left here a prisoner, starved to death, and your fate might never have been known."

"Bless us all, no," replied the cunning janitor, raising his eyes sanctimoniously. "Give me my share and let me depart and embrace my family."

"Hang your family," muttered Jack. "I believe now that you have robbed me, and if I were not so awkwardly placed I would squeeze your windpipe for you until I ascertained the truth."

Jack, however, deemed it best to dissemble.

"Good father," said he, "now we have money let us enjoy it. You can purchase me better food than this horrible stuff, and maybe procure me some indulgences."

"I can, but it must be strictly between ourselves. My son, to-morrow is the twenty-second of the month, and then commences the fast of the Ramadan. We must then for one whole month abstain from eating and drinking, and even smoking, between sunrise and sunset."

"As a good Mahometan I know that," replied our hero, indignantly. "I would very much like to witness the opening ceremony. I am a native of Mecca, where my father is a prince, and there it is very grand."

"So it is here," replied the gaoler, thoughtfully, "If you very much wish to go you shall, but——"

"I can reward you for any risk or trouble you are put to. Here is money, get me some clothes in lieu of these soiled ones, and I will never forget you when I am once more free, for my parents are rich."

"I am assured of that. But if I thus serve you I must secure myself. I shall be armed, and as I forfeit my life if you elude my custody, I shall shoot you down like I would a Christian dog if you attempt to play tricks or endeavour to escape."

"Fear not," said Jack, laughing. "I shall be liberated soon. Go hence at once and attend to my requirements. Don't be long, and I will offer up a prayer for you during your absence."

"Hemmel Abu is your slave," said the gaoler, deprecatingly. .

Then sweeping the money into his bag, he secured the neck of it, and concealing it in the folds of his garments left the dungeon.

Jack felt quite relieved when he was gone.

"Confound the old rascal," he exclaimed. "I know he did well over that deal or he would not be so satisfied. I shall be glad, though, if I can only worm myself into his confidence and bribe him to let me have a blow of fresh air."

Our hero was getting awfully weak owing to his incarceration. The bad food and the pestilential air were working upon his youthful frame.

Now, however, he felt as lively as a cricket, he danced about, sang snatches of his favourite songs, and played duck stone with the black bread and onions to pass away the time.

True to his word, Hemmel was not long absent. When he reappeared with an attendant, his only son, they were both loaded ; one carried a basket of food, and the other carried the clothes and a jar of filtered water.

"There, now you can go," said Hemmel to his son, when he had deposited his load on the table, and Jack, who was as hungry as a wolf, quickly overhauled the contents of the huge basket.

"By the prophet," he exclaimed, bringing out a knife and fork and a clean cloth, "this is business, Hemmel Abu. Why you ought to be sainted. White bread, water melons and plantains. Now what do you think of the bunch of henna ?"

"Very good, very good," replied the gaoler. "You eat while I show you the garments."

Our hero wanted no second bidding. He had not partaken of anything so sumptuous since he left the stronghold of the Red Sheikh.

Having reduced the cold fowl to a skeleton, he then commenced on the slices of roast kid, whilst Hemmel, with a profusion of praises, undid the raiment and showed it to him.

"There now, is not this fit for the son of a prince of Mecca ? Who ever saw such splendid morocco shoes ? What follower of Mahomet ever wore a richer turban ? I declare such things as these make me wish I was the prisoner instead of the gaoler."

"You can be if you like," said Jack, "I'll change places with you, and give you something to boot."

A low tap at the door at that moment sounded. Hemmel rose slowly and opened it.

"Come in, sergeant, he's busy feeding, so there will be no danger of his attacking you. The young prince, you see, eats as other people."

Jack gave the sergeant a sly wink.

"Yes," said the latter, "he acts on prince-iple when he's away from home. I don't suppose for a moment that he's been able to eat as a prince since he's been here, nor dined with such military honour."

This joke of Tom Atkins raised a laugh.

"Well, Tom," exclaimed our hero rising from his seat, and grasping the young guardsman by the hand, "I am glad to see you. To what good fortune have I to ascribe the honour of this visit ? Have you brought me a free pardon ? or——"

"I wish I had, Jack. Things are in an unsettled state. Arabi, as you have heard, perhaps, is taken prisoner, and accused of inciting the Arabs to set fire to Alexandria."

"Indeed I have not. My friend here, as I must term him, is not very communicative. I'm growing tired of this cage. I wish I could get a letter forwarded to the general or to the Khedive."

"That's impossible just at present. I am here only by the favour of the gaoler, who says he will give us both a treat as soon as the Ramadan commences."

"I shall keep my word, and I hope you will both keep faith with me," said Hemmel, who had been carefully arranging the coloured folds of Arab Jack's new turban. "I am not so young as either of you, but I am just as fond of a bit of fun, though."

"Bravo !" said Sergeant Atkins. "We shall enjoy ourselves, I hope. I like your Mahometan style much—fast and pray all day long, and at night see the girls kick up a fandango."

"That's it," cried Hemmel, with a knowing wink. "I wouldn't be a Frank for a gold mine. Who's that ?"

All eyes were turned towards the door, whose rusty hinges gave a blood-curdling groan.

The gaoler was on his feet in an instant.

Quick as lightning he reached the door, which he had incautiously left unfastened, and taking his lantern from its concealment he leaped into the dark stone passage and glared about him.

No one could he see. Yet that door could not have moved by itself, and there was not enough wind to stir a feather, much less move the rusty hinges.

Drawing a pistol from his sash, he scoured the passages round about, and tried the doors of the occupied cells, all of which appeared to be securely locked.

"That's a mystery," said he, on returning from his fruitless search. "We have aroused the cupidity of some treacherous foe, and probably been overheard. I must see to this, otherwise all our hopes will be blighted."

"I hope not," exclaimed Jack and Tom, in a breath. "If you have other prisoners here, I don't expect you leave their cells open."

"Not I. But for all that in these old vaults there have been some fearful doings, and I wouldn't bind myself to say that they are not haunted."

Jack shrugged his shoulders, and Tom tried to laugh.

"I hope you won't leave my door open," said Jack, with a cynical smirk. "I don't want any ghost walking into my private apartment."

CHAPTER XXXV.

A NIGHT ADVENTURE IN CAIRO.—A NARROW ESCAPE.—BRINGING THE GOVERNOR'S CARRIAGE TO A STANDSTILL.—THE GRAND BAGNIO.—JACK MAKES ANOTHER STARTLING DISCOVERY.

IT was pitchy dark, and although the air in the narrow streets was close and muggy, a cold rain drizzled down and extinguished the miserable lights in the paper lanterns hung over the various doorways to enable the visitors to find them.

Heedless of this, three personages closely muffled, with cloaks hanging down to their heels, and with shawls wrapped about their turbanned heads, emerged from a dark archway in the fortress wall and wended their tortuous way along the ill-paved streets.

"Splash, splash," muttered one from beneath the thick folds of his shawl. "Hang me if it ain't all splash. My fancy moroccos will look dandies by the time we reach the divan."

"Never mind, my good friend. You craved for the fresh air, and now you breathe it. We shall be all right presently. Allah be praised! I have my lantern if we should run against any stray dogs, so that we may see whose calf they rob the most."

"That touches you right home," whispered Tom, the guardsman. "If you are a young prince, you have no business to patronise them paper-made trotter-cases. If you bob into many more holes before we reach our destination they won't be fit even to light our pipes with."

At that moment a closely-shut vehicle, with a lantern tied to the horse's head, drove up behind them, and the driver, not observing the pedestrians in the darkness, forced them close against the wall.

"Look out! Where are you going to?" thundered our hero, who was one of the trio, and who had his left shoulder nearly dislocated by one of the shafts. "You'll come down out of that pretty quick if you don't pull up and let us pass on before you out of this."

"Don't bluster so," answered the driver. "Creep in somewhere out of the way, or I'll drive right over you and flatten you like a postage-stamp."

"Will you?" replied Jack, unmindful of the danger he was risking. And without another word he gave the fellow such a blow behind the fez as flattened his ear against his head in the likeness of the article just mentioned.

"Order! What does this mean?" exclaimed Hemmel Abu, in terrifed accents. "Leave off

fighting! The fellow should have been given in charge of the watch. Are you mad?" he added in Jack's ear. "A nice mess I shall be in if we three are found here brawling in the street."

"I can't help it; I'll knock his head off!" answered the impetuous Jack. "I'll have him down out of that and give him a real doing."

Suddenly one of the side windows of the carriage was lowered.

"What is the grievance? Are we about to be robbed, or have the rebels again taken to murdering?"

It was a silvery voice that spoke, and Jack no sooner heard it than he seized the lantern from the horse's head and flew to the window.

"We are neither robbers nor murderers," said he, glancing into the coach, and then he uttered an exclamation of surprise.

Three young ladies occupied the vehicle, and at a glance he recognised them to be the graceful sisters of Hassan-el-Ahed.

Yes, there were the three—fair Lily, Nina, and Sela—and our hero was anything but pleased to meet them while in his masquerade attire, for he was disguised as an old Turk.

In the *melée* with the insolent coachman, Jack's shawl, which had partly concealed his face, was disarranged, and now his long grey beard was visible, his shaggy eyebrows and his grizzled moustache—all of which he had assumed at the instance of the gaoler, to prevent recognition.

"Close the window, Nina," said Sela, whose auburn locks, looking as bright as ever, peeped forth from the Spanish mantilla she had thrown over her head; "the beastly old Turk will want us to find him a seat, I expect. Why, the old rake has actually dyed his horrid-looking whiskers with henna!"

"So he has!" exclaimed fair Lily, tossing her beautiful head, and raising her delicately-gloved hand to assist her sister. "The venerable old sinner, to come here and waylay us in this manner, when I dare say at home he has a dozen or more wives in his harem!"

Tom and the gaoler could neither move nor speak for laughing, whilst our hero, whose pride was terribly touched, wished his grizzled beard and moustache were at Halifax.

"I beg pardon, ladies," said he, gently preventing the raising of the window, "there is some mistake—indeed there is. I am——"

"Some beastly old gudgeon. Go away!" shrieked Lena. "Coachman, coachman, have you not got a pistol with which to shoot the old wretch?"

Jack was half-inclined to tear off his whiskers and reveal himself, but it was fortunate at that moment that he did not do so.

Presently another vehicle, which came in at the other end of the narrow street, appeared on the scene, and there was a complete block.

The second vehicle was a grand affair, with chocolate and gilt panels and blue silk curtains, two splendid grey horses, and with a footman seated beside the coachman on the box.

"The governor, by Mahomet," whispered the affrighted gaoler in Jack's ear. "I shall lose my place and we shall be bastinadoed into the bargain."

The governor was no less a personage than the officer who received Jack as prisoner at the fortress and handed him over to the care of Hem-

HE LOWERED THE HELPLESS, SUPPLE FIGURE DOWN TO TOM.   *p.* 90.

mel Abu, so that if he chanced to recognise the midnight strollers there would be a fine mess.

It was fortunate, however, that it was dark and that the lanterns were more ornamental than useful, and also that the governor wore spectacles, which at that moment were buried in the folds of his richly-embroidered travelling robe.

"Mahemmed, Kali," he shouted to those on the box, "draw your swords and clear the way. If you are unable, raise your voices and call the watch."

The coachman had all his work to govern the restive horses; but the footman drew his huge sword, jumped down and flashed the broad blade before the eyes of the other coachman, who having partially recovered from the blow Jack gave him, straightened himself up and commenced backing his vehicle into a broader part of the street.

During this confusion and the clatter made by the horses' feet, Hemmel contrived to whisper to his companions:

"We must clear out of this, for if we delay and

are recognised in each other's company we shall not be able to set a foot to the ground for more than a month to come."

Arab Jack was still inclined to be obstinate.

With the impetuosity of youth he would have stood and faced it out, and would actually have gone and made himself known to the ladies, by which time of course the neighbourhood would be raised and the guard most probably summoned from the fortress.

Hemmel therefore did well to get them away, and after traversing several muddy streets he stopped at a low portico, drew them into its shade, and gave three taps at a door.

A slave answered the summons.

Hemmel whispered a few magical words.

Then they were admitted into a dark passage, at the end of which a green baize-covered door was opened, and they found themselves in a brilliantly-lighted saloon.

This was the grand bagnio, into which none but Mahometans were allowed to enter. It was magnificently decorated, and the cushions around

8

on the raised part of the floor were covered with the softest velvet.

A number of coloured slaves were in attendance. They assisted our adventurers to remove their wraps, and without further orders brought them long amber-tipped pipes, ready filled, and a lighted cinder of charcoal.

A goodly company was already assembled, and yet there were seats to spare, for they rose like steps one above another in the form of a horseshoe, and coffee and sherbet were plentifully served around.

Our adventurers, looking like three grave Turks, took their seats on the upper row, and our hero began to wonder what was to be seen, as the music was playing softly in the invisible orchestra.

Presently the centre of the carpeted floor was raised about three feet, and the crimson curtains at the end which appeared to be the wall having been drawn aside, disclosed a scene within that fairly dazzled the senses.

It represented the fifth paradise, with the houris clothed in celestial vestments ready to welcome the true believers to the promised realms of bliss.

Hemmel, who had witnessed the gorgeous spectacle before, took not so much interest in it as Jack and Tom did.

Such a bevy of beauty assembled at once they had never before beheld.

Such busts, such limbs, such features, and delightful heads of hair, of various hues and variously-arranged, bound with a neat fillet or graced with a tiara of glittering jewels.

Gliding gracefully about in various figures to the soft cadence of the silver instruments, the dancers seemed to possess such aërial lightness that their feet actually seemed to be resting on nothing, until the cymbals, tabours and hautboys struck up a wild furore, when the dancers, like so many beautiful butterflies, swept out on to the raised daïs, or carpeted platform, and went through such agile movements as would fairly have eclipsed the can-can.

This ended, the dancers disappeared just like a tropical twilight and gave place to the fakirs or magicians of the East.

Their performance was no less astounding; but Jack's mind was now filled with their adventure of the earlier portion of the night.

When the dancers appeared again he carefully noted their features, and he could scarcely resist calling out when he recognised Hassan's charming sisters.

"Good heavens!" he gasped, "to what circumstance do they owe being here? What has brought them to this debasement—to dance and posture in this scant array for the edification of these gloating, sensual, grey-bearded old sinners?"

What indeed! We shall discover anon.

CHAPTER XXXVI.

ARAB JACK PRIES INTO THE SECRETS OF HIS GAOLER.—THE TORTURE CHAMBER AND ITS TERRIBLE INSTRUMENTS.—THE DEATH PIT. —ON THE RAMPARTS OF EL KALAH.—THE POWER OF WINE.

ALTHOUGH Jack had every comfort his gaoler could procure for him, yet having once again tasted liberty he longed to be free, and even determined that if he could bribe the indulgent Hemmel to give him another airing he would try and make his escape.

"And why not?" he mused, as he sat brooding over his wrongs. "If they suspect me of complicity with Arabi why don't they give me a fair trial. I am determined to stand this cruel treatment no longer—it is tyranny, and I am perfectly justified in escaping if I can."

This reverie was broken by the entrance of the janitor.

"Prisoner," said he, "the opportunity has arrived when I can gratify your wish of enjoying a walk on the ramparts and viewing therefrom the enchanting scenery; but let me repeat my warning—the least treachery on your part will meet with its merited reward."

"If you doubt my faith why do you offer to trust me?"

"Because I like you. I have prisoners here whom I would not trust outside the doors of their dungeons—and one especially, a Moor, Ababa by name, one of the lieutenants of the great Red Sheikh, the scourge of the desert."

Our hero gave an involuntary start.

"The Red Sheikh!" he exclaimed. "I was a prisoner of his at one time. I would like to see this terrible Ababa; I might recognise in him one of the cut-throat robbers who plundered the caravan of which I had charge on its way to Mecca."

"What good would that do you?" said the gaoler, not seeing his way clear to accede to the proposition.

"Merely revenge; I might taunt him with his misery, and that would, in a measure, compensate me for the injury I suffered at his hands."

"There is truth in that; but the doctrine of the prophet is to forgive our enemies and let him punish the wrong-doer."

"Aye, that is so; but how many practise it? For instance, how is it he is in prison? Why am I languishing here?"

Hemmel Abu was silent. He bit his lip and at once changed the subject.

"I am not a lawgiver," said he, "therefore I decline arguing. Will you swear by the prophet that you will obey my behests if I conduct you to the ramparts?"

"I have sworn. If you are ready I will go at once."

"It is well. Here is the disguise; speak but little, yet see all, for your voice ill accords with the ancient appearance you must assume."

Arab Jack made no more ado. He was growing quite an adept in making up. But he did not like acting the *rôle* of old man when there was a chance of coming in contact with beautiful ladies. He considered it was sacrificing his youth.

To attain his ends, however, he would assume any form, even that of Satan. So he soon arrayed himself in a patriarchal robe, and off they started to view the delightful scenery that had been so vividly described to him as to set his whole soul longing to view it.

Hemmel always carried a lantern with him, a small affair, the light of which could be turned on and off at will, and by its aid they began the distasteful journey through the subterraneous passages.

It was not by this way that he left the fortress

when they went on their nocturnal rambles, it was by a secret means of egress known only to the gaoler.

Jack, however, had no particular choice so long as he got out of his wretched dungeon, into which daylight never shone, and in which the lamp at times burned so dim that he would have been better had he been in total darkness.

"There, Mahoud (I must give you a name), that is the door of Ababa's dungeon; but as I have reason to believe he is ungrateful for my kind attendance upon him, I have a mind to remove him into one in the lower gallery."

"That will kill him outright, I suppose," said Jack, bluntly.

"Not it, or I would not grant him such a favour. The cell is damp, both the rats and the water find their way into it, but not sufficient to cause sudden death."

"Ah," said Jack, affecting to be careless about it, "then that's all right. But what place is this, the door's open."

"That is one of the torture chambers," answered Hemmel; "but I have not a light strong enough with me now to show and explain to you all its beauties. Step in here."

He pressed open a low door and Jack, not without a little misgiving, followed him in.

It was dark, but the gaoler soon produced a torch from a hole in the wall, and lighted it from his own lantern.

"Now what do you think of this?" he queried, as the torch flared up.

Jack looked around. He could see nothing but a large iron cage in one corner and a peculiar-shaped brazier in the centre of the stone floor.

There was a large wooden frame against one wall, which frame Jack considered was the bedstead, but he was surprised when Hemmel opened the top of it like a box, and showed him the inside.

It was fitted so that a man, or even a woman for that matter, could be placed within it and fixed so as to undergo the terrible torture of bastinadoing. But why its extra strength, and why was there so much iron about it.

Such were the only queries that troubled Jack, but the gaoler very soon settled that point by giving an explanation that made him shudder.

"This instrument," said he, "is the devil's daughter; the arms and clamps you see here are supposed to be her limbs, and with them she embraces the victim who is married to her."

"Very nice, certainly," said our hero, with a shrug. "Then he is not only bound to her heart and soul, but hand and foot?"

"Yes; that is called the wedding ceremony," he explained, "such as adjusting these endearments to the limbs of the honoured swain; and this is the marriage dowry."

He pointed to a short staff hanging on the wall, which was tastefully bound round with fancy coloured wools, and to which was attached a number of thin iron rods in the fashion of a cat-o'-nine tails.

"Yes; this is the dowry," he added, as Jack unhooked it from the wall. "You see we make a bright charcoal fire in that brazier, and heat the rods until they are red-hot, and then we flog the bridegroom over the bare soles of his feet."

Jack was so incensed at the cold-blooded

manner in which he spoke, that he felt very much inclined to punch him on the nose.

"I can scarcely keep my hands off him," he muttered to himself. "But for what crime is this particular favour reserved?" he asked.

"Several," replied the janitor. "For instance, if a prisoner was to escape from this fortress, and was brought back, he would have as many scourges with the devil's tail as his constitution would bear, and then lay in the holy cradle until he died or got well."

"But no one could live after that!" exclaimed Jack.

"Some have, when they possessed hard-soled feet. And this cage here is for eunuchs who desecrate the sanctity of the harem."

"It's rather small," suggested our hero.

"Yes; it's three feet high, the same across, and five feet long over all, and those knobs on the bottom form a very nice cushion, I assure you."

"You wretch!" thought Jack. "You seem to gloat on these horrible torments; but I daresay you are showing me these merely to terrify me in case I meditate an escape. Have you ever seen a eunuch put in it?" asked Jack.

"I have. Three. The last one admitted an English artist into the harem of Suleiman Pasha, to take a sketch of it, as he said. The artist disappeared, and the eunuch died in that cage after enduring all the pangs of the unfaithful. And he's buried there," he added, fiercely, clutching Jack forcibly by the arm as he shrank from him in horror. "You were nearly joining him and becoming one of his companions."

"What do you mean?" thundered our hero, prepared on the instant to seize the hilt of his yataghan.

"See for yourself," was the stern reply, as the janitor held the lantern and pointed to the rear of the angered boy.

Arab Jack turned, and a cry escaped him.

In the damp stone floor close to where his heel had been, there was a square black hole. How deep he knew not; nor was he aware by what means it had been opened.

The terrified boy drew back. So sudden was the sight and so narrow was his escape that his brain reeled, and he was afraid of going too near for fear of falling into it.

It was quite a relief when he found himself on the ramparts with the balmy evening air kissing his pale damp cheek.

"Ah! now," exclaimed he, "I feel for the moment happy. What a sight! What a view, Hemmel! I should think it is the grandest in the world."

"There are few, I believe, to equal it," returned the gaoler. "But don't speak so loud; other ears than mine may hear you, and——"

"I can't help it! Explain to me some of the scenes. What a sheet of flat white roofs, cupolas, minarets, and domes, all gilded with the glorious setting sun!"

"Hush! not so loud. That towering dome and its accompanying minarets belong to the mosque of Mehemet Ali. It is built of beautiful alabaster, veined with white and yellow. And that is the mosque of Sultan Hassan. Those cupolas are some of the tombs of the Egyptian kings.

"How grand!"

"Eh! Sultan Hassan's is the grandest mosque

in Cairo. It is built, like the structure on which we now stand, El Kalah, of the stones brought from the smaller pyramids ; and its beauty was so much admired by the king who built it that he cut off the architect's right hand, so that he might not excel it."

"That was a shame !" exclaimed Jack, unmindful of the character he was assuming. "I'd have punched his head, the gossoon. What water is that over yonder ? "

"The Nile, my bold prince. It touches the base of this town and winds away up yonder a thousand miles or more between its green banks through sandy deserts, and——"

"Yes ; I have heard of it, although it is far away from my desert home. And are they the pyramids, and the Sphinx, and such like."

"They are ; and a grand and wonderful sight they look, even from here. And the sandy background, and the variously-tinted hills."

"It is a sight, Hemmel, and I thank you for it; but I shall never rest until I have been close up to those pyramids. I have always had a desire to touch the Sphinx and sail upon the Nile."

"You must do neither, my prince, whilst you are my prisoner. Come on, Mahoud. Have you seen enough ? "

"I could dwell here for ever," replied Jack. "Oh, Hemmel, how happy you must be to be able to come up here after inhaling the fœtid air of those darksome dungeons !"

"Do I not need it ? Can I go and come the same as you can ? "

"How do you mean, Hemmel ? "

"Why, although you may die in these dungeons, or, for that matter, be strangled with the bowstring, yet there is a chance that you will be liberated."

"And what do you mean by the bowstring ?"

"Why, if they bring you in guilty of treason towards the Khedive, they will garotte you with the bowstring. I don't suppose they would go to the expense of having a boy like you hung."

"Oh, thank you !" exclaimed Jack, thrusting his hands into his pockets, and looking all the impudence he was capable of. "A boy, eh ! And with a beard like this ! But why, pray, cannot you forsake the dungeons any more than I can ? Can you not discharge yourself from the service ? "

"No. I am sentenced to serve till death. As soon as I am discharged, no matter for what neglect, my life will be forfeited."

"And yet you have risked so much," said Jack, seriously, sinking his voice.

"I have for you, and will again while I like you ; but if you once make me your enemy your time will be short. Now let us return. I have gratified your desires. See, the sentries are being posted about the ramparts for the night."

Jack's heart seemed like a lump of lead that night.

As he lay on his camelots, or blankets made of goat's hair, which the governor had ordered him to be provided with, he wished he could cry, but the fountains of his eyes seemed dried up, and the pulsation of his heart seemed to have ceased.

"Escape ! Escape !" The word seemed to be ringing every moment in his ears, and more than once he awoke with a start and fancied that there was a figure flitting about in his cell.

Unable to sleep, he got up, tried the door, and then picked up the lamp. After which he counted the remains of his cash, and taking up his yataghan, which he always kept ready to his hand, he removed another stone from its setting, in case he might need to work another charm.

And thus a month passed, during which time the gaoler could not, by promises or other means, be persuaded to let him have another midnight ramble, and Tom Atkins was only permitted a few times to smoke a pipe with him in his cell.

But Jack, nevertheless, had not been idle.

He had found out something, and that by very careful watching and keeping his own counsel.

The young guardsman, on joining them in one of their smoking bouts, brought with him some wine, thinking it might be beneficial to the prisoner, and forgetting that Jack was supposed to be a Mussulman, offered it to him, whereupon Hemmel, who had never tasted wine in his life, and was strictly forbidden to do so by the Koran, was tempted to taste it also.

"Allah, forgive me !" he exclaimed, as soon as he had done smacking his lips. "If the prophet forbade his followers such good stuff he was a fool. Why, it bringeth the delights of the fifth paradise even into the darkness of this dungeon. What must it be to those who take it in the Frank's saloons ?"

"Heaven, of course," said Tom ; "without the trouble of getting there. Drink, boys. This came out of the chinquins I found at the battle of Tel-el-Kebir."

The gaoler was rather shy before Jack.

Had he been alone with the sergeant he might have drank deeply, for the taste suited his palate, and its genial influence so cheered him that he began singing verses of the Koran instead of repeating them.

As it was, he drank very sparingly and only sang himself to sleep, of which opportunity to chat Jack and his visitor took advantage.

"You are a fool, Jack !" said Sergeant Atkins, "to stay here incarcerated in this hole. If I were you, and an English lad as you are, I'd find some means to get out of this. I don't advocate murder ; but I am sure I should knock this fellow on the head and run."

"What, after the kindness he's shown me ?"

"Yes ; that is, after the kindness you bought. It's only for the money you gave him and he robbed you of, coupled with the hope of getting more, that makes him so amiable towards you ; and I'm sure he got a good round sum for that gem, for he's been a robber and a cut-throat—that's why he's here."

"But how can I get away if I do knock him down ? I can't find my way out alone, and then there's the keys."

"He's got them about him ; and if you're plucky you can do it to-night. I took stock of the secret way by which we got out to go to the bagnio. Trust a soldier to find his way about old castles and dungeons. What do you say ?"

"But what of yourself ?"

"I'm all right. I've got leave off till morning, and I have not to mount guard till to-morrow night. We can lock him in, you know, leave the key in the door, and let his boy find him in the morning."

"Good, Tom ; I'm off. You ought to be a general for your concocting."

"So I shall be some day. I know where to go to when we get out. One night when I went past the bagnio I met with some splendid young ladies, who invited me to their house, treated me like a prince, and invited me to call on them when I liked, in honour of Tel-el-Kebir, but for which, they say, Cairo might have been sacked by the rebel Arabs and laid in ruins like Alexandria."

"Then, let's go at once, and leave this ghostly place behind, for I've been bothered with a sort of mystery of late, and once when the door was unlocked and Hemmel and I were talking I could swear that I saw the door open and a dusky face peer in."

"That'll do, then. Take hold of this lantern. I'm fair on the job, as they say ; but, hold, did I tell you I had a letter from my adorable ?"

"What, the young lady I saved ?"

"Yes ; and what do you think ?"

"I can't guess now, you've made me anxious to be off."

"Well, she visits the bridge every Sunday she gets out, and carries a stone from the barrack parade and plants it on the seat near the spot in commemoration of the event."

"Capital ! You'll do, Tommy Atkins. That's as good as the yarn about the sailor's lass, who planted a cherry-stone on the beach where they last parted, thinking that when he came back he could tie the boat to the tree, and they could both 'sit down and pick the cherries and eat them."

"That's a clincher, Jack. There are no marines about, are there ? Look out ; he seems to be growing restless."

The worthy pair then kissed their hands to the drowsy gaoler, and took their departure, locking the door, as they agreed to, after them.

Aided by the lantern the young soldier soon led the way, and after a deal of twisting and turning he stopped at a low iron door, undid the lock, and the pair passed through, closing it securely after them.

"Now stand fast !" said Tom. "Up and round we go. Hold on to me."

Arab Jack did as he was bid, and on Tom touching a spring, which he had some little difficulty to find, up and round, as he described it, went the little box room or lift they were in.

There was but little noise, yet round and round it went more than a hundred times, rising rapidly at each turn, just after the fashion of a music-stool.

Presently it stopped, and then Tom opened the door, and out they stepped into a long stone passage, at the end of which there was another small door, which Tom opened with a mysterious-looking key, and into the air they went.

"So far free, thank God !" muttered Jack. "Make way for liberty ! Britons never shall be slaves !"

It was a lovely starlight night, and they only waited to close the door, when off they went, laughing quietly to themselves, as they glided along under the high walls.

But suddenly a cry was raised. There was a commotion amongst the soldiers on the ramparts ; but only one word reached them—that was FIRE !

CHAPTER XXXVII.

THE BURNING HOUSE.—ARAB JACK PERSONATES THE BRAVE FIREMAN.—GALLANT RESCUE OF FAIR LILY AND NINA.—TOMMY ATKINS SAVES JACK AND SELA FROM A HORRIBLE DEATH.

"FIRE !"

How magically that small but impressive word acted upon the movements of our adventurers.

To Tom's military mind it naturally occurred that they had been discovered by the guard on the ramparts, and that the order was given to fire upon them.

"Keep close, matey," said he to his companion, "Let's edge along under this wall. That confounded abutment commands this lane, and I fancy I see a rifle barrel pointing out of that loophole."

"We are in for it, then," replied our hero ; "but it's not so much for myself that I care as for your safety. Should you be discovered in my company you will get it pretty stiff."

"But I'm not going to be caught if I can help it. If we gain the corner there is a narrow street in which the overhanging houses will help to screen us, for they make the place almost dark even in daylight.

The commotion on the ramparts increased, the great alarm bell was rung, and amidst the uproar Jack and his chum glided along like two spectres until the lane before spoken of was reached.

"Thank God ! we are safe from the bullets," said Tom Atkins. "Now we can give them leg-bail. Come, pull a foot, and mind you don't stumble over some drowsy watchman."

The warning was only just given in time.

Scarcely were the words out of Tom's mouth when a burly watchman scrambled to his feet and rushed out of one of the narrow entries.

How he heard the bell at all seemed a wonder, for his head was swathed in a large blue handkerchief, and his ears completely covered.

"Allah, preserve me !" he exclaimed, in a state of utter confusion, as he held up his lantern and struck the heel of his stave on the cobbly stones. "What's this, are you robbers ? I arrest you in the ——"

"Arrest that," vociferated our hero, giving him a blow between the eyes. "You've arrested our progress, and I've a mind to drub you with your own staff."

The watchman had no time to resent the blow.

He raised the staff, certainly, but it was only to evince his surprise.

Such a blow he had not anticipated, and of course he was blind for the time, whilst the claret flowed from his wounded proboscis rather freely.

Having thrust him aside the pair then passed on, and on gaining the next turning, which was their intended destination, they discovered the true cause of the ringing of the alarm bell.

One of the large buildings was on fire, and the flames bursting out from the upper windows showed that it was well alight.

All this had happened so quickly that it occupied less time than it has taken to record it, so that the apathetic Caireans, who were at no time very lively, were aroused from their first sleep.

"Good heavens !" exclaimed Tom, "that is the very house we are bound to. What a pity such a fine old building should be burned."

"Don't talk like that, Atkins. If the ladies you

spoke of are in that house their lives are in jeopardy. Perhaps the inmates don't even know the place is ablaze."

"Perhaps not," cried Tom, gazing up at the carved latticed windows. "I'll pull the bell ;" and suiting the action to the word, he gave such a challenge to those within that he soon raised the house.

By this time lights were appearing through several of the lattices, a sign that the drowsy inhabitants were moving, and had it happened in a different country windows would have been thrown up.

As it was, such an infringement of the privacy of a house amounted to a crime, as, according to Oriental etiquette, none but very particular friends are allowed to peer into another's domicile.

And even then the males and females are separated, for no man may gaze upon the faces of another man's wives.

But time, precious time, was fleeting.

Neither of our adventurers was acquainted with the fire-engine department, therefore they could only depend upon themselves, but as the alarm-bell still continued to ring, it was probable that some sort of an engine would shortly appear upon the scene.

Several persons were now collected in the street. Few of them, however, seemed inclined to render assistance.

"Can't we burst open the door," thundered Jack. "Perhaps the inmates are stifled in their beds."

This suggestion appeared so likely that Tom at once flew to Jack's aid and endeavoured to force the door; but it was one of those stout old carved oak structures that are not so easily forced, neither could they make any impression on the panelling.

"Get a ladder, somebody," at length cried Jack, shouting as loud as he could in Arabic. "Is there no one here estimates the sacrifice of human life?"

"Allah be praised! here is one who has a soul," exclaimed one of the crowd, and taking a huge key from his girdle he unlocked an adjoining gate and brought forth a ladder and a rammer such as is used in laying stones.

This action set several of the onlookers to work. Some raised the ladder, whilst others banged at the door, and soon after a figure was observable through the lattice-work that protected one of the upper windows.

The ladder was not quite long enough to reach this window, and if it had been none of the crowd seemed to care about mounting it ; they each one seemed to be waiting for his neighbour to make a start, and to be searching for some mysterious article in the pockets of their baggy breeches.

"Stand aside, Tom, and let me go up," cried our hero, who was already grown excited ; and so, snatching a staff from the hand of one of the onlookers, he placed it between his teeth and ran up the ladder like a cat.

The ladder, as we remarked, was not, however, tall enough to reach the window, but Jack by steadying himself against the wall managed to mount to the top rail and clutch the window-sill, which window was eventually opened, so that he could draw himself up and look in.

And what a sight !

The room was partially filled with smoke that poured through a fissure in the opposite wall, and by a flame which had burst through the floor above and was devouring the carved wood ceiling. He beheld a lovely being stretched insensible and apparently dead on a couch, and another one lying recumbent over the back of a chair, where she had fallen, overpowered by the stifling smoke.

Jack, unused to such scenes, was horrified at the sight.

The fragments of the burning ceiling were beginning to fall, and it was evident it would soon set fire to some of the light drapery, in which event the apartment would soon become ablaze and be like a furnace.

A thousand agonising thoughts flashed through Jack's mind in a moment.

In the features of the lovely being reclining on the couch he recognised those of fair Lily, and in the other he beheld the beautiful dark-eyed Nina.

"Heaven aid me !" he gasped, "and give me strength to assist them. Come up here one of you and see what can be done."

Aided by the staff he forced the window open a little wider, and tightening his fingers upon the ledge he drew himself up, and after a struggle managed to gain admittance to the room.

"So far," he muttered, struggling to get breath, "Now which one shall be first ?"

Then he examined the curtains and looked around for something in the shape of a bed-sheet; but there was nothing of the sort in view, so quick as lightning he tore off his turban and untied its many folds.

"This is tight work," muttered Jack, as he fastened the end of the long cambric rope round the waist of the unconscious Nina, and then carrying her to the window he lowered the helpless, supple figure down to Tom, who by this time was already waiting upon the ladder.

How Tom managed seemed to be little short of a miracle.

Guiding the figure as it was being lowered until he gained a place on the ladder where he could get a hold of his fair charge, he undid the loop with his teeth, thus allowing Jack to haul up the cambric, whilst he descended with all speed with the swooning lady.

By this time there were plenty of ready hands to receive her.

And one, a Greek woman, who had been attracted to the spot by the shouts and cries, offered at once to take her to her own house.

"Yes," said the woman in compassionate tones, "I will give her shelter, for who knows what troubles may visit one's self, being ignorant of what an hour may bring forth ?"

"Good, bravo !" shouted the crowd, whose energies appeared to be exclusively confined to their jaws. "Hurrah ! Well done, brave Ingleese !"

One of the foremost to join in this shout was the Arab watchman whom Jack had practised on ; and quite unmindful that he had been made a victim to the act, he roared at the top of his lungs and beat time on the stones with a huge oaken staff.

Meantime, however, Nina was carried away, and the young guardsman, once more mounting the ladder, stood ready to receive his precious charge, which he did after the same manner as the first ; and Jack bade him good-bye in case he might not see him again.

"What do you mean ?" cried the young sergeant. " Do you think I am going to desert you ?"

"No; but I may not leave this house again alive. I already feel like a half-roasted chestnut, and I mean to see whether there is anyone else about whom I may rescue."

"Do so ; but I advise you to be careful. The people of Cairo may reward noble deeds, but they can't insure you your life. I shall be up here again in the twinkling of a bayonet."

By this time the crowd collected was all excitement.

As Tom descended, the manner in which they showed their sympathy was exceedingly emotional.

Some wept, others wrung their hands, and many strong, sallow-faced, yet chicken-hearted men, actually shed tears.

And this was about the whole of their exertions. But let us in the meantime follow the daring adventures of our gallant English boy.

Having satisfied himself that there was no one else in the room, he at once set about to discover the fate of the golden-haired Sela, whom he felt certain was somewhere in the burning house, and this was attended by some danger.

Two articles in the room caught his eye at that moment—a handkerchief and a water bottle—which he requisitioned at once, and thus made a wet cloth to tie across his mouth and nostrils.

" I believe I'd do for a fireman," thought Jack, he went to the room door and prepared to receive the rush of smoke on opening it.

"Whew ! What a cloud ! It's enough to choke a dozen savages."

The black and brown mixed volume of smoke was overpowering, and drove him back ; but he kept his footing, nevertheless, and fortunately retained his self-possession.

" One, two, three," he counted, so as to regulate his movements, and thus braving the smoke and darkness he felt his way in the passage outside.

Perfectly satisfied by the appearance of the house that there were more than two rooms on the floor, he felt about the walls in the hope of detecting a door, in which employment he nearly lost his life.

By some means he had reached the head of the stairs, and over-balancing himself, he had barely time to clutch at the banisters and save himself from falling. With a half-muttered cry on his lips he regained his equilibrium, and then further pursued his search, which led to his discovering another door, which he at once opened.

The room within was full of smoke.

The atmosphere also was fearfully hot and oppressive.

But our bold hero cared not a fig.

He was bound on an errand of mercy, and he would not flinch from it.

Throwing himself on his hands and knees, he crept into the room, and under the smoke he made his way around it, feeling about him as he proceeded.

" None, none ! there is no one here," he mentally ejaculated, when suddenly a sound—something that resembled the noise made by slow breathing—arrested his attention.

" Yes, it is right ahead," he muttered. "Push

on Jack—faint heart never rescued fair lady ;" and so saying he made his way towards the sound.

Presently his hand touched the bosom of a voluptuously-formed figure, whom he doubted not was a female.

" Joy ! I will save her if she is alive ; and if not, I will rescue her beautiful soft flesh from the devouring element."

But if he intended doing so he must be sharp, for the house seemed to be one mass of flame internally, from the roof to the basement.

Arab Jack had his yataghan tucked up under his clothing just in rear of his left arm, and this to some extent impeded his movements, but not much.

He, however, managed to draw the swooning girl off the ottoman on which she was lying, and down on his hands and knees as he was, dragged her from the heated room.

Jack's long absence from the window was now commented on by those in the street.

Had he succumbed to the fierce, withering heat, or had he fallen through the floor, was the question on every tongue.

Tom Atkins was almost beside himself with protracted suspense, and unable to contain himself longer, he crept in at the window and sought about for his chum.

Strangely enough, the first place he hit upon was the door, through which he groped his way, when suddenly coming upon something, he was thrown down and stretched at full length.

What his thoughts were at the moment is beyond description. It seemed to him that his life was thrown uselessly away ; but he gathered fresh courage, however, and then he discovered that the obstacle over which he had fallen was the one of which he was in search—Arab Jack.

To regain his feet and obtain some inkling of his chum's position was but the work of a moment, and with a strength, which under other circumstances he would have been incapable of, he drew both Jack and the girl to the window.

His appearance, with his smoke-begrimed face, was hailed with enthusiastic shouts by those below, and the firemen and watchmen, now mounted on several ladders, used their utmost endeavours to assist the trio to reach the ground.

The roar of the devouring flames and the ruddy glare in the sky rendered the scene appalling, for now the inhabitants could be seen on the housestops around wringing their hands and calling upon Allah to check the dire calamity.

The fire engines, such as they were, proved of little service in such a strait.

The scanty supply of water was rendered useless by the leaky state of the hose, so that the usual Oriental remedy was bound to be resorted to, such as pulling down the houses at both ends of the street, and thus checking the flames by confining the conflagration within a limited area.

Crash ! Crash !

The roof fell in, carrying with it several floors; and other houses, owing to the inflammable materials used in the party walls, were now added to the general destruction.

Clang ! Clang ! Clang ! still tolled the fire bell ; then a terrible, heartrending shout rent the air, and the burning edifice fell with a loud crash, burying all beneath it!

CHAPTER XXXVIII.

THE CRAFTY MALTESE FOE.—BARGAINING FOR JACK'S BIG DIAMOND.—A PLOT TO DESTROY OUR HERO.—REIS MAHOUD IS TAKEN INTO THE CONSPIRACY.—HOW THE TREACHEROUS MERCHANT WAS SOLD.

ARAB JACK had no more knowledge than a child unborn of how he was rescued from the burning house.

When reason dawned upon him he found himself lying on an Arabian bedstead, with a fair girl bending over him, moistening his lips with wine, and bathing his heated brow.

This was Sela, and no attention that was necessary did she omit; and when he opened his eyes and fixed them upon her she gave a joyful cry.

"Thank heaven," she exclaimed, clasping her hands. "Now is my prayer answered. O! how pleased I am to witness the restoration of my brave preserver."

"What has happened?" queried Jack, in surprise. "Have I had a repetition of Tel-el-Kebir? Speak, Sela—end this suspense, for I know something strange has transpired to bring me here."

"Hush, you must not talk so," replied Sela, placing a glass of cooling sherbet to his lips. "You have been suffering for weeks from a devouring fever; but now you shall soon gain strength, and your every wish shall be attended to at my untiring hands."

Jack would have gone into the whole detail if he had been permitted; but the fair girl put him off, telling him, however, that they were in the house of a friend of her brother's, a Maltese merchant, who was immensely rich, and was deeply indebted to her brother Hassan.

"Ah, have you heard of your brother of late?" said our hero, catching eagerly at her words. "Have I told you how we were captured by the Red Sheikh, and how I left him in the stronghold of the desert robber?"

"You have not," exclaimed Sela, now forgetting her own prudential warning in her anxiety for her brother's welfare. "Pray inform me if he is well, and how you chanced to meet again after being separated in Cairo?"

Jack was so revived by the refreshing odours of the flowers placed about the room, and the invigorating nectar which she made him at intervals sip, that he was enabled to tell her a good deal of the story, which so astounded her that she scarcely believed it real.

"It's true, nevertheless," replied Jack; "and that yataghan, which I must have lost in the fire, I would not have parted with for a diamond."

Sela smiled.

"It is not lost," she said. "I have it under my care. But speaking of diamonds, there is one beauty set in the hilt that would purchase the good graces of a sultana."

"That was given to me by an Indian nabob," said Jack, proudly, "as a grateful acknowledgment of my saving the vessel in which he and his daughter were voyaging up the Suez Canal."

"Then you prize it, of course. At the same time, it seems too valuable a sword to carry about with one on dangerous expeditions."

"Not such as the one in which I was last engaged. But you have not told me the cause of the fire, and how I was conveyed here."

"No, that would tax my powers too much. We only know that the curiously-constructed old edifice was destroyed, and that the fire commenced in the next street. It was a double house, you see, and the fire took place in the one at the back of us, and worked its way through into our apartments."

"That accounts for you all being overcome by the smoke. Was any one burnt?"

"Yes, the dwarf, who had been our faithful servant for so many years; but all the rest of the inmates escaped, for you see that the house in which the fire originated was attended by a guard of English soldiers from the fortress, who were entirely ignorant of what was passing in our street."

At this juncture the conversation was interrupted by the entrance of the doctor, who, although pleased with the recovery of his patient desired that he should enjoy perfect quiet for a few days.

Jack, on the other hand, wanted to be up and doing.

"I know I shall rebel, Sela, I feel like it," he said. "I cannot lay here when I am able to get about. I have determined to ascend the Nile. I should like to go right on to Sennaar or Khartoum."

"Just the journey I should like myself," said Sela, her large eyes sparkling with enthusiasm. "My sisters have gone to Rosetta for a few months, and if you go away I shall be left here cheerless and alone."

"But I can't take you with me," said Jack somewhat perplexed.

"Why not? I can be your page. I can fight, and if I had a little sword like your yataghan I could wield it with more effect and a great deal more courage than those cowardly Egyptians."

"What!" cried Jack, starting up into a sitting posture with delight. "Give me your hand, Sela. Why you talk as though you had already been in a skirmish. What a pity it is your name ain't Sam, or something of that sort."

"I'll take any name, Jack," she replied, tossing back her long golden hair. "You ask, have I been in a skirmish? Well, you should have seen us when we were turned out of our house in the suburbs of Alexandria. The rebel Arabs burned and pillaged most of the houses, and those ruffians with whom you had the *melée* set upon our place as soon as my brother was gone; but we fought them and got away, or you would not have seen us in Cairo."

"Well done!" exclaimed Jack, more astounded than ever. "If you like to go with me in search of your brother Hassan, I can raise some money on my jewels, and we'll go in mufti, as the Mahometans express it. What say you, Sela?"

"I'm on. Anything for a quiet life. I'll just drop a few lines to my sisters. To-morrow we'll make preparations, and will take leave of my friend here, who, I am sure, will be sorry to part with us."

Sela, however, was not so well acquainted with the habits and character of her Maltese friend as she supposed she was.

Maltese Joe, as the merchant was termed in the bazaars, was a money-grubbing old mole and the veriest slave to avarice. He had caught sight of Arab Jack's yataghan, and of course examined the costly jewels in its hilt, and the very thought of their value troubled him night and day.

Could he have surreptitiously obtained possession of the weapon, and stuck to it, he would have done so, but Sela stood in his way, so he was all the while concocting and endeavouring to hit upon some treacherous plan.

As soon as he heard that Jack was about to dispose of the diamond he went almost mad.

"Such an adamant," he mused to himself, calling the gem by its ancient name, "must have adorned the breastplate of Aaron the high priest. It is the 'Urim and Thummim' of history, for of a truth it is *light* and *perfection*."

He rubbed his thin white hands, and the evil glitter in his eye was almost as fierce as the sparkle of the diamond.

"Can I not substitute for it one much inferior?" he thought; "the boy will never know the difference. Or if not, I might dispose of him as I have disposed of many others. We shall see."

So saying, the evil old wretch actually went at once to put his vile thought into practice.

Ringing a small bell he summoned an ill-looking object from the cellar below and began giving him instructions.

"Is the reis, Mahoud, returned from Damietta ? If so let him be here at midnight with an ass and a couple of strong sacks for panniers. I have some merchandise for him to convey for me."

The ugly wretch who had been father to as many murders as would have filled a respectable Newgate calendar, then salaamed, and putting a greasy old fez on his unkempt head, glided serpent-like out of a small door into a very narrow and exceedingly dirty lane.

With an ambling gait he then proceeded to the waterside, where there were a number of small vessels moored, and inquired for the reis, or skipper, Mahoud, who was then busy taking in cargo ready for sailing the next day.

This was good news for our crafty Maltese merchant.

Having summoned our hero he informed him that he had found a customer for the diamond. "But," he added, "you must not fancy it to be the famous Pigot diamond, which was valued at £40,000, which was won by a young man at a lottery, and then sold to the pasha of Egypt for £30,000."

"I shall entertain no foolish fancies," replied Jack. "That diamond, so I have heard, ornamented the state sword of the great Bonaparte, but as I am no snivelling Frenchman I don't wish my yataghan to be mistaken for his old tin sword. Mine is for cutting down traitors, not playing at puppet show."

"Yash," drawled the merchant, opening his yellow eyes in surprse, and reminding Jack very much of the sun-dried crocodile that hung as a sign over the merchant's door. "Yash, my good gentleman, you very good boy, very brave."

"And very honest," sneered Jack, "as I want you to be. What is it you have to urge in condemnation of *my* diamond ?"

"That it ish verra coot, but de cutting is not proper ; it ish worth von thousand poundsh, and den I must pay von hondred to have it polished."

"All right," said Jack. "Dub up, old man, and then I will square off the few debts I owe you. I am hard up just now for a little ready cash."

"Den I can only advance you a little just now on account. De merchant no come until de bazaar shall be closed to-night."

"Very well," said our hero, "I'll keep the gem until then. You might be cutting and polishing it, do you see, before the bargain is struck, and I might not be too very well satisfied."

"Yash, I understand, Monsieur Ingleese," said the crafty Maltese. "Joe do plenty bis'ness mit all mans, so know how to deal every ting fair."

"I am not going to be gulled by you," muttered Jack as he ascended the stairs, and having sought Sela, he recounted to her his interview with the artful old sinner.

"Ah," said she, "it is as I suspect, Jack. The conversation I overheard between him and the slave nigger whom he works to death polishing ivory and such like, in that miserable den underground, explains his detestable plot. Take nothing at his hands in the shape of victuals or drink, or if you do, take an antidote soon after, which I will give you."

"I shall act on your advice, Sela, you may depend upon it," said Jack. "That he's an artful old devil I feel assured, and that, as you say, he would not scruple at putting us both out of the way to obtain the diamond without price, or at least make what to us would be a fortune out of it. Now what do you say if we try and do the old beggar instead ?"

"I am agreeable to anything, as I said before," replied the laughing girl. "And as Nina used to say when she was in her teasing moods that my bright golden locks were ginger, you will find the old adage 'ginger for pluck' is quite true, and that I shall be prepared as readily as yourself for any rough and tumble sort of work."

Jack gave a true schoolboy laugh.

"Why, Sela," said he, "it is a pity you are not a boy. But as you are going to adopt the disguise of the male sex, you should also adopt a male name."

"Call me Selim, then ; there you have it," said she, laughing till her sides shook. "If I go with you, mind, I shall want none of the namby-pamby ; I want to see some life."

An hour later a smart handsome young fellow, elegantly attired, might have been seen upon the wharf, where a host of small craft with tall tapering masts and yards were taking on board bales of coloured calico, beads, and Brummagem ware for Assouan.

This youth was no other than our adventurous Selim.

She had chosen her own disguise, and looked quite a treat compared with the clumsily-dressed merchants, who wore something like a dressing-gown reaching to their heels, girded at the waist with a gaudily-coloured sash, and a turban or fez, some of which were of various colours.

Selim's attire was something after the style of a young corsair.

Morocco boots reaching almost to the knee, pointed in the front and adorned with a silken tassel, red silk hose, blue silk breeches slashed and buckled at the knee, and a white shirt or caftan with broad sleeves and reaching to the same extremity, over which was a corsair vest or jacket without sleeves.

The latter was handsomely braided, whilst the sash that bound the kaftan or loose shirt was of the richest Damascus silk, as was the handkerchief which concealed the handsome braids of her golden hair, which was bound in folds around her head something after the fashion of a turban.

A couple of silver-mounted revolvers and a long Toledo dirk completed her outward attire, whilst a little dye just gave her hands and face the tint it was necessary for her to assume.

The reis or skipper of the boat that was to convey Jack and Selim up the Nile was just superintending the fitting up of the deck cabin for the convenience of his passsengers, when Selim arrived on the quay.

"We shall be ready to start at sunrise," said he in answer to her questioning, "and I have shipped a cook that can defy the whole world. Step aboard—mind how you come—and see how snug I've made your quarters."

Selim was quite delighted with what she saw, and so anxious was she to be sailing on the bright waters that she felt inclined to sleep on board that night.

But she thought of Jack and the crafty Maltese, Joe, so she retraced her way to the merchant's house and entered it by the private door.

Arab Jack was anxiously awaiting her, and having desired her to throw a light robe over her sumptuous dress they prepared to attend the invitation of the merchant, who desired them to join him in his apartment and sup with him.

"Now," said she, giving Jack a small bean, "be on your guard, place this in your mouth, and be cautious what you eat and drink."

The fawning old sinner was delighted when he found them so readily, as he supposed, fall into his snare.

He assured Jack that he had been offered the best price in the market for the diamond, that he would advance him one hundred pounds (Egyptian) on the bargain, and desired him to let him have it forthwith, so that when the merchant came there might be no delay, as in that case he might alter his mind.

"Agreed," said Jack. "Count me the hundred down, then I will entrust to you the gem. We are not Jews, and therefore have no need to haggle over the bargain."

"Deshidedly not, my good friend." And so with this understanding the money and the diamond changed hands.

CHAPTER XXXIX.

DIAMOND CUT DIAMOND.—ARAB JACK AND HIS FEMALE CHUM DEFEAT THE VILLAINOUS PLANS OF THE WILY OLD MERCHANT.—THE DUMMY VICTIMS.—HOW THE REIS WAS SHOT. OUR WORTHY PAIR HAVE ANOTHER STARTLING ADVENTURE.

IT was drawing towards midnight when Maltese Joe, having wearied himself with watching the tardy movements of the hands of the clock, took up his small lamp and ascended the rickety stairs.

He had put on a pair of old carpet slippers, but in spite of this precaution the old woodwork would at times give a creak and cause him to mutter words to himself that would shock ears polite.

Otherwise the old place was still as the grave, so that he could hear himself breathe. Yet with a stealthiness he had acquired by long practice he gained the landing and opened the door leading to the apartments of his intended victims.

It was to Jack's bed that he paid his first visit, and there to his satisfaction he beheld the prone form of the boy, drugged to such an extent that he could not recover consciousness for many hours, even if he did not fall asleep in the cold arms of death.

Yes, there he lay, but to make assurance doubly sure the old wretch turned down the coverlid and exposed a portion of the pale face and swept his hand over the victim's limbs.

Then, with a ghastly smile, such as a fiend only could assume, he repaired to the chamber above, in which Sela had slept since the fire, and there his investigation was the same.

"Dat ish well," he muttered, as he descended again to Jack's room. "Now for de gold ; it ish in de bag, and I dare shey he did as I desired him—put it under ish pillow."

The sinful old wretch trembled in every limb, and his hand shook as though he had been stricken with the palsy, yet he paused not, but crept to Jack's bed, and placed his long bony fingers beneath the pillow.

The gold ! Yes, it was there. The bag seemed just as heavy as it did when last he weighted it. Nothing had been taken out : he felt quite certain of that.

"Ah, vat vos that ?"

He paused and glanced around him in a terrified manner. It seemed to him that the curtains had rustled, but he was not certain, and through the gloom he pictured to himself a pale face with a dark pair of eyes glaring at him.

"Bah, it ish only fancy," he muttered to himself, "Dere, now de clock strikes twelf. De reis will be here, and I must be ready."

Grasping the bag in his trembling hand, he crept down the stairs again, and when he was gone two grinning-faced figures appeared in the room.

"What do you think of the wretch, Jack ? I am glad we stayed to witness his fiendish treachery. I would like to see how he will handle the lay figures, and place them in the sacks."

"So should I," returned Jack ; "but I am afraid the experiment would be dangerous. You see, he is rich and powerful, and might upset all our plans as it is, when he finds out how he is duped. When he goes to count the gold, for instance, and examine the diamond by daylight, he'll go fairly mad."

"So he will when he brings his evil accomplices here to assist in removing the dummies. What a lark ! Had we not better make our escape at once by the window ?"

Selim, as we must now term our disguised heroine, had scarcely uttered the words when the room door creaked, and they had barely time to conceal themselves behind the hangings when the merchant entered the room.

Jack had darkened his bull's eye, so that old Joe could not observe any difference in the appearance of the room, and so finding all was still he whispered to his accomplices to come in.

"Is that the boy?' queried the reis, pointing to the outlined figure on Jack's bed. "If so, we had better not disturb him till we have secured the girl, for, you see, in these matters it is better to work systematically, for if the boy should happen to come to he might kick up a shindy, disturb the girl, and then we should have to resort to the very measures you wish to avoid."

The trembling sinner glanced round the gloomy apartment in evident alarm.

The pale face and the dark eyes seemed to be observing him still, and glad enough to leave the scene, if only for a few minutes, he led the way to the upper room.

"Now," whispered Jack, "we must delay our departure no longer. The slave and the reis would be awkward customers for us to encounter, for you may know by what the reis said that he is a desperate fellow, and would not hesitate to commit murder to obtain his ends and purchase his own safety."

He had scarcely spoken, when there was a loud commotion overhead.

Something was thrown heavily to the floor, a volley of fierce oaths succeeded it, and then there was a trampling up and down the room.

"Confusion to us! The very saints are against us," cried the reis. "The insult of this trickery I would blot out with blood if I could only drop athwart the hawse of the villains who enacted it."

Then there were heavy footsteps on the stairs. Selim opened the window, stepped out on to the wire-rope ladder, and was down in the side street in an instant.

Jack followed his companion just as the footsteps reached the door, and closing the latticed frame, which opened outwards, he placed an iron bolt in the hole he had previously bored, and thus prevented it being opened from within.

"I should like to take the ladder away, so as to kept up the mystery," said Jack, when he stood by the side of Selim; "but, as it is, we had better move off, and take a circuitous route to the quay."

Selim was quite elated at the novelty of her situation. And so away they glided in the darkness, disturbing several dogs who were dosing in the roadway as they proceeded, until they reached the houses of the more opulent, enclosed in their high, gloomy walls.

As they emerged from this street the report of a firearm startled them, then there was a clamour of angry voices, and the name of Allah was uttered in connection with expressions of less reverence.

"Ah, we have got you, then," exclaimed a voice that Jack remembered having heard somewhere before ; and ere he could recover from his surprise a couple of armed men presented their rifles at him.

"What is the matter?" cried Selim, in alarm, stepping from the shadow of a buttress which had concealed her. "Are we in the hands of lawless robbers and compelled to defend our lives?"

"I know nothing of you," cried the commanding voice which had first spoken. "We mean to arrest this prisoner, who has just escaped from the fortress. You, from your appearance, seem to be some jaunty coxcomb out for a night's spree. I advise you to go home, or pass along and not interfere with our duty."

"Not until I have learnt by what or whose authority you molest my friend here. You may be the governor of the fortress for all I care—you shall know who I am in the morning."

Jack as yet had not spoken.

He was so startled that he could not frame his lips to disguise his voice.

"Well," said he, when both sides had endured some moments' suspense, "what is this terrible crime of which you so wantonly accuse me?"

"There must be some mistake," replied the governor, who was all the time wondering with what family of note the handsomely-clad youth, as he took Selim to be, was connected. "But under all the circumstances I ought to take you to the guard-room and detain you until morning. Since the blundering Ingleese have taken possession of the citadel we seem to have nothing but escapes from the fortress."

"That is not our fault, so you had better let us pass quietly on our way," said Selim, "for in either case, whether you arrest me or my companion, whose respectability I can vouch for, it will go hard with you on the morrow."

One of the soldiers still held his rifle at the present, but the other one had lowered his, and was glancing towards the far end of the street, where a dark figure seemed to be dodging in and out of the various entries.

"There, look yonder, officer," said the man. "Shall I fire?"

The governor had not time to reply before the soldier who had his rifle cocked and presented let fly, and a fearful howl proclaimed that the bullet had struck the dodging figure.

"There's your man," cried Jack, who just then caught sight of a four-legged animal, the leading of which had caused the ambling motion of the pedestrian, and the blessings he heaped on the man who shot him was evidence enough to prove to both Jack and Selim that the wounded miscreant was the reis.

"Whoever he is, he's got the bullet instead of you," exclaimed the governor, starting off at a brisk run. "It won't do for me to run amuck and shoot everybody without knowing what I'm about."

Arab Jack and the disguised Selim made themselves scarce as soon as possible, glad enough to get off so scot free, but they had not proceeded far when the creaking sign over a barber's shop came tumbling down upon them, and almost immediately it was followed by the form of a man.

"Dash you, what does this mean?" thundered Jack, drawing his yataghan on the instant. "Scarcely have we got clear of one set of night brawlers than we meet with another. Who are you, curse you? I have a mind to alarm the watch."

"I hope you won't," replied the fellow, in a tone that showed he was labouring under some strong excitement. "I have but just escaped from a set of blood-seekers who threatened to shoot me, mistaking me for a vagabond who has escaped from the calaboose."

"Who are you, then?" demanded Jack.

"An honest sailor, who having come on shore for a bit of a spree lost his way, and is now trying to get safely down to his ship, but I doubt very much if I shall, if I go on in this way ; hearing your footsteps, I climbed up on to this sign out of your way, and you've witnessed the result."

Arab Jack's heart was softened by the tone and manner of the man.

"If you are a sailor," said Jack, "we are going down to the quay and will show you the way. Three are no company they say, but three are better than two in a place where we are at any moment liable to be murdered."

"What say you, Selim?" added Jack.

"If the third person is honest," replied Selim,

guardedly. "Some say it is not wise to make strange companions, even in the desert."

"Then I am honest enough, if that's all you fear," said the man. "I am a stranger here in Cairo, and I would get out of the place with all the speed that's possible."

In this manner they reached the quay, and as daylight was breaking Jack and his female chum went on board the vessel they had taken passage in.

CHAPTER XL.

SAILING ON THE NILE. — OLD CAIRO. — AT-TACKED BY THE DESPERATE NILE PIRATES. —DARING CONDUCT OF JACK AND HIS PLUCKY CHUM. — SELIM'S LIFE IS IM-PERILLED.—LORD WOOLBERRY NARROWLY ESCAPES BECOMING A MURDERER.

THE skipper of the commodious craft was very obliging. He had coffee and a sub-stantial repast prepared for the voyagers, among whom were not only Arab and Egyptian merchants, but Europeans, two of them being Englishmen.

Jack was all about, as the saying is, then. It was quite a treat to hold conversation with his own countrymen, who took him for a well-learned Mussulman, as he could talk so freely of their country.

A strong fleet of vessels of all descriptions, nuggers as well as boats of heavy burden, were prepared to go up the Nile as soon as the morning wind set in. Pipes and cigars, therefore, were brought into active service, whilst the usual bustle preparatory to the setting of the sails was carried on.

The reis being shorthanded, went ashore to engage a couple of smart sailors and procure his bill of lading in the meantime, and soon after Jack descried the fellow who fell off the front of the barber's shop among those who were set-ting the tall, pointed sails.

"Selim," said Jack, "we must keep an eye on that customer. Do you know, I suspect he is the fellow they were searching after for having escaped from the fortress El Kalah."

"You do !" exclaimed the girl, mischievously. "Well, it is nothing wonderful, for birds of a feather, it is said, flock together, you know——"

"Yes, yes," said Jack, interrupting her ; "but I see something of more importance in the affair than you do."

"What is that ?"

"I believe his name is Ababa. There was a prisoner in there of such a name, and if it is he, he is the lover of the slave girl Zela, by whose connivance I was enabled to escape from the stronghold of the Red Sheikh, whom I told you about."

"Then I wish he was back again with his sweetheart and that Hassan was here in his place. I am sure my brother must be tired of his capti-vity before this time. He was always of a roving disposition, and never cared to stay long in one spot."

It was pleasant weather, the voyage was delightful, and the fresh breeze after being stived up on shore was quite invigorating to our young adventurers.

To Selim it was just the same as a school girl going out for her treat, and she could not help remarking to Jack how jolly it was.

"I have never been up this part of the Nile before," she added ; "and now, dear Jack, I hope we shall see a few crocodiles, and also have a shot at some of them."

"So you shall," said Jack, "and I'll have one or two boiled ready for you to practise on; but perhaps we may have some other sort of amphi-bians on which to try our powder."

Our hero was not far out.

The wind blowing both fair and strong, the reis kept the craft sailing until it was opposite Old Cairo, where one of the tall lateen sails was brailed up to the yard and the vessel hove to.

This being the site of the Egyptian Babylon, the Englishmen naturally wanted to take a cur-sory view of the place and to listen to some ex-planations respecting it.

"The Jews," said the reis, who was very com-municative, especially after partaking of a glass or two of wine, "have a synagogue at Old Cairo, and the Catholics a convent and a church ; but the Coptic priests possess the most precious spot of all, a grotto or low chapel in which they say the Virgin lived some time with the infant Jesus when they fled into Egypt. And that," said he, pointing to an island directly in front of the city, "is Roudda, or the gardens, in which the Mekkias or Nileometer is situated for measuring the rising of the Nile, and in whose splendid galleries the Arabs and Egyptians sit at ease smoking their chibouks and drinking coffee, and watching the rising of the water which is to irri-gate the land, and thus enable the government to regulate the taxes."

Steering the vessel across the Nile in a westerly direction, he then pointed out the town of Ghizeh, surrounded by its date trees, and in the distance, standing in their glory, the pyramids, still pressing the ground where the ancient Memphis stood.

Some of the voyagers wanted to go on shore, but the reis would not give consent, for a fair wind was blowing, and he wanted to make the most of every chance of reaching Assouan.

Our adventurers were also anxious to see the cataracts, and they were delighted to view the two immense triangular sails belly out and sweep the vessel along with amazing rapidity against the swift current.

Eight leagues above Old Cairo is the little mud village of Sheik Itmaam, and there they stopped for the night, and were quite amused with the number of date trees which surrounded and interspersed the huts, whilst the white herons which perched among the green boughs gave a dazzling beauty to the scene.

But all this was changed when supper was over and darkness set in.

In spite of the smoking that was carried on to a late hour, the mosquitoes invaded the sanctity of the mosquito curtains, and tired every one out before they allowed them to sleep.

Everyone turned in except the sailors, who slept under an awning in the forepart of the vessel, leaving one of their number to keep watch ; but he, like the rest, worn out with the heat and toil of the day, dozed off as well. Consequently the first thing that was heard was a thump against the vessel's side, and to the consternation of the sleepers, who were thus suddenly awakened, they found the vessel boarded by a score or more of the bloodthirsty Nile pirates.

Jack sprang out of his hammock in a moment and discharged his revolver at a head he saw at

JACK GRASPED THE PALM OF HASSAN.   *p.* 108.

the window of his caboose, and a desperate encounter ensued.

"Selim," cried Jack, shaking the hammock of his chum, who still slept throughout all the noise, "rouse out, my hearty, the pirates have attacked our wooden walls!"

Selim waited for no more than this. As they all had, according to custom, lain down with their clothes on, they were of course all armed ready to repel the attack, and the thieving Arabs met with such a reception as they had not bargained for.

Jack hit the fellow at whom he fired, but the ball was not sufficient to give him his quietus.

He sprang on one side, crept in at the window of the next compartment, and with his long stiletto-like knife inflicted a nasty wound in the fore-arm of one of the passengers, whom Jack, judging from his appearance, took to be a weak, sickly boy. Then the ruffian fell to the deck with the death cry, as it seemed, of his victim ringing in his ears.

Our hero by this time was in the body of the

boat, yataghan in hand, slashing at every fez or turban he did not recognise. He feared to use his pistol lest in the darkness he might shoot any of the crew.

Close to Jack the plucky Selim, too, was doing his level best. With dirk and pistol he was working away, much to the discomfiture of two dusky ruffians who were endeavouring to enter the cabin, from whence cries of pain still emanated.

One shot missed, but the next shot struck one of the ruffians in the cheek just as the reis rushed up from below, calling on his men.

The pirate with the bullet in his cheek gave a most hideous yell, and staggering to the side fell over into the water, which so unnerved his companion that he took to his heels and hid among some of the bales.

Meanwhile the other passengers attacked the robbers in other parts of the ship, so that several were badly wounded and one dead before the skipper could get a word out of any of his crew.

While he was swearing and yelling at the top

of his voice. Arab Jack, who had just disposed of a troublesome customer, slipped into the cook-house, and setting light to a piece of fresh-tarred rope, which the cook had placed ready to light his fire with in the morning, illumined the scene.

The pirates on finding their nefarious actions thus exposed were all taken aback.

"Fly !" yelled their leader, showing the way himself to their boat, which was fastened alongside.

But our hero checked his progress, and called on the passengers to stand firm, as most of the crew had deserted them and were now seen making for the shore.

It was a long swim, with the water rushing like a mill-race, but to them it was a task of little difficulty, urged as they were by a twofold incentive.

Not only were their lives in jeopardy if they remained on board to defend the vessel, but the whole of their valuables, concealed about their persons, they were in danger of losing.

To Arab Jack, therefore, the skipper was greatly indebted for his aid, and our hero well earned the praise he afterwards lavished upon him.

Barring the pirate captain's way, he engaged him blade to blade, and so desperate was the assault that Jack not only wounded him, but made him howl for quarter.

"Fiend of darkness !" Jack yelled, "I'll quarter you. Hand me your sword or I'll run mine through your blackened heart."

"This to thine, then," retorted the pirate, savagely, making a fresh lunge that almost threw our hero off his equilibrium. "Allah is with me ; he strengthens my arm."

And so it seemed, too.

He was a very Hercules in stature, and the blows dealt by his strong muscles were terrific.

Jack, however, possessed superior skill, and fortune turning in his favour just in the nick of time, he beat the pirate leader back and forced him against one of the masts.

It was strange that it should so happen, but it was nevertheless true, and Jack, availing himself promptly of his momentary advantage, seized the end of a rope that was fastened round the mast, and running with it round the base of the lofty spar thus bound the pirate captain a prisoner to it.

The rascal was perfectly astounded when he found himself thus made fast, and he made desperate efforts to cut the rope, but failed.

At length, however, Jack snatched the cutlass from his grasp, and then went to the assistance of one of the Englishmen, who was beaten down upon one knee.

A couple of pirates had beaten him down, and as he was bleeding fast from a wound in his arm, it was evident he would soon be reduced to a weakness which would force him to give in.

Arab Jack only just interfered in bare time.

"Cowards !" he thundered. "Does it take two of you to slaughter an aged and wounded man ? Hence with you. Thus do I consign you to your doom !" With a couple of swift blows he gashed open the cheek of one of the dusky ruffians and wounded the other in the neck.

The oaths that followed these actions were of the most awful character ; but Jack paused not to comment upon them, but following up the attack with increased vigour, he forced one of

his adversaries over the side, whilst the aged passenger disposed of the other.

At this juncture our hero observed the other Englishman, with rage pictured in his every lineament, levelling a revolver at some one in the starboard after deck-house.

Casting his eyes in that direction our hero beheld Selim bending over a lovely-featured individual lying in a hammock slung to the beams of the deck-house.

Jack could not take his eyes off this lovely vision until he heard the lock of the revolver give a sharp click, and then he turned and struck aside the weapon, which otherwise would have settled accounts with Selim in this world.

"Hold ! What are you doing ?" roared Jack, horrified at the act of the Englishman. "That is my companion. Why should you attempt his life ?"

"Because his foul lips have polluted those of my daughter, whom I so disguised, thinking it would be for her safety ; and now that horrid boy, your companion as you call him, has in some way discovered our secret, and this is the result."

Jack, in spite of the seriousness of the case, was compelled to laugh right out.

"They have discovered each other's secret," he said, sinking his voice ; "strangely enough, my companion is also a girl."

"Good God ! you astound me !" gasped the English gentleman. "I have been on the very brink of committing a murder. Accept my everlasting thanks for having thus preventing me having her blood on my hands."

Jack until now had not looked well into the features of the speaker, but now he saw that the gentleman was ingeniously disguised.

"Great heaven !" Jack exclaimed, "you certainly are Lord Woolberry, whose daughter and himself I rescued from the rebel mob during the massacre at Alexandria."

"Indeed !" gasped his lordship, giving an involuntary start. "I am glad to see you : but how is it you are not in Massowah with my dear friend Signor Varnoni, to whom I introduced you after I saved you from the vengeance of the Arab water-carriers ?"

Jack briefly explained, taking care, however, not to mention anything that was detrimental to himself, and then they both entered the deck-house, where Selim was consoling and alleviating to the best of her ability the sufferer's pain.

When Jack entered the wounded girl replaced the sand-veil with goggles in it which she had worn, and once more she bore the appearance of a boy, which highly amused Selim, as their cases were so much alike.

"It is a wonder I have not killed your nurse, my darling," said his lordship, addressing his daughter. "Whoever would have thought that two individuals were masquerading in the same form on board the same vessel ?"

CHAPTER XLI.

TOM TRYSAIL TURNS UP AGAIN ON THE MAN-OF-WAR'S STEAM LAUNCH—DISPOSAL OF THE DEAD AND WOUNDED PIRATES—ARRIVAL AT ASSOUAN—ASCENDING THE CATARACTS—THE SAND STORM—THE CROCODILE AND THE NILE BOATMAN—A HORRIBLE DEATH AND A TERRIBLE REVENGE.

DAY was just breaking in the east when the last of the pirates was either driven overboard or secured, and then the reis turned his attention to the cowardly conduct of his men.

"I believe," said he to our hero, "that the job was planned before we left the quay. Some of my crew belong to this place, and I believe they were in collusion with the pirates."

"Then they must be punished," said Jack. "People are not going to be robbed and murdered with impunity. What do you say to manning a small boat and going ashore to see the El-belled (village chief)?"

"Just what I wish. You have guessed my thoughts to a turn. Can you pull a boat or steer?"

"I can do both," answered Jack. And with the handiness of a sailor he set to work casting loose the boat and hooking the tackles upon her so as to hoist it out.

"I don't think that fellow's in the swim," said the skipper to our hero when he had an opportunity to draw him on one side, pointing to Ababa. "He did well, and assisted us greatly in ridding us of those desperate fiends."

At that moment the steam launch of a British ironclad rounded a point and appeared to their view.

"This is a godsend," said Jack, who was now regarded in the light of a genuine hero by all on board. "We will hail her, and hear what they say of our doings."

As the steam launch drew near, Jack recognised in the bow the thick-bearded visage of Tom Trysail, who was on the look out, and waved his hand with joy on beholding our hero safe and sound.

The lieutenant rushed up from below on his vessel being hailed, and steering close alongside he beheld in the cold grey light the ghastly relics of the terrible affray.

"I have not time to assist you," said he to the reis. "I am carrying important dispatches. Put the wounded and dead pirates in their own boat, tow it ashore, and let the authorities take charge of it."

The reis acted on this advice.

The dead and dying were placed in the boat and towed ashore to the skirt of the village, whilst those who were less hurt were securely bound and fastened to the ringbolts in various parts of the ship.

The village chief was astounded when he heard the news, but he protested indignantly against the accusation of the sailors who belonged to the village of collusion with the dastardly pirates.

From the statement of one of the wounded, it transpired that some of the pirates were part of Reis Mahoud's crew, his vessel being detained owing to the bullet wound in his shoulder, which caused them to desert.

"It is a serious case," said the village sheikh, "and I must go with you to Assouan. So you must make room for me and my servant and my baggage and camel."

It was of no use demurring about this.

The reis knew that for this service his cargo would be taxed to pay the sheikh, who wanted to make as much ado about it as possible.

"A camel, eh!" said Jack to his chum. "Well, that's good goods. Selim. We have come for something on this adventure up the Nile."

Some of the sailors having been collected, and soundly rattaned, were then put on board, and the vessel was taken to the wharf, where the camel and the other effects were embarked, much to the amusement of our young adventurers.

The reis piloted his own vessel up the river, and after one or two stoppages they arrived at Assouan, where our boys (save the mark!) had the pleasure of gazing on the First Cataract.

Arab Jack and his chum left the vessel, taking with them Ababa, whose contract with the reis was then completed.

Jack and his suite, as we may now term them, stayed only two days in Assouan, to view the chief features of the town, and then they joined a party which was going up the cataracts, the same as themselves.

Steadily the boat sailed up to the first gate, as it is called, and Jack began to wonder how they could ascend it, for it seemed a task of no mean pretensions.

However, on arriving there they waited for the morrow's dawn, which gave our adventurers an opportunity of riding round the neighbourhood on the magnificent quadrupeds which hail from Jerusalem.

By dawn, as luck would have it, a favourable north wind blew, and increased in violence until it assumed the proportions of a stiff gale, which was hailed with delight by the skipper.

The crew, almost naked, having set the sails and hauled up the anchor, then prepared for their difficult labour, and the skipper having ascended the roof of the deck cabin addressed them. "My lads," said he, "if you pull the boat up over the falls you shall have plenty of backsheesh, but if you fail you shall have a taste of the kerbash, which I have carefully preserved in pickle."

Our hero also got up and gave them a few cheering words, after which they threw off their kaftans, or loose blue shirts, and naked as the proverbial robins, jumped into the stream.

"Bravo! Good!" cried Jack, as their heads appeared above the foaming water, and with two long ropes one-half the crew, by prodigious efforts, gained a rock on one bank and the opposite half the other.

Arrived at the foot of the fall, the vessel became stationary, and hung as it were staggering against the weight of waters which rushed in heavy volumes over the bows.

Had the wind lulled or the men let go the ropes the boat would have swung round with awful rapidity, and with dangerous results. As it was, however, the boatmen pulled like niggers, hauling and screaming with all their might, and after a series of stupendous efforts they shifted the ropes from rock to rock, and at length it seemed as if their labour was rewarded.

But this was not so.

The rope that was fastened to a crag on the starboard side broke, and away went the boat until she dashed against a rock, which nearly shattered her.

The captain, however, was equal to the occasion.

With oaths and promises, he after awhile got the boat's head pointed up the stream, and another attempt was made, which in the end proved successful, and the first gate of the Nubian cataracts was passed.

Half a mile further on the Second Cataract is situated, and after a short rest the crew went at it again, and got the boat over it with greater ease than they accomplished the first ascent.

"Well done!" cried our hero. "I will stand coffee all round for this performance, for you deserve it ; and I feel proud to acknowledge you have laboured so gallantly."

"Backsheesh, ya Howdaji," was the Arabs' answer. "Backsheesh! Backsheesh! Ya—ha, we work much plenty!"

Their claims being satisfied, the captain looked up at the sun, and, turning to our hero, said :

"I wonder whether we can pass the two next cataracts by sunset? I should like to sleep in Nubia to-night."

"So would I," said Jack. "What do you say, Selim? Especially if there is any better sleep to be had there. I hope there are not so many gnats and sandflies there as we have hitherto been honoured with."

"There are plenty of mosquitoes ; but we may have worse plagues than them," replied the skipper.

And verily his words were too true.

Jack had no sooner rewarded the boatmen than they turned lazy, and wanted to go into a village where they were known to see their friends, a request that was readily replied to by showing them the long canes or kurbashes.

"We mustn't be too hard on them, skipper," said Jack. "They worked hard while they were at it, and we must give even old Nick his due."

"Yes," said the skipper, "we shall have our due very shortly. I can see it coming ; we may look out for squalls."

The rest of the passengers were not a very lively lot ; but they were very agreeable, so that when the skipper's prophecy was fulfilled they kept close in their cabins, and showed not their faces until the storm ceased.

And what a storm was that!

The wind blew fearfully from the desert, bringing with it such clouds of hot sand that the passengers were forced to retreat under awnings and rush into the cabins at times ; and then even, when both windows and doors were closely barred, nothing was free from its gritty influence.

As soon as the storm ceased, the boat was cast off, and the wind being unfair, the boatmen had to haul the boat along by sheer strength.

Jack and Selim found plenty to amuse their minds.

As they walked along the banks their ears were constantly assailed by the cry of 'backsheesh,' and the sigh of the sallia and the creak of the shadoog, as the lazy oxen turn them from sunrise to sunset and raise the water to irrigate the land.

Their next stoppage was at Kalabsheh, a distance of between forty and fifty miles above Assouan, beneath whose cool leafy palms the boat was moored.

Here there was another rapid, but not so large as those they had passed, but it compelled them to moor for the night and start business early in the morning.

In a dead calm, Jack and Selim with several of the passengers put off in a small boat to visit the temples of Beytel-Welled and Kalabsheh.

Having clambered up the hot glaring rocks to the former of these, they found it consisted of two chambers hewn in the solid face of the rock.

At the upper end are two niches, each containing three sculptured figures in high relief, and on the walls outside are sculptured in a very beautiful manner the victories of the great Rameses.

As Jack had read a deal about these, he was exceedingly interested.

The Kalabsheh is the ruins of the largest Nubian temple, but is of much later date than the Beytel-Welled, but it is said to be built of the stones of a much more ancient temple.

"No stay here till dark," said the boatman who acted as guide ; "bad mans come here at night, rob, murder, and leave the body to fester in the sun."

"Let us return on board, then," said Jack, with an uncomfortable shrug ; "the place looks dismal and lonesome enough without adding to it fresh horrors."

But for all that fresh horrors were in store for them.

In ascending this cataract the men had to go naked into the water as before, and Jack, who was watching how they were carrying a line across to the opposite rocks, was startled to see a huge crocodile leave the sedgy reeds on the bank and make open-mouthed for one of the poor fellows in the water.

The man, who was battling with the flood, did not observe the enormous creature at first, but when he did so he gave one piercing cry, and seemed to fall a victim to the monster at once, without so much as an effort to escape from its voracious jaws, or the least struggle.

Arab Jack, paralysed though he seemed, flew to the cabin for a revolver, and taking steady aim shot the "temsak," as it is called, on the tip of the nose, causing it to kick and flounder in the agitated water.

But the brother of the unfortunate man witnessed the scene not only with a feeling of horror, but a sensation of deadly hate.

Putting the large knife with which he was armed to clear away obstacles between his large ivory teeth, he seized a pole with which he had been wading, and thrusting it under his arm sprang into the stream and swam out to the monster who was now the living coffin of his brother.

The water was still red round about the spot when he reached the snorting creature, whose hot fœtid breath was poured into his face, but the dusky swimmer was not dismayed.

He gazed fearlessly at the great horny eyes, and the tremendous jaws, which, as the top one was raised like the lid of some huge chest, disclosed the terrible rows of jagged saw-like teeth.

The "temsak" sprang forward to seize him, but quick as lightning he poised the long pole in his hands, just as a tight-rope walker balances his bar, and raising it above his head he hurled it crosswise between the jaws of the snorting crocodile, and then dived beneath its breast.

"Bravo, bravo!" shouted Jack, who was all excitement. "Selim, try your hand at a shot. See if you can put a bullet in its eye."

The brave girl, however, was too unnerved to do so.

The shock occasioned by the witnessing of so horrible a scene as the devouring by those jaws of a human being was enough to appal the stoutest heart.

The crocodile, however, had this time found its match.

The pole, now fast between its jaws, and in which its teeth were embedded, both impeded its forward progress and prevented it from going under the water.

All operations now ceased, every eye being fixed on the pair, the crocodile trying desperately to free itself from its encumbrance, and the man endeavouring to clamber up on to its back.

These were moments of fearful anxiety and terrible suspense.

Once or twice when the man essayed to climb on to the hard scaly back he was thrown up into the air, and descended into the water with a fearful splash, when the huge creature would endeavour to kill him with its tail, which if it could have struck him with, would have settled the question in a moment.

At length, however, the man succeeded in his object, and sitting astride the monster's scaly neck, clasped his knife firmly in his right hand, and reaching out buried the long blade to the very hilt in the left eye of the writhing monster.

CHAPTER XLII.

THE JOURNEY TO THE MONASTERY. — SURROUNDED BY BEDOUIN ARABS.—TREACHERY OF ABABA.—ANOTHER DEATH STRUGGLE FOR THE BIG DIAMOND.—SELIM'S ABDUCTION.—ARAB JACK WOUNDED AND DISCOVERED BY THE TROOPS OF THE MAHDI.

THE shocking death of the unfortunate boatman and the revenge of his exasperated brother had scarcely died out of the minds of the voyagers when a fresh disaster occurred.

On reaching one of the upper cataracts, the boat being detained on some frivolous pretence by the sheikh, Jack and Selim, accompanied by Ababa, hired some camels and a guide and paid a visit to a Coptic monastery. This was situated in a barren plain, in which the inhabitants were secluded from other habitations and the rest of the outer world by a chain of lofty mountains, whose summits seemed to tower into the sky.

As they approached the wall the sight was one of oppressive grandeur, for it seemed to be more like the abode of the dead in that vast solitude than the habitation of the living, and Jack expressed his views concerning it very freely.

"Well," said he to Selim, who seemed deeply interested in the journey, "how would you like to live there all your life, shut up within those grey, cold walls, without a window to look out of, or anything cheerful to view, even if you had windows?"

"Not much, Jack; but if I had your cheerful company it might not be so bad. You see, society makes all the difference."

Jack did not see the dark scowl that crossed the features of Ababa, who overheard her words.

Had he done so it would have rendered him at ease.

The dark-skinned robber, for such he really was, and for which he had been incarcerated in the fortress of El Kalah, had suspected Selim's sex, and now he felt sure he had discovered it.

Love and jealousy, therefore, entered his evil-disposed heart, and dark thoughts concerning the fair girl took possession of him.

"Yes; she must be mine," he muttered, as he glanced sidelong at her delicately-tinted skin, which was of the smoothness of ivory, and as soft as a piece of velvet. "I may never more see Zela, and if I do, what of that?"

Soon they reached the walls, which being of the same colour as the sand, were not visible at a distance, and having found the portal or small iron door in the lofty wall, they dismounted and knocked for admittance.

"Who art thou?" responded the voice of some being who was invisible from the outside.

"What want you? Why do you disturb our solitude?"

"We are poor travellers," replied Jack, boldly. "We come hither to seek rest and food, and to receive the holy father's blessing."

"You can have all you require," replied the voice; "but we cannot let you in here. Robbers may be lurking about, and if I should open the portal and the Bedouins were to enter, we should be all murdered and stripped of all we possess."

"But we are peaceful enough," exclaimed our hero; "and when once inside, if any robbers were to attack the place, could we not help you to defend it?"

He scarcely had spoken when a party of Bedouin Arabs, mounted on fleet steeds, appeared round the corner of one of the walls, and the leader, Abdallah, spurring impudently up to Jack, demanded his surrender and the sacrifice of any valuables he and his party might have about them.

Ababa drew back a pace from our hero and made a sign to the robber leader, who thereupon raised his voice a key higher and demanded their weapons.

"If you want mine," replied Jack, defiantly, "you can have it—in your heart. Here is my yataghan. Raise but your hand against one of my party, and I will show you how I can use it."

The robber chief smiled and bit his lip with vexation.

"Boy," said he, "Allah has ill-bestowed his blessing upon you. Do you not see that we out-number you threefold? Such arrogance cannot be tolerated. See, already your number is diminished."

This was true. But Jack had not observed it till that moment.

The guide he had hired, and paid before starting, had turned his animal about, and mounting its back was already galloping away over the soft sand.

Jack uttered a fierce expletive on discovering this.

He would have sent a bullet after the treacherous guide had he not felt the necessity of preserving his ammunition for a more serviceable season.

Whilst turning his head, the robber chief took advantage of the movement, and bringing his prancing steed by a touch of the rein to our hero's side, he tried to seize his yataghan and wrench it from his grasp.

"Confound your impudence!" cried Jack,

springing back a couple of paces on the instant. "I have said I will only part with this with my life, and, furthermore, I have sworn it."

The rest of the Bedouin party gazed on with sullen avaricious glances.

They saw that the hilt of the yataghan was ablaze with jewels, and that the big diamond, which now shone gloriously in the sun, was worthy a struggle to possess it.

Jack, however, although the chance of victory was so much against him, allowed not his courage to falter, and then for the first time he became suspicious of Ababa's fidelity.

On turning towards him to see what sort of a demonstration he was making, he found him ogling the beautiful Selim and whispering something in her ear.

With his quick perception, Jack read the fellow's villainy in a moment. But he was so placed that he could not chastise him on the instant.

Giving Ababa one of his warning looks, however, he made him understand that he had discovered his treachery. And then Ababa threw off all further disguise.

"Abdallah," said Ababa to the robber chief, "I have no valuables about me. I have been persecuted and robbed by this fellow here. Take him and do with him as you will. I shall take no part in his favour. But remember that I shall expect my share of the spoil."

Both Jack and Selim were astounded at this announcement, and stood upon the defensive.

"Stand off!" cried the plucky girl, as Ababa advanced and offered to lay hands on her. Then, drawing her dagger, she would have thrust it into his breast.

But at that instant one of the banditti, obeying a sign from his chief, stepped behind her and seized her hand, and a struggle ensued.

Jack made no more to do than to cut the Bedouin down at once. And this was a signal for the whole party to dismount and fall upon our now helpless adventurers.

Arab Jack used his weapon with determination. But although he drew blood from several of his assailants, and actually wounded the subtle Ababa, he was overpowered eventually.

"Strip him!" cried the robber chief, who was foaming with rage. "No doubt he has gold about him, and for this bloodshedding he shall pay dearly."

Jack's eyes seemed to start from his head, his lips were parched, and the agony of his chafing soul was almost unbearable.

"Demons!" he cried, "if you strip me, may the curse of Allah and the wrath of his prophet fall upon you! Here, under these holy walls, the outrage you are committing amounts to sacrilege."

The Bedouin chief laughed hoarsely, and his grim humour was taken up by his men.

"Seize him!" he thundered. "Ababa, assist in his arrest!"

Ababa did not quite relish this.

To stand and look on suited him much better than positive deeds.

He had witnessed our hero's prowess, he knew he was as true and as tough as steel, and he feared that terrible blood-stained yataghan.

But matters had gone too far now for Ababa to retract, and the Bedouin chief gave him to understand that he was to be obeyed.

"Ababa," said he, knitting his dark, fierce brows, "dost remember how I saved your life when I was simply a lieutenant in the army of the powerful Red Sheikh? If so, do as I command you—risk that life, which I might now claim as mine, in serving me."

Ababa was all of a tremble, and his dusky features went yellow with fear, for our hero stood there like a young Apollo, faultless in every limb, and looking that defiance and scorn which showed his hatred of Ababa's treacherous conduct.

"Now, honest chief," cried the daring boy, "as you respect fair play and the honour of your friend here, give him one of your scimitars, and let us try each other's prowess."

Ababa was quite half a head taller than Jack, and proportionately built, whilst the work he was accustomed to should have rendered him twice as hardy. Yet Ababa showed no wish to try the contest, so Jack indignantly struck him with the flat of his sword.

Ababa's eyes blazed fiercely at this degradation before his fellows, and snatching a sword from one of the wounded Bedouins he fell upon Jack with such fury that those around thought our hero incapable of withstanding it.

But Jack was not wholly taken by surprise.

His blade flashed like lightning through the air, and the clash of steel caused the monks to mount the wall of the monastery from whence they kept their look out, and could now gaze down upon the scene.

"Hold! Cease this strife, my sons!" shouted the Coptic priest from the walls, "or I shall call down upon you the curse of heaven, and you shall die some horrible death in the desert!"

The superstitious Bedouins, although thirsting for the brave boy's blood, were awed by these terrible words, and for a moment they seemed to waver, when the voice of the chief again commanded them.

"A truce with his threats," he thundered. "Are we not all true Mussulmans? Lay on, and end this miserable altercation; no good can come to any of our band by yielding!"

Immediately a shot from one of the number, who stood behind his horse and rested his firelock on his saddle, passed dangerously close to our hero's head; and then in the smoke occasioned by the gun the robbers made a rush, and our hero was borne down.

Jack uttered a groan as he sank, bleeding and stunned, to the ground; and then a rummage of his person for the gold Ababa declared he had about him was commenced.

It was found hidden in his sash, and a noisy dispute ensued as the chief divided the spoil among his equally avaricious followers, all of whom declared that next to the chief they were entitled to the lion's share.

It was merciful to Jack that he was unable to witness this dastardly proceeding, but to Selim each moment was an age of torture.

"Cowardly scoundrels!" she hissed, drawing a revolver. "Desist from this iniquity this moment, or I will——"

But she had not time to utter more.

The crafty Ababa crept up behind her, and wrenching the weapon from her hand, struck her on the head with it, rendering her senseless.

Abdallah was enraged at this.

"Fool!" he hissed, turning upon Ababa, sharply.

"Why did you strike that boy after you had disarmed him of his weapon? Give me the pistol, and dread my summary vengeance for acting without orders."

At this moment a change was effected in the scene.

A party of mounted men were seen for a moment on the spur of a distant hill, and just as suddenly as they broke into view so did they disappear down a slope leading to the defile.

Then shortly after they were seen on the plain, and enveloped in a cloud of white dust they made towards the walls of the monastery.

The new comers numbered about a score, and were armed with spears and pennoned lances, which drew forth an angry expletive from the chief as they drew near enough for him to recognise them.

"They bear the Mahdi's colours, and among them I see Faggish, the leading chief of Osman Digna," he shouted to his men. "To horse at once every man of you? Let us fly ere we are trapped by the wild sons of the Soudan."

Ababa, looked around him in dismay, and seemed as if the very fiend of Hades possessed him, and making his camel kneel he placed the prone figure of the swooning Selim across the saddle. Then he mounted himself, and getting the animal into its fastest speed, urged it over the plain, whither he was pursued by a detachment of the coming horsemen.

The Bedouin Arabs also fled, leaving Jack on the ground prone and bleeding, and disappearing round the wall of the monastery, allowed the Soudanese to come up unmolested.

"Allah be merciful! whom have we here?" exclaimed Sheikh Faggish, as he swept on the scene and dropped from his saddle. "By the beard of the prophet, I declare it to be the young hero who showed such daring on the outskirts of Suakim."

These words threw the listeners into a state of wonderment.

None of them recognised the young hero, although they might perhaps have seen him before.

Faggish was down on his knee beside the boy in an instant, and placing his hand to his heart outside his tunic he declared him to be still alive.

"Give me some water," he cried, to one of his followers. "I hope he'll come to and explain how he got into the hands of the crafty Abdallah."

Then resting Jack's head on his knee, the stern-looking chieftain poured water down the poor boy's throat, and soon he showed signs of animation; but the blow he had received was a severe one, and in all probability it might be his last.

The sheikh then took Jack's yataghan and examined it, and his eyes dilated largely as he beheld the dazzling diamond.

"This is the Light of Golconda," he said to himself. "I should like it to be the Light of the Soudan."

The fierce warriors, who formed a square around him, gazed on the priceless gem in wonderment, and every one wished that it were his, as well he might do.

Then the sheikh mounted his horse and took Jack up on his saddle, and some of his men having taken charge of the camels, which were straying, they reformed and departed towards the south.

———

CHAPTER XLIII.

A STUBBORN FIGHT.—JACK IS TAKEN PRISONER BY THE EGYPTIAN ARMY.—IN HICKS PASHA'S TENT.—THE TROUBLES OF MAJOR MARTIN.—JACK DENOUNCED AS A SPY.—THE PENALTY IS DEATH.

WHEN Jack returned to consciousness he was lying on a mound of soft sand with a skin of water for a pillow, surrounded by lofty, rugged hills, between which the fierce midday sun poured down upon him as if a dozen blasting furnaces were at work above him.

He was stiff and sore, and his head seemed to have swelled to the size of a balloon, whilst his wet turban, which was laid upon his brow, felt as if it had been dipped in scalding water.

"Am I alone?" he muttered, feebly, shading his eyes with his hands and glancing from side to side. "No, by heavens! There is Sheikh Faggish, and those armed warriors wear the Mahdi's uniform. Ah! now I remember being attacked by the thieving Arabs. But where is Selim? How came I here?"

His movement was noticed immediately by the keen eye of the Soudanese chief.

He sprang to his feet on the instant, and leaving his men smoking and quaffing some liquid out of their small leathern bottles, made towards the wondering boy.

"Well, how are you getting on?" said Faggish, making his gruff voice sound as pleasant as he could. "It is well for you I recognised your face. You are the young dervish who in disguise so astounded us at Suakim, and afterwards so won the favour of the Mahdi that he entrusted you with the caravan bound to Mecca, and also with a cabalistic message to Arabi Pasha."

These words were quite a boon to our young hero.

They brought everything back to him in a moment.

"I am the young Mahdi," he replied, proudly. "Allah be praised for bringing me thus far on my return journey! News has reached you, of course, that the caravan was attacked and plundered by the desert robber, the Red Sheikh."

The Soudanese chief made a devout sign, ground his teeth, and beckoned to his men, who were gazing searchingly towards him, to approach.

"This is, as I told you, the young Mahdi. Bring him drink and food. And when he blesses us with a few verses of the Koran we will pursue our way to El Duem."

"Humph!" ejaculated one of the ruffians, with a scowl. "We have been travelling night and day, and now we have a chance to rest, and plenty of good water in these wells, you still say advance."

"I do, Akka. Will you obey, or am I to call upon the young Mahdi to denounce you as a renegade, a Copt, an infidel dog of a Christian? I see now why you wished me to take the route past the Coptic monastery, the haunt of that cursed Arabian thief, Abdallah."

The swarthy-skinned Akka was silent. He drew his long robe about him, adjusted the knives and pistols in his sash, re-arranged the green and crimson cloth about his head, and casting a sidelong ominous glance at Jack strode away.

Faggish knelt down, and with his own hands

raised our hero to a sitting posture, when Jack recounted to him such portions of his adventures and mishaps as he thought fit, all of which the chief noted down carefully in his memory, grinding his huge yellow teeth at such portions as displeased him, by which time a couple of his fierce followers returned.

"Allah preserve you!" exclaimed our hero, raising his eyes sanctimoniously, as they laid down beside him a mat basket containing dates, parched maize, and a couple of dried roots.

"May the beard of the prophet never grow shorter!" he added, as a gourd of water was placed in his hand, and then having repeated several verses of the Koran he fell to as if he had eaten nothing for a month.

"I feel as fresh as a cucumber after that," muttered Jack, as he steadied himself on his feet. "I'm in the hornets' nest again, I perceive, and I must keep my weather eye lifting and be prepared to work any kokum. I must beg, too, a piece of green ribbon, or if we fall in with others of the tribe, in spite of all Faggish may say, my life will not be worth a burnt farthing."

Jack then produced a small pocket-book from his breast and wrote with red pencil, in the Arabic most common in the Soudan, several verses of the Koran, which, after appealing to Faggish to restore to him his yataghan, he distributed amongst them.

Faggish's verse was, of course, longer than the rest, and Jack took heed to select one which weighed heavily with his appeal, so that the sword was returned to him with only the one ruby which Jack had made use of in the dungeons of Cairo missing from its hilt.

The Soudanese then pinned the verses to their dress with the long spiky thorns of the mimosa; and Jack having bestowed upon them a blessing in the words he had heard made use of by the Mahdi, they put the water-skins and bags of provender upon the camels and started off.

Jack rode on a horse in their midst; and the man who gave up his long-tailed steed to him mounted one of the camels, and led another by a leathern thong.

For hours they rode thus in silence, two outriders regulating their speed, except when they scoured off on either side to examine a dark clump of scorched-up verdure, or gaze down into the deep rifts which had been scooped out by the desert whirlwinds.

At length it was night, and myriads of winged insects seemed to come from nowhere, and play about their faces; so that they were glad to pull down their turbans and headcloths, leaving just sufficient room to see their way by the light of the rising moon.

Jack, though deep in meditation, allowed nothing to escape him.

He could judge from what transpired that they were making for a chain of hills, in the dark hollow of whose side he could see the fitful glimmer of a watch fire.

"That's our camp," said the sheikh, spurring up to Jack's side. "Your eyes are young and sharp, keep a look-out for a messenger, either on horseback or on a dromedary. We shall halt presently for a few moments, and then off we go for another fifty miles."

"You'll have to tie me on, then." thought Jack; "for I am not only galled, but exhausted.

They talk about Fred Burnaby's ride to Khiva, why that was a penny donkey jumble to this."

At length they halted but only, as Faggish said, for a few moments.

Jack had some water and dried dates, whilst the warriors pulled at their leathern bottles; the animals had a mouthful and a drink, and away they went at a headlong pace as before.

Arab Jack was a good horseman, but this was beyond all jockeying, for the plain was in some places deep, soft sand, in others hard, rocky and rough, and in some places strewn with loose boulders interspersed with thorns.

"Ah, look there," our hero presently exclaimed, pointing to a rapidly advancing figure on horseback.

"I observe him," answered the sheikh, "on his yellow-grey mare; he comes, as I expected, to meet us with some news."

Jack was astounded at the rapidity with which the scout wheeled in amongst them.

His dress, like the mare, being of the same colour as the sand, allowed him to approach close to them before he was perceived.

"Allah Akbar," shouted the chief, giving the password. "Ride on to yonder clump, we'll talk as we go."

Jack pricked up his ears.

"The infidel dog, Hicks Pasha," vociferated the scout, "is on his way from Omdurmann to El Obeid to give us battle."

"Ah! What force has he?" asked the excited sheikh.

"Ten thousand five hundred horse and foot, six thousand camels, horses and mules, and as much stores and loot as would purchase the eye of a mahdi."

Faggish leant over in his saddle and whispered to the scout, who then altered his strain and glanced occasionally at our hero in the uncertain moonlight.

"Our forces," he continued, "now under the holy banner of the Mahdi—the green flag of Islam—number three hundred thousand. That is three hundred to one, and we hold the key to the wells, so cannot we smash them? Aha! Can we not revenge our losses in our attacks on El Obeid, hack and hew them as we did the Egyptians and Bashi-Bazouks at Bara, pierce their eyes out as we did those of they who came against us from Berber and Khartoum, when we routed Abd-el-Kader, who dared to march against the Mahdi's vizier previous to this white-faced Christian, Hicks Pasha, raising his sword against the true followers of the prophet?"

Arab Jack was so horrified at what he heard that his hair fairly stood on end, and seemed to raise his turban from off his head.

"Good God!" he mentally gasped. "What can I do to prevent this intended massacre of such an enormous army?"

"Aye, that we will," cried the other horsemen in answer to the speech delivered by the excited scout, closing in around him as they rode swiftly and noiselessly along; and they would have incautiously uttered their war cry had they not been checked by the voice of their leader.

"Where are they now?" asked Faggish, suddenly. "At Duem?"

"Yes. It took them twelve days to crawl those thirty miles. There they halted with their enormous train. I was there also, and having learnt they had decided on the Shah route, we sent a band there before them, so that when their brigade rode the fifteen miles out, they found barely sufficient water in the wells for their own horses."

"Aha, aha !" laughed the villainous Soudanese.

"It's a pity you didn't poison them," said Faggish.

"I'd like to cut the devilish throats of the lot of you," thought Jack, fumbling at the knife given to him by the waterman.

"Thus he is compelled to take the winding caravan route," continued the scout, "about double the distance ; and I have taken care to provide them with a trusty guide. Aha ! Two hundred and twenty miles instead of one hundred and twenty ! That must do them. No water and no rest. For you may depend upon it we harassed them a bit every day. Oh, Allah !"

The braggart scout reeled in his saddle after winding up his speech with this sudden exclamation. A bullet from an unseen hand, but by the report evidently an Egyptian rifle, buried itself in his lungs, and caused the blood to ooze from his mouth.

Then he reeled and fell, and presently a fusillade whistled about all their ears, one bullet cutting a clean piece out of Arab Jack's turban, and another stripping off the piece of green ribbon he had so recently fixed on his breast.

"Golly, that's a shaver !" gasped Jack. And the next moment Sheikh Faggish drew his scimitar and led his troop towards the gulley whence the firing proceeded.

But if a little more caution had been displayed it would have served their purpose better, for scarcely had they entered the ravine when they were surrounded by Egyptian cavalry, and the voice of an English officer in Arabic called upon them to surrender.

To Jack such an order was awfully galling.

To surrender without a struggle, to yield without firing a shot, or so much as the satisfaction of striking a blow, was quite against his grain.

"Never !" said he. And drawing his yataghan he made one random thrust at an Egyptian, who, enraged at the act, and in consideration of the Egyptians numbering four to their one, spurred his charger towards him, and unhorsed him with the shock.

The fight though short was terrific. Pistols against carbines, and then sword to sword, until the Soudanese were most of them annihilated. The rest, including Sheikh Faggish fled, and Jack was taken prisoner into the lines of the Egyptian army.

Arrived there, Jack was never so much astounded in all his wanderings.

Being the only one taken alive he was conducted at once to the magnificent and spacious tent of the general in command of the large army of which the Mahdi's scout had informed Sheikh Faggish.

"Well, Colonel Farquhar," exclaimed Hicks Pasha, "what is your account of the wells ?"

"Bad, general. I rode forward thirty miles, and the wells in that direction would scarcely provide the wants of my brigade. They are muddy, bitter, and would make even the camels sick."

"Then we must change our route. Did you gain any tidings of the enemy ?"

"None, until I reached the Sange Hamfeud Pass, when I surprised the party to which the prisoner belonged."

General Hicks frowned threateningly when our hero was brought before him.

"A spy," he said, turning to those of his staff who surrounded him. "What say you, Lieutenant-Colonel Coetlogen, and you Captains Walker and Massey ?"

"You are silent. Well, my opinion is that they push a boy like this close to our lines to be purposely caught, thinking his youth will claim our commiseration, and with his brain full of information be let go ; but you may depend upon it, Major Martin, whose right name, by-the-bye, no one on my staff knows——"

"What !" gasped the major, interrupting him, " not know my name ?"

"How can they, when one day you sign it Martin, thus describing yourself as something between a polecat and a weasel ; and the next Marten, making yourself out to be a bird of passage ?"

"That, sir, is according to circumstances. One day you sign yourself general, and the next pasha. How do you account for that ?"

"My dispatches, major—my dispatches !"

"Then I claim the same privilege. If you make a weasel of me and send me out ferreting I am there ; and if you make a bird of passage of me and send me to the furthermost parts of the Soudan I am there also. Now, pray, what else would you have me to do ?"

The major was growing excited and very red in the face.

"Nothing, my dear major ; calm yourself. When our *Graphic* friend here, Mr. Vizetelly, seems more at ease I will get him to curtail your name by one-half, and add on S to it, for you are certainly a son of Mars ; and why should you not bear your father's name ?"

The major stroked his moustache, and the colour of his face made up for the absence of his scarlet tunic when he retorted :—

"You may decapitate the major, and curtail the S, and let me have earl instead ; and then you will see whether you get on better with your Earl of Mar than with your modest major."

"Gentlemen !" mildly interposed Colonel Farquhar, "this is skirmishing without orders. General," he added, saluting his superior, " what decision have you come to respecting this spy ?"

"The same as I was about to explain to you when our major's name stuck in my throat. Young or old, he is equally guilty, not only of being a spy—a rebel—but actually using a naked sword against one of our troops."

"And the penalty ?"

"According to the Articles of War—DEATH !"

CHAPTER XLIV.

THE BLOOD-RED ARM UPSETS THE MAJOR.— A FALSE GUIDE.—THE DOOMED ARMY.— ATTACKED IN THE DEFILE. — DEATH OF BRAVE GENERAL HICKS. — SLAUGHTER OF HIS OFFICERS, AND TOTAL ANNIHILATION OF THE EGYPTIANS.

ARAB JACK turned pale when the dread word was uttered so determinedly by General Hicks.

The fierce glances of the British officers, who closely scrutinised him, were enough to terrify him.

At length recovering himself sufficiently to speak he declared boldly :—

"I am no spy, no rebel, and as to putting my yataghan to the use I am charged with, I swear I never raised my weapon but in self-defence."

Jack spoke this in his own native tongue, and the effect it had on the general and his staff was electrical.

If a shell had suddenly exploded in the tent they could not have been more astounded.

Hicks Pasha broke the spell that bound them.

"Strip him," said he. "If he is a boy of our own country, disguised in the Soudan, and found acting in concert with the rebels, his case is doubly suspicious. Strip him, some of you. He may have some private missive concealed about him."

"That shall be done in a twinkling," exclaimed the major, stepping forward. "Although I command the artillery in this arduous campaign, I would rather blow a spy from the muzzle of a gun than I would shoot the Mahdi."

"Obey my orders," said the general, giving him a fierce glance. "You will shoot the Mahdi when I tell you."

Thus rebuked, the major violently seized hold of the prisoner, and having stripped off his upper garments exposed his blood-red arm, at the sight of which fatal stain the major gave an involuntary start.

"What," exclaimed the pasha, winking at the other officers, "has the sight of a little blood frightened my bold major ! You have discovered a curiosity that would suit old Barnum. What's that round his neck ? An English sixpence. And that formidable dagger knife, too, tied round his waist !"

"They are mine," said Jack, with a flush on his open countenance. "On the plate is inscribed, 'Will Wiggins,' the name of its previous owner, and this coin is sufficient guarantee that I would not raise my hand against the officers of my queen."

"And that birth-mark, what is its history, and what is your name ?"

"They are secrets, both of which I mean not to divulge. There is my note-book, in it you will find various mems. ; and as to my sword, which you have thus basely maligned, it was presented to me as a souvenir of honour."

"Well done," exclaimed the pasha, delighted with his bold unfaltering speech, which won for him the good opinion of the officers also. "If my present army was one-third its magnitude, and composed of such bold British hearts, I would be the happiest of men. What say you, boy, will you take temporary service with me under the Egyptian banner ?"

"I will," cried Jack, "if you return to me my yataghan."

This was done and the officers dispersed, Major Martin returning to his duties with the air of one perplexed.

"That mark ! that mysterious stain !" he muttered. "How strange it should occur on the same forearm. The boy, too, would be about my son's age, if I make allowance for rough usage and the climate."

The noise and bustle of the enormous camp soon drove these dull thoughts from the major's mind—thoughts of home, where, thousands of miles distant, dwelt the wife and family on whom he doated.

As to our hero, Jack, he was as merry and light-hearted now as any brave and unflinching boy could be.

At dawn the camp was broken up, and the army being formed in an oblong hollow square they proceeded.

Day after day passed on, and weeks succeeded weeks of agony, toil, and privation, for one guide, on whom they most relied, and engaged at Khartoum, had led them into a wild and waterless region, among barren hills and narrow gorges, through which the devoted ten thousand, with their great hampering of baggage, camels, and mules could scarce force their way.

Hicks Pasha and his otherwise experienced officers were now in a region to them totally unknown, out of the track of caravans, and utterly unable to extricate themselves.

Still they pushed on, at the aggravating snail-like pace, with the courage of true British heroes, and deprived themselves of the precious drops of water, and other necessaries of life, to assist in alleviating the fearful torments of the sick, who fell like sheep around them.

Let us pass over the sufferings of the next few days, days of madness to some, stolid despair to others, and gallant devotion to many, among whom was our brave boy adventurer.

"Thank God, I have my health and strength," muttered Jack, as the weakened and parched-throated army, led on by a fresh guide, emerged from a narrow gorge into a broader defile, where they found a little muddy water, over which a picked few stood with their loaded rifles to keep the gasping wretches from spoiling and wasting it in their efforts to alleviate the violent pangs of thirst.

In that defile, however, they were enabled to lie down and enjoy the heavy night-dew that fell, saturating them to the skin, which was a relief for a time ; but, alas ! brought on pains of ague, rheumatics, and fever.

Until the morning which succeeded that eventful and soul-harrowing night, Jack had not been able to catch a glimpse of the new guide, nor hear from whence he came, or whether he was one selected from among the mule and camel drivers.

But as Jack stood by the general's tent on that memorable November morning he saw a man come out, and in his features he recognised the treacherous guide of the caravan.

Yes, it was Ali Lobah, the Berbereen outlaw, he who had shared with Jack the conflict with the Nubian lion, he whom our hero had beaten off the sacred camel's back.

Jack was about to confront and challenge him, but the crafty villain, no doubt recognising our hero, slipped in among the babbling throng and was lost at once to sight.

"Curse him," cried Jack ; "he is the villain sure enough. I would like to cut out his thrice guilty heart ; his presence here can bode no good, and——"

His speech was cut short by a yelling shout from the Egyptians, the rattling of musketry, mingled with the clash of steel, and the unearthly yell of the Mahdi's dervishes.

Horror, was it possible !

Was the weakened and almost disorganised army attacked in that deadly defile !

Too true ! They were hemmed in at both ends as though in a vault, with mountains on each side, which presented the appearance of precipitous rugged walls.

God save us!" gasped our hero. "Surely this is a visitation for our sins. Last night I dreamed of my loving mother ; she was an angel, and beckoned me to look on a darkened film which, as it cleared away, disclosed to me the form of my too, too-confiding father, and my sister and brother, whom I feel within myself I shall never again see."

"But I will not die a coward!" cried Jack, clenching his white teeth and searching about him for a rifle.

He had barely time to snatch one from the dying grasp of a Bashi-Bazouk and point at a coal-black visage peering from a gulley on the top of one of the heights, when a bullet whizzed past the back of his neck, taking a couple of curls with it as a perquisite.

Hicks Pasha and his staff soon rallied the greater portion of the Egyptian troops, whom, from their lack of confidence, he ranged in lines three deep, whilst others at every opportunity worked the cannon.

For a couple of hours the unequal battle raged with terrible severity, and although, owing to the narrowness of the position, neither party could show the other a broad face, terrible execution was wrought.

Shouts, yells and groans filled the air as the Mahdi's dervishes, like howling demons, tried to force the square, and were driven back with a deadly shower of lead.

Their great discomfiture was the crowsfeet or spiked iron balls which the Egyptians plentifully threw out, thus crippling the enemy's feet, and preventing them rushing in an overwhelming body upon the devoted and entrapped army of Hicks Pasha.

All day this lasted, but at night the firing was not so continuous. Yet for all that it was harassing. None slept. The groans of the wounded and the cries of the tied-down camels rendered night supremely hideous.

The next day was worse.

The water, such as it was, thick as mud, was now like clotted cream, so that the wounded in their agony disposed of mud and all, whilst many brave men were seen to glue their lips with the blood that issued from their own wounds before they were bandaged.

But in face of all this the Egyptians held their ground until their rifles grew heated, the brass field pieces were also hot, and on the third day Hicks Pasha was slain.

It was a terrible moment that.

Farquhar and several other of the Egyptian leading officers were desperately wounded, and the dead and dying were huddled about amongst the camels in the most ready places they could find to quietly rest.

Arab Jack was like a crimsoned demon. He flew from post to post whenever such a place seemed weakened, and having had his rifle shot from his grasp he fought yataghan in hand, just as a British boy should do.

"Hurrah! Down with the Mussulmans!" he yelled until his voice dwindled to the croaking of a frog. But, alas! just as he parried a spear thrust from the neck of Martin, the bold major fell with a ball in his breast, and the Mahdi's fanatical followers broke the square.

Then, like an egg broken at each end, the exhausted ranks gave way ; a panic ensued, supplemented with reckless and barbarous slaughter.

"Save me! save me!" cried a German-like voice in Jack's ear. "Me mill be kilt ;" and looking round he saw to his supreme disgust a fair-haired, terrified-looking wretch, with his knapsack on his shoulders and under his arms tightly locked his paint-box, satchel, and portfolio of sketches.

What became of him Jack did not know ; he turned away to assist Captain Walker, who had fallen with a broken arm and a shot wound in his leg.

But our gallant hero was very soon overwhelmed.

The Soudanese horsemen, with their long-staffed, broad-bladed spears, made a sudden charge, carrying all before them, in the midst of which Jack was knocked down and trampled under foot.

From that moment Jack's mind was a blank until he found himself a prisoner in the Mahdi's encampment, lying amongst a host of wounded wretches who were so ruthlessly treated that they speared themselves to end their sufferings, repeating a verse of the Koran as their last breath left them with a parting gulp.

Jack was horrified.

He closed his eyes and longed for the bliss of unconsciousness to return again.

CHAPTER XLV.

IMPRISONED IN THE FORTRESS OF EL OBEÏD.— A MYSTERIOUS VISITOR. — JACK HEARS STRANGE NEWS AFTER MANY MONTHS.— TAMING A GAOLER.—THE TREACHEROUS SHOT. —JACK ESCAPES FROM HIS CELL AND WITNESSES STRANGE SIGHTS FROM THE RAMPARTS.

IT was a glorious morning when our hero looked out of the loop-holed window of one of the upper chambers in the fortress of El Obeïd, and gazed upon the wonderful and mysterious Nile.

Whilst he was watching the boats with their broad sails breasting the sluggish stream, he was startled by the sudden striking up of a band beneath his window, which almost distracted him with the discordant sounds of tom-toms, cymbals, and other rude instruments, supplemented by the firing of cannon from the ramparts.

The wall was too thick, and the loophole too narrow for our hero to look out and observe what was going on below, so to deaden the noise he rattled the chains that were rivetted to his ankles and wrists, and walked up and down his cell, the only furniture of which was a bundle of rushes and a water jar.

Suddenly the door opened, and thinking it was his gaoler come with his coarse food, he cast a scowl towards it, when he was surprised to see that his visitor was a muffled figure, wearing the robe of a dervish.

"It's only me ; don't be alarmed!" exclaimed the intruder when the door was banged to and the massive bolt shot. "I have been weeks endeavouring to gain admittance into this cell, and now I am here let us waste not a precious moment."

"Who are you?" demanded Jack, shouting loud to make himself heard above the din of the booming of the artillery. "I have languished here a prisoner for months, and few visit me unless it be to cruelly load me with taunts, in addition to the weight of these galling chains."

"Not so loud ; these walls may have ears. I am Hassan-el-Ahed, your staunch friend, though you left me so scurvily in the fortress of the Red Sheikh."

"My friend ! " exclaimed our hero, disdainfully. "Do you think that starvation and confinement have so weakened me that I fall thus easily into your trap, and yield to the foul accusation of my vile accusers, who charge me with having betrayed Arabi Pasha to the English ?"

"Hush ! " replied his visitor, throwing aside the cloth which coiled about his head, the end hanging down over his face. "Behold, I am Hassan, who took compassion on you when you first arrived in Alexandria."

Jack no sooner caught sight of his face than he sprang forward and clasped him by the hand.

"Good ! Your presence is like a cup of cold water in the desert to this almost blighted heart. Has the Mahdi gained another victory?"

"Nothing of great importance. He is now collecting all his forces and preparing an army to walk through Berber into Khartoum. All his emirs are assembling on the plain without the walls, and Nur-el-Sham, his sister, is organising a band of Amazons."

"What, the Light of Syria ! " exclaimed our hero, clasping his hands as that lovely vision which had so enamoured him was in imagination presented to his ardent view.

"The same. That beauteous creature whose lustre so enthralled you as to cause you to become the rival of young Digna. He knows you are in the Mahdi's power, and he is the cause of your persecution. Every vile means he has used to incite the Mahdi to kill you, and would use bribery to compass your death were not the place of your incarceration kept a profound secret."

"Curse him ! " exclaimed our hero, bitterly. "One day we may meet, and then my trusty yataghan shall avenge me. One word more, and then I will reveal all that has happened to me during the many months of our separation. Is there any chance of my escaping from these bare stone walls ere my mind gives way under the horrible torture of this imprisonment ? "

"Your hand again, Jack. Think you I have used all the wiles and cunning of a jackal to scent you out if I had no hope to offer you ? Cheer up, lad ! It is a godsend that no one has by chance seen through your disguise. Had you once been pronounced a white man and a Christian your life would be sacrificed with all the refinement of torture that these savages could invent, unless you renounced your faith and became a Mussulman."

Jack grasped the palm of Hassan tenaciously with both his manacled hands, and glared fixedly into his eyes.

"Would the sin be greater," he gasped, "if I became a Moslem in reality, than practising this deceit?"

"Certainly," replied Hassan, pointing with his liberated hand to a distant part of the cell. "Take example by yon scorpion and tarantula. They are both making for the pitcher, they both need water to preserve life, and when they meet, which they are bound to do if they go on, they will fight to the death."

"That is the force of circumstances," said Jack, with a shudder. "To that water pitcher, when asleep, I have many a time owed my life. They fight, as you say, till one or both dies."

"Of course. To gain the means of existence they risk all, and so must you. As long as your heart's good you need have no fear. To get out of this you will still have to practise deceit, and dissemble, for Mahomet Achmet still thinks you a Moslem, and I have filled his ears with such prophecies of your future that he will again take you into his favour."

Jack stared at him in amazement.

"Then if I get my liberty again I must pay off old scores and quit this barbarous Soudan. I have witnessed enough carnage and torture to satiate the most ardent veteran," he said.

Drawing Hassan to the loophole to enable them both to get a gulp of fresh air, he then recounted his adventures. And when he described his visit to the bagnio, the fire, his escape with the disguised Sela from the wicked old merchant's house, the narrow escape of Sela being shot in the cabin of the Nile boat by the English nobleman whom he and Hassan had rescued from the murderous mob in the square at Alexandria, and, lastly, the abduction of Sela by the treacherous Ababa, Hassan reeled against the wall like one about to faint.

"Hold ! Spare my feelings," he gasped, and placing his hand to his brow gave vent to a terrible vow of vengeance.

"Ababa ! Curse the villain," he hissed. "He whom I pitied from my heart when I heard the sorrowful tale of Zela. But, there, the slave girl was true to me, and aided my escape ; and though I have registered a vow in heaven to be revenged, yet if my sister is safe I feel that for Zela's sake my heart will be feeble enough to forgive him."

Jack was silent.

The noise and shouting in the square below was modified, and the booming of the artillery ceased.

Shaking off the sickening qualm, Hassan then took from beneath his robe a flask, which he placed to his lips, and afterwards handed to Jack.

The latter thinking it was water, and of a superior quality to that which was supplied to his cell, took a good gulp, the result of which was to send a sensation through his veins as if they had been charged with molten lead.

"That is dervish water," said Hassan, as the boy stood breathless, and with his eyes starting almost out of his head, "the war elixir, such as they use before they make their wild fanatical charges in battle."

"S'—so—I should think," gulped out Jack. "It nearly choked me at first, but now I feel as if I was on springs, and every fibre and sinew of my limbs are as well-tempered steel."

As Jack handed him back the flask, the harsh grating of the door attracted their attention, and the gaoler made his appearance.

On observing the flask he made a host of abject apologies for the intrusion.

"My son," said the dervish, "it is my duty to report you to the Mahdi, whose seal gained me admission to this prisoner. You have disturbed me in my holy duties just as I was preparing him for the realms of paradise, and ——"

"Allah forgive me," groaned the terrified

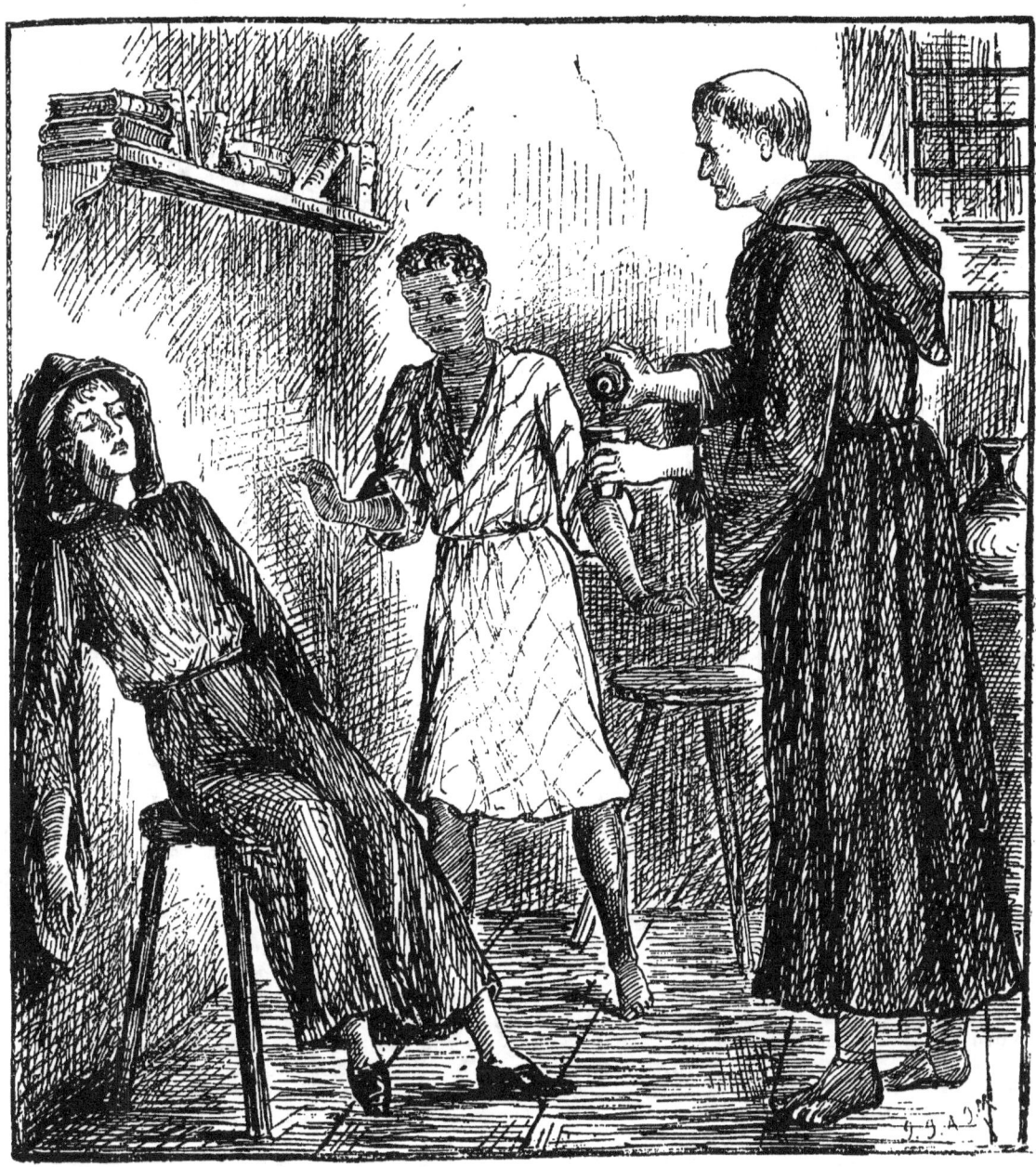

HE WAS THRUST TOWARDS A SEAT.   *p.* 118.

wretch, placing his spear against the wall and falling down on his brawny knees. "Spare me, spare me! I have always done my duty to the prisoner and never asked him for backsheesh as others do."

"That I have heard," said Hassan, seizing the spear and striking the kneeling figure across the shoulders. "Arise! I will punish you no further; but I warn you to be careful in the future; the bastinado will be your portion if you again transgress. Take this," handing him a verse of the Koran, "meditate well, and save your soul from eternal damnation."

"Poor devil!" said Jack, as the fellow slunk out and closed the door, "he can't read a blessed word of it. He is a true Mussulman, though, and a trusty warder, for though he treats me with a blunt civility, he takes good care I shall not get out."

"You could go now, for that matter, but I don't want you to jeopardise your future. Sheikh Taber and Abdul Ahad, the Mahdi's standard bearer, both deadly enemies of yours,

have returned from an unsuccessful raid on Massowah and Kassala, and as I passed through the camp I heard them at high words with Sheikh Faggish, from which I learned that he rescued you from amongst the piles of slain after the horrible slaughter."

"Did he?" said Jack, with a start.

"Yes, and you are supposed to be the only survivor—leastways, when they pillaged the dead they speared every soul they came across who had life, and you would have been served the same."

"Well, how was I spared?" queried Jack, anxious to end the suspense.

"Faggish and his party came across you half-buried in one of the great heaps, and rescued you from the hyenas and vultures who had poured down from the hills and were disputing with one another over the ghastly feast whilst the victorious savages reaped their harvest of plunder."

"Then to the devil, or, rather, to Faggish, I must render his due, although if it had not been for my feeble resistance he would not have escaped when I was made prisoner."

"He confesses that, and attended you well, it appears, when you were raving and delirious, and to his forbidding your clothing to be removed for fear of it being stolen is due the escape you have had of being detected."

"Good heavens," exclaimed Jack, "how wonderfully all things are ordained ! A cat has nine chances of life, whereas I appear to have about ninety. I begin to wonder what will be my next extraordinary adventure."

"That ! ' vociferated Hassan, as a musket bullet entered the loop-hole, and flattened against the opposite wall near to the ceiling.

Hassan sprang to the opening, and being taller than Jack, he could just see a cloud of white smoke hovering above the turreted roof of a house opposite, and through the mist a figure making for the tower in which was the staircase.

"There's treachery ! That shot was intended for you, Jack," said he. "Give me the bullet. Ah, this was fired from an Arabian matchlock."

In picking up the missile our hero observed that the scorpion and tarantula were writhing near to each other as if in deadly torment, which was a proof that they had impregnated each other with their poisonous fluid.

Taking a couple of sticks, which he kept for the purpose, from beneath the rushes, he with them raised the hideous things one by one and dropped them out of the loop-hole.

"Would that I could deal thus easily with all my enemies !" said Jack ; and a few minutes later he was alone.

But the lesson taught by that bullet through the loop-hole had not been lost upon our hero, Jack, and he ardently longed to discover who that cowardly enemy could be, especially if the bullet was really meant for him, as Hassan had just declared that the place of his incarceration was kept so profoundly secret.

When the gaoler paid his next visit there was a marked difference in his behaviour.

He entered the cell with as much deference as he would the abode of a holy emir.

Jack on the first stir of the bolt pretended to be pursuing his devotions, and professed to be telling his beads, each one of which was supposed to be a chosen text from the Koran.

Hassan had provided Jack with the necessary articles to carry out their plans, and given him instructions how to act, and the present instance showed that the janitor's credulity had been already wrought upon.

Jack continued his devotions, and repeated in so loud a voice the name of Allah, and the promises he held forth to the true worshipper, that the gaoler was rooted to the spot, and listened to him in fear and trembling.

Then turning his eyes full upon the now abject dupe, he demanded with the pomposity of a vain-glorious street spouter :

"Are you saved ?".

Jack did not need a Salvation trumpet to assist him when he uttered those words.

The janitor bared his head and prostrated himself before him, thus inviting Jack to put his foot upon his neck, which our hero did ; and then with mock solemnity desired him to close his eyes.

Then the daring boy took a small parcel from beneath the rushes, and slipping noiselessly outside the door and gently closing it, he softly shot the bolt, and then slipping on a loose gown he bound his head with a green silk handkerchief and glided up the narrow winding stairs which led to the battlemented roof of the fortress.

Jack expected to find one sentinel at least stationed there keeping watch and ward, but evidently the duty for that day had developed upon his gaoler, who was now bolted in the cell.

"All to myself, eh ! A clear course," said Jack, joyfully inhaling the fresh air. "All the better. I can make my observations with less restraint." And immediately he commenced his survey around.

The sight he beheld after so long immunity from the outside world was almost too much for him ; it dazed his eyes, and almost bewildered his youthful brain.

The plain beyond the southern wall was dotted with innumerable tents, decked with banners, and men, camels and mules seemed to fill up every vacant space that intersected the vast encampment.

On the side nearest the river there was a compact body of about two thousand horsemen, gaudily attired, and each section marked by a banneret or flag, whilst a flotilla of flat-bottomed boats were conveying across the stream what Jack supposed was the army of Amazons alluded to by Hassan.

On the plateau away from the river there was a disorganised host.

In the various patches he could distinguish the wild tribes, mostly bareheaded, by their straight black hair, or by the almost bare shaven crown and the peculiar manner in which some of them plaited their long hair with a mixture of feathers and Dongola grass.

Above the whole glittered the many-shaped blades of a myriad of spears, so bright, so dazzling in the fierce Soudan sun as to render the sight painful to the eye.

Bordering on the camel track leading to Berber there was another mass—the regular troops of the Mahdi, most of whom were armed with Remingtons, and other weapons, the spoils of Hicks Pasha's army. .

Jack's quick eye took all this in at a glance, and then he directed his attention to the scene below, from which arose a discord of sounds, intermingled with shrieks, groans, and heart-rending appeals for mercy.

Taking care not to let himself be too much seen he glanced down into the square, and beheld several unhappy wretches nude as they were born being prepared for execution.

A number of posts were fixed in the ground in the form of a square, and between each two of these a culprit was chained to rings in the form of an **X**, facing outwards, with their arms somewhat above the level of their heads, and so wrenched as to force their chests forward with an outward curve, thus tightening every tendon and muscle, and making the bravest groan and shriek as if he were extended on the most torturing rack.

Squatted around on their mats, and under the shade of the date trees, were many notables, stroking their grey beards and smoking their long pipes as complacently as if they were witnessing some clever performance of legerdemain.

Behind these were grouped the ordinary spectators, some kneeling, others standing, and those who could afford the luxury seated *à la* flying angel on the necks of burly porters.

Then the tom-toms and trumpets struck up, and the two executioners appeared, who each took charge of a couple of the victims, and commenced to dismember them with their formidable instruments.

Arab Jack's knees trembled so violently that he was compelled to resort to the contents of the flask Hassan had left with him to steady his nerves.

It was not, however, out of any morbid curiosity that Jack looked on : far from it. Being in Rome, as the saying is, he was naturally anxious to learn what Rome did.

CHAPTER XLVI.

HORRIBLE EXECUTION OF THE TRAITORS.—A BEAUTY AT THE BATH.—ARAB JACK IS MENACED WITH THE KNIFE OF AN ASSASSIN. —THE OFFICER OF THE GUARD.—HASSAN TURNS UP AT AN OPPORTUNE MOMENT.

EACH of the executioners had his body well oiled, and a strip of red cotton tied about his loins, and wielded in his sinewy hands a bright scythe-shaped blade fixed to a long bamboo reed.

This they flaunted before the eyes of the doomed victims until they worked them to the most frenzied pitch—goaded them to such madness that they fairly foamed, and every muscle of their frames stood out in strong relief.

Then each fiend, with an artistically-cruel flourish, and at a preconcerted time, struck off one of the fingers of each of their victims, performing a sort of dance in the meantime, and springing from one victim to another with the agility of a wild cat.

At the sight of the first blood the onlookers sent up a shout, while a naked barbarian marched around in the open space between them and the executioners carrying a banneret, on which a verse of the Koran, the name of the Mahdi, and the following words were inscribed :

"Allah is our hope ! Behold, ye, the doom of the traitor ! "

In this manner the torture was protracted for a couple of hours, by which time the toes and fingers of the victims had been pruned off, as it were, and portions of their noses and lips sliced off, so as to give an imposing effect to the scene.

At length one of the victims seemed about to succumb, when the executioner, not daring to let him thus escape, finished him by chopping off one leg below the knee, and then the other, thus leaving him suspended by the arms.

The head of the wretch then fell back, exposing a hideous sight to those in that direction, when, with a skilful turn of the wrist, the executioner laid open the chest and abdomen without touching a vital part, and placing a ball of inflammable gum in the orifice from whence the bowels slightly protruded, set light to it, causing it to burn with a bright and almost colourless flame.

The shrieks and yells which succeeded this drowned the cries of the other sufferers, and Jack, expecting each moment would be the victim's last, turned from the sight in horror and disgust at such barbarity.

Another pull at the flask, however, rendered him himself again, and proceeding to another part of the ramparts he found there, mounted on wheels several six-pounder brass Egyptian guns.

They were so placed as to command the city gates and the navigable course of the river, across which groups of scantily-clad figures could be seen coming from between the hills, making for the boats moored to the bank.

" Some of the Amazons, I suppose," muttered Jack. " I have now seen enough. I'll just make my way down below. Ah ! Where does this door in the wall lead to, eh ? "

Jack had noticed a high wall spiked at the top, but he never dreamed that it parted off a portion of the roof until he saw the door, and then he gave it a push.

It yielded, and peering through Jack discovered that it was set out with plants and flowers, like most of the flat roofs, which led him to suppose he was over the governor's house.

As no one was there he tripped gently across to the opposite parapet and looked down upon a sight that nearly took away his breath.

In the walled-in garden beneath, which was laid out like some place of enchantment, with its marble walks, trees, fountains, and odorous flowering shrubs, was the queen of the governor's harem, attended by her slaves.

She was taking her mid-day bath, and, consequently, like her maids, had no other covering than her silken hair, which enveloped her shoulders like a gauzy veil.

Although Jack knew the terrible penalty if he were caught, yet he could not for the moment tear himself away, so sublime was the scene compared to that he had previously witnessed.

" Well," muttered Jack, " what a contrast. Where do those withered old wretches pick up such beautiful white women ? Why her limbs are as delicate as the alabaster on which she reclines ; whilst as to her maids, two of them are as black as bog wood and the other two as yellow as amber.

Jack was so enthralled that there is no knowing how long he would have stayed gazing on the fairy-like scene had not a sudden dislodgment of a portion of the coping upon which he was leaning warned him of his peril.

" If that had fallen," he muttered, catching it in his trembling hands, " it would be all up with me. But how is it that this door is left undone —that's a mystery ? Does that old gudgeon of a gaoler possess a false key ? At all events I'll be off before it leads to worse events than those which befel King David through his gazing from the housetop at Bathsheba."

So saying he took one more cautious look down, and then glided on tip-toe through the door.

Descending the winding stairs he listened at the cell door, against which the inveigled gaoler was beating with his naked feet, keeping time to it with oaths, and making as much impression as if he was hammering at a milestone.

" Go it, old brick," muttered our hero, turning away, and then he began to wonder how he would find his exit into the street.

It was no easy task.

The fortress was constructed somewhat on the principle of the White Tower in the Tower of London, and seemed to be all staircases, corridors, large rooms, and mysterious doors and cells, in which Jack had no doubt state prisoners were then confined, all of which he observed as he hurried along until he reached the guard-room.

About fifty grim-visaged soldiers wearing the Mahdi's uniform were grouped about, some engaged in a game of chance, others smoking in deep thought, whilst a few seemed to be discussing the daily topics.

Arms of various descriptions were ranged about; among them a couple of swords which Jack easily recognised as having belonged to the officers of Hicks Pasha's army.

One fellow, who sat opposite the door, on raising his eyes and beholding an apparition, as he supposed it, wearing a green handkerchief, staring at him, dropped his jaw in terror, and seemed as if his eyes were about to start out of his head.

Jack disappeared on the instant.

It was no part of his plan to alarm the guard and be detained before he was outside the walls of the fortress.

At length, after pursuing a number of tortuous passages and descending several winding stairs, he found himself in a courtyard, where, through a row of stout iron bars, he saw a number of native prisoners all huddling against each other and fighting to get to the front, so as to obtain a breath of air.

"Water! Water!" they kept continually crying, which reminded Jack of what he had read of the terrible Black Hole in Calcutta.

But the guard who paced before the bars took no heed of this cry.

He salaamed to Jack, and taking a huge key from beside the pistol in his sash, unlocked the portal in the great gates, and stood at the salute as our hero passed out.

"Thank God!" muttered the grateful boy as the portal closed with a loud bang behind him. "I wonder what crimes these poor wretches are there for? If I had been packed there I should have snuffed it."

Thus musing, he had scarcely proceeded a dozen paces when a fresh danger menaced him.

A black-bearded, bare-headed, almost nude savage sprang like a tiger from behind an abutment, and with a long gleaming knife held dagger fashion made a fierce, deadly aim at Jack's breast.

So quick and sudden was this that our hero had only bare time to draw back as his keen eye detected the glimmer; and then as the fierce Kordofanee went forward with the force of the blow, he like lightning seized him by the nape of the neck, and jerking him backward, brought him to his knees.

"Well done!" exclaimed a voice. "I have been watching the rascal for some time. He is brother to one of those who have suffered in the square yonder."

A tall, swarthy fellow, dressed as an officer of the guard, then interposed between Jack and his intended assassin, and dashing the weapon from the hand of the guilty ruffian with a blow from the heavy manacles he held, he seized both of the culprit's wrists, drew them behind his neck, and shackled them.

"There!" said the officer, bowing to our astounded hero, whom, owing to the green handkerchief about his head, he took for one belonging to the highest order of the dervishes. "Will you now come and charge the infidel with his heinous crime?"

Jack was so confused at that moment that he was unable to reply.

It was not likely that he wanted to re-enter the fortress, from which he had so recently escaped, and where, perhaps, he would get into some hitch which might result in his being imprisoned again.

In his unhinged state of mind, too, he might commit some error that would end in his own destruction.

At this critical juncture it was fortunate for him that Hassan came to his aid, and he quickly demanded of the officer an explanation.

He recounted how he had watched the accused hanging about under the walls and crouching between the abutments, as if waiting for some one for whom he watched with excited eyes.

"'Tis false!" yelled the baffled wretch. "This is the viper," glancing at Jack, "who gave false evidence against my brother, and sent him to the shambles? Loose my hands; give me my knife; let me send him to the regions of the damned!"

"Mad," said Hassan, glancing at the officer. "Take him away, place him in the black hole, and there let him await judgment."

The officer saluted, and motioning a couple of soldiers, who stood by, to take charge of the prisoner, offered his services to conduct Jack and Hassan clear of fresh danger.

"Thank you," returned Hassan. "For this courtesy you shall not go unrewarded. Conduct us to the eastern gate. I have a missive here," producing from his garment a scroll, "which summons me and this young dervish, of whom I was just now in search, to the presence of the Mahdi."

The officer took off his fez and bowed so profoundly that his moustache almost touched the ground, and shouldering his sword as a mark of honour led the way through the gaping crowds, who verily believed that a relation of the prophet was among them.

Once clear of the walls and under the shelter of the trees, which shielded them from observation, Jack told him of his adventures in the fortress, at which Hassan and he heartily laughed.

"Why, that was the governor's Circassian bride, Jack," said Hassan. "She's got pink eyes, teeth, and nails, they say—you ought to have seen them. She's all the talk of the fashionable bazaars. She once graced the Sultan's harem at Constantinople, and was sold to her present master when he made a political visit to the Porte as a favour, and for a very large sum."

"What, is she only a secondhand bit of furniture?" said our hero, in whose estimation she was lowered exceedingly.

"Aye. But for all that there are plenty of old devils who would give half their lifetime to see her, especially as you saw her."

"Well, if I'd known as much as I do now I wouldn't have deigned to look at her," said Jack. "I'm sorry I didn't let the coping stone drop, and I regret not withdrawing the bolt so as to let the poor miserable gaoler feast his oblong eyes on her."

"Hush! we are noticed through being on foot. See you that the very meanest journeying towards the Mahdi's pavilion are mounted on asses and mules?"

It was true. And the emirs and dervishes, and head men of the tribes, were mounted on superb camels and chargers magnificently caparisoned.

Among them Hassan pointed out the Emir of Berber, who with a gorgeous retinue was come to do honour to his master, bringing with him the taxes, and therefore in a blissful state of confidence that he was bound straightway to the seventh heaven.

CHAPTER XLVII.

ARAB JACK BEFORE THE MAHDI.—THE FAIR APPARITION.—HOW JACK WAS AVENGED.— THE MAHDI'S AMBASSADORS, EMIR PAIN.— OFF TO KHARTOUM.—JACK GIVES THE RUSSIAN A DOSE OF COUGH MIXTURE.

JACK and Hassan stood in the Mahdi's presence alone, save for a little white camel which reclined on one of the ottomans, and was supposed to have its head always pointing in the direction of Mecca.

It was a magnificent pavilion, divided into many compartments, the one in which our adventurers stood being the grand audience chamber.

The walls were heavily draped with damask, and hung at intervals with tapestry of choicest workmanship, depicting scenes in which the Mahdi was represented working miracles.

The damask was hung mostly with war bannerets, inscribed with some promise to the faithful, sumptuous divans were placed around, and beneath them costly mats, the floor being covered with gorgeous carpets in which the foot sunk noiseless at every step.

The ceiling was one enormous transparency, on which was displayed a well-executed likeness of the Mahdi, and the names of Allah and Mahomet Achmet in large coloured letters.

The subdued light, and the quietness of the vast area, gave it a tone of religious calm, in which the voice of the Mahdi was so modulated that it seemed like that of an angel speaking from above.

The Mahdi was standing, and wore a purple robe, on which in Arabic letters the names of the various tribes who had assisted him in the great battles were embroidered in gold, giving him the appearance of some great necromancer.

On his head he wore a high broad turban of green plush silk interlaced with cords of silver and gold, his feet being encased in a pair of holy sandals, which were reported to have made the pilgrimage to Mecca over one hundred times.

On one finger of each hand he wore a plain gold diamond ring, which sparkled brilliantly at every movement, though not sufficiently to eclipse the small but magnificent starlike gem he wore in the front of his turban, and which from its brilliant fire was named Ner-el-Daum, or continuous light.

On either side of him was a raised daïs. on one of which rested the Koran, and on the other the Kalifa, a revised version of the former, in which the name of Mahomet Achmet was substituted for the name of the sainted prophet.

"So their tongues have imparted lies," said Mahomet, when Hassan, who was speaking, had finished. "Their hearts are filled with envy and deceit, and the serpent of remorse hath not yet sought their vitals."

"Every word the good dervish hath spoken is true," replied Jack, on whom the eyes of the Mahdi were now inquiringly fixed. "The caravan and its costly relics were defended to the death, and your message through it all was preserved and delivered by me into the hands of your servant Arabi. His defeat was entirely owing to the subtle craft of the infidel, who crept down upon the lines of Tel-el-Kebir like a thief in the night,"

"And yet that offshoot of Osman Digna hath declared you betrayed him, and that if it had not been for the clever tact of the guide, Ali Lobah, whom you so bitterly denounce, my sacred army would have succumbed to the wiles of the infidel, Hicks Pasha, Berber would still be in rebellion against me, and like Buri and its zerebas have been pillaged by that crafty Engilshman."

Jack listened with deep attention, although for the life of him he could not understand half he said.

He had never been to Khartoum, although he had heard it was the capital of Nubia, as El Obeid, which he and Hassan had just left, is the capital of Kordofan ; nor had he heard that General Charles Gordon was there, the very Englishman the Mahdi alluded to.

"I deny all of these accusations *in toto*," replied our hero, boldly. "And Sheikh Faggish, were he here, could substantiate my words that I wielded my sword nobly against the Christian dog of an officer before I was taken prisoner by Hicks Pasha's army, and that I even then wrought hard against the infidels by spiking their guns, so that they could not bring them into action."

"Humph," ejaculated the Mahdi, "I have heard two versions of this. I have also been told that you speak Ingleese like one of their own people."

"Being a native of Mecca," replied Jack, with all the impudence he could assume, "I have mixed with the wise men of every clime, and learnt many tongues."

The Mahdi started.

He had found a treasure in Jack which he little expected.

"Then you can explain the chronicles of the Chaldeans. Do you know anything of Moses ? can you tell me how he worked the miracle of the fiery serpent, and above all things by what means the waters were divided in the Red Sea ?"

"I could explain all these at a more fitting time," answered Jack, evasively. "You crowd too many questions upon me all at once. I am but a youth, and if your wise sheikhs and learned fakirs cannot reveal to you the oracles, how can I without time for prayer and divine inspiration ?"

This answer was so pointed and adapted to the purpose, that not only the Mahdi, but Hassan was astounded.

This gave Jack redoubled courage, and boy as he was, he looked the very picture of a young Mahdi.

He and Hassan had been conducted to the baths, and supplied with perfumed linen before they entered the sacred chamber, so that with his brown curly hair flowing from beneath the green and white folds of his turban, Jack looked a picture of both health and beauty.

Jack detested a lie. and therefore as he had been compelled to tell one, he was obliged to turn his eyes away from the mesmeric orbs of the Mahdi.

In doing so he caught sight of a vision that made him start.

Between the slightly-parted folds of the arras was a beautiful wax-like face, and a pair of dark eyes that seemed to penetrate to his inmost soul.

"Nur-el-Sham," he murmured. "Oh that we were alone! The unveiling of her fair features before me shows that she regards me with special favour."

"What a shame," he added. "Her very presence seems to draw me to her, and yet I dare not speak. Why did she appear at all to torment me?"

"Have you ceased praying?" at length said the Mahdi, who had been anxiously watching the motion of Jack's lips.

"I have," was the boy's quick reply. "I await your instructions."

"They are, then, that you hie with all speed to Khartoum. Seek an interview with Gordon, and use all your efforts to prevail on him to renounce his false faith. Mention to him our God, extol to him our prophet, and assure him that if he will come over to us he will find the Mahdi's hand a friendly one."

"All that will I do."

"And not to him only must you make this sacrifice. In the Mahdi's land, which will soon extend from pole to pole, there are many tents, and joyful shall be those who are found worthy to encamp within them. But," added the speaker, "spare not deceit. He is the white, the false Mahdi. Ply him with cunning, and whatever your success, ill or well, great shall be the reward of your service."

"Come this way," he continued, approaching the damask hangings and pressing them aside. "Herein I will show you a proof of my speedy justice and judgment. Close your eyes."

The place they entered was like a small room, draped with black, in the centre of which was a table on which was a lamp.

"Look now," said the Mahdi, after a suitable pause.

Jack and Hassan opened their eyes, and found the place in darkness, but on the table something seemed to throw a light, and they could see multitudes of people, camels, horses and tents; some of the groups being stationary, others moving about.

"Behold!" said the Mahdi, pointing to a group with his finger.

The twain did so, and in the centre of that group, which was formed by a gaping crowd, they distinctly saw the man who attempted Arab Jack's life.

He was naked, with the exception of a small bib or apron, which hung from his waist half-way to his knees, and on either side of him stood an executioner.

To the right was placed a huge stone, about three feet square, and on the left a brazier of lighted charcoal in which were several long irons.

Then the Mahdi touched a wire, and the report of a cannon was heard, immediately after which one of the executioners took an iron from the brazier and branded the felon between his shoulders.

Whilst he was howling and dancing, the other executioner caught the fingers of his right hand in a pair of pincers, and drew the hand upon the stone block, and held it there until his companion raised a sharp scimitar and severed the hand.

To the stump of the mutilated limb the red-hot iron was then applied, and amid the culprit's howls and shrieks, which were as food for the crowd, the executioner seized hold of the agonised wretch, bore him backwards on to the stone, forced open his jaws, and seizing his tongue with the pincers, drew it forth, and then cut it away at the root. Then the searing iron was again applied, the wretch was thrown on and lashed to a hurdle, and was borne towards the city gate.

"That," said the Mahdi to Jack, "is but one proof of what I have spoken. That wretch was thy lying and would-be assassin. His hand assailed thy life, and his tongue assailed thy character; now both to him are lost for ever."

Returning to the council chamber, he then equipped them for their mission, presenting them with turbans which they could change from green to red, white, blue or yellow, with a little clever manipulation, just as circumstances might require, a "prophet's" seal, and a letter of introduction to the Emir of Berber.

Scarcely were they equipped when a big turbaned haughty-miened personage strode into the presence chamber, preceded by the usher, who announced in a high tone—

"The Mahdi's foreign ambassador."

"Emir Pain," explained the Mahdi, turning towards our adventurers; "my right hand. You must be proud of his acquaintance."

One glance showed Jack that the ambassador was a European, and his pointed moustache pronounced him to be a Frenchman.

Moreover, Jack recognised him as a coxcomb who once insulted him when he was looking into a newspaper kiosk in Cairo.

"I'll take him down a couple of pegs," thought our hero, "just for his insolence. Pain?" said he, stiffening his lip, and glancing round at the cocky ambassador in proud disdain. "Pain? Yes; I have heard of an Ingleese fakir who makes fireworks for their grand durbars."

The shoulders of the ambassador began to move uncomfortably about, as if he had some parasites in that quarter.

Hassan, now he understood the drift, was enjoying the fun with Jack immensely.

"Yes," said he, determined to put a capper on the joke. "The fakir of the Ingleese is grand ambassador to the Mahdi of Fire and Sulphurdom."

The ambassador now fairly winced, like a sick camel when overburdened with a load, and he would have given the world if he had been able to vent his spleen.

It was a consolation to him, however, to see that the dignity of the Mahdi was also touched, for he began eagerly to explain.

"My Emir Pain also make fireworks, lay mines, cut the wires, teach my soldiers how to shoot, and write my letters for the Egyptian paper, which go shoot, bang, fire!"

"The old fool," said Jack to Hassan, when they were fairly on their way. "Emir Pain seems to be twisting the Mahdi round his thumb."

"Not he; they are a pair of scorchers well met. Why that ambassador," lowering his voice, "was a communist in the Franco-Prussian war, and he would as soon fill your bags with petroleum and set fire to it as he'd eat a boiled frog."

"I'd like to try my yataghan on him," replied Jack. "Why, blow me!" he suddenly exclaimed, "here's the bloated Russian I gave a

drubbing to at the entrance of the Suez Canal."
So it was, and a poor, starved, miserable wretch he seemed.

"I have been beaten and robbed by the Arabs," he explained when Jack gave the word for his party to halt. "For three days I have had neither food nor drink, and I feel worse than a snowed-up bear—that can find nourishment only in sucking its paws."

"That's shocking," said Jack, whose disguise was too complete for him to be recognised. "I have some oil here from the Mahdi—to whose camp I presume you are bound."

"Yash, yash!" gasped the Russian, clutching the leathern flask and letting the contents pour down his throat just as if it were entering a well.

Arab Jack tipped Hassan one of his mischievous winks, and the pair did a good giggle in their sleeves.

The oil was that drawn from the castor tree, which in its raw state is so nauseous in smell and taste as to make the strongest horse sick.

It was medicine for one of the camels, which had a cough, and when the Russ removed his thick lips from the bottle he gave a cough louder than that of two camels.

Then he rubbed the front of his robe, tore out several tufts of his hair, did a war dance on the sand, and after twisting his features into every form of contortion, tried to stand on his head.

"Damme!—you cot for damme," he yelled in his horrible lingo.

And then, having thrown himself down, and thought himself for some time a garden roller, he sprang to his feet, swore a dozen big oaths, and taking to his heels was soon lost in the swell of the desert prairie.

CHAPTER XLVIII.

GENERAL GORDON IN KHARTOUM.—HOW THE CARAVAN WAS ASSAILED.—ARAB JACK AND HASSAN ARE MADE CAPTIVES BY THE EGYPTIANS.—JACK AND HIS CHUM ARE BEFORE THE GENERAL.—JACK'S YATAGHAN CAUSES A SENSATION.—TWENTY-NINE YEARS AFTER.—CONSIGNED TO THE WATER DUNGEONS.

IT was evening in Khartoum, and motley groups just aroused from their siesta were beginning to move about, some collecting in knots under the broad-leaved palms in the square, while others repaired to the coffee divans or the wine cafés to discuss the all important events of the day.

All were anxious, from the richly-clothed merchant to the wretched mendicant, for a terrible crisis hung like a cloud of doom over that beleaguered city.

At each of the gates double guards were posted, and upon the walls the gay colours of the Egyptian soldiers, with their glittering bayonets, stood out in bold relief against the clear blue sky.

In the vicinity of the palace all was bustle and excitement.

Military officers and civic dignitaries kept moving to and fro, or ascending the great marble steps to the grand hall which led to the state chambers of General Gordon.

The Governor-General of the Soudan, himself, was at that moment seated on a richly-appointed throne in the magnificent audience-chamber, conversing with one of his high dignitaries, who was clad in a long flowing robe, and wore a bright crimson fez with a tassel which hung half-way down his back.

"And this, Martin Bey," said the general, "is the last insult heaped upon me by that Dongolan fanatic. He invites me to come to terms with him, meet him at Buri, and embrace the odious faith of Mahometanism. Is the scoundrel really mad, or does he account me an impostor like himself?"

Gordon dropped the parchment scroll he had been reading, on the floor, and trampled it under foot.

"That is a most fitting answer to it," said Martin Bey. "The arrogance of the foul impostor increases day by day. It is a wonder his emissaries were not slain. The youngest of the two envoys has been terribly maltreated by our men."

"Indeed," replied the general; "let me hear more of this. He is but a boy, you say. Where is the officer who had command of our brigade?"

Martin Bey made a sign to one of the door-keepers, who, drawing aside the heavy curtains which obscured the entrance, admitted the officer to the presence of the great man.

Gordon received him with a dignified air.

"You were in command of the troops whom I sent out to convoy the caravan from the Dhoum pass to the southern gate," said Gordon. "State what occurred."

"With a hundred chosen horsemen, your excellency, I waited in cover for the cavalcade, which consisted of one hundred and twenty camels loaded with grain, and having exchanged salutes with the chief I disposed my men in such a manner that if we fell in with any of the Mahdi's forces we could beat off any number of them with but little loss to ourselves."

"Did you alter your course?"

"Yes. I took the track west of the sand hills and made for the wells, where we intended to water. But, before we reached there a party of Hadendowas, who had crossed the Blue Nile the day before, under the powerful sheikh, Moosab, attacked our rear, and almost simultaneously a band of the Amaras swept down from the hills and assailed our right flank and front."

"Hemmed you in, then? You must have kept a bad look-out."

"We were trapped. My advanced guard was cut off. The enemy seemed to spring up, as it were, out of the earth. But we fought them well. Twenty-five of my men were unhorsed, and we lost nearly half the caravan."

"Worse and worse," exclaimed the general. "With half a handful of English troops I would have brought that caravan in. My instructions were that every precaution should be taken against a sortie from Buri, whose rebellious garrison will now be relieved from a state of famine by your stupidity."

"I crave your Excellency's pardon," said the officer, bowing, and falling on one knee. "If Hassan Pasha and Syed Pasha proved treacherous to our cause, and suffered death by your orders, I desire that your humble servant may at least be above suspicion."

"That is a subject for another court," replied the general, firmly. "Proceed."

"Having beaten off the Mahdians, I recovered the dead and wounded, re-formed the caravan, and proceeded hitherward smartly by the El Duem and Khartoum route, when suddenly I was startled by the firing of my videttes, and on riding forward I discovered a party of the Mahdi's Arabs—six in number—with whom my outriders, mistaking them for a detachment of our late assailants, had had a most desperate encounter."

"Six, in all ?"

"Yes, Excellency. Two of whom were already dead, two stretched *hors de combat*, and the others down on their knees craving abjectly for quarter, which I granted, and then learned that the dead Arabs were servants to the other two, and that the two spared ones were El Obeidan guides."

"Did you question them further ? "

" I did not, your Excellency. I learned that the two wounded—one a mere boy—were envoys from the Mahdi to the Governor-General of the Soudan, then in Khartoum. So I brought them hither, and they are now in the fort awaiting your Excellency's further pleasure."

"Humph ! " ejaculated the Governor-General. I will give you an order to have the prisoners brought before me."

Turning to one of his Syrian scribes, one of whom sat on his right hand and the other on his left, he whispered to him, and a few moments later the officer bowed himself out of the audience chamber with the order for the governor of the fort.

When the prisoners were brought in the governor and the bey were alone, and they both evinced signs of surprise as the captives were uncovered.

They presented a ghastly spectacle.

Their heads were swathed in blood-soaked bandages, and their clothes appeared as if they had been dyed in the crimson fluid.

"Well," Gordon said, fixing his calm blue eyes on Hassan, "you are from the Mahdi—the bearer of his blasphemous message ? "

"No. I am not his messenger," replied Hassan. "My companion is the Mahdi's anointed. I am but my friend's disciple."

Gordon gave his shoulders an uneasy shrug.

"We are getting some more of it," said he to the bey. "Raise up the sick boy's head, and let us hear what he has to say."

"I am the messenger from the Mahdi," said Jack, trying to speak out bold. "But I am not one of his followers. I am an English boy, and your Egyptians and Bashi-Bazouks have tried all they know to kill me ; and they have robbed me of my sword and knife, both of which I prize as dearly as my honour."

"Is that so ?" demanded the general, addressing the officer, who had retired to a respectful distance with the bearers.

"The sword and knife are here," replied the soldier, stepping forward and unfolding a cloth. Then, at the general's request, he handed the yataghan to Gordon.

"A splendid weapon," said the general, examining the yataghan, which was covered from hilt to point with ominous dark stains. "Ah ! what is this—this crest ? Your glass, Martin Bey. I can scarcely trust to my naked eye."

"Yes," he added, fixing the glass to his eye, "it *is* the Gordon crest, and beneath it, in Chinese characters, the word 'Pekin.' This I engraved with my own hand, Martin Bey, and, further, see, here is the date."

Touching a spring with his slightly-agitated hand, one of the large gems flew up on a hinge, and beneath it was inscribed " Kin-tching, October 20th, 1856."

The general was so moved with emotion that he actually let the weapon drop from his hand, but with the elasticity of his youthful days he sprang to his feet and regained it with a joyful expression.

"Strange ! " said he, glancing round at the dial on which was the moveable date of the month. "Twenty-nine years ago this very day this weapon was presented to me by the Emperor of China when we destroyed his gorgeous palace."

"But it is mine, now," exclaimed Jack, excitedly, forgetting his wounds, and springing to his feet. "If you are General Gordon you are not going to bounce me out of——"

"Peace, young man ! " exclaimed the general, reprovingly. "If I wished to rob you you could not hinder me. I could put you to death if I so chose."

"I care not. You may murder me if you will, but I won't stand to be robbed before my eyes. The yataghan is mine, and I have carried it with me many, many miles. It has been my friend, and protected me all over Egypt and through the Soudan."

"That is possible enough to be true," replied the general, who was equally as excited. "But you have not said from whom you obtained it. I will not assume you stole it."

"What ! " cried Jack, stamping his foot, and almost foaming at the mouth. "Stole it did you say ? No, sir. That was presented to me by a wealthy Indian nobleman, and——"

"Enough. It was to him, my friend, I presented it when in Bombay. Be calm. Your brain is heated, my son. You shall have some tamarind wine."

Arab Jack was so excited that he actually made a movement to spring upon Gordon, when the Bey and Hassan each clutched him by the arm and forcibly restrained his impetuosity.

By this time General Gordon had possessed himself of the knife, opened the blade, examined it minutely, and even moved aside the plate on which the name of Will Wiggles was engraved.

Martin Bey eagerly watched the general's features as he so attentively examined the huge knife, when the general suddenly made them all start by exclaiming :—

"This is another of my Chinese trophies. Beneath this plate there is the name of American Ward, the famous sailor-general, who besieged Shanghai, and was killed in battle when fighting by my side. I presented it to one of my Gravesend waifs when I started him off to sea. How you came to possess it is a mystery to me."

Jack's impetuous spirit would not allow him to stand more than this.

"I bought it of a lighterman," said he, "on the Thames. Return it to me. Give me them both, or I will curse you."

"You are vile enough for anything, I believe," answered Gordon. "Your association with the false and blasphemous Mahdi already condemns you. I wonder Salvation Booth allowed you to escape his net. You would have been an ornament to his fanatical army."

This speech so angered Jack that he lost all control of his temper. He struggled so desperately with those who held him, that his white kaftan, or loose shirt-like blouse, which was considerably slashed and torn, was rendered sleeveless, and he stood a pretty sight before the astounded general and those around him.

"Away with him! Take him to the lowest water dungeon beneath the east gate," thundered Gordon. "Has the vile serpent of the Soudan sent this young viper to scoff me?"

Scarcely were the words uttered than our hero was seized as roughly as if he had been a bale of jute. Strong arms thrust him into the chair which had brought him, and when he was firmly strapped down, he was hurried away in a fainting condition from the presence of the Governor of Khartoum.

CHAPTER XLIX.

IN THE DUNGEON WITH THE RATS.—A VOICE IN THE DARK.—THE MAN OF MYSTERY.—TAKING THE OATH.—LITTLE SAMBO TURNS UP AGAIN.—GENERAL GORDON FORETELLS HIS UNTIMELY FATE.—MARTIN BEY UNFOLDS A FAMILY MYSTERY.

"WELL," gasped our hero, when he found himself alone and a prisoner in the horrible water dungeon under the east gate of Khartoum, "if this is the meek and merciful Gordon, give me the tyrant Arabi Pasha, or even the Mahdi, before him."

Jack was in total darkness, yet he rose painfully from the wet stone floor, and with his hands outstretched before him he felt with his feet until he gained one of the walls.

Horror! He shrank back as the tips of his fingers reached it. It was not only wet, but thick with slime, and cold, clammy snails dropped away from his touch.

"Good God! how long am I to be buried in this living tomb?" he gasped. "I shall go mad, I shall die. Ah! what is that—a rat."

A huge rat, a perfect monster, flew at his throat, and fell at his feet as he dashed it away.

Then it made at him again, but this time as it sprang upon the boy's heaving chest, he seized it by the neck with both hands and dashed it to the stone floor.

"Curse it, I hope it is dead!" exclaimed Jack. "I would fight a man rather than one of those beastly vermin. It is horrible—and in the dark, too!"

"That is but one, the first of a great many," said a sepulchral sort of voice, that made our hero start, "one out of thousands."

Jack's hair stood on end as he turned his face towards where the sound proceeded from.

"Who are you?" he demanded. "Be ye mortal or demon, speak again, in the name of Allah, I conjure you."

"I am a friend, seek to know no more. I hear you are tired of your living tomb."

"Then you have been listening, overheard me," vociferated Jack, straining his eyes in the vain endeavour to pierce the inky darkness. "What seek you? Money! I have none. At what price do you value your services?"

"Nothing more than your oath of secrecy. Although I am your gaoler, I am a prisoner like yourself, awaiting death."

"And am I to die?" exclaimed Jack, starting.

"Of course. I have it from your own lips that you cannot survive this long. Now I offer you freedom, for by your aid we may both escape from this place of horrors."

"But why are you here?" asked our hero, thoughtfully. "Are you also a hater of the haughty governor?"

"I am one of the persecuted. I am here because I stick to the good sheikh Faragh Pasha. The White Mahdi is afraid to punish those who are guilty, and therefore tortures one who only complains of being half-starved and being shut up in this citadel, when by opening the gates to the Mahdi we might not only have plenty, but a sure passport to the gates of paradise."

Jack listened to this big speech in a state of feverish excitement.

"The man speaks fair enough, whoever he is," he thought. "Why should I humble to this General Gordon, who on a foul pretext robs me of all I possess, and even refuses to let me depart with my answer to the Mahdi?"

"Well, what do you say?" exclaimed the mysterious voice, breaking the painful pause. "Shall I administer to you the oath?"

Jack was desperate. Another rat touched his foot, and he sent it flying with a horrible scuffling sound and a squeal that rendered the darkness ten times more horrible.

"Yes, go on," he vociferated. "I will swear to anything if it only gets me out of this."

The oath was a terrible one, but our hero, considering the circumstances, listened to it calmly.

"I swear," said he, as soon as the mysterious voice finished.

"By Allah and his prophet?"

"I do."

"And with a hope that you will be eternally damned, and go to everlasting darkness with the pale-faced Christians if you betray me?"

"I have sworn it."

"Then come this way and let me feel your hands. There—so; steady. I will pull you up through this hole if you have the courage."

Jack's lips were parched, and his tongue clove to the roof of his mouth.

"Ha—have you no light?" he feebly faltered.

"None. You must trust to me. If you are afraid remain as you are."

"I am not afraid," answered Jack, boldly. "Give me your paw, whoever you are. I would shake hands with a Christian dog rather than fight these confounded rats."

Jack was himself again, then.

Feeling above his head he caught hold of a pair of hands, and springing himself up he found himself suddenly jerked upon his chest, with his head and part of his body through a hole in the wall.

"Hough!" gasped our hero, as he felt all the wind jerked out of him. And then a pair of strong arms lifted him bodily through and placed him on his feet.

In an instant, then, and in darkness, the pair of hands slipped on to him a monk's robe, with a cowl, which was drawn up on to his head, and then he was seized by the hand and dragged hurriedly along.

Up steps, through dark hollow chambers, and along corridors, some of which he could see were thickly loopholed, they went, and having ascended a winding staircase, the walls of which were so narrow that they had barely room to pass through, they stopped at a door.

Against this the mysterious guide made a scratching noise with his thumb, on which the door opened and Jack was pulled into a chamber where there was a light.

For some moments the exhausted boy was unable to face this, feeble as it was.

However, he was thrust towards a seat, a cup of palm wine was placed in his hand, and with a muttered thanksgiving he poured it down his parched throat.

Then for the first time our hero caught a glimpse of his strange guide, the apartment, and a little negro boy who answered the mystic summons at the door.

"Has the father been here?" queried the mysterious man, who wore the habiliments of a monk the same as Jack.

"No, me seed no mans," said the boy, who wore only a strip of dirty rag about his loins. "Sambo no been sleep. Yah, yah."

"Then I must leave you for a while," said the strange being. "Now, no tricks, mind. I shall lock the door."

Without another word he then strode away, the huge key grated in the lock, and Jack and Sambo were alone.

There was no bed in the room; two three-legged stools and a box for a table were the only furniture.

In one corner there was a pile of closely-cropped camel skins, and bundles of faggots to make a fire.

"No speak you. Hush, him listen!" whispered the little nigger in Jack's ear. "Me prisoner here; big leetle fool, run away from Massa Arabi's yacht."

"You did? Are you the Sambo I know? Were you ever on board the 'Dromedary?'"

"Plenty dromedaries; me feed 'em."

"I mean were you ever in a big ship?"

Sambo opened his big black eyes.

"Big ship—steam—England," he exclaimed.

"Yes," said our hero. But not caring to make himself further known until he was more acquainted with his strange companion, he was silent, and made a gesture as much as to say he needed sleep.

Sambo understood him, and very quickly transformed the faggots and the camel skins into beds, sheets and pillows, and Arab Jack, being pain-stricken and weary, threw himself on one and slept as if he reclined on a bed of down.

That night neither General Gordon nor the bey sought repose.

Morning found them seated in a private room surrounded with papers, which strewed the sumptuous carpet as well as the table.

"So the news is too true; this last despatch fully confirms the treachery of our professed friend, the black sheikh. Colonel Stewart, poor Power, and the French consul have all been basely murdered. O that I had some one I could trust to go and avenge their deaths!"

"Ah! If you had some one you could trust! You confide too much in some already. That Faragh, to me, as an Englishman, is not worth his bread."

"I know it; I feel within myself that he is a traitor. Yet what can I do? If I behead him the whole garrison may rise in arms. I am placed in a false position by my own countrymen. Why does Gladstone hesitate, knowing well that I am surrounded by such savages?"

Martin Bey, who was leaning with both hands on the table, uttered a dry laugh.

"Because," he said, sarcastically, "you have not presented him with one of your medals. Like Jumbo, he wants feeding with hot buns, you know."

"Aye! He wants presenting with an axe. If he were here I would employ him as headsman, and give him a grant to rise every morning and chop down one of our beautiful palms."

The bey indulged in another laugh, but the general looked worn out and hollow-eyed with his harassing night's work.

"Never mind," said the bey, cheerfully. "General Wolseley is on his way to our relief."

Gordon sighed.

"On his way! It is two months nearly since we heard they had surmounted the First Cataract. He must have Gladstone's axe tied to his heels."

"Or be suffering from Bright's disease," laughed the bey. "The Cabinet itself seems to be all talk, just as if it was filled with a lot of washerwomen."

"I feel too sad to joke, Martin," replied the general. "You may laugh at me, but I am sadly put out concerning that boy. Is it not strange—does it not seem a fatality—that he should bring that message from the Mahdi, and have those things in his possession, which I have not seen for so many years?"

"It is strange; but I see nothing fatal about it, general."

"I do, then. To-day, which is the twenty-first, I shall write to head-quarters again concerning my resignation. They seem to care not whether I live or die. I cannot hold out much longer deluding these people with false hopes. I may tell them the English are coming, write them out cheques on the British Government as payment, and give them medals for their warlike deeds; but all this may be turned into a mirage by the Knight of the Silver Axe. Have you not heard the story of the wood-chopper who let go his axe while he spat on his hands?"

"When he dropped it on his mate's toes."

"'Tis the same with me. Whilst he is cutting my stick I am hobbling about lame, and I do believe I shall die here before they reach me with their aid."

"Oh, no—no; don't be so desponding — You have a few friends who are true,—Kashim Elmoos and Abdul Ahmed, not forgetting myself. who, if you are about to give up and die, will not stay here to be murdered."

"You'll try to reach home?"

"Of course I shall. Look at what I found in my Coptic boy's pocket."

The general took the card offered him, and read—

> *Gordon Martin,*
> *The Observatory,*
> *Notting Hill.*

"Why, that is your brother. Is he alive?"

"No; I have a London newspaper announcing the death of himself and his son, quite a boy, you know, on the Hartz Mountains."

"How strange! It seems as if we were having a day of days, Martin Bey."

"It does; and you'd think so more if you

knew how it was I came out to this hideous Soudan."

"Go on. As Barnum would say, I am open to any novelty just now."

"Well, a few months before the bombardment of Alexandria I returned home from an inspection of our coast forts, which at that time were threatened by the dynamiters, and being tired one evening, I hung my overcoat in the hall, neglecting my usual precaution to take out my pocket-book and plans and deposit them safely in my desk."

"Ah, and some grateful beggar, I presume, stole it."

"I can't say. All I know is that the overcoat, pocket-book, gold, notes, and all my plans were missing, and so also was my eldest boy."

"Your boy ! Good gracious ! You don't say so ?"

"I do. And ever since that young madman almost stripped himself yesterday before us, the circumstance has continually haunted my mind."

"So it should, for your boy was near about his age. Let me see, he was born a week or so after you left Paris after the siege."

"Exactly. He would be fifteen years old this very day, and about this hour, allowing for the difference of time between this and Greenwich."

"How extraordinary ! That was just previous to my starting on my mission to the Danube. If I remember right the poor child had some deformity, did it not? Its head had the appearance of a round shot, owing to one of those missiles striking the roof of the house in which you and your family were then sheltered."

"No, no, not quite so bad," said the bey, smiling archly. "The circumstance was this. I had gone up to the attic where our provisions were concealed, for we were worse off for food there, with the Germans investing us, than even we are here."

"This is quite bad enough," interposed the general.

"Yes. Well, as I said, I had just gone up to the garret to get provisions, and had a cheese and loaf under one arm, and our last bottle of claret, which I had saved expressly for my wife, when in comes a shot, tears away the roof and part of the wall, smothers me with rubbish, and breaks the bottle of claret, the contents of which covered my shirt sleeve, and gave it the appearance of being soaked in blood."

"Ah, that was it, now I remember. And when the boy was born he bore the hideous mark on one of his arms, and now I remember that that young infidel, the Mahdi's messenger, bore a mark somewhat similar."

"He did, and so it set me thinking."

"I should forget it. That vagabond is older by years than your son. Let us hope that he may never turn out such a scapegrace."

"I have hoped, and do hope, if he is living. But a body much decomposed, and answering very much his description in height, age, and dress, was picked up in the river Thames, near Putney, and my wife paid for the interment, believing it to be the body of her son."

"And you."

"I had no voice in it. Through losing those plans I got into sad disgrace, for might they not get into the hands of an enemy ?"

"They might. But I have seen enough in my travels to assure me that all our foreign visitors take away etchings and plans. They may praise up your roast beef and porter, but believe me they like to ——"

"Enough. We are straying from the point. It was through that they sent me as a punishment to Cyprus, thence to examine the battered forts of Alexandria, and so I have been marched about until I find myself in Khartoum, your chief engineer, and head of your Intelligence Department."

"And most worthy you have proved yourself Your hand, Martin. If all were as true, Buri and Berber would still be ours, and we should not have our traitor friends cutting our wires and upsetting our mines. Keep your eye on that fawning Frenchman, Olivier Pain."

CHAPTER L.

ARAB JACK AND HIS GAOLER HAVE A FEW WORDS.—WHAT OUR HERO SAW THROUGH THE HOLE IN THE WALL.—THE MOCK MONK FALLS INTO HIS OWN SNARE, AND JACK PERSONATES THE LOVELY YOUNG PERSECUTED NUN.—JACK'S ADVENTURE IN THE TENT OF THE AMAZONS.

ARAB JACK, although he had taken that binding oath with the sole intention of gaining his liberty, was for days and weeks still a prisoner.

He was fed and cared for by his gaoler, but who the man was remained a mystery, and if Jack ever ventured to make inquiry he was put off from time to time, and even threatened.

"I shall want you when I am ready," was the usual reply. "Your friend Hassan has escaped, and is now a great dervish in El Obeid."

"Then why should I remain here like a caged-up dog ?" cried Jack, excitedly.

"Because I take compassion on you. I will drag you back to your dungeon if you're not content."

"All right," said Jack, who although he humbled to the man had no fear of him. "I've made a bargain with you, and if a bad one I must put up with the loss."

"You've sold yourself to the devil," retorted the man. "I'm the devil ! Look at my shadow."

Turning up the corners of his cowl he placed himself in such a way that when his shadow fell on the wall it looked as if he had horns. and the cord he had round his waist hung down and made a very good apology for a tail.

"Now, what do you think of that ?" said Jack to Sambo, one day. "I don't want to part from you, as we're so jolly, but I'd like to get away from that demon monk."

"Massa no mind me, den. Me nuffin but a arf-growed," said the negro. "Me tell you how to get away quick sharp, same as you left big ship in Alezanda."

Placing his finger on his lip he then led Jack to one of the walls, and motioned him to listen.

He did so, and a splendid little plot he overheard.

A handsome young girl, a Dongolan, that is to say belonging to the province of Dongola, the same as the Mahdi, and the daughter of a wealthy Baggara sheikh (a tribe rich in cattle and horses) was anxious to escape being one of the Mahdi's wives.

Poor girl, she had been almost driven mad by the stories told her by the monks of the black cowl mission, who to get her to join the nuns told her that the Mahdi was worse than a dozen Blue Beards.

In his kaliva, or underground den, where he worked his black arts and conversed with the Soudan devil, they said there were piles of headless bones of the wives he had sacrificed, and that their blood was caught in skins and boiled into a congealed sort of paste for the sustenance of the Mahdian Messiah when he was journeying on his holy missions.

The voice of the speaker was tremulous as she recounted all this, just as if she were in the confessional, and Jack, who was in a frenzied state of excitement, bored a hole in the thin part of the wall so that he could see what was passing on the other side.

There, as Jack expected, he beheld the young neophyte, whose skin was of the purest amber, kneeling before the mystic being who held our hero in such enthralment, her thin dark gauzy drapery serving only to expose more fully the graceful contour of her well-moulded limbs.

"Confound you," muttered Jack, quite forgetting his position at the moment. "You black-skinned demon, I would give half my life this very instant to rescue that angel from your claws."

Arab Jack's valorous deeds were, however, confined to listening, unless he was rash enough to cry out.

"So you will join the Amazons?" said the monk. "Nothing can deter you. Well, then, I will lower you from the wall, there is no other way of leaving, and place you safely in Nur-el-Sham's hands."

"When?"

"This very night when the midnight prayer sounds from the minarets. But the diamond, what of that? Remember I have great outlay and a terrible risk to run to accomplish——"

"Here, here!" she exclaimed, producing it from beneath her plait of hair. "Take it. Anything to get away from this. They have scourged me almost to death to get me to part with this treasure."

"The fiends!" ejaculated the mystic monk, as he ogled the precious gem, his green eye glittering like a serpent's. "Enough! Now, return to your cell, and forget not to be here at midnight, and fear not if the place should have to be kept in darkness."

He opened a small door, she passed through, it closed behind her, and she was gone.

"Aha!" laughed the wretch. "I will have twice this amount for her yet. I will place her in the hands of Nur-el-Sham, as I have said, but Abdul Ahmed, the general's most trustworthy servant and second in command,—myself,—must first be her lord and master."

Jack's eyes were opened now.

"Yes; this is the fruit of a good education," continued the deceitful wretch. "I can blind the general, hoodwink the crafty monks, make slaves of the servants under me, and I will mould that fiery, stubborn youth whom Gordon believes has escaped, to my views before I have done."

Arab Jack plugged the hole and walked away, and the rest of the day he spent in converse with the negro boy.

What their concoctions were must be judged from the sequel.

Before the midnight hour Jack crept through a hole he had made in the wall, and carefully covered it with camel skin, then he opened the door, the secret spring of which he had already discovered, and awaited within the passage leading to a steep flight of stairs until the slight rustling of a dress warned him of the girl's approach.

"Fly, begone, as you value your life!" he whispered. "We are discovered! Death hangs frowningly above us, only suspended by a single hair."

The terrified girl turned and fled just as the door opened, leaving in Jack's hands her veil, which he instantly slipped over his head.

"Ah! here, let me carry you," whispered the amorous wretch, and seizing our hero in his arms he walked away with him through the darkness as if he had been a child.

"She's heavier than I thought," he muttered, as he pressed Jack close to his guilty bosom.

"You must be brave," he said aloud, "for I must lower you in a sling."

Jack spoke not, but relieved himself of a deep-drawn sigh.

Feigning terror, he clung to the garment of the mock monk with dreadful tenacity, so that when he found he was grasping the place where the diamond was concealed he took a piece clean out of the textile fabric.

The rope and pulley were already there, with a stout band attached, which was soon placed round Jack's chest below his armpits, and then, having given the signal to those who were waiting below, the chuckling rogue gave our hero a long parting kiss, and swung him into the little hatch, from which he was gently lowered.

Jack was as mute as a maggot, of course, when he found himself in the midst of the Amazons, a bevy of the most beautiful of whom had very naturally come to receive their lost and persecuted sister.

"I must sham a faint," thought Jack, "or I shall never carry it through;" and so letting his padding of camel hair, which he had stripped from one of the hides, fall against one of the girl's voluptuous breasts, he performed a faint just as if he had practised it for the stage.

As the Amazons had approached the wall by stealth it was therefore necessary that they should leave it in the same manner; and so dropping on all fours, so as to reach the mimosa-bush without being seen by the guards, they placed Jack, Johnny Gilpin fashion, on one of the stout-limbed Hebes, who carried him along forthwith.

Arab Jack quite enjoyed the novelty of his position, although at every step he expected they would be set upon by some of the mock monk's emissaries.

But they proceeded unmolested until they reached the tall scrub, when a body of Arabs sprang up in their path to intercept them.

But the Amazons were prepared for this guerilla warfare.

A party of their sharpshooters, armed with bows, appeared at the given signal from a deep hollow, and poured a shower of arrows into the midst of their masculine foes, who, with yells of execration, were compelled to retreat.

Jack was then carried shoulder high, with an arm round the necks of two of the tallest and finest-made damsels of the band, whilst two

JACK WAS THEN ORDERED TO WRITE, BUT HE STERNLY REFUSED.   *p.* 127

others shouldering his feet, led him in triumph into the grand tent.

Jack just opened his eyes a little way so as to see how matters stood, and his eyesight was most seriously impaired by the vision he was compelled to behold.

Lying around on buffalo robes were a score of damsels, who adopted a style of nudity so as to enjoy the cool air which blew under the raised flaps of the tent.

Jack was now in a predicament from which he knew not how to escape.

Believing him to be their long-lost sister they began to strip him, so as to anoint the stripes and dress the wounds which, as a novice, the young girl had received in the convent.

In doing so they of course discovered their error, and plaudits of joy were at once transformed to howlings and shouts of revenge.

"Death ! death !" cried a hundred voices, for those who were recumbent naturally sprang to their feet, and long tapering fingers with yellow-dyed nails were quickly held forth in eagerness to annihilate him.

Jack seized hold of a piece of calico and covered his arm, thinking that might have given offence to their vision, and not caring to die the horrible death of scarification, he began to consider the best way to plead for mercy.

Glancing hurriedly round he could see there was a vein of sympathy in some of those beautiful orbs, whilst others flashed with vindictive fire, heightened most probably by the occasion and the opportunity to show off a little more maiden modesty.

"M—m—mercy," Jack began, when a couple of short plump hands seized him by his long curly hair. "Mercy, I implore !" But his prayer was cut short by as rough a handling as if he had been a welcher.

"Allah ! Allah !" then yelled Jack, "protect thy servant from the hands of these Kaffirs. Allah Akbar, into thy hands I commend my soul."

Such a prayer as this, delivered in the pure Arabian of which our hero was so proficient a master, could not fail in its desired effect.

Nur-el-Sham, who clad in her Amazon splendour had stood aloof, demanded in a loud voice the clamouring throng to stand aside, and her beautiful eyes catching those of our gallant but unfortunate hero the effect was electrical.

It seemed as though the points of two powerful magnets had been placed in direct juxtaposition to each other, and that they drew each other together with powerful attraction.

Jack struck an attitude at once.

Placing one hand on his heart, and raising the other skyward, he pretended to be invoking the powerful aid of heaven, which in a moment melted the whole assembly into a sublime state of resignation.

"Hamlet, Hamlet," said he, in a language they none of them understood, " is this lady before me really thy father's ghost ?"

Such an appeal, and delivered with such powerful pathos, would have brought down the house of an ordinary theatre, much more so the Amazon assembly in the tent on the plain.

But it was necessary that Nur-el-Sham, for her own sake, had some explicit explanation, so Jack bowed and commenced the biggest fib that was ever breathed into female ears by the most ardent lover.

It was in substance that the monks and nuns, despising him for his being a true scion of Moslem, seized upon him, almost flayed him alive, and then bribed the mock monk to deliver him into the hands of the Philistines, as they denominated the Amazons from sheer scorn, to do their will with him, and put him to death as they chose.

"Ah !" said Nur-el-Sham, whose fine perception, being sister of the Mahdi, was inimitable, "and so they kept our beloved sister, and thus deceived us by handing you over to torture."

"Allah ! it is so," replied Jack, reverentially. "And the heretics will still persecute her if my arm is so weakened that I am unable to make an effort to rescue her."

Such a speech was applauded to the very echo.

Loud clamours arose on all sides deploring the law that forbade such a gallant champion joining their ranks.

"Friend," said Nur-el-Sham, in French, which none of the rest were scholarly enough to interpret, "I am sorry we always meet thus. Some day we may have the pleasure of meeting alone, but for both our sakes it is now necessary we part."

"Allah Akbar ! Allah Akbar !" exclaimed Jack, bowing low. "God is great, and as a true follower of his prophet I must obey his dictates."

By this time the hearts of his vindictive scarifiers were so softened that tears stood in the eyes of many of them.

Nur-el-Sham offered him one of her spare robes, a splendidly-worked silken head-dress, a green scarf that was to be thrown over the left shoulder and brought down to the right hip, and a short petticoat with green and gold fringe pending down to the knee.

Gold trinkets and other presents poured in upon him on every side, and the lady who had carried him on her back in the very reverse style to Lady Godiva, presented him with a splendid bow and a magnificent quiver full of arrows.

CHAPTER LI.

AN AWAKENING IN THE DESERT.—HORRIBLE FATE OF THE PERFIDIOUS COURIER.— A RIDE ACROSS THE PLAIN.—ALI LOBAH AND HIS USELESS PRISONERS. — A WILD-GOOSE CHASE.—JACK HAS SOME FUN OUT OF THE CRAFTY ABABA.

ARAB JACK was, as the saying is, as rich as a Jew when he awoke in the morning with the sun pouring down upon him.

Where he was or how he came upon such a delightful scene he could not imagine. It seemed to him as if he had just emerged from some glorious celestial dream, and that he had been whirled through the air by a bevy of angels.

Beside him there was a beautiful camel tied down by the knee, a skin of water, a bag of dates, and a bottle of palm oil.

"Well, this is a go," he exclaimed, springing to his feet. "Here's a plight I am in. They've bound that place on my arm up very nicely, but as for the rest of my body I feel naked. I must contrive a shirt somehow," he added, "and something to cover my legs, for though I dyed myself all over the very day I served Abdul Ahmed that trick, it will wear off and spoil my character as an Arab."

"And gold, too," jingling the treasures as he proceeded. "Well, it must be true that I was among the Amazons ; but they evidently drugged me ; and played such games with me as I may never know." But there, no matter," he added, as he examined the neat construction of the quiver and bow, "I am all sound wind and limb. I wonder what will be my next adventure ?"

Jack had no idea that the sherbet given to him by the Amazon lasses was drugged, that he had slept for several days, and had been confided by the thoughtful Nur-el-Sham to the care of one of the Mahdi's most trusty and swift-travelling couriers.

This rascal, however, instead of escorting Jack towards the Mahdi's camp, where he could have made himself known, and make his tale good, finding that he had property about him, resolved upon taking him far away into the desert, and there having robbed him leave him to be starved or murdered, just as the case might be.

To effect this he had plucked some narcotic plant by the way, bruised it between his palms, and placed it to the nostrils of the unconscious boy.

But fortune turned in our hero's favour after all, for the rascal having laid Jack down in the place he had chosen for the deed (a beautiful green oasis), he by some means caught the narcotic aroma of his own drug in mistake, and was obliged to walk about in the endeavour to shake the drowsy feeling off.

But his hands and clothes were so impregnated with it that he could not get rid of the overpowering stupor, which caused him to reel into one of the deep valleys, where Jack afterwards saw him, battered almost out of shape, with his dromedary on the brink of the gulf looking down on him.

Jack, however, took no interest in his fate.

He knew nothing of his history, so why should he ?

In his fall his turban had got hooked on a thorn, and Jack almost ventured breaking his neck to get it, as it was an article he really wanted.

"Now, which way shall I proceed?" was Jack's next thought. And as he could get no guidance from the sun he sent up an arrow straight above his head, determined to follow whichever course it should take in its coming down.

"Good!"

In another moment he had packed his traps upon the camel, untied its leg, and mounting its back rode away.

"Ah, you'll be able to find your road about better than I," said he to the dromedary who was gazing wistfully after him, and then fancying he saw figures moving on the margin of the plain he urged on his beast in the hope of overtaking them.

On observing a single rider scouring over the plain the party stopped and bivouacked, and when Jack came up with them he found himself in a nice nest.

It was a band of robbers, composed mainly of the Red Sheikh's disbanded Arabs, headed by Ali Lobah, the Berbereen outlaw, whose treachery Jack had been witness of on two occasions.

But, stranger than all, in their midst they held two prisoners, which Jack, on nearer approaching, discovered to be the perfidious Ababa and Selim.

"My golly, here's a find!" exclaimed Jack. "Can you point me the way to the Nile?" said he to the Berbereen.

"Give your camel its head," answered the outlaw with one of his cheery but deceitful smiles. "If you want company, here's a couple of good companions you can ransom. I'm tired of feeding 'em and finding 'em in water."

"Allah save me!" replied Jack, who was so disguised as to be out of all recognition by those who previously knew him. "I have been set upon and robbed, and left, as you see, in this almost destitute condition."

The outlaw laughed.

"You have more clothes than I can muster," he said. "But who robbed you?"

"A tall spare fellow, who said his name was Ali Lobah."

"Dang him!" burst out the Berbereen, suddenly. "Ali Lobah or Ali Sloper?"

"Lobah," said Jack, scarcely able to restrain himself from laughing outright. "He took my good rifle and left me this bow and some arrows, and cleared me out of every piece of coin I had."

"Was it much?" asked the Berbereen, turning thoughtful.

"The price of a caravan," replied Jack. "He had just left me when I espied you in the distance."

"Then, I'm on. Follow, mates!" cried the Berbereen.

And wheeling round his fleet-footed charger he spurred away across the plain until he and his host were hidden in rising clouds of sand.

"Go on. Follow him!" shouted Jack to the astonished Ababa. "I have nothing for you to steal."

But Ababa was so astounded at finding himself at liberty that he only fooled about with his camel. And Jack, who was full of mischief, fitted his bow and let fly an arrow in a line with the crupper, which struck him about two inches above the saddle.

"Yah—hoo!" yelled the affrighted Ababa.

"Yah—hoo—hoo!" And he leaped up in his saddle and danced about just like a savage at the first taste of powder.

"One to me, you confounded rogue!" Jack hissed. "Do you know me now? Do you remember your treachery when we went to visit the Coptic monastery?"

The fellow recognised Jack's voice; but he was in too much pain to palaver, and if he had the courage he had not the means of withdrawing the arrow without danger of breaking it in.

Jack, as we know, was not naturally spiteful, but this joke pleased him immensely.

"Ya—ha—hoo—hoo!" he cried out mockingly. And then seizing the halter of Selim's camel, he rode smartly away.

"Hold on! Don't take this road," said Selim, when they had proceeded some distance. "Yonder is the Shebacat Wells, where plundering Arabs always lurk. I heard that round-faced robber say so just now."

"Ah, that was Ali Lobah!" laughed Jack. "I have sent him after an imaginary impostor supposed to be representing himself."

Selim laughed, too. But it was the last laugh they had for many days. They were lost in the desert—suffered innumerable hardships, and sometimes were days before they could find a drop of water.

One morning, after they had hobbled their camels and enjoyed a night's rest, they were aroused by a noise which sounded like the din of thunder, and on springing up Jack discovered that the hills to the right of them were completely covered with thousands upon thousands of the Mahdi's troops, carrying innumerable flags, and beating their tom-toms to their wild war-notes.

"By Jove, Selim!" exclaimed Jack, who was afraid to acquaint his companion with his fears. "we must be sharp off out of this; we have drifted down among the rebel horde, and if they discover your sex they'll——"

"Don't worry, Jack, old chum," said the light-hearted girl. "I'm a boy now, you know. Don't keep pestering me with my weakness; I feel as strong as a lion, and if any one molests me why of course I shall give them a few inches of this bit of steel."

"Yes," said our hero, trying to laugh; "but we are next door neighbours to a host of savages; your skin is whiter than mine, and if they get hold of us they'll most likely settle us both just out of amusement."

"Then we must die," said Selim, who for the life of her could not be serious. "We must go some time or other. I dreamt of home, of my sisters, last night, and do you know the scene changed, and I thought that we two were seated somewhere enjoying such a nice little chat with my brother Hassan."

"I wish we were; I should like to see his dear old face again. I wonder where he is."

"Well you would not know him if he is anything like what I saw in my dream. Why he's an old man; but he said he was awfully rich."

"Blow the riches!" said Jack. "All the money in the world would be little good to us here. Now listen to me. I have told you enough to warn you of our danger. Take this stuff we got from that old Turk we found wandering in the desert, and go into that gully yonder and give yourself a good pasting all over."

"And you ?" said Selim, who was now more calm, and began to understand their position.

"I shall go yonder. We must be quick; every moment is precious. Here, take it; go along, do, and make haste back here."

Jack was back first, and he set to work grooming the camels to drive away the tediousness of the time he had to wait for Selim.

Thus engaged he did not observe the reconnoitring parties prowling about.

He did not see the dusky orbs peering over the ridge just above him, taking stock of himself and the two camels.

When Selim returned they both leaped on their refreshed animals, and down they went at break-neck speed into the plain, from which they had only emerged on the previous night.

Whither they were flying Jack did not know. His sole object was to place as much distance as possible between themselves and the barbarian Mahdi hordes, and they spared neither goad nor lash to accomplish this undertaking.

But fate, which had stood them in good need on many occasions, deserted them in this dire emergency.

Selim's camel, as sure-footed a beast as ever crossed the desert, trod on a loose boulder and stumbled, throwing its rider heavily to the ground, and then rolled over down a steep slope.

Once down and set rolling like a ball, a camel has no more power over itself than any other beast, and therefore in its terror it began to cry out.

And it was this that betrayed the unfortunate pair. A party of Arab scouts on the hills heard the cry, and on looking down they saw Jack dismounted, supporting his companion's head upon his knee, and moistening her lips and brow with water.

Such a sight naturally enough drew them to the spot, and Selim having recovered sufficiently to stand, Jack, as was his nature, tried all he knew to keep the camels from the thieving paws of the Arabs.

But he might as well have battled against the wind.

"If I had my yataghan," he hissed, or, rather, cried, in his passion, "I would render an account of some of you ;" and dealing about him with the miserable weapon he possessed, he let some of them see and feel he was no coward.

Selim did the same, but not having recovered completely from the fall, she was soon overpowered, after which Jack was made prisoner and roughly handled.

Then each of them being lashed securely on a camel's back, they were led towards the Arab army, their dusky captors informing them that nothing short of a most horrible death would be their portion.

CHAPTER LII.

IN THE HANDS OF THE ARABS AT ABU KLEA. —HASSAN TURNS UP IN THE NICK OF TIME. —THE EMIR OF MATEMMEH.—ADVANCE OF GENERAL STEWART. — FIGHTING FOR THE WELLS.—ARAB JACK DEPARTS ON A STRANGE MISSION.

"JACK, dear old chum, where are we ? O that noise ! I feel as if I had awakened from a most horrible dream."

"So you have, Selim," replied our hero.

"When we were surrounded by those Arab scouts we fought bravely ; but we were outnumbered, and now we are in the Mahdi's hands."

"Then it was a reality and not a dream," sighed Selim. "I am in such awful pain. My head aches almost to distraction, and brave as I would like to be, yet I feel I am about to die."

"Nonsense ! We have many a day to see yet, many an adventure to share together. Cheer up. Confound the tom-toms ! What a din of voices ! The cannon and musketry are enough to deafen one."

Jack's voice faltered. He was weak from loss of blood, and the cruel cords that bound his wrists were gradually eating their way to the bone.

Fortunately for Selim her wrists were tied with a sash, and her ancles bound together with plaited grass, while Jack's ancles were secured with a camel's halter.

Both were stretched on the rough ground, too, the sharp projections of which indented their lightly-clad flesh and increased their pain to an extent that was almost unbearable.

Arab Jack made several ineffectual attempts to rise to a sitting posture, and once when he nearly succeeded he was brutally thrust back by one of the dark-bearded chiefs of the Kababish tribe who happened to stumble over his feet.

This act goaded the proud-spirited boy almost to madness.

He knew that a fierce battle was being waged between the Mahdi's forces and the English, and yet he could glean no intelligence of what was going on.

Showers of rifle bullets hurtled over them at times, and cries and groans spoke of some of the Arabs being hit, while now and again the boom of artillery rent the air and caused a diversion among the rebel hordes of the Mahdi.

As our hero lay listening to these terrible warlike sounds a rocket burst over his head, and some of the inflammable material falling alongside of Selim, singed her golden hair and caused her to scream and faint.

"Allah !" said a voice, "that's a strange cry for a warrior. By the beard of the prophet, I would swear that it proceeded from a woman."

This speech was uttered in a very low tone, and in tolerably good English, which caused Jack to roll his eyes around, and then he discovered the speaker.

It was a warrior dressed as a dervish in a long dark dress, with a green sash and a yellow and red shawl folded about the head.

In his hand he held a broad-headed spear, a scimitar was girded to his hip, and on his chest and back were letters of red cloth referring to one of the great promises held out in the Koran.

A hundred or more dervishes similarly clad were also about ; but this one especially attracted Jack's attention, and glad enough was he when he saw his face.

"Hassan !" he cried. "Hassan-el-Ahed, have you forgotten the prophet's anointed ?"

Hassan-el-Ahed, for it was he, gazed down on Jack in wonderment and alarm.

Who was it among that wild fanatical host would utter his name, where he was known as Hassan Ali, the dervish of El Obeid ?

Until then he had not noticed the prisoners, and when he did he was puzzled to recognise Jack in his strange disguise.

"Hassan !" Jack again called.

"Yes," answered he. And kneeling down added, "My son, what is your need ? do you desire me to administer to you the last rites due to the faithful ?"

"Allah, I do," whispered Jack. "Don't you know me—am I so altered that——"

"I recognise nought but your voice. How came you to be a captive ? I must at once get you your release. Who is that boy ? Your companion ? "

"Sela !" gasped Jack. "She is almost dead. Quick, Hassan, render her assistance."

The dervish gave a start, and every limb of his stout frame trembled.

"Good heavens !" he muttered, falling on his knees by his sister's side, "how am I to rescue her from this imminent peril ?"

Quick as lightning he snatched a small dirk from his breast and severed the bonds that held her, and then placed to her lips his gourd of consecrated water.

"She revives, Jack, she comes to ! " he gasped. "Oh, that we were once more back to our home in Alexandria !"

"Don't funk," replied our hero. "All will come right in the end. Cut these cursed cords from my wrists ; they burn me like red-hot wires !"

"Do I dare to ?" exclaimed Hassan, glancing round. "Ah, here comes the Emir of Metemmeh. You saw him at the assembly of the holy durbar. He is consulting with the chief of the Hamara Arabs."

The pair of notables to whom Hassan referred were dismounted and holding a heated discussion, in which the English infidels were frequently referred to.

"Allah is great, and by his aid we'll annihilate them—the accursed dogs, the haters of our race, the robbers of our land, and destroyers of our faith !" yelled the emir, excitedly.

"They are such !" hissed the Amara sheikh. "We are ten to their one, and when we lure them on we will show this Herbert Seymour and his host that their utter destruction is far easier than was the slaughter of Hicks Pasha and his Egyptians.".

"Allah, grant it so ! They must not reach the wells of Abu Klea, at any rate. Once they are swept away, Gordon and Khartoum must fall. By-the-bye, Faragh Pasha and Abdul Ahmed must be communicated with at once. And—Ah ! who have we here ? Hassan Ali, the dervish of El Obeid !"

"Where else should I be ?" said Hassan, gravely, making a devout sign to the emir and his companion. "Where danger threatens the Moslem flag there should the servants of the true prophet administer."

"Allah be praised !" said the emir, returning the salutation. "Before another dawn I hope to see our flag victorious. Ah ! see you yonder, the dogs are forming in square. Now is their defeat registered in the holy records of Mecca !"

The plateau on which they stood was faced with a natural breastwork, which afforded excellent protection from the shots of the British army down in the valley.

Therefore they could converse somewhat at ease, watch the manœuvres of the English, and dodge down when they heard the whistling of the artillerymen's shots.

From what Jack overheard he concluded that the battle must have been raging pretty fiercely for some time ; but now, as the gallant little band under General Stewart moved forward, it was likely to bring on the final issue.

Selim (we must still call our heroine by her assumed masculine name) was by this time sufficiently recovered to understand how matters were.

With her poignard, which through all perils she had always kept near her heart, she severed the cords that held Jack's hands, and handed him the gourd which her brother had unintentionally left by her side.

"Now I feel myself a man again !" he exclaimed, then aloud. "Allah be merciful ! May he bring victory to his host !"

The emir caught the words, and suddenly turned.

"Who is this ?" he asked of the dervish.

"The persecuted messenger of Mahomed Achmet."

"How came he here, and in this plight ?"

He was sent by the Mahdi to Khartoum, where he was imprisoned, menaced with death, escaped, and——"

Hassan had no need for further invention.

A round shot struck the face of the rock above them, and a shell burst not far away, dislodging for a time a party of black riflemen—picked shots — who, commanded by several renegade Europeans dressed in the Mahdi's uniform, were directing their attention to the officers of the British regiments.

"Clear out of this !" yelled the Hamara chief, who seemed suddenly transformed into a madman. "They've got our range, and, by Allah, we must give them our reckoning."

Arab Jack was now free, and rose stiffly to his feet.

"Do you want a messenger to Khartoum ?" said he to the emir.

"I do ; but you seem in a plight not fit for such a journey."

The emir eyed him and Selim up and down, and a pretty pickle they both appeared to be in.

Their garments, torn and threadbare, were coated with a thick paste of sand and blood, and their faces wore a mask of the same composition.

But appearances, in dress especially, were not noticed in the desert. Happy was he who needed no other garment than a strip of calico round his loins and a piece of green rag around his arm or neck, to point out that he was a follower of the Mahdi.

Having descended by a steep gorge into the ravine where the tents were pitched, the party entered one over which the Soudanese flag was flying, and the emir wrote in Arabic cipher a note for Faragh Pasha.

"Equip him well," said the emir of Metemmeh to one of his dusky lieutenants, "let him want for nothing, give him two of our most trusty and intelligent guides, and the rest I will leave to his own discretion."

The Amara sheikh was already mounted, and the emir having concluded, left the tent, and springing on to the back of his fiery steed joined him, and they spurred to their respective commands, which were speedily to be engaged in that deadly onrush which broke the British lines.

"Confound you ! May you both be killed !" thought Jack, as he watched their departure.

Little did he think, however, that his words would be prophetic, and that one of the fiery pair would actually penetrate on horseback into the very heart of the British square.

Jack was sadly disappointed when he heard that Selim was not to accompany him.

"No," said Hassan," she is my sister, perhaps the only one I have left, and I will see after her welfare. Here is a bottle of dervish water to cheer you on your way. Good bye."

CHAPTER. LIII.

THE JOURNEY TO KHARTOUM.—THE TRAITOR FARAGH PASHA.—JACK'S INTERVIEW WITH GENERAL GORDON. — THE WARNING. — GORDON'S PRESENTIMENT AND FATAL PREDICTION. —TREACHERY.— UNCERTAIN FATE OF THE GENERAL.

JACK parted sadly from his friends, but with the elasticity of youth his spirits were soon as buoyant as ever.

"I wouldn't have come alone, though," he muttered, "if I had known it. If there was a chance I would throw myself in the way of the English, and go on with them to Khartoum and demand of General Gordon my yataghan and knife."

This stuck so in Jack's throat that he was compelled to take a pull at the flask of dervish water, which made him merry, and set him singing, much to the amusement of the Arab guides, who thought he was practising some new selections out of the Mahdi's revised edition of the Koran.

In this manner he whiled many a long day of the tedious journey. Sometimes he camped out, and at others he put up at the sheikh's house of some half-deserted village, where he practised his deceitful art, and made them think he was really a saint from Mecca, which brought him in alms and insured him the best entertainment.

On leaving Berber Jack fell in with a party of the Mahdi's followers, who on learning that he was a fakir of the holy prophet (which statement was of course enlarged upon by the guides) fell on their faces before him and worshipped him.

They were on their way to the emir of Omdurmann, a relation of the Mahdi's, at whose court our hero met with a grand reception.

He assembled his notables and held high entertainment in honour of the boy fakir, as Jack was termed, and clothed him in the most sumptuous robes, and even took the massive gold chain from his own neck and placed it round our hero's.

The plumpest and prettiest girls were also made to dance and sing before him, whilst others with additional charms, swelling busts, and flesh like the softest velvet, handed him sherbet and fanned him till he was gently wafted to the land of zephyrs.

In return for this our hero was necessarily expected to do something extraordinary, and having learnt several sleight-of-hand tricks he performed wonders with his magic sixpence, the hole in which he declared was the work of the prophet Mahomet himself, and had been presented to him by an angel in a dream when he was asleep near the tomb at Mecca.

The dervishes looked grave, and marvelled much when Jack by his sleight-of-hand tricks produced the silver coin from the eyes, nose and ears of the emir's favourite slave girl.

When he did the handkerchief trick, causing the coin to appear and disappear at will, they were astounded.

"Allah is good! Allah is great! Allah is marvellous!" they kept on ejaculating, until at length growing jealous of the favours showered upon the boy fakir, by the emir, they were pleased when they escorted him to the boat on his way to Khartoum.

Once arrived on the outskirts, Jack dismissed his guides, and soon obtained an interview with Faragh Pasha, who met him in the cabin of one of Gordon's steamers that lay moored near the gate of the citadel.

The interview was strictly private, and the two-faced Faragh took the document Jack gave to him with an oily smile.

"So the English dogs are beaten," said he to Jack, when he had cast his eyes over the mystic characters. "Allah is victorious."

"It may be so," replied Jack, using the same crafty tone. "The battle was waging hotly when I left, and——"

"I must get you an audience with the general," whispered Faragh, interrupting him. "Gordon is a fool! He still holds out, and yet he sees that Khartoum must eventually fall. Perhaps if he hears the truth from your lips he will come to reason, open the gates of the town and avert a most horrible slaughter."

Jack felt the hand of the villain tremble as he clutched our hero's shoulder, which made Jack grin within himself immensely.

It was his earnest wish to get an interview with Gordon, and here was the fulfilment of his desire.

"I will see him," he whispered softly. "But what of my life?"

"I will answer for it. Throw this shawl about you and fold this handkerchief round your head, then follow me in silence and all will be well."

One hour later Jack in his strange attire stood in the presence of the Christian martyr.

They were alone, for the crafty traitor had arranged it should be so, deeming it best for the safety of his own head not to be seen in the affair.

"Well," said Gordon, calmly, "so you bear ill news of the British arms."

Jack bowed.

Then he went to the table and wrote on a slip of paper in English :—

"Beware! Faragh Pasha is a traitor to your cause. Are we alone?"

The general took the paper and read it with thoughtful brow.

"Too sadly I know it," he murmured. Then fixing Jack with his mild blue eye, added aloud:

"We are alone,—are you? Methinks I have seen that face before."

"True, sir, we have met here," replied Jack, boldly. "Remember, you took from me my yataghan and knife, and then consigned me to that horrible dungeon below the gate."

Gordon started.

"Are you the boy?" he exclaimed, an indignant flush mantling his noble brow. "When I ordered you to be brought before me I was told you were dead. Merciful heaven, who are you, mysterious boy?"

"A waif! a London arab!" replied our hero, his fine eyes brightening with enthusiasm.

"Drifted on the tide of fortune I have encountered many perilous adventures through Egypt and the Soudan, and now I am here."

"Your name ?"

"Arab Jack."

"What else ?" exclaimed Gordon, clutching him by the arm. "What of that fearful mark ? Can you give me an explanation ?"

Jack shuddered.

"All I know is that it is a birth mark," replied Jack, falteringly, "and in some way connected with the siege of Paris. My dear mother——"

Jack broke down here. His speech failed him. When he thought of his parents he could go no farther.

"Good ! Then your name is Martin," Gordon exclaimed, pleased to see the tear that welled from the brave boy's eye. "Your uncle was slain in the army of Hicks Pasha, and your father left here but a week since with the harrowing conviction that you were his son, whom he now mourns doubly dead."

Jack listened intently to the recital which the general outlined to him in a few brief words.

"Then it is my father," he exclaimed in agonised accents, "the parent I so cruelly wronged. O my poor mother ! and she, too, mourns me dead. God give me strength to once more return to her and crave forgiveness."

The lips of the strong man quivered as he gazed on the brave boy's emotion, and an inward prayer was muttered in the penitent's behalf.

"Cheer up !" said the general, at length. "You are a child of fate; the yataghan and knife shall be restored to you. Be seated and recount to me some of your adventures."

Jack did so, and the general was astounded at our hero's recital.

"You are a *Gordon boy !*" he exclaimed, excitedly, "one of those *waifs* such as I would gather to my bosom. Fate has willed that you should pass through all these trials. You are a child of sorrow and acquainted with grief, yet your die is cast, and there may still be for you a bright hope in the future."

"Thanks, thanks !" cried Jack, brightening up at the last consoling words. "If my parents live, and that power you speak of should enable me ever to meet them, my remaining days shall be devoted to their comfort, and my whole soul engaged in atonement for the past."

"Brave boy !" muttered the general, as he approached his escritoire, and produced from one of its secret drawers the yataghan, the knife, and a well-worn Bible. "Take these, and whenever you turn over the pages of this sacred book, think of Gordon, whose time on earth is, I feel, drawing to a close."

"But what of the bright hope you held out to me ?" said Jack.

"You are young," replied the general. "I feel that my country has deserted me—betrayed me as Samson was sold to the Philistines by his wife. They have bound me with withies, shorn my locks, put out mine eyes, fettered me with promises instead of bringing me gold, and now they make sport of me ; but mark me, boy, when I am wearied out, and been solely on my supports, Faragh Pasha and Abdul Ahmed, Khartoum must fall as did the house."

As he spoke, the big diamond in the hilt of the yataghan dropped out, and Jack, clutching it up quickly, placed it in his breast.

General Gordon turned terribly pale.

"This is an omen," he said ; "the hour is at hand."

Jack was startled.

Taking up the yataghan and knife, he was about to receive the Bible from Gordon, when the curtains that screened the grand entrance were thrust aside and a party of armed men with Farag Pasha at their head rushed into the reception chamber.

Gordon pressed the holy book to his lips, and snatching a sword from beneath his vestment stood ready to defend himself bravely, when another figure stepped from the arras behind him and dealt him a blow on the head.

Arab Jack was so astounded that he was unable to move.

He was seized and firmly bound before he could even raise his hand in the general's defence.

Then he was thrust to one side, and with agony beheld the brave general stripped ; and the traitor who had dealt him the foul blow donned his vestments.

Gordon was not so stunned as not to understand what was going on.

"Traitors," he scornfully hissed, "why do you not divide my vestments among ye ? why do ye not cast lots for my fez ? Crucify me you may, but the false doctrine of the Mahdi I defy. I believe in the eternal God."

Jack fainted as Gordon, still clutching the Bible in his bleeding hands, was dragged away to a secret door and disappeared, and when he came to he found the heads of the treacherous rebels in close council.

"Allah ! it must be so," said he who had usurped Gordon's place ; "I demand it. Admiral Khasmel Nus, with two of the steamers, five hundred or so of the faithful garrison, and what stores we can rake together must be sent down to Gubat, and carry with them a letter I will indite to the British general."

"Good !" exclaimed Faragh. "But who is the scribe—whom can we trust when on secrecy alone depends our success ? "

"The young Mahdi, the boy dervish," suggested Abdul Ahmed. "I know that he can write and speak English as well as if he were a real Christian dog."

The pretended Gordon, a fellow about his height, of sallow complexion and blue eyes and moustache trimmed and dyed the colour of Gordon's, clapped his hands and made a sign to the guard who stood over our hero.

This was a stalwart Soudanese with bare arms and legs naked to the knee. He carried a Remmington across his shoulder and grasped a long broad-bladed spear, with which he motioned Jack to approach the council table.

The false general stood aside and allowed our hero to stand in his place, and writing materials were placed before him, with a copy of Gordon's writing.

Jack was then ordered to write, but he sternly refused, although the eyes of the council of ten were fixed vengefully upon him.

"I command you in the name of the Mahdi," shouted the usurper ; "write, or die like a Christian dog—behold !"

Jack looked up, and there, suspended above his head by a single horse-hair was a massive sword, and the keen edge of the Soudanese spear was held ready to sever that hair at the word of command. Bold as was, the brave heart of the boy fairly sank as he gazed up at that terrible instrument ; and then he suddenly bethought himself of the role he was playing, and the words of hope uttered by General Gordon.

CHAPTER LIV.

UNDER THE HANGING SWORD.—THE COUNCIL OF TEN COMPEL JACK TO WRITE THE FALSE DOCUMENT. — CAPTIVE AGAIN. — LITTLE SAMBO.— THE FALL AND MASSACRE OF KHARTOUM.

ARAB JACK stood, like Damocles of old, with the terrible sword suspended above his head, his fine eyes glowing with fervour as he glanced heavenward and implored the divine aid to guide his actions.

He was still fearless, however, so much so that Faragh himself held his sword to his throat to intimidate him.

"Then I must yield," he said, desperately. "Do you call yourselves true followers of the prophet to force me to forge the handwriting of a Christian dog? Though I yield, the sin still lies upon your own heads."

There was a commotion among the council of ten.

Their case, however, was desperate ; they had crossed the rubicon, and now it was too late to retract.

The message Jack was compelled to write was very simple to look at, but very significant in its importance.

It ran thus :—

"Dec. 29th, 1884. Khartoum all right ; can hold on for years.—C. E. Gordon."

"Well," thought Jack, "if General Herbert Stewart ever gets this, he will surely smell a rat, for this is January the seventeenth, and they say that if the steamers evade the traps laid for them they cannot on any account reach Metemmeh before the twenty-first."

After this reasoning Jack felt easier in his mind. "I will struggle against it all," he said, "and live."

But he was surprised to find himself suddenly seized, and half dragged, half carried towards the secret door through which Gordon had disappeared, and he was still further astounded after being led through a labyrinth of subterranean passages to find himself in the very chamber into which he had been led by Abdul Ahmed after his liberation from the water dungeon.

Little Sambo was still there, and pleased enough was he when they were alone to find himself once more in company of our hero.

"Whar massa been?" he asked. "Long time away. Next time you go Sambo go—eh?"

"Yes," said Jack, "but we must first discover the means. Whisper low; we may find out soon how to make our escape."

Next day Jack discovered that he was thus immured merely to be made a catspaw of by the council, who not only ordered him to write false reports and orders, and sign them in the name of Gordon, but forced him to do so by placing his feet on gradually heated plates of iron.

No mortal could stand against this, neither could Jack, so he yielded to force, and by this means he could get a considerable view of what was passing on the forked branches of the river and in the principal parts of the town.

It was thus he was enabled to witness Gordon's steamers weigh anchor, and glide away down the Nile out of sight, and see the disaffected groups crowding the streets and squares after they were gone.

The false general had to be very busy just then.

The people clamoured so for food, and complained so much against the delay of the British, that the usurper had to show himself at the windows, or on the housetop of Gordon's palace, and address them in conciliatory terms to pacify them.

At length Jack noticed that the guards on the city walls were reduced, and that Faragh Pasha marched the body of the troops away from the principal gate of the citadel, outside which the besieging Arabs were massed in terrible force.

"There is something wrong," muttered Jack, one evening as he watched the hubbub in the town. "What is it? a crisis certainly is at hand."

Scarcely had the words passed his lips when a body of armed men rushed up the palace steps, the double gate above mentioned flew open with a crash, and the Mahdi's forces with maddened yells rushed into the principal streets and commenced a slaughter that was horrible to behold.

Shrieks and yells then rent the air, the populace fled hither and thither, blood was shed in all directions, and corpses, mangled and gashed, strewed the streets.

Presently there was a commotion on the palace steps.

Swords clashed and revolvers flashed, and a desperate struggle waged for some time.

Then a robed headless trunk, in a dress similar to that worn by General Gordon, rolled down the steps, and Faragh Pasha rushed towards the gate with a bleeding head.

Arab Jack almost fainted at the sight.

"Sambo," he gasped to the little negro boy, who clung tremblingly to his side, "we must find our way to the pulley in the wall and make good our escape. If we stay here we shall be massacred."

"Come, den," exclaimed Sambo, his dark eyes brightening at the thought ; "dis way, Massa Jack, dis way."

A terrible explosion shook the place as Jack and Sambo flew down the winding stone steps to their prison chamber, where Jack sought his yataghan and knife, and various articles useful for their disguise.

A roll of green mosquito curtaining served to make them sashes and turbans, and a Malayan creese with a long serpentine blade and a haft, surmounted with the head of that reptile, formed a formidable weapon for the little negro boy.

A loaded revolver was seized by Jack, and having gained the loop-hole, he fastened the end of the pulley rope round Sambo's waist, lowered him to the ground, fastened the rope to the cleat and then slid down it himself.

When about half down, however, a voice above startled him.

"Cursed Anglaise, die, die!"

Arab Jack looked up.

"Emir Pain!" he exclaimed. "Ah! 'twas you who represented the false general. Take that!"

Jack drew his revolver, and aimed at his would-be assassin's head, but he only wounded him in the shoulder, and the traitor, with a fearful oath, severed the rope with his scimitar and allowed Jack to fall heavily to the ground.

Luckily for our hero he fell, cat-like, on his feet, and with a parting shot he and Sambo took to their heels, round one of the bastions, and were soon lost in the gathering gloom.

Khartoum was ablaze in many parts then, and the shrieks of the victims and the yells of the fanatical Arabs told of the fell work that was going on in the betrayed city.

"Khartoum has fallen. What is brave Gordon's fate?" exclaimed Jack, as he watched the lambent blaze as it lit up the sky.

CHAPTER LV.

A NIGHT OF HORRORS.—JACK AND SAMBO SEEK SHELTER IN THE RUINS.—OUR HERO RESOLVES UPON A DESPERATE RUSE.—HE OVERHEARS THE VILLAINY OF MR. BRUIN AND THE ARAB REIS.—THE THREAT.—JACK GAINS A BLOODLESS VICTORY.

"WE'VE had a narrow escape, Sambo," said our hero when they reached a place of apparent safety. "But we're not out of the wood yet, remember, so keep your ears and peepers open, and don't utter a sound louder than that of a snail."

The little negro boy, brave as he was, could not help shuddering.

The sounds of the carnage and the shrieks of the victims were appalling.

Mingled with the crackling of burning woodwork were the shouts of strong men fighting for dear life and the lamentations of women and children pleading for that mercy which was denied them by their ruthless murderers.

Then the loud shock of some terrible explosion smote the ear, and myriads of sparks were sent hurtling into the air, whilst the Mahdi's hosts, mad with disappointment at not being able to join in the sanguinary fray, added to the fearful din their horrible shouts.

The evening was terribly close and oppressive.

A hot south wind that blew up occasionally from the Nile was anything but refreshing. It seemed to wrap round one like a sheet, and wafted the sulphureous smoke from the fierce conflagration in whirling eddies round about the outside of the walls. Arab Jack's brain fairly reeled with excitement.

"Good God!" he gasped, "this is more terrible than all. If there was some fighting to do it would string my nerves. What are the English about, I wonder, that they have not arrived before this?"

Jack and Sambo were sheltered in the ruins of a sort of pavilion or bazaar, which had been pulled down out of sheer wantonness by the Arabs, who had taken possession of Gordon's remaining steamers, and every boat and other vessel they could lay hands on.

From this position Jack could get a good view of the Blue Nile, on which side of the city they were, and stretch his gaze along the shore, which was literally alive with armed savages, who waved their spears and rattled them on their horn-like shields of raw hide to add to the din and confusion.

"Sambo, I can't stand this, dashed if I can," said our hero at length, turning to his anxious companion. "Do you feel any fear, are you afraid to go where I go?"

"No, Massa Jack."

"Can you swim?"

"Yas, berry good, too."

"Well, then, we'll have a try for the other side of the Nile, for if we stay here we shall be starved, if not slaughtered. Halloo!"

Jack uttered this exclamation in a louder tone than he intended, for on placing his hand on the negro boy's shoulder he found he violently trembled.

"I thought you were not afraid?" he added softly in his ear.

"No more me am," returned the negro, with chattering teeth. "Me swim in the Nile, but not so far across as dis, and not in dark. Me see crocodile eat many mans down um riber."

"Ah, I see. But we are not going to swim if I can help it. I mean to have a boat. But, you see, we may get pitched overboard, and then we must use our flippers."

"Yas, bery good, me no care for dat," said Sambo, endeavouring to smile. "Crocodile worse dan shark you know, no swim away from him; he like alligator."

Jack, although he was in anything but a merry mood, could not help laughing.

"No crocodile would eat you," said he, "while you wear that holy turban. Look yonder. The boat moored to that boulder of rock is the one I intend trying for."

Sambo looked in the direction indicated.

There was a vessel with two masts, and with several people dressed in Mahdi uniform about the deck, whilst the Mahdi's banner floated at the masthead.

"She big ship," said Sambo, rather downcast; "too many peoples for us to fight; we no kill all dey mans."

"We'll try for it. Those we can't kill we must frighten. Look yonder, quick. You see there's no chance of our escaping that way."

As the roof of some large building fell in, the flames that shot up illuminated the stream, presenting to the eye a spectacle of sparkling grandeur.

Below, at the confluence of the White and Blue Niles, there was a mimic fleet of men-of-war blockading the two streams, and preventing all craft from leaving Khartoum by water.

"There," exclaimed Jack, excitedly, as a steamer shot clear of the point, "that is the vessel on which I was received by Faragh Pasha. The traitors are determined to cut off all news and communication with the British army. I wish I had wings to fly, Sambo."

"Yas, so do me. Wish I was on board de 'Drumderry' again. Dis wus nor being sea-sick. Wus nor having knives frowed at nigger."

As the glare went down it left everything in blacker darkness, in which the lanterns of several vessels could be seen moving as further reinforcements were conveyed from the opposite shore.

"Now, Sambo," whispered Jack in a determined voice, "make ready your weapon, and then take hold of one end of my sash and follow me. Not a word, mind. Keep silent, for remember if we are not careful we may throw our lives away."

Without another word the pair crept from the ruins, and taking a devious course, so as to evade a party of Amaras who had just landed, made for the rocks, and after a while made out the outlines of the craft they sought.

"Now then, gently does it," whispered Jack. "Don't breathe louder than you can help ; they are talking, and I want to hear what they say."

"Confound it, I am sorry we were so late," said a voice Jack recognised as being familiar. "We've lost a fortune through your delay, and that crafty Frenchman will have the laugh of us, and the treasure, too."

"Allah forgive us, it cannot be helped now. If we had once gained an entry to the city and aided in the slaughter we should be as happy as princes. It was your fault, though, Mr. Bruin. You Russians are too headstrong and conceited. Why did you stay to palaver with that confounded old sheikh ?"

"Because he disputed my honesty. Did he not say that my Arabic was Dutch, and that I was not commissioned by my government to spy and report all the actions of the English, and render all the aid and information I could to the Mahdi ?"

"He did."

"Then why should I stand it ? Did I not tell him that as the Suez Canal was a bar to our getting by that way to India, that the Holy Czar meant to make a road through Afghanistan, and that as the cursed British whelps are hampered and muzzled in the Soudan he will strike a blow, just as if it was by accident."

"Before Allah I am witness to that."

"Then, I repeat, why should I sit like a bear sucking its paws ? Russia is a big country, you know, and can do a lot for Mahometans when they unite. Sky-blue ! can I use an expression stronger ?"

"Allah forbid ! You have said enough. You should have hastened with your message to Sheik Abdul Ahmed."

"Sky-blue ! did I not ?"

"You dallied, and we are too late. Emir Pain has done the trick for us, and he will find the oil jars full of gold. Oh Bruin, Allah forgive you, you've been our ruin."

Jack knew not whether to laugh right out or give vent to an expletive.

His brain was on fire while he listened to the infamous treachery of the Russian ; whilst the grave and disconsolate speech of the Arab quite tickled his fancy.

"You confounded rascals," he muttered, when he controlled the risibility of his features, " you are a nest of Judases, and I now feel no compunction in giving you your quietus."

He was creeping nearer to the craft, which was lying with its rope fenders hanging over the side close to the smooth face of the rock, when suddenly he was startled.

The Arab had filled his pipe and struck a vesta to light it, when the flame, small as it was, betrayed our hero's presence.

"Allah Akba !" burst like a thunderclap from the Arab's lips ; "Allah Akba !"

"Amen," responded Jack. " Amen."

Then followed a few moments of suspense as the pair stood gazing at each other and the light slowly waned.

Each one naturally enough endeavoured to read the other's thoughts, and as Jack was the intruder he considered it the best for him to break the ice.

"Well," said he, putting on the most injured look he could assume, and making his voice sound gruff, " what are you doing on board my nugger ? Where is my dragoman ? where is my reis ?"

The Arab started back astounded.

"This is my vessel," said he.

"Is it ?" answered Jack. "Then you will please to explain how she became yours, and what has become of my crew."

"By the true God, I know not what you mean. Who are you—where are you from ?"

"That you shall soon know," answered Jack, who had noticed the Arab take particular notice of his green turban. " I am the Chief Fakir of Omdermann, and I bear a firman from the Mahdi which I am now on my way to deliver to the Emir of Berber."

"This is strange," replied the Arab, making a devout sign. " But how came you to leave your vessel here ?"

"That question I would only answer to the Mahdi. I have been in Khartoum, thence on to the holy prophet, and now I have to cross the river in all haste."

"Allah will aid you," replied the Arab.

In fact, he scarce knew what to say, for the cursory view he had obtained of our hero's features led him to suppose that he was conversing with a man past the middle age instead of a boy.

Jack had pulled the green turban well over his brows, and the sweat and dust gave his cheeks the appearance of being wrinkled, while his gruff voice completed the deception.

Jack, with all his cunning, however, was somewhat puzzled how to act in the emergency.

From what he had overheard he knew that he had a crafty customer to deal with, and what was more he had no doubt that there were too many on board for him and Sambo to cope with effectually.

"I'll work on his fears," he thought, as an idea flashed to his relief. " Are you the reis of this craft and a true follower of Islam ?" he asked.

"I am, thank Allah and his prophet. I can read many verses of the Koran, and I once made a pilgrimage to Mecca."

"Good !" exclaimed Jack. " You are to me as an angel in disguise. Set your sails, cast off your ropes and waft me across to the eastern shore."

"What !"

"Put me and my dervish boy across to the opposite shore."

The Arab was so astounded at this peremptory demand that he let fall his pipe, the clatter of which on the deck caused the Russian and several others to come up from below.

"What's the row ?" said the Russian, deliberately sucking his fingers, which were dripping with some oily substance. "What's up, skipper ?"

Arab Jack replied " I am the Fakir of Omdermann." I am now conveying a message to the Emir of Berber, and as my vessel has disappeared mysteriously from these moorings, I demand that you put me ashore on the other side."

"Skyblue ! I am not the capitano," exclaimed the Russ. " If I were I would have you whipped for one bad imposter. How many beans can you count in the dark ?"

Jack's mettle rose at this.

"Look here," said he ; " Allah shall aid me in

resenting this gross insult. At yon camp fire there are hundreds of Amaras, and to the left there are as many Beggaras ; both thirst for the blood of the Christian and infidel dogs. If I but say that you deny the Mahdi, and persecute his true follower, they will flay you alive and tear out your nails with red-hot pincers."

At that moment the moon, that had been veiled by the clouds of smoke, broke forth, and disclosed to our hero the pale faces of his listeners, who, taken aback by this terrible threat, seemed to be transformed to statues of stone.

"You dare not ; they would not believe you," gasped the Arab, who was the only one who had power to speak.

"My word and my yellow passport will be enough to convince them," answered Jack.

There was a tone of irony in his voice, as he drew forth a long yellow scroll which was covered with mystic characters in various coloured inks.

"Look there," he said, when he had unrolled it, pointing to a signature at the foot of the scroll. "That is the signature of Mahomet Achmet. Dare you deny it ?"

His listeners gazed on in silent awe.

Not one there was sufficiently schooled in the language to decipher the characters, much less to deny it.

"If such is the case," said the Arab, who considered that the most easy way to get out of the difficulty was to dissemble, "I will unmoor at once, and sail you across ; but what baksheesh shall I promise my men for their trouble ?"

Jack noted the abject leer in the crafty fellow's eye, and he grinned to himself as he thought of how little of the baksheesh would fall to the lot of the sailors.

"Any sum you can afford to give them," he said, boldly. "The servant of the prophet carries no worldly treasure."

The Arab gave a shrug.

"Suppose they refuse," he said, in an undertone, slavishly rubbing his hands.

"Then I shall signal to the Amara and Beggara sneikhs. They will hasten hither, I shall denounce you, and they will put every one of you to the most horrible torture, seize your craft, and divide amongst them your cargo and treasure."

The Arab forgot his sanctity and uttered a deep oath.

"By the wells of Shebacat, which are the most holy, I declare this is some villainous plan to rob me. Allah is good, but you, dam devil, are like the kamsin (hot southerly wind) of the desert, you sear all, scorch all up."

"Tut, tut ! a truce to this nonsense," said Jack, who was growing tired of the parley ; "every moment's delay is to me important, and is dangerous to the Mahometan cause. The British may be here by to-morrow's dawn, and you know they will deeply avenge the death of their hero Gordon."

"If he is dead," returned the Arab ; then suddenly checking himself, he added, "Allah knows best ; if he is alive the English will give any sum of money for his ransom."

"Skyblue !" exclaimed the Russian, stamping his platter-like foot on the deck. "They no care whether he live or die. Khartoum fallen, they will now run back home again like one geese. Skyblue ! they no fight like the Russ."

The Arab turned pale, and placed his huge slippered foot on the Russian's toe to enjoin caution, a movement our hero did not appear to notice, but of which he took particular stock, as the saying is.

By this time the cries and groans that all the while had emanated from within the walls were subsiding. The bright flames were succeeded by clouds of smoke, and a cool breeze began to ruffle the surface of the water.

"Well, what is it to be ?" demanded Jack, at length. "Are you to cast off, or am I to ——"

"Step on board," replied the cringing Arab. "Allah will protect his children from all harm."

By the time Jack and Sambo were comfortably settled on the after-deck, the Arab sailors flew aloft, let fall the canvas, and the sharp-prowed nugger sped swiftly across the waters of the Blue Nile.

———

CHAPTER LVI.

THE FIERY CROSS.—"DE DEBIL ABOARD DE NUGGER."—ARAB JACK USES HIS MAGICAL DIVINING ROD. — SUCCESS. — THE RUSSIAN JONAH IS CAST OVERBOARD.—A FISH DEVIL. JACK SELLS HIS TALISMANS, AND DEFEATS THE CRAFTY REIS.

THE splendid vessel had barely got way on her, when our hero's mischievous propensity began to assert itself once more.

Taking a stick of phosphorus from a small vial which he always carried with him, he crept to the after-mast when all was still and made the sign of the crucifix upon it, and then crept back to his former position.

The fellow at the wheel on raising his eyes and observing the strange glow set up an unearthly yell.

"Massa Reis, Massa Reis," he shouted, "here, quick, come look ; de debil aboard de nugger !"

"The devil's more likely in your soul," replied the reis, as he came shuffling and panting aft. "Curse you, what is the matter—have you all gone mad ?"

"No, look, look, see ; hell fire, all alight ; burn the ship."

The skipper turned, and he set up a yell more loud than that of the helmsman.

"Allah be praised—Allah d-d-e-e-fend ?" he raved, madly tearing his hair and stamping his foot.

Jack, who was leaning on the taffrail watching the silvery fish sporting about the rudder, and Sambo, who was crouched under the rail, nearly burst their sides with laughter.

The mate, startled by the skipper's cry, came rushing aft, knocking over one of the crew who sprang out of some hole in front of him, and he fell over a couple who were lying at full length near the galley, whilst the Russian rushed up from the cabin and nearly broke his thick skull against the side of the companion hatchway.

The oaths, groans, and howls thus occasioned were something terrific.

The man at the wheel was unable to steer.

He caused the nugger to yaw from one side to the other, while he turned the wheel round backwards and forwards at a fearful rate.

"Hard up ! keep her off !" yelled the reis, as the vessel swung up in the wind, and her large, white, pointed sails shook and rattled until every timber of the ship trembled.

"Yah, yah, me can't ; debil got hold of steering ropes. Allah, Allah, we shall all die !"

"Skyblue !" yelled the Russ, rubbing his head. "I'm killed, I'm gone ; me dead."

At that instant one of the sails shifting over caused the rope sheet to strike him in the neck ; and he let out another yell, which could be heard on either shore.

Fortunately for all hands the mate kept his presence of mind.

The attendant to the sail rushed to the wheel and implored Arab Jack, who was calmly watching the fun, to pray to Allah to deliver them from the spell.

"I can't ; it's in your own hands," replied our hero, who was secretly enjoying the dangerous lark, which might have been the cause of their running into some other vessel. "There is a Christian dog on board, a Jonah !" and he immediately began repeating aloud about a dozen verses of the Koran.

"Allah protect us, then !" cried the mate, who was a giant in size. "Show me the Christian dog, and I will at once throw him overboard."

"Aye, do," implored the reis, who was like one just recovered from a violent fit. "Throw him overboard whoever he be."

"We must trust in God," replied Jack, who then went on muttering his incantations. "But," he added after a while, "I have my divining rod, one I brought from Mecca ; by its aid I can find the culprit and divine the mystic symbol you see upon the mast."

"Well done ! do, do," shouted several.

Jack then took a small wand from his breast, and approaching the Russian, who was leaning with his back to the companion-way, holding both hands to the sides of his head, and uttering a few cabalistic words, Jack pressed the stick to the lower part of his waistcoat. For several minutes he held it there.

Then he described three circles in the air with his left hand, after which he removed the divining rod.

Then such a shout rent the air.

Prayers were mingled with execrations of rage.

On the base of the Russian's waistcoat there was a yellow light, from which issued a noxious, sulphury fume, which assailed not only the olfactory organs but the stomach, and made every one of the crew feel as sick as if he were being tossed on the briny ocean.

The Russian's feeling were, of course, extremely awful.

Not only did the sulphurous odour assail him, but the thought of the awful and damning circumstance drove him almost mad.

"There stands the culprit," said Arab Jack.

"The Jonah," gasped the mate.

"The Christian dog," returned our hero. "The infidel who, in professing to be a Mahommedan, spat on the prophet's beard."

There was a pause for a moment after this.

The captain was in league with the Russian, and he scarcely knew how to act.

He would have had no compunction in throwing him overboard, neck and heels, if it had not been for that. As it was, he feared he might be accused of complicity with the Russian, whose idea was to get Gordon stowed away, buried, so to speak, in one of the deep dungeons or underground vaults, or confined in some lofty turret chamber (as Raleigh was in the Tower of London) until the British nation offered a heavy ransom for his release, his whereabouts, or even a knowledge of his fate.

But of that we will say no more at present.

The pause, which had lasted only a moment, and was one of painful silence, was broken, and the mate in a loud voice demanded that the culprit should be thrown into the Nile.

"Spare me ! spare me !" cried the Russian, who was now ten times more abject than he was arrogant before.

"Keel-haul him ! let him walk the plank !" shouted a renegade Greek.

The moon was now riding high in the cloudless heavens. Every face was as plainly seen as if it were day.

The prisoner glanced eagerly around, but in not one of them could he read the least pity.

"Stay, all of you—let me speak," said the skipper.

All were silent.

"What death is he decreed to die ?"

"Drowning ; let him drown !" shouted several.

"But, supposing he is seized by a crocodile !"

"All the better ; Jonah was swallowed by a whale."

"But he escaped."

"Tie a rope to him then, and if he is swallowed by a crock and he still lives, then we can haul him up again and hang him."

It was the mate who spoke.

The captain's eye glistened.

It was just the very suggestion he would have liked to make had he dared.

"Quick, a rope !" he shouted, and willing hands soon seized upon the Russ, and the rope was tied round him under his arms.

The next minute he was borne aft, and the dusky crew stood ready to pitch him overboard.

"Hold ! avast !" cried Arab Jack, holding up his hand warningly. "Dog as he is, let us give him a chance to pray to his false deity ; the devil already waits to bear him to his unhallowed regions.

This was strong reasoning. Nevertheless, the voice of the fakir was hearkened to, and the Russ, who was as cold and bloodless to look at as stone, was saved from being hurled headlong into a watery grave.

It was from a motive of humanity that Jack caused this delay, although at the same time he revelled in the suffering the Russ endured.

The vessel was rapidly nearing the opposite shore, and if he could only delay the execution of the sentence long enough, the life of the wretched Russian might be saved.

At this juncture a squall from the south-east called the attention of every one of the crew.

The big sails flapped, then filled out, the nugger heeled over, and her flat bottom made rapidly towards the shore. The mate, however, had not forgotten the sport that was in store for him.

"This way !" he shouted to several of the crew, when they were liberated from their duties, and by their aid he liberated the culprit, who was firmly lashed to one of the stanchions, and with a loud " whoo-whoop " he was plunged over the stern into the sea.

Then followed a loud splash, one deep heart-rending yell, the waters hissed, and the Russ, with his head above water, was being towed astern.

"MY JACK!" SHE CRIED, SUDDENLY STARTING UP. *p.* 144.

At first his brain whirled, so that it seemed as if he were about to faint; but the cold water revived him and brought him to consciousness and a full appreciation of the surrounding horrors.

Being towed through the water at such velocity caused him no little pain, and the deep sobs that burst from him showed how the immense pressure of the water affected his chest.

At length, however, the nugger shot into a little creek in the bank, the sails were brailed up, and, as the little craft came to a standstill, the Russian was enabled to touch bottom with his feet.

"Now Sambo," whispered Jack, "we must be off like a pair of birds. There she grounds."

As he spoke, the nugger ran up on to the soft sands, and remained fast.

"We must now bid you adieu, Master Reis," said Jack to the Arab skipper. "Mr. Bruin, as you style him, is enjoying a nice bath. What a pity he was not born a water-spaniel."

"Perhaps he was, the false-dog!" retorted the artful skipper. Perhaps he was. Before you go,

good fakir, can you not oblige me with another antidote against his madness, for fear he again bites?"

"I can, Allah be thanked; but this is asking too much of me, I fear. Can you not give a little assistance in return, in the way of money, to help us on our way, as we have none; as you must remember before you agreed to run us across, when you wanted money down."

"So I did; but that was only baksheesh for my crew, all poor fellows, work hard, never grumble, and have big families."

"That is the cry everywhere," muttered Jack to himself; "they all plead large families, and because I have neither chick nor child, I suppose I might starve."

"Come, what say you?" he added aloud. "Mark you, the evil spell I have removed from your craft I can return to it again. On your return voyage you may perhaps go down with all hands. Remember I am the bearer of a firman from the Mahdi."

"Confound my ill-luck," muttered the Arab

skipper; "I wish you had never come on board." Then aloud, "How much do you require?"

"Fifty pieces," replied Jack, opening and shutting his hands in true Arab fashion. "Ten, twenty, thirty, forty, fifty."

"A fortune; more than I clear in a voyage," exclaimed the reis. "I cannot do it."

"Liar!" Jack was about to reply, when a strange commotion was heard in the water under the stern, and the voice of Mr. Bruin was heard shouting and yelling in terrible accents."

Every one flew aft, and glared over the taffrail.

"Yaw, yah, yoo, boo," yelled the Russ, his terror seeming to increase each moment. "One debil! one debil!"

"It is so," vociferated Jack, who was equal to the occasion. "It is the devil, the fish-devil; same as swallowed Jonah."

In spite of the sand which had been stirred up and mixed with the water, our hero detected the silvery scales of an enormous fish with a black back, and horns on its head like a silurus.

"There, there it is!" Jack cried out again, in a voice that was enough to set the boldest heart on the flutter. "It will kill him, I know it will. Give me room. By the prophet it will make a hole in the ship!"

Little Sambo was almost dead with fright, and his unearthly noise added to the terror of the crew.

"Allah! Allah!" they shouted, as they leaped about and tore their matted hair.

"Allah!" exclaimed Jack, disdainfully; "he will not help you. You are a set of outcasts, you have defiled the prophet's beard."

The reis clasped his hands, rolled his eyes, and stood like one stricken with palsy.

In the meantime the Russian was half-drowned.

The fish, which was one of the largest species in the Nile, and somewhat resembled our jack-pike, terrified by the explosions, had sought shelter in the mouth of the wady; and when the nugger glided in and disturbed it, the affrighted monster endeavoured to make its way out into deep water, and in doing so darted against the Russ, threw him off his feet, which he had just gained, and kicked up a rare ado.

In this way both the Russ and the fish got fogged.

The fine sand and light clay-like deposit made the water thick, so that neither of them could see clearly.

Mr. Bruin, of course, could feel the cold slimy thing dart against him, and slide from his hands like a conger eel; and as the conger is a man-eater, and by some denominated the sea-devil, the Russian, who had seen them in the Black Sea, at the termination of the Russian war, as large as sea-serpents, thought it was one of the hideous creatures come to devour him.

In the confusion the fez of the reis fell from his head on to the deck, and Jack, picking it up quickly, slipped his right hand within it, and held it up to the sky in such a way that the interior was quite dark.

"There," said our hero.

He held the fez arm-high, and moved it towards the reis, who naturally threw his head back until both his eyes were fixed on the inside of the crown.

"Now," cried Jack, "what do you see? The

wisdom of Allah is great; a second Jonah is to be cast into the sea. Are you prepared?"

The face of the reis went green, white, and purple, all in succession.

"I'll give you the pieces," he gasped; "double them if you will give me absolution."

"Hand them over; no shirking."

Jack took a couple of tablets from the folds of his dress, and showed them to the affrighted reis.

"Follower of the devil," said he, "one of these tablets is worth ten thousand pieces; but as I like you, and as there is more joy in paradise over a sinner that repenteth, than over a rich emir who has never sinned, I will give you the pair, one for yourself, and the other for your mate, in exchange for one hundred pieces of gold."

The reis, as Jack anticipated, was, however, not so ready to part.

Avarice was his forte, and for lucre he would have sacrificed his very soul.

Jack, however, was not to be done; his inventive genius was already at work.

"Cavil but one moment, and they are lost to you for ever," he said, in a stern voice; and dangling them before the Arab's eyes by means of several long white hairs which were attached to them, he added, "These are hairs shorn from the holy camel of Mecca. They would pay the ransom of an Abyssinian prince; whoever shall possess them shall die happy and go to the——"

"Devil! devil! de devil!" yelled the Russ; "come quick, kill him, or he scoff me alive."

This appeared very probable.

The voracious monster was circling round him, charging at him open-mouthed now and again, so that those on deck could actually hear his jagged teeth clash.

Such a predicament was enough to appal a bolder heart than that of the Russ.

"Drag him up," said Jack to the herculean mate, "he has had enough now. I will give you a charm so that he may do you no further injury."

When the mate obeyed, Jack could no longer restrain his laughter.

Such an abject miserable figure as the craven presented was not often seen.

His legs were bare up to the thighs, the garment having been torn therefrom, and his dark, dingy skin was lacerated and torn in many places.

Meanwhile, that is while the mate and our hero were enjoying the fun, and the renegade Greek was whispering mysteriously to his fellows, the Arab reis slipped below, and presently appeared with a string of gold coins, with a square hole in the centre of each.

He handed them to Jack.

"Are they all right?"

"As correct as the sun," pointing upwards.

Jack counted; there were ninety-nine.

"Liar and knave!" he said, drawing his yataghan, which he carried concealed in its usual place, "I have a mind to confiscate the lot, and strike off your treacherous head for your pains."

Jack's eye flashed as brightly as the precious bauble in the haft of his weapon, as he erected his magnificent form and stood ready to deliver the blow.

"Hold, I pray you, good fakir," cried the mate, springing forward. "You said that one of the talismans was for me. I will give you the hundreth piece of gold."

"Nay, you shall not. I will not take it," cried our hero, wrathfully. "The bargain was struck, and he shall fulfil it."

Awed by the threat, and quailing under our hero's fierce glance, the artful reis then produced from the capacious pocket of his baggy breeches the missing coin.

"That's better," exclaimed our hero ; and having secured the string of pieces in the folds of his raiment, and placed the loose coin in his pocket for immediate use, he handed one of the tablets to the reis, and the other to his mate.

"Let us now depart, Sambo," said Jack, clutching that worthy by the arm. "Such company as this is not meet for a young dervish. Let us on to Berber. Can you, Master Reis, direct us in the way ?"

The skipper at once assented, and pointed to a defile between the rising hills, about a mile distant.

"There," said he, "at the end of yon gorge you will find caravans passing your way ; but have a care whom you trust, for the track is lined with bands of robbers, who would murder you, be you Mahommedan or Greek, for the pieces you have about you."

"I'll take heed," replied Jack, "and especially of you," he muttered to himself, for he had noted a treacherous shifting glance in the eyes of the crafty reis, and he concluded that if any plundering was to be done he, the reis, would be the most likely one to do it.

The mate presented Sambo with a bag of dates and a gourd of filtered water.

Then, having cast one more contemptuous glance at the Russ, who was heaving up the sand and water with more noise and less decorum than a drain pump, Jack led the grinning negro boy ashore.

"Now then, step out and keep your eyes open," said our hero to his youthful chum ; "the Arabs seem to be flocking towards Khartoum like a host of vultures. Let us thank fortune that we have crossed the river without swimming and without fighting. It would be awkward if we had to travel with our eyes and arms in slings."

"Yas, Massa Jack, me look out ; see plenty Arabs coming dis way, both sides. Ah ! see dem heads dere in mimose bush ?"

CHAPTER LVII.

AN OLD ENEMY AGAIN ON THE TRACK.—A TREACHEROUS SHOT.—SAMBO HAS A CLOSE SHAVE OF HIS LIFE. — THE OUTLAW'S SIGNAL. — THE DESERT ENCAMPMENT. — JACK'S LITTLE AMOUR WITH THE SHEIKH'S DAUGHTER.—A GLORIOUS FEED.—STARTLING APPEARANCE OF THE OUTLAW ALI LOBAH.

ARAB JACK cast his eye immediately in the direction indicated by Sambo ; but smart as he was he was only in time to see the heads disappear and catch a cursory glance of one round face.

It required all Jack's presence of mind to prevent his starting, and thus betraying that he recognised the face.

"That is the confounded traitor, Ali Lobah, the Berbereen," he said to himself ; "where the hawk flies there is quarry of some kind. What is he doing here ?"

Jack would have started in reality if he could have had his question answered.

The outlaw guide, with a band of desperadoes had blockaded the pass, and was watching for all stragglers who might have made their way out of Khartoum.

From his position, a clump of mimosa on a piece of rising ground, he had watched the arrival of the nugger, and seen the gold pass into Jack's hand ; and, what was more, his keen eye, which could discern anything accurately for miles, had seen the blazing glitter of the diamond in the hilt of our hero's yataghan, when he raised it to strike off the skipper's head.

But the crafty Berbereen was as artful as a fox, and having recognised in our hero the young Mahdi, of the Holy Caravan, he shrank from attacking him openly as a fox would from attacking a wolf.

Finding that his ambush was discovered, owing to Jack's double pair of eyes, he now proceeded with still greater caution.

As yet he was not aware that our hero had recognised him.

He knew that Jack's eye spotted him and that is all.

"Confound the little demon," he muttered, alluding to Sambo, as he drew his myrmidons back into the scrub.

"Forewarned, forearmed," muttered Jack, as he became cognisant of his danger.

"Stick close to me, Sambo," he said ; "they'll attack us in the ravine ; "roll your eyes about, and look behind you if you can, but don't turn your head."

"Yas, Massa Jack, me look all the same as one fly," returned the little hero, as he brushed a handful of those active little creatures off a big date plum and thust it into his mouth.

Jack's mind was actively employed the meanwhile, as they entered the passs or gorge, through which was a broad camel track.

Jack was surprised to find a stream of water running on one side of it, and as many bones strewn about as would make a fortune in London.

Steep hills were on both sides, one with a face almost as smooth as a wall, and the other rugged and retreating backwards.

"A nice spot for an ambuscade," thought our hero. "This is something like the trap into which Hicks Pasha was inveigled, barring the stream, which if they had had matters would have been different."

Jack took a good drink out of Sambo's gourd and then told him to refill it, he (Jack) keeping a good look out the while for any treacherous action, which he knew must come, though he could not tell how soon.

Then they journeyed on for nearly a mile, Jack keeping his yataghan ready for service, and his revolver, in which there were several shots.

"Bang !"

Jack drew his pistol and faced about.

The shot came from his rear, and from one of the rugged breaks just described a wreath of white smoke was curling.

"Curse you, you murdering assassins !" cried our waif. "I'd like to have you at the point of my steel, whoever you are."

"Don't stand ; keep on ahead," he whispered

to Sambo. "I'll walk backwards. If the two of us can't fall in three deep we must form a movable square."

"Yas," replied the cheerful little negro, brightening up, and loosening his creese, which was hid up the sleeve of his loose kaftan, or shirt, as Jack called it; and then he commenced stowing away the dates at an enormous rate.

Jack, in spite of the seriousness of the occasion, could not help laughing.

"You're a scorcher, Sambo," he said, encouragingly, "a fair hot un. You ought to be sent to the North Pole instead of the Soudan."

"No sar; Norf Pole no good to Sambo; he too fly; no flys Norf Pole. Pole too high and slip'ry for dem to hang on."

"Go on, faster, you shambling blue bottle," cried Jack, who kept touching against his heels. "Steam on, we're beating the rascals; they can't crawl over those jags as fast as we can walk on level ground."

He had scarcely spoken when another bullet whistled through the air, and passing over Jack's left shoulder cut through Sambo's turban and grazed his head.

"Yah, yah," yelled the negro, springing several feet forward, and then bounding along like a ball, or rather leaping like a kangaroo.

Sambo maintained his speed until he had placed a good distance between him and Jack, when he eased a little, and snatching off his turban began rubbing his woolly head.

Our hero just cast an eye on his movements, and then looked about him for the clever marksman. But seeing no one to fire at, he took to his heels also, and on reaching Sambo he discovered the other entrance to the gorge, through which he could see the open plain beyond.

"Hooray! we are getting somewhere now," said he, his cheeks all aglow. "Hooray! I declare this run puts me in mind of the skeedaddle I did down Villiers Street, on to the Thames Embankment."

Sambo, who of course knew nothing of what he was alluding to, gaped at him with open mouth.

"You run like dis before, massa" he gasped. "You hab debil's chase, you, like dis, sar?"

"Yes, Sambo, something like it; but come on we have no time to waste; pull up yer socks, nigger."

Sambo heeded the advice.

Scrambling up the few dates he had left, he thrust them in his mouth, threw away the bag, slung the water gourd over his shoulder, and then started off at a quicker pace than before.

"Bravo!" said our hero, following suit.

Then three rapid and successive reports awoke the echoes of the valley.

Three separate shots, which Jack had no idea was the robbers' signal.

On he went, his chief object being to gain the open, which they both eventually reached.

A fresh surprise awaited them there.

On the edge of a bright patch of verdure an Arab encampment was pitched, numbering about thirty tents. Upon the grass, horses, camels, horned cattle and sheep were peacefully grazing, whilst fowls, ducks and pigs, were amusing themselves in their primitive fashion.

All else was quiet, and not a human soul was to be seen, but presently the yelping of a score or more dogs announced the presence of our visitors.

Jack, although fully cognisant of the Arab's cunning, had no idea that this was a ruse.

He was so taken off his guard by the surprise engendered by such a scene, as to be quite unconscious that anxious eyes were watching him.

Presently a young Arab appeared at the mouth of one of the tents, with a gun slung over his shoulder and a sword in his hand.

"Peace!" shouted Jack, drawing a white handkerchief from his breast; and then he made the sign which is a sort of freemasonry among them.

"Welcome, come on, enter," said the youth, taking off his fez and bowing in deference to Jack's green turban.

Sambo had put his in his breast to preserve it from further mutilation, so that he was bareheaded, and of course was of no significance.

At the entrance of the tent Jack paused; but the sheikh, a man of about sixty, beckoned him in, and prostrating before him, craved his blessing.

Jack, having glanced round at the group to see that all heads were uncovered, then went through the formula without delay, and taking a parcel of small dried chips from his pocket, distributed them about.

"Venerable father," said Jack, "I am the Fakir of Omdermann. I am from Khartoum with a firman from our victorious Mahdi to the Emir of Berber."

The sheikh, who was squatting on his mat, moved not a muscle.

He bowed gravely until his face nearly touched the earth, and then he resumed his listening with the same composure.

"As we have fasted many days," pointing to Sambo, whose black eyes were rolling, as the saying is, all over the shop, "I beg you will supply us with food, and afterwards if you can spare us a camel or a couple of horses, the servants of our lord the Mahdi will be grateful."

Jack paused, and so did the Arab sheikh. The former awaited the answer, the latter waited to hear what reward or recompense would be offered.

Jack tumbled to this at once and was needled, for he had blessed the sheikh and all his host, and furthermore, given them all a talisman that would allow them to peer in at the gates of paradise, if even they were too wicked or too poor to gain admittance.

"My father is dumb," said Jack, artfully.

"Allah forbid," was the grave reply. "Abka is only weak in articulation; he have no teeth; false ones he have made, but he has no gold to set them in."

"Oh," said Jack, pretending to awake suddenly from a dream. "I have one gold piece, and ——"

"No more?" cried the astonished sheikh; "and yet you come from Omdermann and Khartoum."

"I am not a merchant or trader," replied our hero, tartly. "If you refuse my request, I shall say amen; but beware."

Abka made a sign to one of his young men, who telegraphed it to the further recess of the huge tent, and presently a beautiful, partly-nude girl made her appearance.

She carried on a red earthen tray pipes already loaded and lighted, one of which she handed to her father and the other to Jack.

Then she spread a crimson mat, and with a graceful curtsey and a no less bewitching smile, desired our hero to be seated.

Jack deferentially bowed to the blushing girl, and taking a small gold necklet from his breast-pocket—which necklet, by-the-bye, he had intended for the Emir of Berber's favourite slave, when he used her as a medium in his miraculous performances—handed it to her.

Such a present set the dark girl's eyes aglow.

"Thank you, thank you," she said in her beautiful flowery language ; "thank you one thousand times ; me wear this for your sake ; part with it, no, never."

Jack bowed his acknowledgment so low, that his face came dangerously close to hers ; and she, delighted by the precious treasure, and tempted by the close contact of Jack's smiling and handsome face, gave him a kiss.

"Waugh ! waugh !" cried the sheikh, pretending to be angry ; but the young girl, knowing her father's ways, took no heed of his reproach, and so, hugging Jack fairly round the neck, she gave him a full dozen more, and Jack was quite delighted.

The girl, who in vulgar parlance knew her book, then gave Jack an extra one for makeweight.

Then, whispering in his ear, and giving him one of those warm seductive glances that strike right home to the heart, she darted away.

Jack and the sheikh then both smoked on in grave silence.

"Well," said Jack, when he could restrain himself no longer, "what about the food, the horses, or the camel ?"

"I cannot yet say," answered the sheikh, solemnly gazing at Jack through the thin vaporous cloud of smoke ; "I shall give you food, but as to the cattle, no, no."

He shook his head, and pretended to be suffering from either extreme anguish or sorrow.

"You have broken the sanctity of my house," said he, "and now what guarantee have I that if I supply your wants you will not run off with my daughter ?"

"Allah forbid !" exclaimed Jack, raising his eyes hypocritically ; "what cause have you to judge me thus harshly ?"

"Your conduct just now. By the beard of the prophet I am grossly insulted. Five hundred gold pieces would not purchase my maiden daughter ; one kiss of her virgin lips was priceless till you polluted them."

"Well," said Jack, taking the cool amber from his mouth, which was not half so delightful as the soft, warm lips of the voluptuous maiden, "I made her a gift, but I would not have polluted her, as you choose to term it, had it not been for the accident which brought us so close together, and which I could not avoid. I am sorry, father, that it should have happened under the roof of your desert house ; but I saw no sign when I entered declaring that you were a jellab (slave dealer)."

"Allah forbid !" replied the crafty Arab ; "Allah forbid ! I merely said it in jest. You have bruised my heart in taking liberties with my daughter ; but you have a gold piece and I will give you food on that account."

"I have one, only one," said Jack, sharply. "That you can have. Quick, give us some food ; we are as famished as Pharaoh's lean kine."

Jack's olfactory organs were aroused.

He smelt something savoury cooking, and being tired of the pipe, he wanted to set his teeth to work.

Therefore he handed the coin to the avaricious sheikh, who accepted it with many servile thanks, and in due course the repast was served up ; but it was not in accordance with Jack's present taste.

It consisted of a great heap of white dough pancakes, to which were presently added two earthen bowls, one containing oil, the other butter, mashed up with a quantity of powdered sugar.

Hungry as Jack was, the sight of this mess did not tempt him to set to ; but the eyes of Sambo, whose appetite was always like that of a jackal, seemed to devour the whole lot.

This was a favourite Arab dish, and to the sons of the Arab sheikh it was quite a luxury.

Without any invitation they gathered round, squatted within arm's reach of the dishes, and baring one arm, broke off a large portion of bread, dipped it into the oil, and then rubbing it into the mixture of butter and sugar, threw back their heads and dropped the dainty goody goody into their open mouths.

Then they all sucked their fingers, and the old sheikh made a sign to Jack that he was welcome to follow suit.

"No," said Jack ; "I gratefully decline ; I am not up to that sort of tack to-day. I can smell fowls boiling in the distance, and I should like a small slice of lamb."

"You shall have it," said the sheikh, pretending to be abashed.

Jack was glad when the sheikh's own dinner was served.

It consisted of a large bowl of soup, in which the fowls cut up floated about, with plenty of onions, small dough balls, and other tempting niceties.

Some white bread and a couple of wooden spoons finished the preparations, and as Jack and the sheikh both fed out of one bowl, Jack opened his shoulders and fell to.

Jack was death on the solids.

He did not care so much for the soup ; it would blow him out and spoil his appetite for the lamb-chop, a couple of which he could smell, and hear spitting and fizzing over the fire.

When these were served up, with nice white bread, and steaming hot coffee, Jack felt as if he was on the right track for heaven.

The repast over, Jack felt as if he could scarcely move.

"I'm as tight as a drum ; and as to smoking," he thought to himself when pipes were again brought, "I don't care about it."

Jack was so engrossed with his pleasant thoughts, and so enraptured with the girl, who pressed his hand as she handed him his pipe, that he did not notice the anxious and eager glances the sheikh keep casting towards the door.

Presently, however, something darkened the opening, and on turning his head Jack beheld Ali Lobah and a couple of dark-browed ruffians standing there.

"Morrow to you, good sheikh," said Ali Lobah, bowing obeisance. "So you have visitors, I see ; how is it they have not paid toll for crossing my frontier ?"

"I know not," replied the hoary Arab, raising his eyebrows as if in surprise. "They are too poor, I suppose ; they came here begging food and assistance, and they would not do that if they had money."

"That's a sure thing ; but have they not paid you for your hospitality ? "

"The secrets of my house are best known to myself," replied the sheikh. "If they owe you anything, why not demand it from them. You are king hereabouts, and what is due to you, is your due."

Jack needed no more to see through the affair at once.

The sheikh evidently was a traitor.

"Get your creese ready," he whispered to Sambo, "we are in the den of a wolf ; we shall have to fight like blood and thunder."

CHAPTER LVIII.

ARAB JACK IS THREATENED BY THE DESERT OUTLAW.—THE DEATH TRAP.—DOWN IN THE PIT.—FACE TO FACE WITH A HORRIBLE DOOM.—THE ARAB MAIDEN TAKES UP THE DEFENCE OF OUR HERO, JACK.— BOUND WITH THOINGS.—FRESH TREACHERY OF THE SHEIKH AND ALI LOBAH.

LITTLE Sambo was alert on the instant he caught the words of warning.

"Me ready," he whispered, giving Jack a sharp pinch.

"Well," said Ali Lobah, when he entered the tent, "it is not decorous to enter a stranger's house to make terms, but as he is sheltering a criminal——"

"Liar ! " cried Jack, interrupting him; "if you allude to me, I am no criminal ; to yourself that name would be best applied ; I am——"

"A defaulter, then, a cheater of revenues," interrupted the outlaw coolly, and as such, "if you do not shell out, I shall arrest you."

"Scoundrel ! what do you mean ?" gasped Jack, choking with pride and honest indignation.

"Ay, and if I cannot find sufficient about you to satisfy my claims, I shall sell you for a slave."

"This is insolence," he thundered ; "arrogance intolerable. Do you know who I am ? "

"I care not ; you may be devil for all I know. So shell out all you have, or I'll show you I am king of the desert."

"You'll get your desert," muttered Jack, grinding his ivory teeth, "if you dare molest me. Stand off ! "

Then he drew his revolver and sprang to his feet, but before he could complete another movement, the carpet on which he had sat sank beneath him, and he fell into a deep pit made in the earth.

Sambo, who at that moment approached him, fell in also, and there they were below both struggling together.

"Ha ! ha ! " laughed the brutal outlaw, hoarsely. "Ha ! ha ! you are trapped, my young tiger ; now where is your boast ? "

"Confound you," Jack yelled ; "you have broken my spine ; let me once get sight of you and I'll riddle you with bullets."

"Thanks, noble stranger ; we shall see."

Ali Lobah spoke, but he took care not to go near the opening of the hole.

At a signal from him a large square board was brought and pushed over the opening, and on this was piled a heap of damp matting, evidently with the intention of excluding the air from below.

The voices of Jack and Sambo were now reduced to a minimum.

Presently Ali Lobah took a plug out of the earth a little distance away, and down this shaft, which led into the hole, he began to pour lighted charcoal, which was brought to him in a camp stove, not much unlike a perforated pail.

"Cowards ! " Jack yelled. "Cowards ! We may die, but we shall be avenged."

"Bang ! bang ! bang ! "

"It's all over," laughed the outlaw ; "the shooter is of no further use ; we can let them out now. That is the way to draw the teeth of vicious young tigers."

Jack heard the words as plainly as if he had been alongside the speaker ; his heart beat and his fingers convulsively clenched as he longed to be at the throat of the inhuman monster.

The hatch and the cumbrous mass were then drawn off ; but the fell vapour had nearly done its work.

"They are all quiet, my son," said the sheikh to one of his young men ; "fetch them up, bring them to me, but take care the young spitfires use no knives."

The young Arab made no bones of his work ; unhooking a rope that was fastened to the roof pole of the tent, from the side, he slid down it into the smoking pit, and fastening a rope that was thrown to him around Jack's limp body, desired those above to haul away.

This was soon done, and up Jack came holus bolus, as limp as a wet rag, and looking the picture of death.

The fresh air, however, brought him to a little, and in a dreamy sort of state such as is induced by the vapour of charcoal, thinking it was the sheikh's daughter who had hold of him, he threw his arms around Ali Lobah's neck, and held him firmly.

"Help, help ! " thundered the outlaw ; "he's choking me."

It was a death-like sort of tenacity with which he clung, and Ali Lobah reckoned upon every minute being his last.

The old sheikh was not able to render him the least assistance.

"Boys," he said, hoarsely and feebly, "see what you can do ; don't stand there looking on as stolidly as the sphinx ; are you all turned into stone, or has the devil set his cloven foot on you ?"

"He has set it on you, petrified your heart," cried the daughter, coming forward from the inner room. "You have murdered the noble youth, you know you have ! Was it for this dastardly work I blew up the charcoal ?"

"Hist ! you have done so many a time before," said her father.

"Yes ; but not to scorch the skin and choke the life out of a handsome boy like this," she retorted.

"You are in love with him, then ?"

"Maybe I am, maybe I am not. Though you are my parent, and guide my movements, you are not the keeper of my heart."

The eyes of the lovely Arab girl glowered like those of a tigress.

"Father, if I am still to call you such, let

not this cruel thing be. I warn you, if you do, that I, hitherto your dutiful child, will cause you such sorrow that you shall repent of it every hour of your life."

"In what way ?"

"I will consort with the young Israelite, who is mad to gain my hand, Ishmael the ivory merchant. I will become a renegade, a Jewess; and when you next see your daughter she shall present you with a little Jew."

The Arab sheikh sprang to his feet, and stamped and swore just as if his senses had left him rightaway. "Curse you! curse you! daughter or no daughter," he yelled, until the foam fairly fell from his lips.

The Arab girl stood statuesque and immovable all this time.

Her bare bosom, which protruded above her scanty corset, was swelling and heaving, whilst from her dark eyes flashed darts of fierce fire, just as if she were really one of Israel's dark daughters.

Arab Jack in the meantime was lying in a state of semi-consciousness.

The powerful Berbereen, succumbing to his fierce grasp, had fallen senseless.

Jack, as was stated, had fallen upon him.

As he lay he could hear all that was passing, but he was held in such a state of lethargy that he could not move.

He heard the Arab girl's voice plainly enough, and, strange to say, he fancied she held him in her arms and was supporting him, and that he was fondly clinging about her neck.

Therefore, when he did come to with a sort of spasmodic revulsion, one may imagine his horror, disgust and surprise on finding himself clinging to the half-dead and hoarsely-breathing Berbereen. "Good God!" he muttered, releasing his hold and springing to his feet. "Good God! where am I? what is all this? am I really the victim of some horrible hallucination, or the sport of some hideous dream?"

Two of them a little in the rear were attending to Sambo, whose nostrils they were fumigating with some sort of incense, and in the midst there stood the lovely Arabian girl, the very acme of love and beauty, facing her unholy parent, whose grey hairs should have guaranteed his respect for his child. For one instant she took her fierce flashing eyes off her father and fixed them on Arab Jack.

"Stranger," she said, her pink lips parting like the petals of a beautiful rose, "you are a Moslem, a fakir, one brought up in the holy rites, which teach that women have no souls, but I would give myself to you body and soul, if it were only to get clear of this cruel and unnatural ——"

She paused for a word, for a name. Her eloquence was spent; the desert child had exhausted her speech.

Jack was almost beside himself.

The presence of that earthly angel, as he considered her, wiped out all recollection of how he had nearly been suffocated, and in all probability roasted alive.

"I have money and jewels enough," he thought "to make her happy." "What if I declare myself to her ; declare I am no Mahommedan : tell her I am a Christian?"

Fortunately, however, a circumstance happened that prevented all this.

Just as Ali Lobah was coming to, a large caravan hove in sight, and some of the desert robbers rushed in to acquaint their leader with the fact.

"It is a slave caravan," answered one in reply to a question from the sheikh; "two hundred men and a thousand girls, young and old, all fit for market at the bazaar."

"Where to is it bound?"

"Half to Berber, half to Shendy. It is a treasure—if we only capture a part of it."

Meanwhile Ali Lobah was so far recovered as to understand what was passing.

He forgot all about Jack, and having caught a word about the approaching caravan, his rapacious heart rose and swelled at once. There was a sign of plunder.

"Keep well out of sight," he said, excitedly, his frame trembling from his recent mauling. "Babel, you see after the band; attend to signals; those here can hide in the pit, and the chief of the caravan will of course enter here."

"Of course," echoed the sheikh, who was, if successful, sure of a good share of the spoil. Then, beckoning two of his sons to his side, he whispered: "Bind and gag these tarantulas; we'll draw their stings when we have more time; they are our legitimate prey."

This was said so quietly that Jack was seized and thrown on his back and bound wrists and ankles to a long pole, which the Arabs picked up and walked away with easily.

Sambo was trussed up like a fowl, and the Arab girl was threatened with a long doubleedged knife if she did not retire.

She needed no persuading of that sort.

She gladly retreated to the rear, for there Jack was conveyed, and as he looked ill, she lavished upon him all her attentions.

In the meantime the caravan approached, and as the fleet of the desert drew near to the one at anchor, the sheikh sounded his horn, just as ships might hail one another at sea.

All was silent in the traitors' camp for some minutes, and then one of the sheikh's sons went out and blew a corresponding blast on a curly ram's horn, which was a sign of peace and welcome.

Scarcely had the echo died away when the caravan was brought to a halt, and before the baggage camels were unpacked the captain of the caravan, as we will call him for distinction, with two of his officers, left their vessel, so to speak, and mounted on splendidly-caparisoned dromedaries, rode towards the camp of the traitors.

Sheikh Abka received his guests with all the fawning and flowery speeches he could muster; pipes and coffee were served, salt and bread was placed for those who chose to partake of it, and a rare fuss was made until Abka had fairly thrown the dust in the other sheikh's eyes.

Wine is forbidden by the Koran; but as the unscrupulous do many things contrary to their laws, it is not likely that they neglected the good things of this world; so wine was brought, and the captain and his officers imbibed pretty freely.

But, alas! the wine was drugged, and the victims were soon past the power of detecting the difference, and Ali Lobah, coming from his concealment beneath the pile of mats, very soon arranged the treacherous programme.

He slipped off the outer clothing of the guests,

and himself and the two robbers who had hidden in the pit quickly disguised themselves in their gay attire, and having made themselves up, so to speak, they mounted the dromedaries, and off they went to the bustling encampment.

CHAPTER LIX.

HOW ALI LOBAH SOLD THE CRAFTY SHEIKH.— HORRIBLE FATE OF THE SLAVE DEALERS.— THE BOY CAPTIVES CROSS THE DESERT.—THE HALT.—A NIGHT ALARM.—SURROUNDED BY THE AMAZONS.—SHOCKING DEATH OF SHEIKH ABKA. — LEILAH BECOMES AN AMAZON.— JACK TAKES HIS LAST FAREWELL OF NUR-EL-SHAM.

JACK made good headway with his courting the lovely Arabian girl, especially after he prevailed upon her to loosen the thongs of the little negro boy.

He made all sorts of promises, none of which he saw it possible to perform, and wound up by telling her fortune.

They were thus engaged when Ali Lobah returned to the encampment, where Sheikh Abka sat fuming and fretting like a porcupine.

"Well, eh, how are you getting on?" queried the sheikh, trembling in every limb.

"It's all done, all settled. Our get up was so immense that their wives, who were awaiting their spouses' return, took us for their lords, and hugged and kissed us till we should have melted away."

"Yes, yes; but how are you going on?"

"Well, we have sorted out the stock, and I intend taking one-half the caravan and leaving the other to be divided between the captain and his mates. I shall make a start as soon as the moon rises; and now I've come to bid you adieu."

"But what of them?" pointing to where the drugged men lay.

"They are your guests, your prisoners, or what not. If I were you I should drop them down the pit straightway, and bolt with half the caravan I shall leave behind."

Abka dropped his pipe, and stared at his visitor as if he scarcely believed he was there.

"This is robbery," he said, a tear stealing to his eye.

"So it is; but I'd have you be sharp, and not fool away the time. If Aben Mahoud and his officers sleep off the drug, and awaken before you are out of this, you'll not get a smell of a share."

The chafing sheikh needed no reminding of this. He knew very well that Aben Mahoud, as he whom we termed the captain was named, was a man who stood no fooling.

He was a man, too, who knew nothing of mercy. You might as well try to reason with a hail storm as with him.

So when Ali Lobah left, Abka's only course was to act on his advice—lower the three drunken slave-dealers down into the pit, get his own caravan under weigh, and then by showing a formidable appearance plunder what he thought fit from the remnant of the slave caravan and do what he could with his two other prisoners.

Precisely as the moon rose Ali Lobah, true to his word, set sail over the sandy ocean, keeping his destination to himself, and leaving only a line of foot-tracks in the sand, which were soon obliterated by the night winds.

Abka then collected his most trusty sons, and bade them dispose of the slave-dealers, who were lowered down the pit, the entrance closed up, and sand and earth thrown over it to obscure its vicinity.

The shaft, however, down which the burning charcoal was thrust, was left open, so that they might have air to breathe and barely sufficient to keep them alive.

"What care I whether they live or die!" was his answer when one of his sons, more humane than the rest, reasoned with him.

Taking time by the forelock, however, he quickly summoned his followers, and told them he was about to pillage the broken caravan, which was visible from his tent, urged them to break camp at once, and incited them by enumerating the profits they would get by the night's work.

To such men, whose occupation was plunder, he had no need to say more.

By midnight the slave caravan was plundered, the best of the slaves selected from the gangs, and with the healthiest of the camels Abka set off, striking the trail for Berber.

Jack and Sambo had a most horrible time of it.

Although the sheikh forbade them being ill-used—as he had a silent dread that Jack possessed some invisible power—yet they were ill-fed, and kept in chains for many long days and nights.

They might have been starved, in fact, had it not been for the Arabian girl's kindness; and they would have been robbed had she not put it about that Jack, if he was not an agent of the Mahdi, was versed in the art of necromancy, declaring that he had foretold her something to her advantage which she was sworn not to disclose.

The superstitious old sheikh, therefore, let them remain unmolested; but he was afraid to liberate them for fear that they should disclose the horrors they experienced in the pit, by which means it was likely the place might be sought after and the remains of the slavers and his own cruel trickery be discovered.

During this journey, although Jack's clothing was almost reduced to a collection of rags, his yataghan, with its valuable jewels, was never discovered by the sheikh, nor exposed to the gaze of any one of his followers.

This was owing to luck more than anything else, for it was no honied time. Jack's camel, besides being tall and lanky, had a touch of the rickets, which, of course, kept our hero in continual motion the whole of the day.

"Ah! what town is that?" queried Jack one evening when they halted in view of the walls of a large city.

"Berber," replied the Arab girl.

"Good! Then my troubles will soon be over. Once inside, and I can get an interview with the emir, I'm all right."

"Ah! then you will leave me," said the girl, sadly.

"I can't very well leave you while I am fixed up in this manner," replied Jack. "Look how cruelly my flesh is cut and torn. Can you not loosen these bonds? The agony I suffer is almost past endurance."

This appeal, delivered in one of Jack's most touching tones, won her sympathy. Braving the risk she ran, she set him altogether at liberty, so that Jack only had to watch his chance to release Sambo and run.

That night, however, brought a strange scene.

Whilst the caravan was wrapped in slumber, and the watchers were dozing at their posts, a cry was raised that the camp was surrounded by armed ruffians.

All was panic and confusion then.

The guards, on whom the sleepers had most depended, were missing; worn out with a fatiguing day's march, they had thrown themselves down on the hot sand, and, using their matchlocks for pillows, had fallen asleep.

The old sheikh was like a maniac.

"Leilah," said he to his daughter, "I believe you are the cause of all this. Have the magician boy, as you call him, brought before me at once. Let me hear what he has to say about it."

When Arab Jack was brought before him his rage towered higher and higher.

"Ah, angel of mystery!" he exclaimed, "you are the plague-spot that's blighted my caravan. First, you defy me; then you wean from me my daughter's affections; and then you place me in the hands of the daring outlaw, Ali Lobah. Can you in any way assist me in this strait, or am I to offer you up as a blood-offering to Mahommed, whose blessed beard, through you, I have spat on?"

"Abka," said Jack, "you Philistine! the blood of the innocents condemns you. To me and mine you have behaved abominably; but to those poor wretches you have dragged across the burning desert in chains—those weeping mothers whom you bound by the neck to the yoke-poles, and towed foot-sore and bleeding—you have done worse! You goaded them with the lash when they fell exhausted, and now the angel of Allah hath come to avenge them! The Amazons are upon you! Behold!"

There was a whizz in the air, and the sheikh saw that the roof of his tent was pierced by a thousand arrows.

"The Amazons!" he exclaimed, thickly, as if a big lump stuck in his throat. "It was predicted by my mother that I should die by a maiden's hand."

"Die then, at once," cried a stern but silvery voice, which rang like a charm through the canvas edifice. "I am Nur-el-Sham, the sister of God's chosen prophet Mahomet Achmet, the Mahdi of the Soudan, the liberator of the slave. Die then, I say. It is not our province to war against men, but fiends like you die, and I—I will protect your orphan daughter;" and the Amazon Queen buried her dagger in the breast of Akba.

"Allah, Allah! be merciful," gasped the miserable wretch, clasping his hands to his breast as if suffering intense pain. "What of the boy? the boy?" glancing piteously at Jack.

"He is free! From the moment those arrows made a communication between here and heaven his bonds were severed."

Then she glanced around, and suddenly her eyes came in contact with those of our hero, when she started as if she had suddenly received an electric shock.

Until then she was not aware that the prisoner, who her scouts had informed her was with the sheikh, was the boy Mahdi in whom her brother had such faith, and for whom her modest bosom had beaten, and her virgin heart secretly yearned.

No; but she only gave him one glance of her fervent passion, and then she scowled at him with a look of withering hate.

At that moment there was a commotion, one loud piercing shriek—a sound like the death-rattle in the throat of a dying man—a sob—a gasp—and the next moment Leilah was seen supporting the corpse of her father in her rounded arms.

Let us draw the veil.

"Well," thought Jack to himself next day as he and Sambo stood in the tent of the Amazon Queen, "it's awkward for a fellow to be placed like this. Here's fifty of the loveliest girls I ever set eyes on, and yet I dare not give one so much as a kiss, by Jove! If I were the Mahdi I'd marry the whole lot!"

The music struck up, and the queen, followed by her body guard, entered, looking more beauteous, in Jack's eyes, than ever.

The queen led Leilah by the hand, and immediately commenced the form of introduction preparatory to her joining the maiden army; after which the pavilion was cleared, and our hero and Nur-el-Sham were left alone.

Seated side by side on a soft divan, they then held an hour's delightful chat, at the end of which the queen said:—

"Although I love you, I could never be yours. Your wandering life makes you like a bee roaming from flower to flower, and Nur-el-Sham, having once parted with the key of her heart, could never lose sight of the keeper."

Jack could not speak; he accepted her warm kiss, and that was all.

"We part now," said she; "but I advise you to shun the walls of Berber; you will find enemies there. Go on to Dongola, if you like, and spread news of the Mahdi's victory. Here are papers that will procure you assistance on the way. But I will provide you with camels for your journey."

"Farewell!" she added. "May Allah protect you!" And then, with a sorrowful glance, she gave our hero the parting kiss.

CHAPTER LX.

JACK'S PASSAGE DOWN THE NILE. — OLD FRIENDS AGAIN MEET.—HOMEWARD OH!— ON BOARD THE "DROMEDARY." — THE WANDERER'S RETURN.—HAPPY HEARTS.— NEVER TOO LATE TO MEND.

OUR hero, aided by his disguise, money, and a large roll of papyrus, on which was written in Arabic verses of the Koran, found no difficulty in procuring a passage down the Nile for himself and Sambo.

At Abu Hamed he heard of the murder of Colonel Stewart and his staff, the death of Earle, and later on the wounding of Sir Herbert Stewart and the heroic death of the brave Colonel Burnaby.

Jack was almost worshipped at each place they stopped at. Had he declared that he could walk upon the waters of the Nile, as Peter did upon the sea, they would have believed him.

At one place he landed he saw Sir Charles Wilson's steamer on its way to Khartoum, and Jack shouted to Bo'sun Benbow that Khartoum was fallen; but that gallant tar declared he was not to be caught with that pinch of salt.

Landing above Gubat, the party took the camel route to Korti, on nearing which Jack and Sambo collected alms, and then threw off their Mahdi disguises, giving a sufficient reason for so doing to the travellers by the caravan.

From Korti, Jack took boat for Dongola, where he fell in with Lord Woolberry and his daughter, who warmly congratulated him, and on learning Jack was bound to Cairo, his lordship offered him a passage in his yacht, which was then getting up steam.

"But what of my soot" (suite), said our hero, jocularly; "this negro boy, who escaped with me from Khartoum?"

"He shall come with us, of course," said the young lady, with one of her most winning smiles. "And you, Arab Jack (I know you by no other name), can occupy the cabin we prepared for Martin Bey."

Jack started.

"Martin Bey," he exclaimed, trembling like an aspen-leaf. "Where is he?" turning to his lordship.

"On his way to Alexandria. He is summoned by the Khedive in all haste to inspect the forts, and could not delay until I settled my private business."

Jack and Sambo were suitably attired, and enjoyed the passage down the Nile very much, our hero enlivening his lordship and his daughter by recounting his adventures and hairbreadth escapes, which not only amused but astounded them.

On reaching Cairo, Lord Woolberry accompanied Jack to the palatial mansion of Signor Varnoni, who they learnt was then at the Italian consulate in Massowah, but his secretary handed our hero a letter which was sealed and addressed to his courier, Arab Jack, and left with the secretary in case he might at any time turn up.

The letter ran thus:—

"False Scoundrel,—Your massive gold chain and other valuables I have placed in the custody of the Mudir of Suakim, who will deliver them to you on personal demand, and also have you flayed in accordance with the rules of the Soudan, for abducting his fair niece, the lovely Nubian girl, whose parents are of high standing, and are driven to madness by her loss and uncertain fate. —Your indignant and misguided friend, Signor VARNONI, Agent of the Italian Government, Massowah."

"Good heavens! what do you think of that?" exclaimed Jack, handing the letter to Lord Woolberry. "I will write a reply at once denying this false and cruel allegation. It was Osman Digna, not I, who abducted the voluptuous girl, who, so far from being fair in my eyes, was as black and shiny as a nugget of coal."

As they rode back to the yacht his lordship commented freely upon the epistle, and desired our hero to bear up, advice that our hero little needed, as they passed the various spots which Jack recognised as the scenes of his former adventures.

Jack took a farewell glance at the towers of the fortress El Kalah, in which he had been confined, as they steamed down towards Alexandria, where, on arriving, he was astounded to behold Hassan - el - Ahed and his three lovely sisters conversing on the quay.

"By Jove!" vociferated the excited boy, leaping ashore as the yacht touched. "By Jove! Hassan, old boy, how the deuce did you arrive here?"

"What, Jack, my blooming young Mahdi!" exclaimed Hassan, clasping his hand with joy, "my brave fireman, my noble Jew-cheater, my —my everything but brother-in-law."

"Ah!" cried Selim, throwing her arms about his neck and kissing him, "I knew we should see you again."

Jack was nearly smothered with the kisses and caresses of the three enraptured girls, whose conduct awakened a sort of jealousy in the heart of his lordship's daughter, who from the quarterdeck of the yacht witnessed the joyous proceeding.

But an explanation ensued, and Lord Woolberry, who was as delighted as the rest, and was the *beau ideal* of a thorough English nobleman, invited them on board to dine, and the vessel having been moored off in the stream, the evening was passed in music and dancing, to which enlivening entertainment his lordship invited many notables of the town.

Jack, what with the wine and the excitement, was somewhat elevated when he retired in the small hours of the morning to his berth; and then he had a dream—a sort of vision which warned him to leave Alexandria at once and return to his home.

That vision was of a lady draped in black bending over the form of a drowned boy, whose features looked calm even in death.

She was fondling the light curly hair with her fingers, and gazing abstractedly at the left forearm of the boy, from which the skin had been torn by the keel of some vessel passing over the corpse, and when she raised her head he beheld the pale face and tear-dimmed eyes of his disconsolate mother.

Jack sprang from his cot and made instant preparations for going on shore.

Revealing his intentions to his anxious friends, he hastened to the office and booked his passage in the next steamship that was to leave for dear old England.

That ship chanced to be the "Dromedary," the very ship in which Jack had sailed from Gravesend as a poor London waif and friendless stowaway.

Jack joined his tears with those of the ladies as he and Sambo took the last parting leave of his friends, and the kisses lavished upon him made his lordship and Hassan almost wish they could change places with him.

His presents, hastily collected, were costly in the extreme, whilst Lord Woolberry not only gave him a draft for a large sum on his London bankers, but letters of introduction to his friends.

The captain of the "Dromedary" did not recognise Jack until some days after they left Egypt, and then it was through little Sambo, who in his position of valet to our hero did not fail to ake down the arrogant midshipman, Marcus, a peg or two.

Jack, still dressed as a wealthy Arab, kept the captain at a distance, treating him with contempt and bestowing his attentions lavishly upon the invalided soldiers and sailors, to whom he represented himself as one of that country against whom their nation were still waging a cruel war.

"What!" cried one of the old salts, who hobbled about on crutches, "a cruel war, darn ye? Ye wouldn't say so if ye'd been wi' Brackenbury's collum at Abu Klea and had a port hole made in yer thigh wi' a darned spear, as did poor Tom Trysail."

"Tom Trysail!" exclaimed Jack, starting back, as he gazed on the pain-shrunken face, buried as it were in the mimosa-like bushes of whiskers. "Tom Trysail, your hand! We last met at Tel-el-Kebir."

Arab Jack soon explained who he was, and the scene that followed is best left to the imagination.

"Then you know Tommy Atkins," said one of the soldiers who had been listening with quivering lip, and who had an arm in a sling and a patch over his left eye.

"I did," said Jack, turning. "Allah be merciful! is it you? Why with your ghastly visage and that moustache you look like a death's head stuck behind one of the lines of Tel-el-Kebir."

"I have been knocked about, Jack, since I lost you at the fire. I have been home since, seen Polly—God bless her!—who spoke of you, and I have been to Suakim and got this," meaning a lost finger, "since, in one of the night attacks, when I gave Abdul Ahad, Osman Digna's standard bearer, his quietus; and these," pointing to his arm and eye, "are souvenirs of the rush on McNeil's zereba."

"God bless you!" cried Jack. "I mean, Allah preserve you! I suppose Polly has raised a pile of stones on the bridge as high as the monument."

The invalid gave a grim laugh, and many a weary hour the trio passed yarning about their escapades in Egypt and the Soudan, until the white cliffs of Old Albion hove in sight, and the "Dromedary" was moored at Gravesend.

"Halloo! take your togs ashore, mister furriner?" said a gruff voice, as Jack leant over the bulwark watching a barge being moored alongside.

"No thankee, Mister Wiggles," replied Jack, interlarding his speech with a few words of Arabic.

The lighterman was astounded on hearing his name pronounced, and when Jack showed him the knife he was almost startled out of his wits.

"What! are you the London Arab as I cast adrift on the world out of my craft? Lord love yer! give us your oar, my lad, and——"

A tear stood in the eye of the honest lighterman, his utterance was choked until Jack gave him a stiff glass of brandy hot, and then there followed a scene that needs no depicting.

A swift train conveyed Jack and his valet to town, and a cab took them, dressed in their Oriental attire, to the West End.

But, alas! many changes had taken place during Jack's three years' absence from home.

His father's house was now occupied by strangers, who directed him to the abode of a relation, Mrs. Gordon Martin, who resided in the neighbourhood of Berkeley Square.

It was dark when Jack alighted from the hansom at the corner of the street and proceeded on foot to the house, which he well knew, and as he stepped up to the door and was about to knock his ears caught the strain of a female voice within singing the last verse of a popular ditty; it was the last line in fact—

A boy's best friend is his mother.

Jack started. The sweat oozed from his sunburnt brow, and he leaned on the railings for support.

A dead silence followed. Then there was the murmuring of voices; wine was evidently being passed round, and from what he gathered by a short speech now and again it was a birthday party.

Jack was so absorbed that he scarcely remembered the mission upon which he was bound.

He was enthralled, and he listened with quivering limbs and bated breath to the next song.

It was sung in a plaintive strain and stung him to the very soul :—

Where is my wandering boy to-night,
　The boy of my tend'rest care,
The boy that was once my joy and light,
　The child of my love and prayer?

Oh! where is my boy to-night?
Oh! where is my boy to-night?
My heart overflows, for I love him, he knows;
　Oh! where is my boy to-night?

Jack's brain reeled, his senses seemed to have deserted him, and he would have fallen had not Sambo lent him his support.

He recovered himself, however, as the following verse was pathetically carolled forth :—

Go for my wandering boy to-night,
　Go search for him where you will;
But bring him to me with all his blight,
　And I will love him still.

At the last cadence Jack seized the knocker, and was about to rat-tat at the door, when a series of moans arrested his hand, followed by a scream that went like a dagger to his heart.

"My boy! my boy!" shrieked a female voice hysterically, which voice Jack recognised at once as his mother's.

Sobs followed, and then our guilt-stricken hero shook all over as if he had been seized with an ague. Then the door opened, and a female distracted in appearance rushed out, and brushed past the excited boy on the way for a doctor.

Jack, taking advantage of the open door, rushed quickly in, and sought the room from which emanated the sobs and a confused murmuring of voices.

"My mother, your son!" he exclaimed, wildly as he made for the couch on which a female reclined surrounded by agonised friends.

Jack recognised the pale-stricken features immediately.

"Stand aside! Give her air; I am her son, her long-lost son, her blighted boy. Mother! mother! oh speak, look up, it is your wandering boy returned, guilty but repentant. Oh God, she will die, and her death will be on the head of her son, Jack Martin!"

The guests, both male and female, drew back aghast at the sudden appearance of this strange apparition ; but the voice of the long-lost boy had struck a chord in his mother's heart.

"My Jack !" she cried, suddenly starting up. "My boy ! my boy ! it is you I know, in spite of this strange disguise. My prayer is answered, my vision has come true. My boy ! my boy ! It was not your remains I followed to the grave. What parent have I wronged, what mother's heart have I robbed of her only solace ?"

A cab rattled up to the door, and, a tall sun-burnt, noble-looking man entered the room, followed by the doctor.

"Ah, what is this ?" cried the stranger. "Who is this Arab that thus fondles my wife before I am dead ?"

"Your son, Jack," exclaimed our hero, recognising his voice. "Ah, now I am persuaded I saw you in company of General Gordon in Khartoum. Father, father, forgive your erring son."

Let us pass over explanations that are too minute to detail.

Mrs. Martin was overjoyed at the return of her husband, who had been sent on foreign service as a punishment for not taking better care of the plans of the forts, which were in his coat pocket when it was stolen, and the restoration of her darling boy, whom she at one time mourned as dead

And the heart of the widow of Gordon Martin was rejoiced, for she discovered in her nephew the poor boy for whom she had left the suit of clothes and the half-crown at the station on the Underground Railway, and that he had used the ticket which she had lost in the terror and confusion caused by the discovery of the boy lying between the metals.

"Hurrah !" shouted Jack, when it was all comfortably settled. "Hurrah ! Cheer up, Sambo ; I have gold and treasures enough to make us all happy. Hurrah for the London Arab and the Boy Mahdi of the Soudan !"

A week later a convivial party met in one of the most fashionable houses in the square, among whom were the noble guardsman, Tommy Atkins, and his faithful lass, and Tom Trysail, the true-hearted and jovial British tar.

The former are married now, and enjoying the treasures Tommy brought from the East, and the latter is pensioned off, having served his full time.

Flash Luke died raving mad in the Military Hospital at Cairo, and Drury Lane Dick, having repented of his ways, is doing well.

As to Jack, he is now leading a quiet life, devoting his whole care, as he promised General Gordon, to his fond mother, who never tires of hearing her boy waif's recital of his TRIALS, TROUBLES, and ADVENTURES in EGYPT and the SOUDAN.

THE END.